Buffalo Nickel
A Memoir

Floyd Salas

Arte Publico Press
Houston
Texas
1992

This book is made possible through a grant from the National Endowment for the Arts, a federal agency.

Arte Publico Press
University of Houston
Houston, Texas 77204-2090

Cover design by Mark Piñón
Photograph by Bill Ashley

Salas, Floyd, 1931–
    Buffalo nickel / by Floyd Salas.
        p.   cm.
    ISBN 1-55885-049-X
    1. Salas, Floyd, 1931– —Biography. 2. Novelists, American —20th century—Biography. 3. Boxers (Sports)—United States—Biography. I. Title
PS3569.A459Z464 1992
813'.54–dc20   91-48217
    [B]   CIP

The paper used in this publication meets the requirements of the American National Standard for Permanence of Paper for Printed Library Materials Z39.48-1984. ∞

Second Printing, 1992

Printed in the United States of America

Each tear is a crystal heart
Count them
Paper spots!
Damp!
Blurring print!
Streaking my thoughts!
But I'll spread them for you
Give the why
Why?
Because I ache in my guts
Because my intestines cramp with memory
And that memory is greased with brain and blood
And this the why
of that.

For my brother Eddy and my Dad and my brother Al

Buffalo Nickel

A Memoir

PART ONE
Buffalo Nickel

1

His big plaster leg took up the whole back seat and he held his crutches next to him. He was eleven and I was almost two. We were taking my brother Al home from the hospital, where he had been put after jumping headfirst off a thirty-foot water tower. I stared at him. He was a spectacular sight to me.

It was the deep depression of 1933. We lived in a mining town called Brighton and my father was lucky to have a job. He had a job because he was a hard worker, the best, a deputy sheriff's son who grew up on a ranch and knew how to get things done, like blow coal out of the tunnel walls with dynamite, so other men could load it.

I remember that tower. My oldest brother, Eddy, who was thirteen and an intellectual prodigy, swung me around by an arm and a leg up there and scared the hell out of me. I caught my breath, got dizzy and nauseous and saw a damp, dark spot on the earth beneath the water spout under the tower.

When Eddy came to bring Al home to get a spanking for selling one of Dad's rabbits for a big jar of marbles, Al jumped headfirst from the tower. That's my first memory of my brother Al. It has set the tone for the rest of his life, as I see it: tragic, but with a stubborn streak of survival in it that has denied defeat.

Oh, he was fun, though. He took me to my first movie when I was three. It was in a red brick building across the dirt alley from our yard in the small town of Lafayette, Colorado. He took me right down to the first row, where we sat looking up. I remember being astounded by the size of the big cowboys in front of me. And somebody behind us was shining a big flashlight down on them. I kept looking back and forth from it to the spinning wheels of the stagecoach. It astounded me. I couldn't figure it out. It was real and not real, another spectacular sight.

Next, I remember this little suburb in Denver called Elyria, where my father worked in a packing plant. Al took me to a house where somebody stuck a rake under a front porch and pulled out little warm puppies. Then, he taught me to shoot little green buds off a tree like spit wads. I was still three then. Then, I remember him when I was four and we lived in a red brick, two-story building on Curtis Street in Denver. We lived on the bottom floor.

My birth broke my mother's rheumatic heart, it is said. She had my little sister three years later, so she had to sleep in the afternoons or she'd die. I remember her lying down in the bedroom. I had nothing to do and would wander around the house.

One day, I was rummaging around and I found the black suit with short pants and white silken shirt that my mother used to dress me in when we went somewhere. I liked it and put it on. Since I was dressed, I decided to go for a walk. I wandered a block down to Curtis Park, which was a big park with a swimming pool. I stayed there all afternoon, had all kinds of fun. I remember playing with these bigger boys who carried me and another little boy on their shoulders so we could wrestle and try to throw each other down. We were the arms, they were the legs. It was great fun.

Then I wandered to the other side of the park, where a woman in an alley told another woman I was the brother of Al Salas. He must have been thirteen at the time. I went back to the park and it must have gotten very late, almost dark already. Al appeared. He said he had been sent to find me and that I was going to get a beating when I got home. I can still see him lying down in the grass next to me: dark, wavy hair, strong-boned face, telling me very seriously that I better put a book under the back seat of my short pants so the whipping wouldn't hurt so much. I took him very seriously, but the book was too big and didn't fit. I did need it, though, because the next thing I knew, I was running around in a circle in the kitchen, hollering, while my mother held onto one of my hands and switched me. Even then my brother knew how to lighten the punishment you got for being too free.

Al put the first pair of boxing gloves on me then. Some cute little blond kid who lived next door was in the kitchen with me. So he taught the both of us how to box, or, rather, he put the gloves on us and had us slug it out on the linoleum floor. And we punched and punched at each other, getting all sweaty and red-faced. I remember it as a rainy day. That's why we didn't go outside. He kept stopping us and pouring hot water on the gloves so we could hit harder. It made the gloves heavier and they splat more when we hit each other. I didn't know then how many fights he was going to get me into during the years to come.

He taught me to tie my shoes, sort of. I don't know how old I was, but I didn't go to school, not even kindergarten, so I had to be four or five. We were living on Welton Street. Our house was pretty and bigger than the previous one, more lighted, too. It must have been cold outside, because we were inside again, and again he was watching me and my little sister. I kept going up to him to get my shoe tied. It kept coming undone. I watched him as he did it. He was getting tired of tying it. I knew he was annoyed. But a little while later, it came untied again. So I sat down and tied it myself. I never asked him or anyone to tie my shoes again. He taught me that without even trying. Before it was over, he'd teach me a lot of things without trying, some good, some bad.

He protected me, too. I had a little dog by the name of Trixie, a little terrier. She was very pretty, black with perfect markings. She had a natural white collar around her neck, white feet, a white star on the back of her head, white tip at her tail and a white throat. She started barking one day at some Mexican kids about ten or twelve years old who had come into the backyard and grabbed my bicycle. When she threatened them, one of them hit her in the nose with a Vaseline jar. She started yelping and ran back to the house across the big back yard. I yelled, "They hurt Trixie!"

Al ran out of the house and, with all the neighborhood kids, chased those guys down to the ballpark on the next block, where Al tackled the guy who had hit Trixie. He then held him down and let me hit him in the face for hurting my dog. I leaned over the big kid, who stared at me with wide eyes, and touched him with my little fist. Then, satisfied, my brother let him up. The kid ran off across the baseball field and never came back to our neighborhood. My brother was a hero to me that day, as he would be on many other days.

The next thing I remember is my father taking me to a boxing match somewhere in Denver. As a small child, things seemed to suddenly materialize before me. There I was sitting next to my father watching the Golden Gloves. I was astounded again. Another spectacular sight. I saw a great big brown man get into the ring. Heavy flesh filled him out, rounding him off. He had black hair and black, narrow eyes. He was fighting a pink man who had hair on his chest. The bell rang and they ran out at each other. There was a big thud and the pink man flew backwards and landed on the mat. Everybody yelled and some stood up, then some man on the other side of my father said, "Who's that? He knocked him out." Another man, in a white jacket with a bony face, who was selling beer said, "He's an Indian!" Suddenly the cowboy movies I'd seen came to strange life again. Another spectacular sight. But that wasn't all. Then they brought out Albert, my brother.

I saw him go into the ring and stand opposite some kid with light brown hair who was built husky, like him. I got worried. He looked tough. Then, the bell rang and they ran at each other. My brother hit him, but got hit back. I jumped up on my seat and, standing on it, started swinging my arms like I was fighting, shouting, "Come on, Albert! Hit him, Albert! Hit him!"

He needed all my help, I could see. I forgot all about the people around me and threw all the punches I could, shouting all the time for him, shouting so much my father told the man on the other side of him, "That's his brother!

That's his brother!" He said it a couple more times to other people who turned to look at me. Little kid, five years old, standing on a wooden seat, throwing punches for his brother. It paid off, though. When it was over, they raised my brother's hand. I was really happy. He had won.

I found out that he would fight again at the end of the week. I couldn't wait to go see him again. For some reason, however, we didn't. But the very next morning after the second fight, as soon as I woke up, I went into my brother's room and touched him, my eyes wide, my mouth open.

"Did you win?" I asked.

He shook his head and said, "No," then he laid back down, his wavy hair dark against the white pillow, his handsome face looking sad.

I was disappointed and lowered my eyes and shut my mouth and walked out. I was going to be disappointed in him a lot, too.

I did well in school. I could read before I even went to kindergarten. I remember my father reading the funny papers about a little kid my age riding down a snow slope on a sled, screaming, "Eeeeee eeeeeeeeee!" all the way across the page. My father made the sound and followed it with his finger. Picture and sound and letter came together and made words for the first time for me. The corner grocer's name was Freeeee-man. I could see that "e" in the word. I read it out after that. So, when I went to school, I could already do that part.

One night, when I was six, I went out into the back yard with Albert to get a pail of coal for the stove. I don't remember why I went with him. Maybe because my mother didn't trust him out alone. Maybe she wasn't home and he was supposed to stay with me. But when we were out by the coal shed, he suddenly said, "Do you want to go to the Epworth Gym with me?"

"Yes," I answered right away, thinking of another spectacular sight.

So, off we went on his new bicycle. My father bought it new for Al because he had stolen one and gotten in trouble over it. It had cost a lot of money for those depression days of 1937: sixty-five dollars. You could buy a decent car for that, then. He sold all the fancy parts off it, a piece at a time, until it was stripped bare, without fenders even. That disappointed me, too, because it had been so pretty. But off we went across town to the Epworth Gym, which was near Curtis Park, where we used to live and where I had so much fun the day I went for a walk.

We got there and Al took me inside. I remember playing around a while, even though I didn't know anybody. But then it came to be seven o'clock and all the little guys had to go home and the man put me out. I told him my brother was inside and that I had to wait for my brother. It got cold and the man kept telling me to go away. I kept saying I had to wait for my brother. But Al didn't come out. I waited there for two hours before he did. I remember how worried I was that he might run off without me. It was nippy, too, and I got bored, besides.

Al finally came out with all the big boys at closing time. The next thing I knew, he said to this other big kid about his age, "My brother can whip yours!" I looked up at this tall, skinny kid who had come out with the big boys. He was at least a head taller than I was.

They made a circle around us in the dark, with just the glow of streetlights shining on the residential street. "Fight!" Albert told me. I turned to face the tall kid, who immediately smashed me in the nose. Blood spurted out of it and stars filled my head. He almost knocked me down, and then he hit me a few more times. Albert stopped the fight, and tried to wipe the blood off my face.

Finally, when the blood stopped, Al said, "Here!" and gave me a buffalo head nickel. I took it, thanked him and got on the bike again. I was a little guy even for six and I fit handily on the handle bar in front of him. He pumped down the dark streets for a long time. I remember how cold it was and that my nose kept dribbling blood. I liked my brother, though. He had finally come outside at closing time, had stopped the fight, and had given me a nickel.

But when we were almost home, he told me not to tell my mother that we had gone to the Epworth Gym or that I had been in a fight.

"Okay," I said.

"Good," he said, then asked me, "Floyd, could you give me that nickel back? I need it."

"Sure." I handed it over to him.

He'd do that a lot to me, also, before it was over.

Al sure was fun, though. He'd take me with him when he had to go get a gallon of fresh milk from the dairy for our Sunday breakfast of pork chops and eggs. That was fun, walking hand in hand with him to pick up the big gallon glass jug with the thick yellow cream caked at the top. We'd stop and take a sip before we got home, and he'd say not to say anything. I didn't.

Maybe I thought he owed me something for the nickel, or maybe I was just naturally a predator. I remember my older sister Dorothy, who was seven years older than I and two younger than Albert, giving my little sister Annabelle and me dinner. She told us that she was saving a small bowl of preserved plums for Albert far up on a pantry shelf. I don't know. Maybe she thought I was a thief, or maybe she just wanted to get them out of sight and out of mind. In any case, I later sneaked into the kitchen and, using a chair, climbed up into the pantry and took down the bowl of plums. I can still see them, pale purple, swimming around in the juice. I ate them down. I was a sloppy crook, though, because the next thing I knew, Al, my fifteen-year-old boxer brother, was home. And Dorothy, who was a good housekeeper and baby-sitter, was showing him the empty plate. Al was right on me.

"Stole my plums, huh?" he said, and slapped me right across the face.

I yelled and started crying as I felt the blood gush out of my nose again. But he didn't try to comfort me this time, and neither did my pretty sister, Dorothy. I was a crook and, feeling sorry for myself, went into my bedroom, where I stood at the back window that overlooked the backyard and cried for myself, for the sting and the hurt. I dabbed at the blood with my mother's lace curtains. Then I got bawled out for that when she came home.

I told her, feeling full of self-pity, "Albert hit me!"

She said, "You shouldn't have wiped your nose on the curtains, anyway!" She knew I was a thief and didn't feel sorry for me either. That hurt a lot, too. Maybe that's why I never became a thief.

Albert did, though. I sensed it was about him when I came home from school and saw Mom walking back and forth in the kitchen. Her green eyes were all wet and pink as she walked back and forth from the table to the stove while cooking dinner. Her cheeks were pink, too, but they often were, because she had high blood pressure, and her skin would get so pink and white, it was almost transparent. This and the heat of the stove could make them burn. But next to her eyes, her cheeks looked worse, now. She sniffled every once in a while and I looked up at her. But she avoided my eyes when she turned back from the table and stepped toward the stove.

I was drawing on my chalkboard, which was located right next to the warm stove, with the colored chalks my father had gotten me. I didn't want her to hurt, but she kept me out of her world and I didn't say anything. I was well trained. Yet, I knew it was about Albert. He didn't come home that night. Often, he wouldn't be around for days at a time. The world was still a wonder to me. I didn't question its turning. My mother took care of all that. My life was well ordered and I never asked when Albert disappeared or where my father was when he left somewhere for months at a time. She and he kept the worries of the world away from their children as much as possible. She kept a six-year-old child out now.

Soon after that, we took a Sunday drive to the town of Golden, some thirty miles away from Denver. Again, nothing was said to my little sister or me. But we saw Al there in a blue dungaree uniform, sitting with a hundred other boys out on the lawn, talking to their families in front of a big yellow building. I remember my mother making sure that she gave him a carton of cigarettes. Then, later, all the boys lined up and took down the flag, and we got in our '31 Model-A Ford and drove back through the settling darkness to Denver. I told my father all about how the Indians lived on the plains of

Colorado, which I had learned in school, where I had gotten an unbroken string of A's. I never asked where Al was. I wasn't told and I didn't question. But I knew he was locked up, though it didn't look like those reform schools for dead-end kids I had seen in the movies.

The next thing I remember, it was summer. I was eight years old and skipping the last half of the third grade to enter the fourth. I was taken to a ranch near Pueblo, Colorado, called "Pinyon" for the pinyon-nut trees. My grandfather and grandmother lived with their sons in an old, long bunk house with only one separate room for them. The house was on land, I heard, that my grandfather had owned before his brother had lost it. His brother had been a college graduate who was county auditor and had power of attorney. He had gotten syphilis of the brain, went crazy and lost the family fortune to his cheating bank partner just before he died in 1927. This was twelve years later in '39. Now, my grandfather worked with his sons as a picking crew on other men's land. I didn't know this. I thought it was my grandfather's ranch and that all the horses were his.

I was surprised to see Al there, with his head shaved bald. It didn't take me long after my mother and father went back to Denver to learn that Al had escaped from Golden Reform School. I found this out because he stole my grandfather's new car for a joyride and wrecked it. Al was always pulling some kind of trick. I liked him, but I must have had some reservations already, because my Uncle Willy saw how much I liked my little dog, Trixie, and, smiling, asked, "Floyd, who do you like the most, Albert or Trixie?"

I looked up into his soft, gray eyes, then at Al, who looked away. "Trixie!" I said, and Uncle Willy burst out laughing.

2

I didn't see my brother again until late September, 1939, in Boomtown, California, an original boomtown from the gold rush days, near the Shasta Dam, where my father and his two brothers had gone to find work in the summer. Its legal name was Central Valley, but it still had the original boardwalks and Silver Dollar Saloon from the Gold Rush days of ninety years before. It was called Boomtown by everyone who lived there. All Albert's hair had grown out and was wavy again, and he was seventeen years old.

We never returned to Denver. But it was fun being with Al and Dad again and with the whole family living together in an old cabin of unfinished pine walls. It nestled in the pine trees, like all the other cabins. My Uncle Tommy and Aunty Dolly lived right behind us with their children.

All the neighborhood boys used to gather in a clearing in the forest and play tackle football on the red earth. My brother was one of the stars and he often chose me for his team. One day somebody centered the ball to him, and he gave it to me and grabbed my hand and took off running down the sidelines. My feet hardly touched the ground. I was flying and all these big boys were running at me, throwing their big bodies at me. But he blocked them off and ran down the field with me sailing along behind him. That was scary and I got some bumps, but it sure was fun. Like when I was five and he had taken me to the City Park near the lake in Denver, where he put me on a rollercoaster with him. It was so scary, I caught my breath and couldn't even scream as the ground rushed up at me and my heart flew out of my mouth above me. He put his hand over my eyes to help me, but, now blinded, too, I fell in darkness towards the ground. Just about when my face was going to pop with red blood, I finally screamed.

In Boomtown, I remember Al getting the boxing gloves out and all the boys boxing in a clearing under the pine trees. Some boy's mother came by, pointed at Al, and said to her son, "You can't box him! Don't box him!" She was being friendly, but she didn't want her son getting hurt. I can still see her. A dark-haired woman about thirty-five trying to keep her tall, slim, dark-haired son with a large nose from boxing. I think they were Italians. Back then, I didn't think anything, I just felt a great sense of pride out there

18

under the pine trees that she feared the prowess of my brother. He was a hero to me.

When school started, my mother told Al to take me to enter school on the very first day. We walked down a red dirt road under the pines for a half mile or so. The school was a commandeered union meeting hall on a hill on the other side of the narrow paved road, the only paved road in town. The unions were strong up there in the late thirties. Just before we had come to Boomtown, there had been a battle between the CIO and the AFL over jurisdictional rights at the Shasta Dam they were building. I heard other boys talk about how the men went around town carrying clubs for a while. I knew my father was with the CIO and, so, I was on his side. But the battle was over when I arrived there with my mother, Dorothy, Annabelle and older brother, Eddy, who had just finished his first year at Colorado University on a four-year scholarship.

Inside the schoolroom, a pretty young blond teacher sat at the desk. When she saw Al, she smiled and showed her pretty white teeth between her red lips and stared at him with her blue eyes. I knew right away she loved him. I could see it. That's when I realized Al was handsome. He wore his dark, wavy hair combed straight back from his big forehead, accentuating the strong bones of his rounded face. Good nose bridge, full lips, large, bright front teeth. Well-built, husky, with thick shoulders and chest. Flawless complexion. His brown eyes, set far back, peered out intelligently at you. I found out later he was supposed to be a good dancer, too.

My father bought a house on the other side of town, in the northeast, by the unused railroad right of way. In the new place, the forest was right behind us. There was only an oak tree in our front yard in which my father put an old car door up in the branches for a treehouse for me.

One morning, I was out on the back porch where Al slept and he showed me a paper flower. I asked him where it came from and he said he paid fifty cents for it.

"Fifty cents? Wow!" I said, really impressed that he had fifty cents to waste on a frill. The only movie in town cost a dime for kids and a quarter for adults. So, to spend fifty cents on a paper flower at a dance was grandiose to me. I found out much later that they gave the flowers out when you paid the price of admission. So he was pulling my leg all the time.

At that time, my oldest brother Eddy had bought me "Tom Sawyer" for Christmas and my older sister Dorothy teased me and asked if I loved Becky, Tom's sweetheart. She embarrassed me because I did love Becky. Dorothy, by the way, after only a month in town was picked out at a dance to run for Boomtown Sweetheart. She finished second to a very pretty girl called Elaine Garber, whom my brother Eddy said, quite seriously, won only because she was better known. But Dorothy thought Elaine was as beautiful as a movie star, and she always said, with awe in her voice, how pretty Elaine was.

That Christmas of '39, I saw Al put on the gloves with my Uncle John, who later won fifteen straight professional fights by first round knockouts before he lost one decision to a fancy boxer. After that, he quit and became a rich contractor. The next thing I knew, my brother was lying on the front room floor face down, eyes closed, arms stretched above him. He never forgot that beating and neither did my father, who had raised John, his younger brother, since the age of seven when their parents had died of the Spanish Flu in 1919.

Not long after that, Al asked me how much money I had saved in my bank.

I answered that I didn't know.

"Get it and I'll help you count it," he said.

I ran to get it.

We sat on the bed to count all the pennies, nickels and dimes, but he kept moving his hands so quickly while smiling at me, that I couldn't keep count. I finally saw him filling his palm with pennies and not counting right. I shouted, "Albert! You're stealing my pennies!"

"I am not!" he said still smiling, showing those big front teeth and making me smile, too. He kept snatching them until Dorothy ran in from the kitchen, took the bank away from him and put it away.

He did cheat me, but he was funny. I didn't want him to take my money, but I couldn't stop laughing. He was funny.

I heard that he also got into a fight with this guy called Bozo, who was an old acquaintance of my father's from Colorado. Because Al, who was now eighteen, beat him up, Bozo came drunk to our house, woke my father up and threatened to stab Al with his knife.

Now, my father was a big-boned man who weighed two hundred pounds and was very strong. I heard the ruckus outside and the next day learned that my father had talked Bozo out of it. It's odd, because twenty years later, this same Bozo would live a couple of blocks from my sister Dorothy. I met him by coincidence one time when I was twenty-nine—not having seen him all those years. During the course of the conversation, he pulled a big, sharp, pointed knife out of his pocket and told me what he would do if somebody ever bothered him. So evidently the threat was real. My father was no coward, but he was also no fool.

I remember walking in the rain into town for some reason with Dorothy and Albert, maybe to go to the show. When we got near the business section along the paved road, where the post office and the soda fountain called The

Big Dipper were, Al wouldn't carry the open umbrella anymore because he felt it made him look like a sissy. I was impressed and made sure that I didn't carry one like a girl, either.

A carnival came to town that hot summer of 1940, when 110 degrees in the shade was not unusual. The carnival featured a traveling boxing show run by a big, brown negro man who looked like Joe Louis, who was at that time the heavyweight champion of the world. The carnival was pitched on a vacant lot across the street from the post office and The Big Dipper Cafe.

It was a big deal to me. I got to go there every night for a whole week or so. One of my big brothers or sister or older cousin would take me. I walked on the swords the sword lady walked on because the soles of my feet were thick with callouses from running barefoot all summer. The fire-eater man used to let me and my little sister into the sword-lady show free. I didn't like the whirling octopus ride at all when my older cousin Manuel, who was fourteen, took me on it. It was almost as bad as being on the rollercoaster with Al. But I liked the fluffy pink cotton candy and the greasy hamburgers and the red soda pop. And I liked the boxing matches, too.

The big, brown negro man had a puffy face, cute, pouty lips and narrow eyes. He liked me, too. He always told me he was going to give me a nickel, but he never did. Although he did let me in to see the fights free every night. He was an ex-pug, a heavyweight, and he had this black, wiry fighter, who was a welterweight of about a hundred and forty-seven pounds. He was long and lanky and muscles rippled on his black body. He didn't wear boxing trunks, but a close-fitting bathing suit. When he was already in the ring, his manager, the big heavyweight, would shout something like, "Boogie, baby, boogie!" and the fighter would snap his hips in a pumping motion as if he was screwing and make all the men laugh. Then he'd fight all comers.

"Would any man in the audience like to fight my fighter?" the big negro would ask from the middle of the ring. Local men in the audience would put on the gloves and take the guy on. A local man would also be chosen as referee. I don't remember right now whether there was some kind of prize offered if you could beat him. There must have been or, except for some crazy young men, nobody would fight him.

In any case, I saw a few men try. I saw my Uncle John, who later turned pro, give it a try. It seemed to me like my uncle was winning until, in the first round or at the break, they stopped the fight because my uncle's eye was cut. When they gave a TKO to the black fighter, all the local people booed. A girl in my class at school told me my uncle had won, too. I agreed, but my father said my uncle, the one who'd beaten up Al with the gloves at Christmas, was chicken and quit.

Early one night I went to the carnival with my brother. He was taking his own boxing gloves to the manager, who wanted to use them. I didn't know if Al was paid for it or not. We were sitting by the ring in the big tent and there was only the big, brown manager and his black fighter, Al, my cousin and me. Men from the gypsy family that told fortunes came in. The oldest gypsy had two stringbean sons, one my size and the other a head taller. Al said a couple of words to them. The gypsy man said a couple of words, and the big brown man said a couple of words. The next thing I knew, I was in the middle of the ring with big boxing gloves on, facing the tallest gypsy boy, my heart pounding.

Now, I wasn't exactly a sissy. The first day I went to school in Boomtown, when they unloaded all the new desks for the Union Hall School on the hill, all the boys attacked each other with the straw padding that was sandwiched between cardboard. I hit some blond kid on the head, he turned and attacked me with his fists. Evidently, I could hit hard. I saw a blond, fifth grade teacher watching and I assumed she would break the fight up right away, like they did in my old school in Denver. But she only stood on the porch and watched us fight. She didn't make a move. I put up my guard, as I had been shown by Al, and jabbed and blocked and countered and made the boy quit.

I had two more fights for the same reason that day, and I won them both, too. I quickly became known as a scrapper, who was handy with his fists, and was asked by the other boys to join their clubs. It was a taste of athletic glory. My cousin, Paul, who went to Denver University and was later shot down in a fighter plane over the Philippine Islands during World War II, taught me how to wrestle and bring down bigger guys by tackling them low on the legs. I was a good rough-and-tumble fighter, the kind of kid who sometimes chased other boys home. The new school principal thought I was too small to play in organized games with the older, bigger boys in my grade, though. He always put me on the sidelines with the other misfits: tall, skinny, awkward boys, round, roly-poly fat boys and tiny boys like me. But he was mistaken, because I could fight.

Now, here I was in the center of the ring, facing a kid a foot taller than me. The tall gypsy boy came at me and I didn't get a chance to dance and box, he was too big for that. But I knew how to keep my head down and stay in close so I wouldn't get hit in the face. From there, I could hook to his head and body with both hands. That's what I did, non-stop, while he pounded on the top of my head and arms. I felt like I was suffocating, but I kept punching and was getting the best of him. I kept driving him backwards toward the ropes, determined to knock him through them, like I had heard a great fighter like Dempsey had done to Tunney. My brother had put me in there and, though I was scared, I wasn't afraid. If I couldn't box and dance around the ring like Billy Cohn, I could slug, and I did. I drove the gypsy kid back toward the ropes. I put all my will and power into it and was doing it, too. He was so small at nine or ten, he could have fallen between the strands, even though he was taller than me. I had him almost to them and through them. My brother shouted, "Hey! Get away from the ropes! Move back into the center of the ring!"

I stopped and stepped back, did what I was told, and Al stopped the fight. He had ruined my plan for a spectacular victory.

The dark-skinned gypsy father then pointed at me and laughed and said, "Your face is all red!"

All the gypsies laughed, as if for this reason I had lost. But I was pale-skinned and my face got red from sheer effort, not from punches. I knew I had won, because I drove him back around the ring and almost knocked him through the ropes. Even my older cousin, Manuel, said right after the fight, "Gee, Floyd, I didn't know you could fight like that!"

So, although my brother had gotten me in another fight, this was legal and I had won without getting hurt. Sometimes, he did me some good. I wish it could have stayed fun like that, but my brother got in trouble again.

Nobody told me anything at home in the cabin at the edge of the woods. I didn't see Al very regularly, so it surprised me to see him come riding by the school in a patrol car. He was sitting in the front passenger seat as the cop car came up the hill on the dirt road, crunching over the hard red dirt. It was recess and the whole school was out on the hill. When the cop car went past all the kids playing in the wide yard, I saw Al staring out the window at me. I raised my hand and waved, a strand of my straight brown hair hanging over my forehead, my mouth and eyes both wide open with the shock at seeing him in there.

Al lifted his hand, but didn't wave it and didn't smile either. He just looked away as the patrol car crept slowly by. I recognized the cop with him, a deputy sheriff called Frenchy, his big red face and thick jowls visible on the other side of Al. Six foot four, 240–260, I'd know now, a giant for those days when anybody over six feet was really tall. I'd heard some adults talk about him and say that nobody in Boomtown liked him, and now here he was driving around with my brother in the car. I thought about it all day at school and looked around for Al when I got home. I went into the big, sunny porch to see if he'd gotten back. When I turned around and saw my mother looking at me, I knew she didn't want to tell me about it. I kept my mouth shut.

Soon after that, my father sold the cabin and we moved down to Oakland, because there were good jobs down there in the shipyards, and also because of Al. Clarence, my tall blond buddy who was a whiz in math and a good athlete, got mad at me once and said, "Your brother's a convict." I think that kind of attitude also had something to do with them moving. My brother Eddy was already working in San Francisco and going to Cal in Berkeley.

My father packed the Model-A Ford. My mother made a bed on some mattresses in the back seat for my little sister and me, so we could sleep the whole four or five hour trip to the bay. Then, we left one evening in October, down highway 99 to the Bay Area.

PART TWO

Brothers' Keepers

1

Larry had given me the ride downtown on his bike. He was in the same fifth grade as me, although he was a head taller and a year older. He lived on Thirtieth Street and Chestnut, a short block from my house on Thirtieth and Adeline. He took me to Payless Market on Nineteenth and Telegraph. It was a huge warehouse-of-a-market, filled with different types of stores and stands, including a market with sundry goods. For some reason, we went in there and the next thing I knew, he was taking a pen out of a drawer, and I did, too. Then I followed him over to a side entrance where he ducked under the turnstile.

I squatted to duck down under the turnstile and sneak out without paying, when steel fingers clamped on my shoulder and I looked up to see a woman in dress clothes, pulling me back into the sundry goods section. Trapped in the pincers of her fingers, I was marched through the stalls, up some steep back stairs and into an office with wide windows that looked out over the entire store. We were right above the stand where the pens Larry and I had stolen were kept. There was a man up there who must have been watching all the time.

I was so scared, I shook. When she asked me my name, I lied and said, Floyd Sánchez, giving my mother's maiden name instead of Salas.

She pointed to the floor beneath a high counter and said, "You sit down under there!" Which I did. Then she asked me what my religion was.

When I answered Catholic, she said, "Catholics don't steal."

I just stared at the floor. She made me sit on the floor under the counter for a long time. I didn't have the slightest idea what was going to happen to me, but I knew I was in deep trouble. I knew my mother was going to spank me and that I had committed a terrible wrong, even a sin, for stealing. I was so ashamed, I couldn't look up.

Finally the woman said, "You come out of there and stand over here!" I got up and stood in front of her desk. She sat behind it and made me empty my pockets, I guess to see if I'd stolen anything else. I had ten cents in my pocket, so I wasn't penniless. But there was also a test I'd taken in grammar school with my name, Floyd Salas, written across the top of it.

"Oh, you not only steal, but you lie, too," she said, and I felt my face light up with hot shame.

"How old are you?" she asked.

"Nine," I said.

"Are you sure?" she said.

I nodded my head, afraid to insist, even though I was nine and small for my age.

"What's your phone number?" she asked. When I gave it to her, she immediately picked up the phone and dialed the number. I remember she asked over the phone, "How old is he?" She listened for a moment, then said, "Seven!" and glared at me as if I had lied to her again. Evidently the person on the phone at home was trying to help me by saying I was younger than I was. She then handed me the phone.

"Hello!" I said, and when my sister Dorothy said, "Floyd! What's the matter?" I wailed, "Oh, Dorothy!" and burst out crying.

I was sobbing so loudly, the woman took the phone from me. I don't know what else she said, but she hung up the phone and looked at me. I was still sobbing, rubbing my eyes with the back of my hand, trying to hide my face. Finally she said, "You can go home now. But don't come here and steal ever again. Do you understand?"

I nodded, still sobbing, and walked out, following her pointing finger to the swinging gate that led down the narrow steps to the ground floor.

I hurried down Twentieth Street to San Pablo in the warm sun, my face feeling stiff from all the dried tears. I hurried north on the east side of the boulevard, past the giant, red granite cathedral of St. Francis Catholic Church, which made me feel guilty again. I'd committed a sin and knew it, and God would punish me for it. I turned my face away towards the Greyhound Bus Depot across the street, which as usual had a lot of people moving in and out of the front door. Then I looked ahead again, up toward Thirtieth Street, where I had to turn left to head home in a few short blocks. I was going to get my just deserts, for sure, from my mother—the second punishment, after the store detective grilling.

When I started across Twenty-Second Street, and crossed over the street-car tracks where the electric B Train was bound across the Bay Bridge for San Francisco, I saw a kid I knew casually from Clawsen Grammar School sitting on his shoeshine kit. He was a brown Filipino kid named Vincent. He and his sister were the only Filipino kids in school. I was so glad to see someone I knew, I stopped to talk to him. Although we weren't friends, I told him what happened to me, saying I was probably going to get a spanking when I got home. He squinted up at me, through the strands of straight black hair that fell across his eyes, and nodded.

"Do you want a donut?" I asked.

He nodded again, so I stepped into a donut shop next to the old fashioned beerjoint on the corner and bought two big, sugar-glazed donuts for a nickel. I stepped back out and gave him one. I stood next to him until we both finished. Then, my face still stiff from the dried tears, I waved goodbye and started up San Pablo towards home.

I was getting gradually more and more scared the closer I got to the house, and I was trembling when I crossed Adeline on Thirtieth Street and saw my white house in the center of the block. It was a pretty house, solidly built, with love seats in the hallway and in the front room, wide rooms on the second story, with big walk-in closets and windows all around. It had been built in the twenties probably. But it didn't look pretty to me then. I was plain scared, and could barely reach out for the front doorknob when I crossed the porch.

As soon as I stepped into the big hallway, Dorothy rushed up to me and said, "What happened, Floyd?"

"I ... I ... " I couldn't finish because my mother stepped into the hall and, with a worried crease between her brows, stared at me through her rimless glasses, her green eyes shimmering with pale light. I started to cry again.

"Come on," my mother said and grabbed her purse from the dining room table and crossed to the coat rack to get her coat. "I'm going to find out what's going on right now!"

I cringed and started crying even more, knowing I was going to get whatever I deserved, but really dreaded having to face that woman detective again.

"You get your coat, too, Dorothy. We're going down there right now!"

"Ooooooooh!" I moaned, getting a taste now of the final day when God would pass judgment on me.

Dorothy got her coat, too, and Mother turned and reached for the door, when Al came running down the stairs from the second floor. He grabbed my hand and ran up the stairs, pulling me after him, refusing to stop when my mother called, "Albert! Albert! Come down here!"

"He's already paid enough, Momma!" he called back and pulled me down the hall and into our bedroom, right at the front of the house. "It's okay, Floyd! It's okay! Just don't do it again," he said. He hugged me and rocked me back and forth. He was back with the family again after being in reform school for six months.

When my sobbing finally quieted down and my chest quit heaving, he asked, "Who took you down there?"

"Larry Andre," I said.

"It's all right for now," Al said, "but don't let anybody lead you into anything like that again."

"Okay," I said, breaking out into another sob, feeling like my chest was going to crack with wracking pain. Suddenly I heard my name being called, "Floyyyd! Floyyyyyd!" and Albert let go of me.

We both stepped to our second story window. I could see Larry out there on his bicycle, looking toward the front door below us, his brown curls falling onto his forehead.

"Did he take you downtown on his bike?" Al asked. I nodded, and he said, "Wait here," and left the room.

I saw him go out onto the porch below me and shout, "You get away from here, kid, and don't come around my little brother again." When Larry looked up at him with a pale, scared face, Al said, "You heard me! Get going!"

Larry didn't say anything. He just pushed off on his bike and quickly pumped out of sight. I felt sorry for losing a friend, but I really felt grateful to my brother, who came back up the stairs and said, "Come on downstairs now. Mom's fine. You're okay. Just learn something from it. Never steal again. You don't want to end up in a reform school like me, do you?"

"Nooooo," I said, squinting my eyes with the hot tears that rolled out again.

"Come on down, then," Al said and, taking my hand, he led me out the door and down the hall to the stairs, where I could hear my mother in the kitchen, closing the refrigerator door. When I walked into the kitchen, still scared, both Mom and my sister turned to look at me. Mom's face was pink from the heat in the kitchen, but her green eyes were gentle. Dorothy smiled, showing that one dimple in the one cheek. I looked over at my brother, who smiled at me, also.

2

Three little kids with canvas bags stuffed with brand new copies of *Liberty Magazine* hung over our shoulders, we'd stopped on the busy corner of Nineteenth and Broadway, when Billy saw a quarter below the grate in the gutter, about a foot below. All three of us crowded around the grate and kept trying to stick something down there and pull the quarter up.

Donald and Billy Skipper were two tow-headed brothers my age. Billy was a potential terror. Billy's straight blond hair hung over his forehead just like Donald's and mine and that of every other kid who parted his hair on the side and didn't use pomade to keep it down. Billy looked like Donald, but was bigger and had a flattened nose and puffy lips, and he was always looking for some kind of rowdy fun. He had the idea of selling *Liberty Magazine*, which came out once a week, to earn some money.

I decided to go with him and Donald downtown that Saturday and sell the magazines for twenty-five cents to make a nickel a copy. We all went together instead of separating, and managed to sell a few copies each. We never thought of going different ways because we wanted to do it together. We must have wasted about a half hour on the quarter, trying to stick our fingers through the iron bars, then sticking a pencil down there, and even managing to touch the quarter, but with no luck. We were still crowded around it when a man came up and watched us for a moment, then said, "Now, don't you boys go steal anything, now."

We were all embarrassed and looked at each other. Then we stood up. We hadn't thought about stealing anything, though we were trying to get the free quarter. We walked away from him and kept on moving around the downtown streets, selling a copy here and there. Maybe I sold three or four copies, like Billy and Donald, then walked home with them. I felt pretty good when I walked in the front door with my bag of *Liberty Magazines* hanging around my neck. Al was lying on the bed in our room when I went upstairs to put my bag down.

"What you got there, Floyd?" he asked.

"*Liberty Magazine*," I said, and slipped the bag off my shoulder and handed it to him.

He looked inside, then looked up, his face intent. "How'd you do?"

31

"I sold three. That's fifteen cents. I can probably earn a quarter next Saturday, if I get started early."

He stared at me for a moment, then his brow furrowed and he said, "I don't want you going downtown selling magazines."

"Why?" I said, feeling like he was picking on me.

"Listen," he said and stood up, putting his hands gently on my shoulders. "Kids who hang around the streets pick up bad habits and get street-wise. I don't want you turning out like that."

"But I get a chance to earn money and it's fun doing it. Besides, I want to save enough money to buy me a bicycle like Larry's."

He looked right into my eyes. His face was set, but not stern, his narrow brows were sharp lines over his eyes. His high-bridged nose made his eyes look deep and dark brown.

"Is that what you're doing it for?" he asked.

I nodded. I did want a bike and it seemed that was the only way I was going to get one. I never thought of asking my father and mother for one. I was treated well, but I wasn't spoiled. My father earned good money, but he was a working man now, no longer the son whose father was a small town deputy sheriff and lumbermill owner, and whose mother had a general trading store in town. And, although the country was finally coming out of the depression after ten long years, there still wasn't much money to throw around. My older brother Eddy went to Cal and lived at home, too, and my father had three underage kids to support. So, I never presumed to ask.

"I'll tell you what I'm going to do," he said.

I waited for him to speak, never guessing he'd say, "I'm going to give you fifty cents a week for spending money. Which is twice what you can probably earn selling *Liberty Magazine*. Now, you save a quarter of that money for a bike, and when you've got five dollars of it saved, I'll put up the rest of the money and go buy you one."

I broke into a wide grin and threw my arms around him. He squeezed me and said, "I don't want my little brother hanging around the streets." I thought of the man who had warned us not to steal and how I'd taken that pen at Payless and got in trouble, and I knew now that's what he was talking about.

3

"I've got the five dollars saved up, Al," I said. He was sitting at the kitchen table with my father after dinner. It was Friday night and I knew he'd been paid for the week. It seemed like it'd taken a long, long time, but I'd finally saved five dollars. I'd counted my money just to make sure. I kept it in a metal box where I had some old flint Indian arrowheads I'd found in the forest in Boomtown. By then, we'd moved from Thirtieth and Adeline to Fourteenth, between Filbert and Myrtle, into a big, stucco, Spanish-style house with red, curling tiles on the roof and a pretty, little green lawn in front with a hedge running down one side. My Aunt Mattie, my mother's younger sister, lived in the bottom flat with her family, including my two teenage cousins, Junior and Julian.

"What?" Al said.

"Yes, I counted it today, and I've got exactly five dollars."

"Already? I don't even have enough money for my car yet," he said, smiling.

I waited, not wanting to say that he'd promised to buy me a bike when I had five dollars saved up, but he didn't say anything. Finally, I said, "Remember what you said when I had five dollars saved?"

He looked away and my father, a big, baldheaded man, looked at me, then at Al, and said, "You said you'd buy him one. Now go do it!"

Al blushed, but slid his chair back in the big sunny kitchen, and said, "All right, let's go."

I glanced at my father, who gave me a big smile with his bright, white teeth, and I ran into our room to get my coat. Then, I started downtown with Al. We only lived six blocks from town and the department stores, now, so we didn't have far to go.

But when we reached a bicycle store at dusk and saw some bikes in a lighted window, he just kept on walking. I ran to catch up to him, wanting to say we'd just passed a window full of them. But he still kept walking and I didn't say anything. Finally, we reached Money Back Smith's, a mens' and boys' clothing store, where he stopped and looked in the window at some mannequins and pointed at one of a young boy in blue jeans and said, "Floyd! How about a pair of Levis?"

I couldn't believe it. He'd faithfully given me fifty cents a week for months now and I'd faithfully saved half of it, twenty-five cents of it, each week.

"No," I said. "You promised me a bike."

"Well, how about a pair of Levis instead?" he said. He didn't say he was short of money. I knew he wanted to get a car himself, but that was going to cost a lot of money. I think if he'd asked me to understand, I would have. But he didn't. He just said, "How about a pair of Levis?" There was a sign on the Levis that said, "$2.95." I knew bikes cost about twenty dollars. But although they were very popular, I already had a pair and shook my head no and turned around and started walking home again.

"Floyd!" he called out. "How about a pair of Levis?"

I kept walking and didn't turn around.

4

"You promised him. So take him down and buy him one," my father said.

I hadn't talked to Al for a whole week. I was still mad at him when I went in for breakfast that Saturday morning. He and Dad were sitting at the table again. Mom was serving them sausage and eggs. Dorothy was washing some dishes. I didn't know where my little sister Annabelle was, and Eddy was in the hallway at the top of the stairs, where he'd set up his desk to study.

"You don't have to pay for it all at once. Put a down payment on it and buy it on credit. I looked in the paper and they've got some good deals at Western Auto Service up on San Pablo, by the Bay Bridge approach."

I knew they were talking about me and I didn't say anything, although the hurt came up and made my chest tight again. Al hadn't offered me my fifty cents this week either. I guess because he knew he'd hurt me the week before.

"How will I get there?" Al said.

"I'll drive you," my father said, and the next thing I knew I was standing in the Western Auto store looking at all the shiny chromed, brightly colored bikes. Another spectacular sight.

"No use getting a small one. He'll only outgrow it," my Dad said.

So we picked a 28-inch black Western Flyer. I could only reach the pedals with the tips of my toes when the seat was tipped down so it touched the frame of the bike. And I had to swing my butt over the bar each time I pumped down. My brother took my five dollars and five dollars of his own and then signed a contract for fifty cents a week until the bicycle was paid off. I was supposed to bring the money in every Saturday.

But once we'd bought it, we had to take it all the way home, so Al said, "I'll ride Floyd home on it, Dad. We'll see you there."

The next thing I knew, I was seated on the frame of the bike between Al and the handlebars and was flying down San Pablo Avenue with the wind in my face. Another spectacular sight. When we reached a corner at a red light, he balanced the bicycle in one spot without putting his foot down for nearly the whole time it took for the light to change. Then he pushed off and stood up on the pedals and started pumping, and soon we were a block down

35

again and flying through the streets on my new bike. He'd come through again. My brother. I looked up at him above me and he grinned down at me, showing his big front teeth. I grinned back.

5

Oakland was a port city packed with people building ships, and soldiers, sailors and Marines going off to war. It was also packed with people who were making money off the servicemen. The streets were always crowded. All the dance halls held dances every night and were always full. All the beer joints went full blast. Everybody had money, and I remember my sister Dorothy telling how a young sailor, who was going off into the Pacific Theater the next day, had burned a ten dollar bill at a dance. There was a price and wage freeze on then, and twenty-five cents would get an adult into a show. The dances cost a dollar at the door. A high-paid shipyard worker made a dollar an hour. It cost fifteen cents for a Jack's Footlong hotdog. Twenty-five cents for pie a la mode. Bar drinks were fifteen cents, too. A Coke and a phone call each cost a nickel. A quart of milk fifteen cents. A man on the A train to San Francisco was shocked when I told him my brand new leather jacket cost ten dollars. He said he'd never paid a price like that for a leather jacket when he was a boy. Ten dollars was a lot of money.

We seemed to have a lot of parties. They weren't formal things, but after Dorothy got married, my mother got my father to buy a big, Victorian house, which had beautiful woodwork and furniture in it. It had an apartment for Dorothy and her new husband, Frank, to live in. Back in those days, everybody was encouraged to make apartments out of attics and basements to shelter all the workers and their families who had come out to join the defense industry. Restaurants were crowded all the time. The shows were filled every night. War was the order of the day. Mass production of defense goods. War and excitement.

My mother usually had big dinners on Sundays and there was always a crowd around the dining room table when I'd get home from the afternoon show. Al would be there, having fun with the family, and not getting into trouble for the first time since he was a little boy. I'd never seen him happier and would never see him happier again. He seemed completely changed. He started training to box again, too. He entered the Golden Gloves and, although I didn't get to see him fight, he won the novice lightweight title of the California Golden Gloves in 1942.

He turned pro right after that. I went to see his first pro fight at the Civic Auditorium in San Francisco. Al came out and went after a black guy. I don't remember the fight very well, but Al kept after him. I remember the guy, who was cute, dancing around to get away, grabbing the rope with one hand and jabbing with the other a couple of times. After four rounds, they gave the fight to my brother. I cheered loudly and liked the fight and the decision, even though it wasn't particularly exciting. It was still a spectacular sight to an eleven-year-old boy.

⊖   ⊖   ⊖

I was really a loner most of the time, since I now lived in another community, centered around 14th and Market, and the kids I hung around with at school didn't live near me.

I read a lot and went to the movies by myself most of the time, and went to church alone, too. I immersed myself in Jack London's *Call of the Wild* and *White Fang* and even read *Before Adam*, about prehistoric, monkey-like human creatures, which haunted me. I read *The Odyssey* all the way through at the back of the room in the fifth grade because the teacher, Miss DePew, thought I was too young and too small to be in her fifth grade and never called on me. It was only when I went into Miss Evans' room in the high fifth and she heard me read one page that she put me into the highest reading group immediately. She then made a sergeant out of me when they gave an IQ test and she saw how smart I was. She encouraged my art work, too, putting it up in the room and the hall. But Miss DePew always discouraged me when I moved back into her room for the sixth grade, which is where I was the Spring of 1942. I would belong to the first graduating class of Clawsen Grammar School after the war had started.

I still did well because I read so much. I started reading biographies at eleven in the seventh grade: Mussolini, Napoleon, Will Rogers, Joaquín Murieta.

In those days, kids could go into a bar, if they didn't drink, which I, of course, didn't. One night I went with Al and two of his boxing buddies and my Uncle Lesher, who was my mother's youngest brother, to a bar up on Market Street, about 19th Street, next to the Greyhound bus garage. It was a typical neighborhood bar in a working class residential area. Market Street was the business street of the community, but mostly had houses on it. My mother's brother, my Uncle Lucio, lived across the street from the bar and we probably came there to pick up Uncle Lesher, who was Al's age exactly, although he was Al's uncle.

I remember some words between Lesher and some guy in the bar. We got in Al's car to drive off, when this guy came out of the bar after us. His car was in the middle of the block. He shouted something at Lesher, then ran into the bus garage, where men were working the swing shift. The entire big garage with the high, wide doors was lit up. He came running back out with a shovel and slapped it into the side of the car. Al pulled to a stop right there and everybody jumped out of the car and ran into the garage after him. The next thing I knew, I was standing outside the garage watching all the guys in the car fighting all the guys in the garage.

It was spectacular. I saw Al charge after one guy—I think he was a black mechanic in coveralls—and Lesher fight with the blond guy who'd hit the side of the car. Al's buddy, this big handsome guy named Manuel Lugo, was fighting this big mechanic who had his head down and was swinging a monkey wrench at Manuel's head. All the fights were going on at once. There was some other guy with Al, too, but I can't remember him. I was too excited to really see much more, anyway. Then the next thing I remember we were driving away from the fight, headed down Market to Twelfth and our big Victorian house. Manuel was saying, "I must have lost my punch. I must have lost my punch."

What a sight it had been! When I told Al that some guy had tried to sneak up on him, he said, "Why didn't you help me?"

I stared up at him with wide eyes.

⊖ ⊖ ⊖

I was starting to learn how to be an altar boy at St. Andrew's Catholic Church. I had made my First Holy Communion and was considered a crackerjack by the priests, who used to smile at me when I came in to help serve mass because I was so little. We got to come in to class a little after nine at Clawsen Grammar School because we served the eight o'clock mass and it took us a few minutes to walk from the church at 36th and Adeline to 32nd and Magnolia, where the school was. I went to confession every Saturday night, not because I wanted to be good or because I felt guilty, but because my schoolmates went to church all the time, so I did, too. I did like the serene beauty of the interior of the church, the way the light came through the stained glass windows, reflected off the beautiful statues, especially Christ's uplifted face with that beseeching look in his upraised eyes, the highlights of his sculptured bones, and the halo that seemed to surround the priest when he spoke from the pulpit.

I only followed what everybody else in church did. I did it all by rote, but there was a deep inner satisfaction, even when my knees used to ache from the long kneeling. I used to daydream in the church and let myself drift into an almost non-thinking state in which I floated on some inner spiritual plane.

I didn't go way up to St. Andrews on 36th Street for either confession or Sunday mass because we lived down on Fourteenth and Filbert. One Saturday night, Al gave me a ride to confession at St. Mary's Church in his 1940 blue Studebaker. He hadn't gotten into trouble lately and he was looking good. With him in the car was a slender blond girl, Eileen, who was the girlfriend of our next-door neighbor June. Eileen started questioning me about what confession was all about. She was sitting next to Al, as I remember, and I was on the outside of the front seat of his Studebaker. I didn't mind telling her about it, but Al stopped the conversation, saying, "Talk about something else, Eileen." They took me to the church and dropped me off. Nobody worried about my walking home at night alone. Oakland at that time was still a peaceful place, but it was going to change fast.

God made the world. God made everything. God would take care of me, so I didn't worry.

6

Mom was dressed in a blue dungaree workshirt and pants, with a bandanna wrapped around her head to go to work in the shipyard when I got up early one morning to go to school. What a sight it was to see my very feminine, delicately boned mother, dressed up like a shipyard worker, with a rust-colored hard hat and everything. The war had come to our house, too.

Mom, who was running a big house filled with people, still wanted to do something for the war and earn some money. So she got a job in the shipyards, like all the other patriotic women. I think she did it for the fun. A lot of the women she knew, all the housewives who no longer had very little children, joined the defense industry to defeat the Japs and the dirty Huns. So she went off to be with the girls.

But it was too much for her. The hard work strained her weak heart. The next thing I knew, she became this pale woman lying in bed with a puffy face and a wrinkled forehead. I would go in to get my lunch money and I didn't like having to look at her. I'd back out and hurry away to school, knowing that something was wrong, but not realizing how serious it was until I came home one day and she wasn't there, but in a hospital ironically called Providence. It was a Catholic hospital that had a small chapel in it.

Al came home from Texas on an emergency furlough. He had tried to join the Marines after the war first started, but they wouldn't accept him because of a punctured ear-drum. But the Army did take him in late 1942. Eddy, on the other hand, had a deferment as long as he stayed in school. He was due to graduate from Cal in August 1943, then either go on to medical school or go into the service. Al was sent down to Texas where, after boot camp, they put him in the military police. It was ironic. He had changed. He no longer stole or even thought of it. And he knew how to deal with lawbreakers, especially the kind of laws soldiers broke, drunk and disorderly mostly, he told us.

I was really glad to see Al, although I was sad it had to be because Mom was dying. We went to see Mom at the hospital. One day when I went to see her after school, Mom said, "Go pray for me, Floyd. Hurry. Hurry!"

I rushed out of her room and went to the chapel and prayed there for a long time, begging God to save my dying mother, pounding my chest with my fist, saying prayer after prayer after prayer.

Eddy woke me the next morning. He was squatted down next to the sofa cushions I'd laid next to my father's bed so I could be near him that night. The house was full of relatives who'd come to be near Mom in her last hours, and other members of the family were using my room. I wanted to be near my Dad. I didn't think about it, I just wanted to. I looked up into Eddy's face. I could see the faces of my Aunt Emma and my sister Dorothy hovering behind him, two beautiful women, their faces long and sad in the shadows. His face by the light near the window was pink and quiet.

"Floyd. There's something I've got to tell you."

I knew instantly what he was going to say, "Mother's dead. Isn't she?"

He nodded his head.

"Momma! Momma! Come back! Come back! Come back, Momma!" I cried and pounded my fist against a cushion. Then I fell on the cushions and sobbed and sobbed.

I saw her in the coffin during the praying of the rosary that night. She had a sore on her lip. Her face, swollen a little, was pink and white, framed by her dark brown, curled hair. The first strands of gray showed in the hair swept back by her ears. Her high forehead was a swatch of pink. Her cheeks were rouged and her lips reddened, but for the brown sore breaking through on her lower lip. I tried to avoid looking at it. I looked at her long, slender, pale white hands, one placed over the other. They were aristocratically delicate, long-boned, nearly transparent, except for the cloudy milkiness along the knuckles and along the flat back of the top hand.

I knelt down next to the coffin to say the rosary out loud with the priest who was leading it. The prayers pounded into me with the thud of my fist against my chestbone. The words of the "Our Father" blowing out of my opened lips. The heavy wet scent of flowers. The thud on my chest. Although kneeling, in my head I could see the sore on her lip turning into a brown bud. The hollows of her closed eyes. Her whole face suddenly swimming in a blurry wet motion before me. Tears spilled out my eyes and down my cheeks in hot streaks. I heard my voice cry out, "Momma, Momma, Momma," as I leaped up and threw myself into the coffin and grabbed her stone cold hands, sobbing, sobbing, the hot tears streaking down my cheeks, my eyes burning.

"Momma, Momma, Momma."

7

Eddy closed the white refrigerator door and faced me. He was dressed in a dark tweed sportcoat and tweed slacks. His long face looked down on me. He had a long nose with a bump on it as if it had been broken. His lips were full. His eyes looked like mine, but were large, slightly bulbous, but exactly the same hazel-green color as mine. I'd seen pictures of him as a boy that I thought at first were me. That's how much we looked alike. Except that I was smaller, of course.

"Floyd. Now that there's a lot of disorder in the house and everybody's very busy, you might not get enough balanced meals, so take one of these every day at some time."

He took a box of vitamin capsules out of the refrigerator and showed it to me.

"Okay," I said.

"One other thing," he said. "Be aware that Dad's going to keep trying to give you things so he can try to make up for Mother dying. It's his way of showing love to you."

His right eyebrow was arched over the eye, with a furrow in his forehead. His face was kind, but serious.

"Yes," I said.

"Well, don't let him spoil you. You can take things from him, of course, but don't let him ruin you because he feels sorry for you. Do you understand?"

"Yes," I said, "like when we went into that roadside bar on the way back from the funeral and he kept trying to buy me a Coke when I didn't really want one, and I told him I didn't."

"That's right," he said. "That's exactly what I mean."

"All right, I won't," I said.

"Good," he said and led me back into the front room, where all the people who'd been to the funeral were socializing.

I heard him and I tried to take the vitamin capsules, like he told me, but I kept seeing my dead mother in my mind. Especially if I was alone, like in the morning or when I went to bed at night, I would think of her, and the sadness welled out of me. I'd look at the vitamin box and know I should take one out and swallow it, but I didn't.

During the week after the funeral my eyes started running tears and kept running tears so often and so badly, they started stinging and then staying red and then finally tearing and stinging and staying red all the time. When I had trouble just opening my left eye without it watering all over me—my eye felt like I was crying when I wasn't—Eddy said, "Floyd, you have to go to the doctor."

He took me to San Francisco near Union Square and the St. Francis Hotel and told the doctor that I would totally cooperate with him and follow his directions conscientiously. The doctor nodded seriously and put medicine in my eye and a white patch over it, then taped it to my head. I wore the patch for about two weeks, then the other eye went blind, and then I had to do it with that eye, too.

But when I at first wore the patch, Al took all the cousins and male friends a block up to MacClymonds High School and played baseball. I was out in the field with my patched eye when the ball came rolling toward me. I squatted down to catch it, but I'd lost depth perception and it rolled between my legs and Al laughed and made fun of me. I wasn't a school athlete and really didn't know how to play, it's true, but I could catch a rolling ball and had been on my grade's softball team in centerfield in Boomtown.

I said, "I couldn't judge it with the patch," but he still laughed at me and I could see the humor in it. It did roll right between my legs. I also fell off a buddy's bicycle, too, in the same kind of way. I was riding on the back paper-rack and, when he turned by Lafayette School, I fell off onto my face. Then I stood up in the hot sun and looked across the street at the kids in the playground who'd seen me fall, and saw heat waves shimmering in front of me.

Somehow, I think the grief of seeing my mother dead made me want to go blind. I can remember sitting in the funeral home at mass the day of her burial, wanting the impossible to happen, for her and me to rise up together out of the coffin and into the sky, so that everybody could see that she was going to heaven and that I loved her so much that I was going with her. I guess I wanted to die, too.

When Al went off to war, and Eddy graduated from Cal and went into the Naval Reserves as an officer's candidate at Northwestern University in Chicago, and my little sister Annabelle went to live with my Aunt Dolly and Uncle Tommy and Cousin John, and my big sister Dorothy lived upstairs with Frank in the front master bedroom made into a studio apartment, my life really got lonely. I couldn't study at school and couldn't think of anything but my mother in that coffin with the sore on her lip and of my father sitting with the lights out in the corner of the big front room, where three high, wide windows made a little alcove. He would just sit there listening to "The Red

River Valley" over and over again on the phonograph, suffering and crying in the dark over my mother.

I not only missed my mother, but also my brothers and my father. He started going out drinking all the time and he would leave me alone in the house. I'd go ask the people who lived in the rooms upstairs if I could sleep on a mattress in their room with an American flag blanket over me, because I was afraid of burglars.

Once my cousin Manuel, who was a sailor, went with me to pick up my father's check at Moore's shipyards at the foot of Adeline Street in Oakland. We had left the front door unlocked. When we came back, my dog Trixie started growling at the piano. Manuel was afraid to go into the room, but I went in with an old shotgun with a broken hammer and pointed it at the piano.

Trixie kept growling at it. I went back to the kitchen to get Manuel and said, "Come on and look behind the piano with me." But he just shook his head and insisted on keeping the swinging kitchen door shut. We'd barely sat down again when we heard the dining room door to the hall slam, footsteps in the hall, then pounding down the front stairs. We realized the burglar had really been in the house when we had come back. It was really scary.

8

A mail truck was doubled-parked in front of the house when I went to answer the doorbell.

"Floyd Salas?" the mailman asked.

I looked down at the big cardboard box on the porch next to him.

"Yes?" I said.

"Sign here," he said and had me sign a lined piece of paper with my name on it.

Then, he pointed at the box and turned around and walked down the stairs. I was really mystified. I picked up the heavy box, turned around and put it on the seat of the big hall mirror with the clothes hooks.

One glance at the return address, which said, "Camp Maxy, Texas," and I knew it was from Albert. I was excited when I tore the box open and pulled out nine leather baseball mitts, almost new and enough for a complete team, with beautiful catcher's and first baseman's mitts.

"Dorothy! Look what Albert sent me!" I yelled. She came out of her apartment upstairs and down the staircase to look at the mitts I pulled out of the box. A pretty, dark-haired young mother now, she was carrying her daughter, Sharon, a little tow-blond, blue-eyed infant.

"You see!" Dorothy said, "Al thinks you can play when you have two eyes, Floyd!"

We both laughed.

Θ   Θ   Θ

Al sat on the stool to Mother's vanity with his back to the big mirror. I could see his square-jawed face and the little knot on the high nosebridge, the deeply set brown eyes, the lean cheeks, his puffy upper lip and the quick tremors of animation that crossed his expressive face.

He was home on Christmas furlough.

He looked great. He'd sent me and Dad copies of the Army base newspaper every time he was in it, which was a lot. Dad had made a big scrapbook of Al's boxing career, to keep with the other scrapbooks which traced the war. Al won the 1943 Texas Golden Gloves senior championship. We were both very proud of him. When I first talked about my boxing champion brother, the guys on my baseball team doubted me until I showed them the scrapbook. Then they admired him, too.

It was as if a glowing spirit had entered the house. Everybody gathered around him. My father, who slept in the back bedroom on the bottom floor, even stayed home. Dorothy and Frank, who had come back from the South Pacific on a merchant marine vessel, came into the bedroom, too. We all sat around in the bright light from the wall of windows at the back and Al told us all about Army life.

His thick shoulders and the wings of muscle under his arms that stretched his tailored tan uniform reflected in the mirror behind him. I could see both his front and back simultaneously. It was as if he was there in fourth dimension. All his words and gestures seemed significant. I was only twelve, but I suddenly realized how much he meant to me. A tense anxiety gripped me that I might miss even a moment of his visit home, the first time I'd seen him in six months.

9

The auditorium was a block big and had a dance floor the size of a football field. Harry James and his band were up on the stage at the far end. I could see his golden horn pointed at the ceiling, shimmering with light. He was one of my heroes. I'd seen him in movies with Betty Grable and other famous stars. I'd been in the auditorium once before when Al had taken me to a professional fight. That night I had seen a referee slap a boxer's face when he cursed at him during a fight. But I'd never seen such a big floor absolutely covered with people.

There had to be five thousand people packed together dancing on that floor. Soldiers and sailors and Marines and guys in civies, dress suits, ties, zootsuits, the women dressed up in slinky dresses and high heels which showed their curving hips and legs. Sometimes circles would form around jitterbugging couples. There were huge crowds around the bars in the big hallway that circled the auditorium on three sides, like a horseshoe starting at the sides of the stage. There was a constant roar of talk and laughter and the hustle of movement as the dance floor throbbed with dancing bodies. It was one of the greatest sights I'd ever seen.

Al led the way from the top of the horseshoe shaped hall to the last door by the side of the band, where we walked in. I couldn't have been more than a hundred feet away from Harry James himself. He was a handsome man with a mustache and dark wavy hair. He wore a dark blue doublebreasted suit and everybody else in his band wore a maroon-colored doublebreasted suit. There were a handful of singers sitting on chairs in front of the band, at the side near me. I'd never seen anyone famous in person before. I just kept staring at him over the pack of people between the hall door and the stage.

"Come on, let's go sit on those chairs so you can see better," Al said, and we turned to the right and sat up in the rows of elevated seats that circled three sides of the dance floor.

Right in front of us, between the front row of seats and the side of the stage, all the local Oakland people bunched up and made circles around jitterbugging couples. It was really exciting, the throbbing big band beat and the couples twisting and turning. I saw lots of older guys and girls from my neighborhood, Fourteenth and Market Streets, and said hello to a few of them, including my older cousins Lee and Sally. Al and Lesher had both stepped down on the dance floor, too, and were talking to people they knew when I heard a sort of rumbling noise, but I couldn't quite make it out because we were so close to the blasting sound of the band.

I stood up in my second row seat and looked out over the auditorium towards the front doors and saw people. Then, I saw the heads of a lot of men, soldiers, sailors, Marines and civilians who were fighting each other. The row of couples in front of me stood up, too, and I stepped out into the aisle between the rows of elevated seats to see better, as the band kept up its big, throbbing beat, playing "Tuxedo Junction." Harry James' big, brash trumpet sang out in quick staccato as the couples twisted and turned and hopped and jumped near me.

I watched, fascinated as the fight seemed to ripple out over the floor and wave down the long block towards us, engulfing everybody in its wake. There was a stamping of feet as women screamed and people swung and swayed and stumbled as they were shoved back by the fighting surge. I couldn't believe what I was seeing. It was incredible. It was spectacular. But the giant wave kept coming and then suddenly swept right through the crowd around the stage and down our side, knocking into Albert and Lesher, who started fighting right away. I could see their heads down, their arms swinging at guys who were swinging at them. Then, the wave came right up to me, and a man suddenly rocked back into me and knocked me off the elevated aisle and down onto the dance floor.

I got stepped on, but managed to scramble up in my little blue plaid loafer jacket and get to my feet again. Then, I saw Lesher fighting someone near me, saw him swing and his fist come flying in an arc, miss the guy in front of him and hit me right in the cheek.

He stopped, green eyes wide in his pink face. "You, okay, Floyd?" he asked and I nodded.

The punch must have already been spent when it hit me, because it didn't hurt at all. He then turned and started fighting this little sandy-haired sailor again. I could see the little guy's wife shouting and trying to pull Lesher off, when, just as suddenly as it started, the giant wave of the fight that had splashed against us seemed to ebb back and all the fighting stopped again. That's when I saw Al pick the little sailor up from the floor, and ask "How about a beer?" The little guy nodded his head and Al waved me to follow him and they walked out the big hall doors and down the hall to the first bar and ordered a round of beers.

I watched as they all talked. None of them had any marks on them. The little sailor's wife, a slender, petite, little brunette woman with a pale complexion, stood behind her husband and told him not to drink with Al and Lesher. But he just ignored her. I heard her say, almost as if to me since there was nobody else there, "They beat him up and then he drinks with them."

I didn't know what to say back to her, but Al and the sailor and Lesher seemed to be doing the right thing to me, being friends after the fight. I told Al I was going to the men's room and walked down the hall and across it about fifty feet, when I suddenly heard a commotion and turned around. There was the little sailor fighting Al and Lesher again. He was a cute little guy and he didn't back up at all, just kept punching until the cops came and broke it up. They sent him and his wife away and told Al and Lesher to stay there. I noticed that the cops didn't put anybody in jail, and I asked Al about it.

"They teach them how to be tough and fight in the service and a lot of them have to be back at base to go overseas and kill Japs. That's probably why," he said. "Here, let's get away from the bar, it's too crowded."

We went and stood on the other side of the hallway, right across from the bar, near the women's restroom. I could hear the sweet tone of Harry James' trumpet blowing a slow one in the auditorium. But I got thirsty and said, "Al, could I get a Coke?"

"Yes," he said and handed me a quarter.

I crossed the hall and went up to the bar, but it was crowded. I was looking for a place to slide in when I felt a hand run down my back and over my butt.

I looked up as a middle aged man with a pot belly and a round, red face, smirked at me and pulled his hand away. I knew he meant evil, but he was twice as big as me. I walked back over to Al, who was talking to Lesher and a couple of other guys.

"Al," I said, "that man over there rubbed my butt." I pointed out the middle-aged man.

"Go hit him in the mouth," Al said.

I walked back across the hall and up to the man, who turned around and saw me just before I reached him and blasted him in the mouth with a wide right hook from my side.

It knocked his head back, and when he straightened up, there was blood on his lip. He started to jump at me. I stood there with my fists raised, not at all scared because of Al. Then I saw him glance across the hall and catch himself with his arms already up and spread to grab me. I could see Al and the other guys all staring at him, waiting, and he stepped back and reached into his back pocket and took out a handkerchief and dabbed at his split lip. He then turned and walked away. I walked back to Al and the others with my hand stinging. I looked down and saw blood on the knuckle that I'd cut on his teeth.

They all looked at me when I walked up and didn't say a word, but I felt glad I'd been able to hit him for molesting me.

"Come on, let's go out on the dance floor and have some fun," Al said. We walked back down the hall and through the big doors and out onto the dance floor. We could barely work our way in because there was a big crowd around a couple who could really jitterbug.

"Come on, I know her," Al said. "Let's go watch. She's one of the best dancers in town."

He pushed his way through the crowd into the front of the circle around the dancers, with me following him.

She was really good. A slender woman with dark, almost frizzy hair and a beautiful, slinky body whose breasts and hips and haunches quivered in unison to the throbbing swing beat, a really fast one.

The couple broke apart to boogie and she slithered back on her high heels right into me. She turned around and said, "Oh, I didn't see you, sorry!"

And I said, "It must be jelly because jam don't shake like that!" which were the words of a rhythm and blues song, and I shook my shoulders.

She grinned and shook her shoulders back at me and started doing some boogie dance steps in front of me. I did some back and she grabbed my hand and pulled me out into the middle of the circle and started boogying with me. I knew how to boogie. I was one of the very best dancers in my junior high school. I had learned it around my older brothers and sisters and my older cousins and so could really do it. We boogied back and forth. I shook my shoulders and slid my feet and rocked my body and shook my knees like a Hawaiian dancer and did the splits and came up rocking. She closed with me and we twisted back and forth in the center of the crowd until Harry James and his big band blew into a rousing climax and ended with a quick stop in the middle of a beat. The young woman burst out laughing and grabbed me and kissed me on the mouth as the whole circle of people around us burst out clapping.

10

One day when I was walking with Albert downtown just before he was supposed to go back to camp, we ran into the two dark-haired twins, Tony and Johnny, and one of their buddies, a fair-haired kid who was as husky as Al. They lived further down in West Oakland and went to Peralta School, about a mile west of my house. They were my age, but a year behind me in school, so I considered them younger than me, even though they were taller and the same age, twelve.

They made some comment when they walked by me and I made some comment back. Not much, we didn't even cuss, none of us.

But after we walked by, Al said, "Go back and hit him for that."

I could fight. I could box and I could hit. Not many young kids can knock another guy down with a single punch, but I learned I could in fights. I got in fights once in a while and won them all, although I did get my head knocked around a few times, enough to teach me to keep my head down and not get hit if I could help it. I hung around with Al, I wanted to be like him, be a fighter, too.

"Now?" I said.

"Now," he said and I ran back to them. They were waiting for a red light on Eighth and Washington Street. When I reached the corner, they turned around and all of them put up their fists. I smashed the first, short husky guy in the nose and the blood spattered all over. But he ducked his head and started fighting and we both slugged it out there on the corner until Al broke us up and took me down the street to his Studebaker.

He was grinning. My T-shirt was spotted with the guy's blood. He drove down Seventh Street and saw a guy he knew, Baby Tarzan, a little featherweight fighter who was standing on the corner with two young women across the street from a creamery on Seventh and Castro Street.

Al pulled over and they waved to him, then came up and got in the car. They asked him how the Army was. One of them commented that he was losing his hair. I hadn't noticed myself, and Al said, "Floyd just had a fight."

One of the dark-haired women looked at me, narrowed her eyes and said, "He looks like he got the worst of it."

"That's the other guy's blood," Al said, and they all nodded. I felt a little proud, and got a taste of bootleg glory again.

I'd fight those twins about three times before I left Hoover Junior High School. Once, when I was delivering papers on my route and was on tree-shaded Chestnut Street near the boundary of their neighborhood, I fought one twin and that other blond kid. But this time my punches made the guy duck down and cover up, so I punched him on his back with roundhouse hooks and hurt him. The other twin was afraid to help him, so the one I was fighting called out, "Hey, Johnny, you gonna help me or not?" But Johnny wouldn't help him, so I stopped and went on my route again. They still threatened me when they saw me, but didn't attack. I can't explain it, but I felt like fighting them every time I saw them. The last time was when I saw them at a carnival on Twenty-second and Filbert Street. I hit one of them in the nose and knocked him down and the other was afraid to fight me again. Later, I saw them looking around the carnival for me with a bigger guy who was about sixteen or seventeen. I didn't hide, but they didn't see me.

Something happened to me, though. Nobody was ever home. I lived mostly alone and would go take money out of the money sacks my father kept the rent money in when I needed to go to a movie or for lunch or whatever. I never abused the privilege. Still, I was lonely, and all the movies I saw were about war and heroism and killing the Japs and the Germans and the dirty Wops. I'd see fights downtown between sailors and civilians all the time. The whole country was geared up for violence. The shipyards went twenty-four hours a day to make ships to carry the guns and soldiers to the front. War, war, war, war everywhere. It seemed to fill me. I wanted to be a hero like Errol Flynn and Robert Taylor and James Cagney and John Garfield and my brother Al. Mostly, I wanted to be like Al. I wanted to be strong and handsome and tough like him. But I wasn't too strong, and I wasn't very tough and I wasn't handsome, it seemed to me. But I tried and got myself in trouble, suspended from school. I wasn't the scholar I'd been the year before. I cut school for two weeks straight once, and, when the nurse showed up at the house to see what was wrong with me, I tried to hitchhike to Los Angeles, but only got as far as Palo Alto and came back.

I was lonely. Although I belonged to the Boy Scouts and passed fourteen tests in one week at Camp Diamond in the Oakland hills, I wasn't happy. I just wanted my brother Al to come home again.

Eddy came home instead. He was on furlough from the Navy, where he taught in a naval college near Boston

"Floyd ... " he said. He hesitated and for a moment I could see frustration on his face, the slightly open mouth, a wrinkling at the corner of his left eye.

I nodded my head to help him. "Yes," I said.

"Dorothy says that Al takes you everywhere with him when he's home on furlough."

I nodded.

"When he comes home for good, he won't do that. He'll associate with friends his own age. So, you can't expect to hang around with him. You've got to keep building your own life."

My heart seemed to start beating hard. I sat up.

"Is Al coming home for good?"

Eddy glanced over at Dorothy, who'd been sitting quietly on a big stuffed sofa chair.

"Al's trying to get a medical discharge so he can come home and turn professional. He could come home for good in a couple of months."

"Wow!" I said and stood up. "I'm going to go to church and pray right now. Right now."

Dorothy grinned, but Eddy's mouth just stretched in a sad, soft smile.

PART THREE
The Pro

1

Dad opened the trunk of Al's Studebaker to put Al's suitcase and gym bag in. We'd met Al when he got off the train at the SP Depot, then walked out to the car in the parking lot. Al was home for good. He'd gotten a medical discharge from the Army as a head case, despite having won Gloves titles in three states: California, Texas and Michigan in 1942, '43 and '44. He was going to turn pro. I was proud of him for being such a brave fighter. I took him at his word that he had faked the doctors into thinking he was crazy so they'd discharge him and he could start fighting pro instead of staying in the service like Eddy. I didn't consider the morality of it. If Al did it, then it must be right. When he stretched his arm out in his khaki-colored sleeve to hand Dad his leather gym bag, I suddenly knew he was home for good. He shimmered through tears in my eyes, Army cap tipped back on his head so the brim pointed at the sky, wide face strong as stone. My brother Al was home. He was home.

I sobbed and sobbed until a middle-aged man, round like my father, who was standing on the other side of the car next to us, stared at me and then rattled off something in Italian to us. He thought we were Italians, too. I could tell he didn't mean anything, but he did stick his nose in our business.

Al said, "Watch yourself, fella," and the man shut up.

"Come on, let's go home and eat steak and eggs," Dad said.

2

I was mesmerized by Harry Fine's gym. I let my gaze sweep over the gym, past the fighters shadowboxing in the tall wall mirrors, mock-punching at their twins in the glass, over the robot-like motions of the boxers twisting their bodies on the exercise benches, the blur of a boxer's fists as he punched the speed bag with a machinegun racket, the tap-tapping of a fighter jumping rope, seeming to hover in flight just off the floor like a humming bird, and two boxers mauling each other in the ring with its black, rubber ropes.

Then, I skimmed my eyes over to the heavy bags in a dark corner, where the bags and boxers punching them made jerking shadows on the old-fashioned mahogany wall panels, where hundreds of fighters posed with cocked fists, bloodless as phantoms, trapped behind the glass walls of picture frames, and up to the hundred or so posters pasted up along the walls above the panels all around the whole gym, announcing all the fights, some great, some not so great, of all the years of fights dating back to World War I in Oakland.

Al was home and he was turning pro and I'd get to come with him to this beautiful place all the time now. I turned and followed Al into the office past Mrs. Fine, who sat at the long counter by the swinging doors at the entrance to the gym. She was a silver-haired woman, thick in middleage, with powdery white cheeks, who was taking some guy's money next to a sign that said fifteen cents.

Inside the office, a wall of windows looked down on Eleventh Street and out across it at the T&D Theater. A big man stood up and shook Al's hand, then sat down and pulled a long, legal size piece of paper out of his drawer and said, "This is the contract, Al."

He'd been a fighter himself and it showed. His big nose drooped crookedly down his face, hiding most of his upper lip with its bashed-in tip. He kept pushing his wire-rimmed glasses up on his nose with his broken hands. The scars on his thickened left eyebrow showed stark and emphatic above a permanently squinted eyelid. His brown, flannel sportshirt hung off his rounded shoulders, sagging across his flat chest, bunching around the wide, sloppy knot of his loud, checkered tie. He carried the stink of a cigar with him even though his nicotine-stained fingers were empty. He looked great to me, like a boxing character in a movie, another spectacular sight.

58

⊖ ⊖ ⊖

Dressed up in my blue gabardine slacks and new shoes, I sat in the front seat of the car between Harry Fine and Mrs. Fine, who squeezed up against me. It was an old luxury Packard from the thirties with deep, soft seats, arm rests on them and a dashboard that looked like fine wood paneling. When we got to the fights, I carried in the water bottles in a bucket and walked back to the dressing rooms. I was very excited. It was going to be one of the most spectacular things I'd ever seen in my life and I knew it.

The whole auditorium was packed. It cost a buck to sit in the gallery upstairs, two bucks for dress circle, the several rows of seats that surrounded three sides of the main floor of the auditorium where I'd seen Harry James and the great big riot. Ringside cost three whole dollars. Al kept getting up in the dressing room and going outside to the men's room on the Tenth Street side of the auditorium. When he came back the third time, Harry Fine asked, "What's the matter, Al?"

"I just threw up," Al said.

"Nervousness. Try to lay down on that shelf over there and rest. Try to relax."

"All right," he said, but then I got nervous, too. I'd never thought that he'd be scared, and now I saw it for myself. I went out and into the other dressing room in the hall by the men's room and saw this big black guy and I realized Al was going to fight him. The guy had to be five-ten or -eleven, at least, and it scared me.

When I went back into our dressing room, which was the same one every week, because Harry Fine had fighters in his stable fighting every week, Al was already getting dressed. He looked good. He slipped on a pair of black trunks with a red waistband and red stripes down the side and the word AL in red on the right leg of the trunks. His square face was lean with hollows in the cheeks and his eyes seemed to hide under his wide brow. His puffy upper lip seemed to pout with a sullen determination. He didn't smile. He didn't talk. He just got ready, then sat with one hand leaning on the back of a wooden chair, while Cocky Johnny wrapped his hands. Cocky Johnny's hair was starting to thin now and his pink, almost florid skin showed on his scalp. One cocked eye looked askew, but the other stared straight down at the gauze bandage he was wrapping around Al's hand. He was a well-known trainer. Later on, when he became more famous in the boxing world, they'd call him "The Count."

Al's short, pale fingers looked stubbed by the time Cocky Johnny got through wrapping his hand. Al made a fist and popped it into his bare hand. Then, Johnny wrapped the other one and Al popped that fist into his wrapped hand. Johnny picked up one small, six-ounce wine-colored glove and slid it onto Al's hand, tied it tightly, then wrapped tape around the wrist to hold it down. When he finished with the other one, it looked like Al's fists were only the size of baseballs. I suddenly realized how small the six-ounce gloves were and how it must hurt to be hit with such a hard ball of padded bone. Then, Johnny picked up a black and red silken robe and hung it over Al's shoulders.

"You ready?" he said. Al had just nodded and straightened up when someone, a gray-haired man, leaned his head in the dressing room door and said, "Curtain raiser! Salas!"

My chest started fluttering as we walked out the door into the big auditorium. I followed them down the aisle to the ring. When Al stepped in, I stepped back out of the way and went to stand at the end of the aisle, where I found an empty seat and sat down.

Al, Cocky Johnny and Harry Fine were already standing in the center of the ring. Al was barechested without his robe, getting instructions from the referee.

I held my breath, then sat up when both fighters went back to their corners. Cocky Johnny put Al's mouthpiece in and Al turned around at the sound of the bell. His head was down, his brow wrinkled as he danced out and circled the big, black guy whose back muscles rippled with shiny highlights.

The guy threw a jab and Al danced back, crouched low, looking a full head shorter, looking almost like a boy next to the tall, rangy fighter. Al circled the guy and then leaped in with a jab himself. When the guy tried to parry it with his right hand, reaching out and exposing his chin, Al threw a long left hook which connected, then another which connected, too, and wobbled the black guy. The crowd cried out and the black guy grabbed Al and held onto him. But the guy's head stuck straight up. I could see his eyes squinting as he held on. Al's head was under his chin, and I knew that was a good sign because, up close, Al was inside the guy's long arms.

Then Al suddenly cut loose with a rally to the stomach, about four or five punches with both hands. When the black guy started to pull away, Al leaped after him with a looping left hook to the chin, catching the guy right on it. He then hit him with a quick right hook from the other side, then a left hook again, all right on the chin, and the guy wobbled backwards this time and the crowd yelled and I yelled.

Al stayed right on him and hit him with another hook and another and the guy toppled to the canvas as the crowd screamed. I didn't realize I was standing up until the referee counted to ten. Then, Al bent down and hooked his arms under the guy's arms and helped stand him up on his feet.

The auditorium went crazy with shouting and stamping and whistling and clapping as the referee raised Al's arm and turned in a circle with him in the center of the ring. I could feel my heart pounding in my chest. My brother was home.

3

"Rinnnnnnnnnnnnnnng!" the alarm went off. I lifted my head from the pillow. It was still dark in the room Al and I shared at the end of the hall at the back of the house on the second floor. Dad's room was right below us on the main floor, next to the kitchen. We had twin wooden beds. I wanted to pull the covers over my head and go back to sleep, but I heard Al jump out of bed and say, "Let's hit it, Floyd!"

I slid out of bed and picked my Levis off the chair next to my bed, slid into them, then sat on the bed. In the dark, by feel, I found my tennis shoes and woolen socks and slipped the socks on, then the shoes, tied them, then stood up and, still wearing my white T-shirt, pulled my sweatshirt on over my head. Al was slipping into his sweatpants, sweatshirt and tennis shoes. I stepped out of the bedroom, into the long hall, turned left and stepped down a few steps into the bathroom at the end of the hall to take a leak. When I stepped into the big bathroom just next to the toilet, I could see the dark silhouette of the city starting to outline itself.

It was still dark, all right, but not pitch black. The shapes of the houses were becoming clearer. I turned on the hot water faucet in the big marble sink, caught the water in my palms and splashed it over my face and woke up. Then I picked up the bar of soap, rubbed it between my wet hands, put it back down in the deep dish carved into the sink surface and rubbed the soap over my face, then rinsed it off as Al came in to wash his face off, too.

He tapped my shoulder with his fist and said, "Let's get moving, Floyd. We've got three and a half miles to go."

We walked in the dark quietly down the curving staircase. As I went down I could see the big, stained glass window in the wall and the dark outlines of the red roses and green leaves of the flowering plant that completely framed the transparent glass in the center of the window.

I seemed to wake up again in the car beside Al as he drove down Twelfth Street through town, coming up on Lake Merrit and the auditorium at the foot of it. Al turned up Fallon Street, past the court house, and parked the car on the west side of the lake, next to the old Oakland Museum, a huge, white, wooden Victorian mansion. We got out, ran across the lawn, down to the water and started running along the wide dirt walk next to the dark water. The cool morning air filled my lungs and within a couple of blocks, my whole body heated up. I felt good.

It was still war time and the whole city was blacked out, except for streetlights, whose tops were painted black. It gave me an exotic feeling as I ran behind Al down past the boat docks next to the water. The lake shimmered to my right. I could see the wooded thumb of land that stuck out into the water on the north side, which seemed like the forest landscape in a Robin Hood story. I felt like a hero, up and out and running with my great hero brother. A feeling of power and joy filled my chest and swelled up into my throat. I lifted my chin and started throwing punches as I ran, just like my big brother ahead of me. He was going to be champion of the world and I was going to be a fighter, like him, and maybe become a Golden Gloves champion, too. Then, as if he had heard my thoughts, Al turned around ahead of me. It was getting lighter now and I could see the big grin on his face as he waved to me and yelled, "Catch up now! And keep punching!"

I grinned back and started running faster. Even though I felt it, I wasn't tired. I just remembered to breathe through my nose, like he told me, and to keep relaxed and let my body carry me along.

4

"Never lie, never cheat, never steal, never drink or smoke," Al said, standing in front of me in the gym, sweating, his flannel robe wrapped around him, his face pink from the exertion of his workout. "And don't take money from people. Always pay your own way. Never be a coward and always be loyal to your buddies."

He'd boxed six rounds with Chester Slider and had done really well. All the fans on the benches had oohed and aahed at this new young fighter who'd been written up as a "crowd pleaser" in the *Oakland Tribune* by Alan Ward, the sports writer. He'd rocked Chester, who was bigger and heavier and a ten-round fighter. Even Harry Fine had come down to ringside to watch.

Chester was a five-foot-seven, brown-skinned black man who walked back on his heels with a little shuffle and fought out of a bobbing and weaving crouch. He had lost eleven fights in a row before he finally won one. He was now a main-event, ten-round fighter who had beaten all the welterweight club fighters in Northern California.

I really loved being with Al. I was accepted at the gym by all the fighters. I even got to punch the bag myself at times. I loved it in that dark cavern of a hall, the mahogany wall panels and mirrors, the smell of sweat, leather, evergreen mint, rubbing alcohol and Vaseline. I found a place to go to every day after school. I went most days, with or without a friend. My brother was happy and all my friends loved him.

None of us could smoke or drink or swear or in any way do anything disloyal or dishonorable. I remember those days as a blur of excitement. I wasn't lonely any more. I went with Al to a lot of places. He stayed home and he trained hard, though he always had trouble with his weight. It seemed like the harder Al trained, the closer attention he paid to me, making sure I went to school, studied and went to bed early and ate well. He had set up a charge account at the Cue Cafe on Fourteenth and Market for me, to make sure I got balanced meals every day, since he often wasn't home and Dorothy had moved out to Richmond to live with her husband Frank and there wasn't anybody around to make sure I ate well. I wasn't lonely anymore. I'd come home and know that Al would get there soon after six and that, on the weekend, we'd go to a movie and maybe even a dance.

My buddies Walter, Kenny, Jack, Al, Charley, David, Warren and George Mohr all loved him. None of them smoked and all of them wanted to be like Al. He was in the newspapers. He was recognized when he went places. And he ran up a string of first round kayos in about three months. It seemed that all I did was go to the fights and see Al knock guys out, big guys, mostly black. His name was put on the posters. I'd see it when I went to the Cue Cafe. There'd be a fight poster in the window with his name on it.

Then one day, he was going to fight in San Jose and, when I got to the gym all dressed up to go with them, Al came and told me there was no room in the big limousine, that only fighters were going, not even Mrs. Fine.

"All right," I said. I understood and walked home from the gym by myself, sorry I couldn't see him fight and knock somebody out, but I was not hurt.

The next day when I woke up and I looked over at him in bed, one eye was swollen and black and there was a cut on it. I suddenly saw that he was looking at me look at him.

"What happened?" I asked.

"I lost a decision to Ernie Sanchez, the new hero of San Jose."

"Oh, too bad," I said, but then smiled when he said, "It was called the best fight of the night, and I was given fifty extra dollars and a new hat for putting on such a good show."

I looked over at the fight poster he'd brought back with him. It had his name on it as the six-round semi-windup. I took a pen and wrote, "Sanchez by unpopular decision."

Al grinned and said, "That's the way to do it. I'll get him next time."

He was sore, though, and I cut school and stayed home with him. We were getting out of the car in front of the house, when the gray-haired lady next door saw his puffed and cut eye. She shook her head and said "You're looking worse and worse. When are you going to stop that fighting?"

Al didn't say anything, but I saw the expression on his face change from a smile of hello to a sullen, narrow-eyed glance at her. It was his first loss, and he seemed to keep silent for a few days. He had to wait for his eye to heal before going back to the gym. That weekend, he went to a dance with a bunch of guys from the Cue Cafe. He brought Don Wixom home with him that night. When I went downstairs the next morning, they were both already up and in the front room drinking coffee.

"This is my little brother, Floyd. You've met him already, Don."

Don smiled at me. His pale, blue eyes looked round and bright under the pale scar tissue that showed in both eyebrows.

"He thinks he wants to be a fighter, too," Al said.

Don let his head rock back and forth with a knowing nod. "Don't we all," he said.

5

Al used to get upset with me all the time now, it seemed. I'd be in the gym watching him work out, and then afterwards he'd send me for something back in his locker and then complain when I brought it out. Or when Chester sparred ten rounds for an upcoming fight, and I was telling Al how many rounds he boxed, Al got mad at me and said, "He didn't box any ten rounds, so don't go around saying he did, when he didn't." He avoided my eyes when Chester came back and said, "I just boxed ten whole rounds, Al." I didn't say anything. I guessed he'd gotten angry because he couldn't spar ten rounds.

In the meantime, Al worked hard, but he didn't seem as happy as he'd been up until that loss to Ernie Sanchez. I'd feel tension when I was around him, like he was ready to snap at me for any little thing. He must have realized it, because he said, "When I'm getting in shape, I get on edge, Floyd." That's all, no apologies, no I'm sorries, just that. I understood or thought I did, anyway.

But that Wednesday night, his manager said he wanted Al to show endurance, not just go knock the guy out, like he'd been doing up until the loss to Ernie Sanchez. So, Al came out and boxed and fought the guy four rounds and won. But when I was going to get a Coke, a young woman who knew him stopped me and said, "What's wrong with Al? Why didn't he knock the guy out?"

I knew that his manager wanted him to build his endurance, but I didn't say anything. Al must have felt bad about it, too, because he was even more testy afterwards. I could hardly turn around near him without him complaining about it.

And when he had to get ready for Nate Husky, another big welterweight, I tried to understand. That Wednesday night, I felt like I was walking barefoot on broken glass around him. During the day, Mr. Mills, the Negro cleaner who ran a shop on Twelfth Street, invited him to a steak dinner in the mid-afternoon. He came back and got ready, but was really silent. I almost dreaded to go with him, but he expected me to and, besides, I really wanted to. So I went and tried to hold my own tenseness in when he barked at me for every little thing. Go get his towel. Go put his shoes away. Go tell Cocky

67

Johnny he wanted to see him. Go do this and go do that. I was getting tired of running around for what seemed nonsensical things.

I was scared when he walked out in his black robe to fight again.

The crowd cheered when Al's name was announced. Everyone expected him to blow the other guy out fast, even if he had only won the last fight on a decision.

It was a tough fight. The guy was big again. Al couldn't seem to get down to one-thirty-five and he always had to fight guys who were one-forty or over, I think, that's one of the reasons he got tired. They wore him down with their weight. Al boxed well, but couldn't knock the guy out, and in the third round he got his eye cut. Then, when the doctor came over to the corner to check it, he tried to hide his eye, but the doctor stopped the fight right then.

Harry Fine was mad. When I followed him and Al into the dressing room, Fine said, "What the hell's the matter with you? He might not have stopped that fight if you didn't duck your head! Now you've got another loss on your record and this one goes down as a TKO! Shit!" Fine spun away from him and wouldn't talk to him the rest of the night.

6

"I'm not going to fight for that guy again. He takes his big third cut from my measly fifty bucks, and then complains when I get cut!" Al said.

He was talking to Dad and me in the kitchen. It was sunny. The lemon tree just beyond the back porch flickered with little yellow globes.

"Well, you can't blame it on your manager, Al," Dad said.

Al sucked in air through his teeth as if trying to keep his temper. "I'm not blaming it on him. I'm too heavy now, anyway. I should get down to one-thirty-five before I fight again."

"You'll feel better after your cut heals," Dad said, but Al didn't say anything.

I waited to see what Al would do. Was Dad right about how he'd feel when his cut healed? I was hoping Al would get that old spark in him again and that we'd go back to the gym. But, although the puffing went down and there was only a thin, pink line on Al's upper eyelid, he never said a word about the gym. I was afraid to mention it.

Instead, Al started going to dances with some ex-reform school Mexican guys from Denver who'd come out to California during the war to get jobs in the shipyards. He took me with them once to a dance hall people called "The Hickey," where a security guard with one cast eye stood guard. I think it was called "The Hickey" because, although it featured rumbas and sambas, it also played country and was corny. I enjoyed the music, but Al got drunk. After we left the dance, we sat in his Studebaker with some guys and they passed around a gallon jug of red wine in the soft light of the car.

A powerfully built guy with thick brown muscles and farmer overalls that hung loosely from blue straps over his big shoulders sat in the back seat. Al kept saying things like, "I'm not looking for it, Bob, but if you are ... ?"

Bob hunched down between his thick shoulders and took a swig of wine.

I knew my brother was a great fighter, but he'd been drinking, and the other guy didn't seem to be drunk at all. I kept my nose out of it, and thank God they didn't fight. I just shook my head with relief and a little bit of sadness when we dropped them off at their place down the block and Al drove home. Here Al was going to fight some big guy in the street for nothing, instead of fighting for money in the ring. He was going to break the law instead of earning respect. I didn't know what to think.

Al started getting drunk a lot after that. He wouldn't go train at all and he started getting a flabby belly. I didn't like to look at him, because it made me sad. He didn't take me with him much anymore, either. So I couldn't believe it when he came home one day, waved to me to follow him, went upstairs to our room and got his tan, leather boxing bag off one of the shelves set into the wall and put it down on his bed. He started taking stuff out and putting it back in, as if he was checking to make sure everything was there. First his boxing shoes, then his mouthpiece, then his trunks, then his jockstrap. When I waited for him to explain himself, guessing he might want to go work out at the gym, he stopped and said, "Do you want to go see Joe Louis in Sacramento? He's going to referee the main event."

"Sure!" I said, but looked down at the open bag. He turned and pulled a pair of white sweat socks out of a dresser drawer, and I watched him throw them on top of his cup and his jockstrap.

"You're not thinking about fighting, are you?" I asked.

He met my eyes for a moment, then looked down at the bag and said, "Naw-naw. Just getting my gear together," and he snapped the bag shut.

"Are you sure you're not going to fight?" I asked. His full mouth got tight and thin. "Don't ask so many questions. You've got a chance to go see Joe Louis. Take it, and don't try to run the show. That's part of growing up."

He was my older brother and I didn't want to say anything, and I did want to go see Joe Louis. But my face must have showed the hurt I felt, because he explained, "Cocky Johnny needs a ride for him and another fighter. He just told me about it. They might need a welterweight." He was trying to apologize for being short with me.

This time, I asked rather than said, "Maybe you shouldn't fight, Al? You're not in shape."

"We'll see how I feel. No use going unless I fight," he said.

When I didn't say anything else, he said, "Get dressed and let's go. I've got to pick him up by five-thirty. It'll take us a couple of hours to get there, and the fights start at eight."

With a quivery feeling in my belly, I reached into the closet, pulled out my blue slacks and little blue loafer jacket and started taking off my levis.

It took a while to get to Sacramento, but I felt the quivery feeling in my stomach all over again when we pulled up on the tree-lined street next to the big, red-stoned Memorial Auditorium. We went straight past the ticket booth to the door. Cocky Johnny said something to the doorman, and he let us right in, pointing to a dressing room down in the front hall. I could see that the auditorium was already crowded. The magic name of Joe Louis, the Brown Bomber from Detroit, had packed the place. Beer butchers in red jackets were already moving up and down the aisles. There was a lot of noise and clouds of cigarette smoke.

Inside the dressing room, fighters were getting weighed and examined by a doctor with silver hair. He took Al's blood-pressure as soon as he took off his coat and rolled up his sleeve. I realized that Al knew he was going to fight all the time. After he got his blood pressure taken, he stripped down to be weighed, and I saw how thick his belly was. The doctor slid the weight down the scale bar, said, "One-fifty," and wrote it down.

Al was fifteen pounds overweight! He avoided my eyes as he took his jockstrap and boxing trunks out of his bag and put them on. When he let the waistband snap back against his flesh, it stretched very tight and the flab rippled just above it. When he sat down to get his hands wrapped, the flesh made a thick slab over the band. I got really worried. I still believed he could be champion of the world, but he hadn't trained and he didn't look fit. He'd always had trouble making weight and had to fight hundred-and-forty pounders. But now, he was going to have to fight a six-foot-tall black guy who was a natural hundred and forty-seven-pound welterweight in trim, muscular shape! I was glad the guy had left the room after weighing in. I didn't want to look at him.

When Al started shadow-boxing to warm up, his back was a square box without any curve down to the waist. I didn't want to look at him either. I almost held my breath when the crowd started whistling and stamping their feet for the fights to start. Then a little man, who looked like a wino, stuck his head in the door and said, "Curtain raiser! Go to the ring!"

I hurried to catch up, followed Al across the hallway and through the entrance into the main auditorium, but stopped just inside the doors and watched Al walk down the aisle. It was dark inside already, with only the lights on above the ring and the announcer, a redheaded man with a microphone, introducing, "Joe Louis! The greatest heavyweight champion in history!"

The crowd broke into loud whistling, clapping and stamping of feet as Joe Louis stepped into the middle of the ring and held his hand in the air. He was a big, dark-brown man in a white referee's shirt and pants, with small eyes and a puffy mouth. He still had his hand in the air, turning to greet the crowd, when Al stepped into the ring.

Joe Louis stepped over to Al's corner, wished him luck, and then crossed the ring and said something to the black guy in the opposite corner. Then he stepped out of the ring and walked down the steps and down the aisle to the clapping and cheering, stopping near the doorway where I was standing. Some people hurried over and asked him for autographs, and the thought also crossed my mind, but the bell rang and the crowd fell silent.

I was just plain scared, watching the white square of the ring at the end of the aisle down under the bright lights. Al came skipping out in a crouch, his hands up. Although he held his arms close to his body, he was so thick, his elbows stuck out. He was short for his weight at one-thirty-five, anyway, and now, fighting a full-fledged welterweight, he was even shorter.

I caught my breath when the tall guy shot out a long jab that caught Al on the forehead. Al stopped, looked at the guy, then fell into a crouch again and shuffled forward, but circled the guy this time. Then, when the guy shot out another long jab, Al suddenly dropped to his right, slipped the jab, and leaped in at the same time, hitting the guy with a long left hook and a quick, straight right that drove him up against the ropes. The crowd cheered. Al ducked his head down and hit the guy with a rally to the belly. When the guy started to fight back, Al hit him with a half a dozen two-handed hooks to the head that dropped the guy flat. The crowd went crazy.

My heart leaped in my chest. I felt like I was going to fly through the air with excitement. My fear was gone. I walked down the aisle, shouting with the crowd, my fist doubled while the guy lay on the canvas and the referee's white arm went up and down with the count.

"Get him, Al!" I shouted as the black guy shook his head, then got to one knee by the count of five and stayed there, letting his head clear. He was a handsome black man, who stood up at the count of eight. The referee wiped his gloves off on his white shirt, then stepped back and waved Al in. The crowd roared when Al charged him, punching with both hands, and drove the guy back against the ropes again. But the guy covered with both hands and caught all of Al's punches on his arms and gloves. I could see that none of the punches were getting through. I saw Al pause, then slow down, then pause again, and when he paused the second time, the guy stuck out a straight left jab to measure him and keep him off. Then he threw a straight right cross that knocked Al flat on his face.

The crowd roared again and I stopped in the middle of the aisle, just before I reached the first ringside row. I dropped my arm and undoubled my fist. I felt like a deflated balloon as Al lay on the canvas. Then my heart quickened again when Al put his hands under himself and pushed up to his knees at the count of six. But he only toppled forward on his face again and was counted out.

The referee waved his hands back and forth over him. But when Cocky Johnny helped him to his feet, Al tried to charge the guy again. The crowd started booing as I turned and walked back down the aisle, my eyes filled with tears. Yet, I could see some guy sitting on the aisle seat in about the third row touch his friend and then point at me and whisper something in his ear, as if he guessed I was Al's brother. I kept walking, sobbing.

7

Al quit training and didn't go to the gym anymore. So neither did I. I hardly saw him. He was either driving a cab or getting drunk and going out to dances with his buddies. He brought home some young woman from the Hickey dance one night.

Al got in bed with me, first, and the girl got in his bed. Then I heard them whisper things to each other. Al said, "You wouldn't mind?"

"No," she said, and he got up and went over to her in his bed. I grabbed my pillow and pulled it over my ears when the bed started creaking, trying to shut all the sound out. Later, he came back to my bed and slid in, and I heard her say something about when she was coming and he said, "Shhhhh," trying to be nice to her, but to shut her up. Finally, I fell asleep. When I woke up in the morning, they were both gone.

I cut school that day. It was depressing to come home. I couldn't look at Al and he couldn't look at me, and I cut again the next day. I kept cutting so much, I got kicked out of Hoover Junior High at the end of the low ninth, on my fourteenth birthday, January 23rd. I was sent to MacClymonds High, a block from my house. I got kicked out of Hoover not only for cutting school, but for leading a gang of guys down to Westlake Junior High School to get some guys who had jumped my red-headed buddy Fred Carge at Lake Merritt. I don't know why, but I felt like fighting.

MacClymonds, although a high school, started in the eighth grade. I remember wanting to take all college prep courses, which I was given. But I didn't really care about doing well in them. I just sat and endured the hours until I could get out and go have some fun.

I let my crewcut, GI-style hair grow out long because my pretty girl Dolly told me she'd like it that way. Then I started using pomade on it to keep it stiff and straight with a pompadour in front. I wore motorcycle dark glasses, called tea-timers, for guys who smoked pot and wanted to cover up their red eyes—although I didn't even smoke cigarettes. The corner grocer told me the glasses were warped and could hurt my eyes. I, nevertheless, kept wearing them to keep my eyes from smarting and watering, they'd been so sensitive since I went blind after Mother had died.

I was invited to a birthday party for Kenny Snyder, who played a great swing trumpet, and I saw that all my friends had started wearing drape slacks with balloon knees and tight cuffs. So, the next day, I rushed out to get the slacks that Eddy'd bought me that were made into drapes by narrowing the cuffs to twelve inches. I wanted to do something fun!

One night, I was eating dinner by myself in the kitchen when Eddy walked in in his naval officer's uniform. I hadn't seen him in a year. I had my dark motorcycle glasses and zootsuit pants on. I'd also tucked the collar of my sportshirt inside the neckband of the shirt and buttoned the top button at my Adam's apple. My hair was greased down with pomade.

His eyes widened with shock at my appearance. Although he didn't say anything at first, Eddy finally said, "Floyd! I didn't recognize you!"

The next day when I came home from school in my Levis, I found that he'd taken scissors and cut my gabardine drapes into shreds. He held them up so I could see them. "This is what I think of your zootsuit pants," he said. He was sitting in the kitchen, with a full-mouthed, serious look on his face.

I had felt really proud of my drapes, but I just looked at them and didn't show the slightest reaction.

"You can't go around looking like some lower class thug, Floyd," he said. "What would Mother think?"

My mouth puffed out and I looked down. I didn't care if he slashed up my drapes, I'd just buy another pair. Dad had a charge account at Money Back Smith's and all I had to do was go get a pair of pants and have the cuffs cut down at Bill's, a men's and boys' clothing store that sold cheap, fancy clothing. But I did wonder what my mother would think. That bothered me.

"And look at your hair!" he said, throwing the slashed slacks on the backrest of a kitchen chair. "It's loaded with grease, like some Filipino."

I didn't say anything, but followed him when he said, "Come in here with me." He led me into Dad's bedroom. Dorothy followed us in. Frank had shipped out once more and she was living at home again.

He sat down on Mom's vanity stool and took a comb out of the vanity drawer and combed my hair down and parted it on the side, the way I had worn it when I was a little boy. I started sobbing. The tears ran down my cheeks as he patted a pompadour into my hair and combed it back on the sides. It was nothing like the sleek look of the time. Even Dorothy felt sorry for me.

I didn't resist because Eddy was my big brother. But I went outside afterwards and went to the playground at MacClymonds to shoot baskets. My hair was just as he'd combed it, when Eddy appeared in his naval officer's uniform. His face was long and serious under the stiff black brim of his white cap. "Floyd, come and get a Coke with me. I want to talk to you," he said.

I stopped playing and walked across the playground with Eddy and up to the corner of Fourteenth, where we crossed the street and went into

Heathorne's Drugs and sat at the counter.

I went with him, but wasn't friendly. I didn't like him making me comb my hair like his. Al was always talking about what a sissy Eddy was as a boy, when he got the highest grade point average in his high school graduating class in Denver. Since Al had come back from the Army, I'd absorbed his likes and dislikes and his rebellious attitude toward Dad, too. So I found myself disliking my brother Eddy and my father, because Al always complained about them. It was going to be a long time before I realized he was jealous of Eddy and resentful of Dad. Resentful because Dad didn't spoil him all the time, now that he wasn't always in trouble. That tendency of Al's to get himself in situations where he needed help all the time had turned into a habit of using people. It was a habit he'd never lose.

Yet, Eddy looked very handsome and distinguished in his uniform and with his cheeks lean from the required exercise at the base.

"Listen, Floyd," Eddy said. "I just went to the school office and checked on your grades. Do you know that your I.Q. is lower than it used to be? It was 140 in the fifth grade and now it's down to 112. That's quite a drop. It means you're not getting much out of your schooling right now."

I could sense the respect he paid me by the serious level of his talk. I didn't look away, although I was ashamed. I hadn't been doing any homework at all. I just did the work in class and nothing more.

"Al and I both had gifted IQs in school and Al's, believe it or not, was two points higher than mine in junior high. When you were a little boy, you skipped grades. Your teachers held conferences on you, and your homeroom teacher took you to the library when you were seven and introduced you to the whole staff so they could help you use it on your own, so they could help you become a scholar. You were allowed to spend an hour a day in the library by yourself. Do you remember?"

I nodded.

"If we'd stayed in Denver, you might have been almost ready to enter college now."

"Already?" I asked.

"They had you on a special curriculum. You were getting an advanced education in a working class school."

"I remember," I said.

His big, green eyes looked down and into my green eyes. "You're running a little wild, Floyd, and I'm afraid you're going to get into trouble, if this keeps up. I don't want you to forget to use your mind, just because I have to go away. I've volunteered for active duty in the Pacific and I'll be leaving soon." His long face showed no emotion.

"You want to go fight?" I asked.

He nodded and I felt really proud of him. He seemed to become more manly just sitting there looking at me. He looked bigger, taller in his dark blue uniform, the white cap with the stiff black brim on his head. I realized that he was two or three inches taller than Al and a bigger man overall.

Eddy was going off to the South Pacific to fight the war, and Al had lied to get out of the service to come home and turn pro. I was proud of Eddy for being so brave and patriotic. Now that Al had quit fighting pro and wasn't a soldier anymore, either, he seemed smaller than Eddy to me. But I couldn't let myself think that, and I quickly asked, "Why, Eddy? You teach in a naval college and could stay there for the rest of the war? Everybody I've heard of keeps trying to avoid combat duty."

"First of all, I consider it my duty," he said, and turned to me with that long-nosed, narrow-faced look. He stared right into my eyes with his soft, yet deep green, eyes which looked like mine but were bigger, almost protruding.

"Secondly, I have to prove to myself that I'm not afraid to die for the things I believe in. This is a personal thing. Mom died a slow, painful death after sacrificing herself for all of us. So, it's a combination of social duty and personal need."

"Need?" I asked. I'd grown up listening to him talk like this and wasn't at all surprised to hear him say that.

"Yes, need. I've got to prove that I'm not afraid to die. I've got to prove to myself that I'm as brave as Mother. She was very brave. I saw her die slowly, my whole life, and especially at the end, the last three months."

He looked right into my eyes again.

"Maybe my own life doesn't seem so important to me anymore, either. Maybe there's an element of willful risk involved that comes from some kind of despair over Mother's death."

He looked away and I sipped at the cherry Coke I was drinking at Heathorne's Drugs. I felt the sullen feeling of resentment fade inside me. Eddy was everything Al said you should be! Brave and loyal. He looked like a statue in profile as he looked out the door and across the street, from under the stiff brim of his cap, down the aquiline curve of his nose, to the little tip that curled over his upper lip. He was really handsome, with hollows in his cheeks, a slender face, a narrow waist. He looked like a hero to me. Yet, he looked so sad and seemed so brave, I didn't want him to hurt. Then all of a sudden, Eddy asked, "What would you think of going to a military school?"

For a moment I thought of looking like him and liked the idea. "Where? When?" I asked.

His mouth twisted in a quick grin. "Let me check into it. At a military school, you'd get discipline and study and camaraderie in a healthy way. Something you're not getting now. You need order and structure in your life."

I looked down at my Coke. "I'd go if you wanted me to, Eddy," I said.

"Good. Now, if Dad will be willing to pay ... That's the catch," he said.

"Is it a lot of money?" I asked.

"Yes," he said. "Probably a couple of thousand a year."

"Wow!" I said. "Dad only paid twenty-five hundred for our house when he bought it two years ago."

"I know," Eddy said. "That's why I said there could be a catch. But the money he's spent on getting Albert out of trouble ought to make him consider it. He could have bought another four homes by now with it. If you get in trouble, it's going to cost him that much just for lawyers."

I looked up at him. I couldn't in any way conceive of anything I'd do costing that much, but I liked the idea of going away to a military school and learning how to march and be a hero like my brother Eddy.

8

"I'm not discouraged, Eddy," I said. I had liked the idea of wearing one of those gray uniforms with the red stripe on the collar I'd seen on a big kid downtown. But Dad wouldn't pay for me to go to military school, Eddy said, even though he made a lot of money on the apartments he rented. Eddy was disappointed and told Dad he wouldn't help pay for a lawyer if I got in trouble. But Dad said two thousand dollars would buy him a new car, if he could buy one during the war. I didn't see them argue, but Eddy told me what had happened and that I shouldn't let it discourage me.

"Try to understand," Eddy said, sitting next to me on a couch in the big front room. "Dad's been suffering over Mother, too. He's lonesome and he's concerned with his own problems now. He drinks now and just sees the expense. He said he could send you to Harvard for what it costs to go to military school. I couldn't argue with that. But you must try to do your best, even if you can't go. And above all, try to understand him."

"I do, Eddy," I said. "I can't forget how he sat in front of that window in the dark for months after she died."

He nodded at me, his face long and sad, then he suddenly smiled and said, "Why don't you take piano lessons? The piano's sitting there not being used and it would give you something to do. I'll talk to Dad and get him to pay for lessons, at least."

"Okay, Eddy," I said. "I want to learn how to play 'Ave Maria.' "

He smiled and touched my hand, then looked down at it and said, "You've got big hands and should get a good spread on the keys."

He pointed down at my hand.

I'd never noticed. I couldn't really tell. They looked all right to me, but I didn't know if they were big or not.

Then Eddy said, "I know you've just been playing basketball, but clean your nails every day. They're dirty. See?" He held up my hand and there was a line of dirt under some of the nails.

"All right," I said.

"I want you to realize how far you can go. I don't want you to lose direction because there's no mother around to guide you. Do you know who Spinoza was?"

I shook my head.

"He was one of the greatest philosophers of all time. He was a Spanish Jew. You're descended from those Spanish colonists who first came to America with Coronado and Ponce de León. One of Mom's cousins is a superintendent of schools in Arizona. You could be a superintendent of schools. You can reach high, if you see that it's possible."

I faced him. I knew he cared for me and was trying to tell me something important. The long line of his nose looked stern. "I'll be leaving tonight, Floyd. I can't tell you where, but I'll be in the invasion forces of the Pacific Fleet."

His expression didn't change when he added, "I'm sorry about your slacks, but I felt it was necessary."

I nodded. I knew he only meant well, and I was sorry to see him go. "Don't be sorry. I'm going to try, Eddy. I'm going to study just like you want. I'm going to go to college just like you, no matter what Al does. Al doesn't want to fight anymore, anyway. I might as well go to college."

Eddy grinned and shook my hand.

9

I heard heavy footsteps on the front porch and then steps down the hall and the heavy slurred voices of men. I guessed it was my father and wondered who was with him. Then the dining room door flew open and he staggered in with his hat twisted to one side of his head and his eyes glassy. A man who looked just like him with his suitcoat unbuttoned over his big belly and his hat pulled down low on his head stepped in behind him. He was a friend from Colorado that Dad had known since he was a boy, and he was glassy-eyed, too. They could have been brothers, they looked so much alike.

I looked at my girlfriend, Dolly, who sat next to me on a couch in the big front room. Her hazel eyes met mine and her sister, Bomby, who was sitting on the other side of her, looked at me, too. They were two pretty, darkhaired sisters who'd come to see me, and I blushed at my obviously drunken dad. But their father was an alcoholic, too, and they knew all about it.

Dad waved his hand in greeting to us, smiled crookedly and staggered through the dining room towards the kitchen, where I knew Dorothy and Eddy were sitting. The man followed him across the unlit room like a fat shadow.

I'd been showing them pictures of my mother from a family album and pointed to a picture of me at the age of nine with my mother and sister above the Shasta Dam, where Dad had worked. I had my fists up and was sticking out a long jab at the camera. I was so skinny my belt curled almost halfway around my waist again. But I was curled up nicely with my right fist in front of my face in a good punching pose. They smiled at the picture and I thought I had distracted them, when I heard Dad's voice from the kitchen. Then I heard Eddy talking in a slow calm voice. Then Dad's voice again and somebody bang against the wall.

"Excuse me," I said and pushed the album onto Dolly's lap and hurried across the big front room and through the dining room. I pushed open the swinging door into the kitchen. Dad was lying on the floor and Eddy and Dorothy were squatted down next to him. Dad's hat was lying next to the refrigerator at his friend's feet.

"Dad!" I cried and bent over and put my arms around his big waist and helped pull him up into a sitting position as Dorothy and Eddy lifted him from under the arms.

"Get behind him, Floyd," Eddy said. He was in his officer's uniform and his words had the soft sound of quiet authority. I stepped behind them and hooked my hands under my father's armpits as Eddy and Dorothy lifted him to a standing position on the kitchen floor. Then I held onto him as they guided him into his bedroom and over to the bed, sat him on it, then laid him down. I lifted up his feet and put them on the bed, too, and then untied his laces and pulled off his dress shoes. I hurried back into the kitchen to get his hat. When I turned, the man was standing in the doorway. I put the hat on Mother's big vanity dresser.

"Wait a second, Dad," Eddy said and turned away from the side of the bed and up to the man. "Dad's ill and he can't entertain you, sir. You'll have to leave."

The man had a medium complexion and long nose like my father and the same style of dark-colored dress suit, the same kind of a hat. His mouth and eyes drooped with his drunkenness, but he turned and let Eddy guide him back past the swinging door and through the dining room, down the hall and out the front door. I watched him walk the man out. I wondered what Dolly and her sister thought and wanted to go back and sit with them again. But I heard my father retching like he might vomit, so I turned and ran across the kitchen into the pantry and grabbed a dishpan from under the sink. I ran back into the bedroom just in time to stick it out and catch my father's vomit. As he lurched over the side of the bed, Dorothy grabbed his thick shoulders to keep him from falling off. I caught my breath at the blood in it. It was all watery blood.

"Dad! Dad!" I cried as he vomited and vomited what looked like a quart of watery blood.

When he finally stopped retching and leaned back on the pillow, I burst out crying.

"Go empty the pan, Floyd," Dorothy said, wiping his mouth with a handkerchief.

I made myself stop crying and turned and carried the enamel pan of thin pink liquid back through the dining room, glancing at Dolly and Bomby. They looked at me, still sitting side by side on the couch in their matching sweaters and skirts, bobby sox and white oxfords.

I was ashamed at carrying bloody slop and didn't want to cry in front of them, either. But I knew they could tell my eyes were wet and red, and hoped they understood and had pity on me.

I stepped into the high hall and into the bathroom under the stairway, lifted the seat and poured the watery blood into the bowl, seeing my mother dead in my mind, scared my father was going to die, too. I flushed the blood down the toilet and hurried back out. I couldn't look at Dolly when I went back through the dining room, but rushed into the bedroom. My father was lying with a pale face against the very pillow I'd seen my mother lying on before she went away to die. I burst out crying again.

"Don't die, Daddy! Don't die!" I cried. Neither Eddy nor Dorothy had turned the light on and his face looked gray and dead to me already in the dim light that shined through the kitchen doorway. I remembered when I'd sobbed when I'd come home for lunch in Boomtown and seen an ambulance parked outside our cabin. He'd hurt his back working on the Shasta Dam. I sobbed and sobbed when they carried him out on a stretcher to the ambulance. He'd gotten well, though. But since then my mother had died in this very bed, on this very side of the bed, I was sure I was going to lose my father now, too.

"Daddy! Daddy! Daddy! Don't die, Daddy. Don't die! Please don't die!" I cried and he opened his eyes, stared at me for a moment with a glassy stare, then suddenly reached out and grabbed me and pulled me down next to him on the bed and kissed my cheek. I could smell the hint of blood and vomit on him, but I threw my arms around him and squeezed him, squeezed him like I'd never squeeze him again, until he stopped kissing me and held me away from him.

His face was blurred through my tears.

"Don't cry, Floyd," he said. "I'm sorry that I can't afford to send you to military school. But I promise you this. I promise you that I won't die and I'll pay your way to any college in the country that you want to go to, if you'll promise me you'll go to college like your brother Eddy."

His eyes were clear, even in the soft shadows of the bedroom, with only the light from the kitchen shining in the doorway.

"You promise me that you'll go to college like Eddy, and I promise you that I won't die. What-a ya say, sonny boy."

I could see both Eddy and Dorothy staring at me from the other side of the bed. Dorothy tried to smile.

"I promise, Dad. I promise," I said.

That night, I went with Dad to drop Eddy off at the Oakland Naval Base. When he got out of the car, he leaned in the car window and said, "Remember your promise to Dad." He glanced across me at Dad and smiled when I said, "I'll remember." Then he shook my hand hard, gave me a tight smile, waved to Dad, picked up his big canvas suitcase and walked through the wire-linked security gate where the Marine on duty saluted him. My chest ached with sadness. I knew I might never see him again. I wished the war would end. I decided I was going to try. I was going to study and my father wasn't going to die.

PART FOUR
The Comeback

1

The tall, thin guard led Al over to the washbasin after he'd fingerprinted him, pointed at some soap and paper towels, then left him to wash off his hands. I watched Al through the little perpendicular window of the county jail door on the eleventh floor of the courthouse. He rubbed soap between his palms as he stood up against the iron bars. The jail office was a clean, pale green. Al had on his cabdriver's uniform of olive-drab wool, short-waisted Eisenhower jacket and pants, very much like the army uniform he used to wear. I hoped he'd look up and see my face in the hall window. But he never looked over. He didn't look at anybody. His face was stiff and silent, wounded, as if his pride was hurt, as if he was deeply angry about being bossed around. But he kept his anger down inside the jail, because he knew he was getting bailed out. I'd rarely seen him like that. Al wouldn't take anything from anybody. I was afraid he'd lost his job, too.

I was seventeen now and working as a page in the public library with plans on starting classes at San Francisco City College in the Fall. It hurt to look at him through that thin, little window, not more than six inches wide, a foot high at most. I was used to looking up to my brother, even if he wasn't a boxer anymore.

I glanced down at the pack of Lucky cigarettes in my shirt pocket I'd bought for him, turned away from the window, then walked down to the other end of the short hall. I had bought the cigarettes for him because he was smoking again, and I'd remembered my mother buying cigarettes for him at reform school. Anyway, that's what you were supposed to do, buy cigarettes for guys in jail. I turned with the clank of a key in the iron door, to see the uniformed chest of the tall guard in the little window, the door swing back and Al step out, the bailbondsman behind him.

"Al!" I said and rushed over, reaching out for him. But Al just stopped and looked at me with his hands down. He barely nodded. His mouth was stiff. I dropped my hands and stepped back to let the bondsman by.

The bondsman glanced at me from under the wide brim of his pearl gray hat, then looked away when I glanced back. He pressed the elevator button and stepped in when the door opened. He had on a black pinstripe suit and wore a thin black mustache like a mobster. The hair of his graying temples curled back along his head between the hat brim and his ears. I stepped in next to him and Al stepped in, too, but still didn't say anything. The elevator dropped with a sigh. The arrow started moving down: 10 . . . 9 . . .

When Al and I were descending in the elevator, I announced, "Al! I bought a pack of cigarettes for you."

He looked at me and said, "You give a guy in jail a carton of cigarettes, not a pack, Floyd." Then he stared straight ahead again and didn't say another word. His chin was high.

"Al," I said, "why don't we go work out today? Then run around the lake tomorrow? Try to get in shape. It'll make . . . "

"I've got a lot on my mind," Al said, still staring at the door. The arrow touched 8.

"But won't . . . "

"Look, Floyd," Al said and looked at me, really for the first time. "I've got a charge against me now. I've got to get some money, a lot of it. I've gotta pay my bondsman here and my lawyer, and feed my wife and kids and find a way to get some money . . . That's the biggest part of it. And . . . "

"But you've still got your job, don't you?"

Al looked at me and shook his head really slowly, as if I was too dumb at seventeen to understand much.

"We'll see if I do. I got busted for pandering, at first, but they might drop it to a contributing-to-a-minor charge, if I can get my lawyer to swing it. The girl working out of the 614 Club was only seventeen, it turns out, but that actually might pay off for me."

He stared at the elevator door again, his heavy jaw set. The arrow touched 6 . . . 5 . . .

I shook my head this time. I didn't know what he was talking about, but I said, "I still think you should make a comeback. Twenty-six isn't too old. Lots of experienced fighters do that."

"Gaaaa," Al growled, clearing his throat, still looking at the door. I shut up and kept quiet the rest of the way down, watching the arrow go by 4 . . . 3 . . . 2 . . . 1.

2

"Naaaaw!" Al said, sticking out his lower lip like Mussolini, all big jaw and bare forehead. His brown eyes looked away. His hairline was higher now, but his hair was still thick enough on top to wave and the shape of his forehead was broad and noble-looking, with the same strong nose, deepset eyes and powerful jaw. In the bright lights of Dad's restaurant, the El Patio, on Nineteenth and Broadway, he looked a little pale from his nightlife style of living.

Dad turned and looked over at us from the cash register. He grinned, showing bright teeth under his black mustache, then snapped a bill into the drawer, slammed it shut, popped a check on the spindle and turned to a waiting customer. Waitresses in Mexican peasant costumes moved around the brightly painted tables and chairs in the room. Woven rugs, Mexican Indian masks and bullfight pictures hung on the stucco walls. The restaurant was crowded. Dad advertised in the *People's World*, a communist newspaper, and he always got a big, leftist crowd, especially on weekends.

"Start fighting again, Al!" I said. "Make a comeback. Become lightweight champion of the world! I'll turn amateur and train with you."

Al leaned back and tucked his chin in. "At twenty-six?"

"Yes! That's not too late for an experienced fighter who's already made a start."

"I haven't had a fight in three years!" Al looked at his wife, Tommy, who was sitting in the booth with us. She smacked her lips and squeezed them together, shaking her head as if the idea was stupid.

I didn't let her stop me. "If you fight, you'll keep busy and stay out of trouble! Look, Dad sold the house and moved out of that West Oakland neighborhood so I could change schools and get different friends. All my close friends moved up to the foothills with us, though, and I still ended up being with my close buddies. But I didn't get in trouble again, because the school and the atmosphere were different. I started reading a lot again. You said it yourself! Start training and you'll stop hanging out at the 614 Club and you'll keep out of trouble, too!"

"Hmmm," Al said and squinted so that the thin scar on his right eyelid glistened like a fishscale.

"If you fight, you'll have a goal to work for, which will keep you busy. That's what's wrong! You haven't fought in three years and you've been drinking and smoking and getting into trouble! You need to keep busy at something you love! You're not just some worker! You need to box! You like the attention!"

"Hmmmm," Al said again.

"You can train me, too, and that way I can help you get in shape," I said.

"What-a-ya mean?"

"I mean, I'll fight, too! You always wanted me to fight. Well, now's the time for the both of us! I'll fight in the Golden Gloves in the Fall and you make a comeback as a pro. You train me and I'll help you get in shape! I'll run with you and I'll go to the gym every day with you. You help me and I'll help you!"

"Hmmmm," Al said and rocked his head. "Why do you want to do this? I thought, you were going to college in the Fall? I thought since you've been hanging out with all those poets and painters in high school and working in that library, that you didn't want anything to do with fighters? I thought you were a big bookworm, like Eddy, now?"

"I'll keep reading. I'll still go to college. I can go in the Spring, after the Gloves are over. I can put it off. You helped me after Mom died and, now that I'm out of high school and have a job at the library and have the time, I'll help you!"

"I don't want my husband gone all the time at work and the gym," Tommy said.

She was pretty and had a creamy pale complexion and slender features, but her mouth was too big, in many ways, from my way of looking at it. He'd met her at that Hickey dance, knocked her up, married her, and then got stuck with her. He spent all his time trying not to be with her so he could have some fun. Yet, I think he needed a woman in his life, now that Mom was dead. But, I don't think he ever wanted a mate, a woman to share his life with, rather a mother to take care of the house and give him maternal affection without tying him down. He really liked hanging out with his buddies, like he did in the Army, and in the gym, and in reform school.

"Would you rather he go off to jail, Tommy?" I said, and her brown eyes widened.

"Ever since he quit fighting, he's been getting in little scrapes. And he's been drinking, too, and you don't like that. You complain that he never comes home after he finishes driving cab, but stays out and gets drunk. What's better, boxing or that?"

She pursed her full mouth and didn't say anything.

Al tilted his head and squinted that scarred eye at me and said, "So, all that Bible reading and philosophy and books on psychology are puttin' you up to this, huh? That's what happens when you read those big books. Makes you wanna do good, huh?"

I nodded and looked straight at him. "Okay," Al said, "I'll go try and hustle my job back. My boss ought to hire me again, I saved him from those two thugs he fired who tried to beat him up six months ago! I'll get Dad to talk to him, too!" Al grinned, his upper lip curled and his eyes went down at the corners, just like a puppy dog. "I just might start training again, too, little brother!" he added.

3

The ringing of the alarm clock made me sense the reality of what I was trying to do. Without opening my eyes, I reached over and pressed the stop button down, then lay there with my arm outstretched, wanting to fall back into warm sleep. I suddenly remembered Al saying he just might do it, so I forced my eyes open to wake myself up.

The illuminated clock hands touched the 6 and the 12. It was still dark outside my bedroom window. The stars were shining and it was clear. I threw my covers back with both hands and swung my feet off the bed and stood up on the cold floor, shivering suddenly, realizing what a monk did every morning of his life! What discipline! Then I turned on my bedstand lamp, took off my pajamas, hung them across the footboard of the bed, and reached over to the chair next to the wall and grabbed my jockstrap. I slipped into it, then into my gray sweatpants, T-shirt and sweatshirt. Then I sat down on the chair to put on my sweatsocks and sneakers.

I was still sleepy and doing everything mechanically but quickly. I had to get Al up, start him training, help him like he'd helped me when I was very lonely in junior high school. I hurried to the bathroom, glanced out the window at the glittering, dark sky and stopped. It was still night. I suddenly felt exhilirated at getting up so early. Running would be a lot of fun.

I went into the bathroom and splashed water over my face, dried it and walked back through my bedroom, the dining room, the back kitchen and up the steps of the narrow boxed-in back stairs on the far side of the kitchen that led to the second floor, where Al and his wife Tommy and their two little children lived.

"Come on, Al," I said, knocking on Al's door, "get up and run!"

There was no answer, so I knocked again. When there was still no answer, I tried the knob and opened the door. I stepped into the tiny kitchen. I tried to see in the darkness, but there was only a slight glow to the white stove and refrigerator. I couldn't see into the front room at all. The bedroom was at the front of the apartment on the other side of the front room.

"Al!" I said. "Get up!"

When there was still no answer, I flicked on the kitchen light and crossed through the front room and into the bedroom, where I stopped a moment to focus my eyes. Al was asleep on the side of the bed nearest me. The big,

fancy mirror of the bedroom vanity reflected the sleeping bodies of Al and
Tommy. Their daughter Anita's big crib was on the other side of the room,
and another, smaller crib for the new baby boy, Sonny, was right by Tommy.

I tiptoed to the bed and pushed lightly on Al's shoulder. The muscles
were thick and solid. He opened his eyes and, squinting up at me, asked,
"What's going on?"

"Let's go run," I whispered.

"Run?" Al said. "I didn't say I'd start training."

"Come on. It's beautiful outside," I said, then shut up when Tommy
rolled over and looked at me.

"Aw, Floyd. Why don't we wait a few days? Until I really decide," Al
said.

"No, let's go now or we might not do it. Come on, Al, get up!" I said and
pulled the covers back from my brother's shoulder. "Let's go do it! Become
lightweight champion of the world!"

Al grabbed the covers to keep me from pulling them down, but squinted
up and said, "Okay! Give me five minutes."

As I hurried out of the room, I heard Tommy mumble something in a
complaining voice. I stepped into the toilet, used it, quickly, and stepped out
into the hall again just as Al opened his door and said, "Give me a minute
and let's go!"

He stepped into the bathroom, was in there a minute and came right back
out. I punched him on the shoulder and he hit me back. I turned and skipped
down the darkened stairs ahead of him. We went out the side porch door.
We both walked quickly around the back of the house, through the darkened
back yard with its several trees, past the barbecue pit and out the front gate
to Al's Studebaker.

"It's going to be great to run around Lake Merritt on a morning like this,"
I said.

"You like this, huh?" Al said as he started the car. He put it in gear and
spun it in a U-turn from the curb and headed down Twenty-third Avenue
to Foothill Boulevard, where he turned right and started speeding down the
darkened, deserted street.

"Yeah. I'm having fun," I said. "It's like old times again, like when you
came back from the Army."

Al grinned and said, "I ran your little butt off, didn't I?"

"I loved it," I said. "I love it now."

"So do I," Al said, as he gunned the motor and raced the car to forty
miles an hour.

4

Curly Upshaw turned on his bar stool down by the bandstand and squinted as if the glare of the sunlight through the open door hurt his eyes. Al had taken me with him to see if Curly would be his new manager. Curly owned the Knotty Pine, a nightclub on 18th and San Pablo. When the door closed behind us, Curly got off the stool and stood up to greet us. I saw how slick he looked with his black, curly hair, black mustache, beige silk shirt, mustard colored slacks, brown suede coat and brown suede shoes with pointed toes. He also wore a big diamond on his finger. His flashiness bothered me. But I tried not to show it. I wanted Al to fight and I was glad Curly was considering being his manager.

"This is my little brother, Floyd," Al said.

Curly reached out and shook my hand. After offering me a Coke and Al one, too, he said, "I hear you want to fight, too!"

"Yes. Amateur. See how I do."

"He got me up at six to run the first morning after I got out of jail. Had my old lady mumbling in her sleep, complaining she hardly got to see me before my little brother took off with me."

"Do you really want to fight, Al?" Curly asked as the bartender put two Cokes on the bar.

"Yeah, I think so. I got my job back today, but I've got to do something besides drive cab. I'm still young and I've only got those three losses: a decision in the best fight of the night with Sanchez in San Jose, a cut eye in a tough fight when I was holding my own against Nate Husky and a K.O. when I hadn't trained in months. But I was never really in shape. If I really got in shape, I could still do it. I know I could."

"When Harry Fine got him to work on endurance and he quit knocking the guys out, he lost his momentum," I said.

Al nodded as if that made sense to him. "There's no reason I can't fight and win," he said. With you as my manager, we could earn some real money fighting main events within a year. If I stick with it, that is ... and I've got my little brother here to work out with me and keep me at it now. He was too young before."

Al tilted his head at me and Curly asked, "If you won those Gloves, would you think of turning pro, Floyd?"

Buffalo Nickel   ⊖ ⊖ ⊖ ⊖ ⊖ ⊖ ⊖ ⊖   93

I put my Coke back on the bar, thought a moment and said, "I'll postpone going to college to get Al training again. I'm thinking of becoming a lawyer, but I haven't made up my mind about anything, yet. I'd have to be really good to turn pro. I'm not sure if I can even win the Gloves yet. I'll keep working at the library while I train and see how things work out."

"You oughta see the books this guy reads, Curly! He could read before he went to school! He talks all this philosophy and theology stuff all the time. And he can gab. He'll make a good lawyer."

I blushed. Al had never complimented me on my reading, ever!

Curly smacked his pink lips under his thick mustache and said, "I bet he will." He turned to Al and said, "Okay! Let's do it! Let's go down to the gym and buy your contract from Harry Fine. Then I'll buy that big rubber cup you said you needed and any other gym supplies you want. I'll pay a month's dues and we'll get started."

Al grinned and shook Curly's hand. But he quit smiling and said, "Let's go to the YMCA first, though. Until I can cut my weight down to 145, at least. Then, when I think I'm strong enough, we'll go down to Harry Fine's."

Al turned to me. "You ready, Floyd?"

"You bet," I said, grinning, too.

5

I winced as Al got mauled against the black rubber ropes by a tough, little lightweight who fought for Curly Mendonca, the most famous amateur fight manager in the country. He would lead the U.S. Olympic boxing team this year, '48, the first year they had the Olympics since before the war. The fighter was a powerfully built little white guy who could box and punch. He was in good shape, whereas Al was only getting into shape.

Al squinted and covered up as the thud-thud of gloves connected to his head and body. We'd already worked out at the YMCA for two months. Al had gotten his weight down to one-forty-five and he felt strong enough to come and work out at Harry Fine's gym again. Curly had bought his contract for fifty dollars from Harry Fine.

Al was beginning to get in fair shape, but he didn't have that power or that ferocious toughness that had made him so feared when he first turned pro. I could see that he didn't have the strength to launch an attack himself. But he wouldn't wear a headgear and already there was a red glove mark on his forehead. He was taking some more shots when the bell finally rang. Al stepped slowly across the ring to his corner where Curly sat on the middle rope. Curly stood up and raised the top rope to let him out of the ring.

"I feel it," Al said, panting as he stepped over the second strand and stood on the ring apron with his arms hanging down and sweat glistening all over his face. Then he stepped down and held out his hands for Curly to untie his gloves.

It was my turn now. I was going to spar with Johnny Ortega, the California Flyweight Golden Gloves champion. I could see Johnny stepping up into the ring. His olive-complected body rippled with muscle. He was only five-three, but he was a tough bomb about to explode at all times.

I'd fought him a few times, maybe ten, the year before, in 1947, when Al and I had worked out a little. Johnny had broken my nose almost every time I got in the ring with him. But I was a year older and stronger. Although I only weighed one-twelve, I was taller and bigger than Johnny. I was going to be a natural bantamweight when I quit growing. The very first time I'd boxed Johnny had been in Alameda at my buddy Walter Soots' house in the Fall of 1946, where I'd broken his nose and he said, "You won this fight, Floyd. But we'll fight again." He won the East Bay Boys Club championship the next year and was one of the most natural fighters I'd ever see, meaning a fighter as a person, a guy who loves to fight and loves to win. That's why he'd turn pro and fight as a contender for ten years, even though he'd never win a world title.

I could see Johnny glance down at me as he shadowboxed around the ring. I wasn't scared, but I knew I was in a fight. Al slipped into his terrycloth robe, wiped the sweat off his face with a towel and wrapped it around his neck. "Okay, Floyd, your turn," he said "You might end up being the only fighter between us. I don't know if I can do it anymore."

That didn't make me feel any better. Even though my heart started beating fast, I still wasn't scared as I climbed up the steps to the corner and crouched down and slid through the ropes. I stepped into the resin box and then turned to see Johnny staring at me. His heavy-lidded brown eyes looked like slits in the headgear and his mouth was set tight. His stomach muscles rippled. His pectoral muscles popped up on his chest. His shoulders were like football pads and his biceps looked like baseballs. There was no such thing as a workout with Johnny; every time he got in the ring, it was a fight.

I skipped around the ring to work off some of the nervousness. I avoided the eyes of the spectators who sat on the bleachers on one side of the ring. Then, I turned and bit down on the mouthpiece as the bell rang. I moved out and held my hands up, gloves in front of my face, so I could just see over the tops of them with my eyes. As soon as Johnny moved in, which I knew he'd do, I stuck out a jab. But Johnny slipped to his right under it and countered with a stiff left hand to my nose, making my eyes water. When he charged in, I danced away, staying out of reach. He moved in to crowd me again, leaping in, and I skipped along the ropes, trying to get away. Johnny caught me in the corner. I jabbed, but Johnny dropped to his left and hooked me with an overhand right to the nose again with a big splat! I saw stars, then caught a left hook to my right eye. I grabbed Johnny and held on, waiting for my sight to clear. Blood was running down from my nose, I tasted it already in my mouth.

"Move away and jab!" Al shouted, and I pushed Johnny back and started dancing away. I managed to catch Johnny with a couple of jabs, but he caught me with another overhand right to the nose. I heard that splat again. It hurt so bad, I knew it was broken again and wondered how bad it looked. I punched to the body when Johnny came in again and caught him with a couple of good hooks which made Johnny cover up for a moment and allow me to dance away again.

"Jab! Jab!" Al shouted, and I danced back, then suddenly stopped and caught Johnny with a solid jab to the face, stopping him in his tracks.

"Again! Do it again!" Al shouted, but when I jabbed again, Johnny dropped to his right and hit me in the head with a left hook. He followed with a quick right hook and another left hook to the head. But I punched to the body again as soon as he got close and made him cover up again. When I hit him with another hook, he caught me with a good one in the stomach, making me wince and grab his arms again.

"Break and move away!" Al shouted, and I danced away. Johnny jumped right on me and caught me with two hooks to the body, almost knocking the wind out of me. I felt the pain spread over my stomach as I kept my arms in and blocked two more hooks to the body. I fell against the ropes, where Johnny tried to maul me with a barrage of punches. I leaned inside and pressed against him, pushed him back, managed to get him off, and then I moved away along the ropes, panting, feeling fatigue, hoping the bell would ring. I was barely able to keep my guard up with the pain aching over my whole stomach. Now, I knew how hard it was going to be to become a Gloves champ and why Al was so hesitant. I wanted to keep Al training, but I wondered if I could keep it up myself!

6

The pop-pop of the fastbag behind me made so much noise I moved even closer to Al, who was down on the slantboard, doing his sit-ups. Already showered and dressed, my damp hair combed back in waves, I'd been waiting for a chance to talk to Al, but I didn't know how to bring up the subject.

Finally, Al leaned slowly back down on the board after doing his fifteenth situp, letting his body relax, his gray sweatshirt stained almost black over his chest from the sweat that had soaked through the T-shirt and rubber inner tube he'd wrapped around his waist. Sweat bubbled all over his forehead. Tipped upside down, his upper lip looked bigger and his eyes smaller than they really were. His wavy hair was wet and laying flat on his head.

"I'll buy you a new suit," I said, "if you make weight by Easter, Al!"

Al squinted one eye at me, the scar making it look like he was winking. "A new suit, huh?"

"Yes, if you make one-thirty-five!"

"You really mean that?" His eyebrows seemed to touch on his wrinkled forehead.

"Yes! A new suit if you make the lightweight limit by Easter."

Al grinned, showing his big front teeth. "Trying to use that nickel psychology on me, huh? Bribing me, huh?"

I grinned and said, "You might call it that."

Al lifted his head again as if he was going to start another sit-up, making a doublechin. "What if I don't make weight? Then what?"

"Nothing. You don't owe me anything. I just want you to make weight."

Al grinned again, his upper lip creased. "You sure there aren't any hidden clauses in this contract?"

"Sure," I said. "I just want you to get in shape."

"Listen, Floyd. In the Army, I used to go out and drink every night, have a few beers, then get some rest and get up and go fight the next night and win! I had twenty-seven fights and won twenty-five of them, half by knockouts!" He leaned his head back down on the board, but kept looking at me.

"I know," I said, "but you only fought three rounds in the amateurs and you start at four rounds in the pros."

Without answering me, he hooked his hands behind his head and curled his body into a ball and touched his knees with his elbows, grunting with the effort. Then he leaned way back again and let his body sink down on the board, looked up and winked.

7

"Al T. says that Speedy's out working the Greyhound Bus Station this morning and I should drop by before we go to the gym, just in case, if I want in," Al said, as we stepped into the elevator at the Leamington Hotel, one of the most expensive hotels in town.

The gray-haired elevator lady smiled and said, "Hello, little lady," to Anita, Al's three-year old daughter, who was dressed up in her Sunday finery.

Anita looked up at the lady with her big, brown eyes and said, "I don't wet my pants."

We all laughed, then smiled again when Anita said goodbye to the lady as we got out on an upper floor.

Al T. was still in bed when we walked into his room, which had a view of Lake Merritt and the Oakland hills. He was sprawled out under a fancy bedspread, but he didn't slide up into a sitting position until the phone rang.

I'd seen him sitting at the bar in the Knotty Pine. He was a thirty-five-year-old guy in dark "tea-timers," rimless dark glasses cut square around the edges like a pilot. He sat there drinking scotch, looking just like a serviceman in a rust-colored loafer jacket and slacks.

"Yeah!" he said into the phone. "Yeah!"

He looked up at Al. There were dark circles under his big eyes. He had a permanently tanned, ruddy complexion. He was a southern hustler, like Curly. There were a lot of them around.

"Yeah!" he said. "Al Salas is already here. He came by just for this. If he wants in, he's in. I'll ask him." He lowered the phone from his ear.

"Al! Speedy's got a mooch down at the Greyhound Bus Station, but Jimmy's already tailing him. You can play tail or let Jimmy do it alone and split with him. Up to you! You got first choice!"

Al looked at me.

"I'm supposed to box with Johnny today. You should be in my corner and you should train, too," I said.

Al must have caught the hurt tone of my voice because he said, "Count me in, Al T., but let Jimmy do it alone. My brother here ... " Al tipped his head at me, still holding Anita's hand.

"Al's in, whether Jimmy's already there or not!" Al T. said into the phone again. "Take the mooch down to that sailor bar on Broadway between Tenth and Eleventh. By Harry Fine's gym, around the corner from the T&D. So Al can be around for the payoff. He's going down to the gym across the street to train his brother. Yeah." He hung up.

"You're in, Al! Good thing you came by."

They both grinned.

"You've seen my kid brother, Al T.," Al said.

"Yeah," Al T. answered, "I've seen him around, with his pretty girl."

He shook my hand. Up close, I could really see the deep circles under his eyes and that his eyes were blood-shot, too. He didn't wear those dark glasses, even in the bars at night, for nothing.

"Anytime you wanna use my Cad, let me know. I'll let you take your little girl out in it."

"Thanks, Al T.," I said, although I had no intention of asking for it. I didn't even have a driver's license yet.

"Well, we better get going," Al T. said, and he threw the covers back. He stood up in his white, silken boxer shorts, which stretched around his thick belly. His flesh hung down. There wasn't any definition to his arm muscles even.

"Take your kid home and get down to the gym with your brother. I'll go park my Caddy down on Eleventh and see you there. We've got some time. It'll take Speedy a few minutes to get the mooch down there anyway."

"Okay," Al said. "Let's move, Floyd."

When we were walking up the stairs to the gym, Al said, "You know why I don't have to wait and tail the mooch with Jimmy for a half a tailing share, like Al T. said?"

When I shook my head, Al said, "Because I can whip Jimmy. He might refuse to split with me, otherwise." Jimmy sat outside in a convertible, already tailing. I didn't know who owned the car: Speedy Upshaw, Curly's younger brother, or Jimmy, a guy around thirty who hung around the Knotty Pine and was always friendly.

"How much will you make?" I asked Al.

"I'll get a split of a third," Al said. "They're taking those discharged servicemen for their bonus money. It's usually about three hundred. Sometimes more. Fifty bucks for me, at least. Not bad for just dropping in to see Al T., huh?"

"Not bad," I said.

"You know how I met him?" Al said. "He came into the Knotty Pine hung over and broke one morning when Curly had me helping out behind the bar. I lent him five dollars. We been friends ever since."

I didn't say anything, just kept walking.

"Al T.'s got a lot of class," Al said.

8

I skipped away when Johnny came tearing across the ring in his usual attack. I popped him with a jab and then skipped away again, quick with fear, trying to figure out how I could be my best against the tough, little guy. Maybe I should just slug it out with him? I was in much better shape now. I kept moving from side to side, back and forth, never letting myself get caught against the ropes, catching an occasional grazing blow, but never anything solid. I began to relax a little. The three months training was finally paying off and, though I didn't get in any solid shots, I didn't get hit good at all either. I went to my corner with the bell and felt a sense of satisfaction, but Al said, "Don't let this guy play with you like that!" and I blushed.

Al plucked the rubber mouthpiece off my teeth, sticky strings of spit clinging to it. I spit a cotton ball into the bucket as Al turned and washed the mouthpiece off over a bucket with water from a quart 7UP bottle. He turned the mouthpiece over to get both sides of it, then lifted the bottle up to my mouth. Balancing it on a finger, an inch away from my full, open lips, Al poured the water into my mouth until I closed it and water splashed on my chin.

"This Johnny's treating you like a punk. He's taking it easy on you. You're not even fighting him! He got you tamed or something? Show some Salas, man! Now get out there and fight. Don't just dance away. You got twice the talent this guy's got, whether he's Gloves champ or not. You're twice the boxer and you can hit harder, too. Now spit and get out there and fight!"

I hoped nobody else could hear him as I spit in the bucket. He stuffed the mouthpiece back in my mouth and shoved me out into the ring as the bell rang.

"Don't wait, Goddamnit!" I heard him say as he stepped down from the apron. Sweat pouring off me, I made up my mind to slug it out with Ortega, just to get over my fear. I'd been thinking of that all morning, anyway.

I peeked out through my gloves to protect myself, with my head down between my shoulders. I shifted my weight forward on the balls of my feet, lifted up on my right heel, stepped forward with my left foot and came down flat on it just as I jabbed with all my shoulder in it. My arm was stiff as a

102

spear as my left hand connected hard. "Splat!" Johnny's head flew back and I heard a murmur in the gym.

"That's the way! Keep working! Right hand!" Al shouted. Sparked by his words, I shot a right glove out with a twist of my shoulders and a twist of my wrist. It connected with another splat, knocking Johnny Ortega back a step to another murmur of the gym crowd. Another wave of strength surged through me.

Johnny dropped into a crouch and hooked with a right hand that caught me on the nose, making it sting and my eyes water. I jumped back.

"Don't dance back!" Al yelled and I leaped in with another left, attacking again, but missed. Johnny hooked with a left, but I shifted back a step with the swing and made him miss. Then I shifted my body forward with the same move, just extending the motion, and caught Johnny with a jab to the forehead. I felt that power and confidence again.

"Keep moving! Keep fighting!" I heard, and I moved in on the tough, little flyweight, who was so powerfully built his body looked like a ball of muscular lumps.

Shifting my weight back and forth like a teeter-totter, sure I could do it now, I stayed right outside the edge of Johnny's reach but close enough to leap in and score because I was taller. In spite of my thick chest, I was built long and wiry, instead of stocky. I had less bulk but as much muscular definition to my spare body as Johnny, even if my muscles were flatter and longer, instead of bunched like his. And there was a washboard of muscles on my stomach which flexed every time I punched. I'd seen them in the wall mirrors. I was strong, too, and I knew it. I scored again and again, leaping back out of range every time Johnny threw.

I could see all the faces looking at me, hear the murmurs, and smell the sweat, the leather and the Vaseline. My blood was pulsing in me. My legs were strong. I felt no fatigue. I felt good as I moved in and out, thinking, watching him when he punched, seeing the opening and beating him to his exposed part before he could score. Jab, jab, then counter with a straight right over Johnny's jab, then throw a straight left after it, two punches every time. When he jabbed, I stepped in, caught his jab with my right hand and speared him with two hard jabs. Whatever I threw, I threw two, maybe three, if he was still open. Then I would beat him to the punch with a jab when he charged in, and I would skip away. I felt good, good. The fear was gone.

The bell rang. I turned and walked back to the corner to Al standing at the ropes with his powerful shoulders over the top strand. He had the 7UP bottle in his hand, already reaching for my mouthpiece, smiling.

"You're ready now!" he said. "You can fight Johnny in that exhibition hotel smoker next week!" And in spite of the fear that streaked through me,

I knew I could do it. Boxing was fun. School could wait.

9

My heart started pounding at the sight of the crowd, the roar of voices bouncing off the walls as I stepped into the hotel ballroom in Santa Clara for the smoker bout. To me, it was like walking into the Roman Coliseum. Puffs of smoke floated in clouds over the bald heads, the gray hair, the pink, puffy faces and pot bellies, the eyes that were all looking at me!

I was in a new, shiny blue and silver Judson Pacific Murphy boxing robe with a silver sash. I was going to fight in front of a real fight audience for the first time. Al had decided I should box amateur with Babe Figuera's Judson Pacific Murphy iron foundry team, because I had gone to Alameda High School with half of them. Babe wanted me on the team, which was all right. But it also meant that I was going to have to keep boxing Ortega forever. I was afraid he was going to break my nose again tonight.

When we got close to the ring, which was set right on the floor in the middle of the ballroom and padded with mats, I could see Curly Upshaw and Roy, his older brother, a highclass pimp, too, with one of Curly's blond whores sitting on the other side of the ring. Al T. was there, too, in his dark tea-timers. They gave me some support, but their presence also put pressure on me, because I knew I had to fight good for them. I was worried I'd look bad.

I could see them all watching me walk up. They made me feel so shy, I ducked my head and started shadowboxing like a welterweight amateur main eventer I'd seen kayo some guy in Vallejo. Babe had said, "That's the way you should fight, Floyd." Babe astounded me because the guy was so good and so tough. He even looked tough with hair on his chest and beard stubble. I never dreamed Babe would think I could fight like that. So, right now I copied the guy, the way he shuffled down to the ring. I tried to fall into it, get inside myself and keep the self-consciousness and fear off. I did not want to see all the eyes staring at me.

I shuffled forward on the balls of my feet, sanding the floor with the leather soles of my boxing shoes, my heels barely touching, hands flickering with subtle feints, barely suggesting punches, the twist of a wrist and turn of a shoulder for a hook, the knuckle point of my fist twice for two fast jabs. I teetered my head and rocked my shoulders to slip a punch and began to feel good. I slipped inside myself, safe from the crowd for the moment.

But I was still scared. I still saw everybody looking at me, still knew they were there. I tried to concentrate on the feeling in my body, and it helped. I floated toward the ring, less a victim now. I could win this fight. I could beat Johnny, even if it was my very first amateur fight ever. I had beaten him in the gym only last week, and afterwards lots of guys had told me how good I looked against him, in front of him. Even Jack Mendonca's fighters said so. I could beat Johnny, I told myself, and squeezed my fists into tight balls in the twelve-ounce gloves. I gritted my teeth and set my jaw. I was going to win! I was determined to win!

I stopped shadowboxing and got scared again when I reached the ring and all eyes turned on me. I stepped through the ropes onto the mats set on the floor and into the bright lights all alone, tense, self-conscious. I walked in a blur to the neutral corner to sand my shoes in the resin box, then back to my corner, where Al untied my belt and slipped my robe off.

Now, I felt naked. The referee was beckoning me. Up close, he was a red-faced man with lines in his cheeks. Johnny stepped up. Babe Figuera, his eyes looking steel-rimmed in his glasses, was behind him, rubbing his shoulders.

With the bright lights shining down on us, Johnny looked like a tiny Atlas, like a miniature body builder at five-three, a hundred twelve pounds. He smiled stiffly at me. At nineteen, there was a toughness in the tight lines of his face from having to work so hard as a migrant farmworker when he was a child. He was supposed to be half Apache and had won every tournament he'd ever entered for two straight years, from boys club bouts to the Golden Gloves.

I could hear the announcer calling Johnny the Golden Gloves champion of California and then announcing my name and weight. But when the referee started mumbling instructions, all I could hear was my heart thudding against my chest: bu-bump! bu-bump! bu-bump!

When we got back to the corner, Al said, "He's going to try and get even with you for the whipping you gave him last week. So keep moving and keep fighting. Don't wait for him to pick his shots. Go get him. Beat 'im to the punch. Keep the pressure on him. He's not used to that."

He jammed my mouthpiece into my mouth and pushed me around to face Johnny at the sound of the bell. I froze with fright for a second when I saw him charging at me. But I caught my breath and danced away along the ropes, fast, running to get time to think. I skipped completely out of the corner and around to the other side of the ring, where I had a safe distance between us and I could see Johnny for the first time, really. Then, when I saw him chugging after me like a little locomotive, I knew I could hit him with a jab right away. All I had to do was beat him. Now I was thinking.

Now I could fight. I wasn't afraid. It was just a fight. I'd been in lots of fights.

I was in another world when I skipped out under the bright lights on the balls of my feet to meet Johnny, my body sizzling as if the mats under my shoes were white hot, skimming over them toward him like a water mosquito. My hands were up and I peeked over the gloves in front of my face, my chin tucked into my left shoulder, my arms like two fence posts in front of my face and body, elbows covering my belly. I was pale from working in the library all the time, but my shoulders were thick and muscular, and muscles rippled on my belly. My thighs were slim but muscular and popped out like turkey legs, knots of muscles above the knees. My calves were slim and muscular, too, with ridges of muscles outlining them.

I started firing with a jab as soon as I got in range to keep him off. But I was forced to jump back when Johnny charged with a flurry of hooks, overhand rights and lefts, grunting as he punched. He drove me around the ring, going all out to get me, trying to knock me out just as Al said he would. Johnny "The Killer" Ortega.

But I suddenly stopped and counterpunched with a quick one-two, left-right, and danced out again as Johnny charged in again. He was still throwing hooks with both hands, barely grazing me, only the slightest turn of my head making the punches slide off instead of connecting full force. And as soon as he paused after missing a couple, I leaped back in again with two jabs, pop-pop, then one-two, left-right, and leaped out again as the crowd started shouting.

Johnny chased me, kept coming and trapped me against the ropes, where he threw a barrage at me and caught me on the sides of the head. He kept punching, forcing me to fall inside the hooks and cover up, take the punches on the arms and shoulders and gloves as much as I could. I felt the sting of them on my face, my forehead, my cheekbone, but none were solid.

I could hear Johnny grunting with the swings, feel his weight pressing against me, leaning on me, keeping me trapped against the ropes. I shifted to my left and when Johnny pressed harder, I quickly shifted to my right and shoved Johnny by the left shoulder to his right, spinning out of the way and sending him sprawling over the second rope.

I heard the crowd cry out with approval as I danced back until Johnny was facing me again. Then I went in again, pop-popping with my left, and I shifted back a step to make the countering left miss and shifted back in with a left-right, one-two. I wasn't thinking of what I was doing. I was just doing what I'd been trained to do, what I knew I could do, anything to keep the fear away.

When Johnny charged, I waited and popped him with another jab, but I caught one to the nose myself. It stung. I danced away, then back in with another jab, then back out again, out and in, again and again and again, jabbing, jabbing, jabbing, crossing with my right every time Johnny charged, stopping the charge, punching back every time Johnny punched, even when dancing back, throwing a flurry of punches as I backed up, short lefts and rights, all of them crosses, pumping them straight out in front of me, "Bam-bam-bam-bam-bam!" inside Johnny's hooks, catching the hooks to the forehead and temples, not letting any one punch get me in the face and landing every punch I threw square in Johnny's face until he finally backed off. Then I waited, facing him until I heard Al shout, "Go get'im!" and I leaped in again.

But Johnny caught me with a right hook that stunned me. For just one second my sight blurred and Johnny fuzzed out of focus, and my head went "Bzzzzzzz." I caught another punch square in the face, and I grabbed Johnny's arms, tied him up and felt myself being pushed back against the ropes.

I could hear the excited voices of the crowd and knew I was hurt and in trouble. I held on desperately until my sight cleared and I heard Al shout, "Move! Move!" And I shoved Johnny back and danced away just as the bell rang.

Johnny walked away. When I got to my corner and sat down, I could see him on the other side of the ring, sitting on his stool. I met his heavy-lidded eyes with my own just for a moment. His eyes looked strangely at me. There was a question in them, the quizzical way he studied me that showed he was surprised, that he respected me for giving him, the Gloves Champ, such a battle in my very first fight. But there was no fear in his eyes. Ortega feared no one.

I was clear-headed now, but the rest of the fight was a blur for me. I started jabbing and connecting again, then let go with a sharp right when he started to come in and caught him right on the jaw. I heard the whole hall shout and saw Johnny stagger back, then just stand there staring at me with his arms down, mouth open, looking surprised.

I stared at him. His eyes were glazed. Yet, I just stood there, as surprised as he was. We stared at each other. Suddenly, I heard Al shout. "Go get him. He's all yours!"

And the whole crowd cheered as I leaped in as Al told me, but Babe yelled, too: "Hands up, Johnny!" and Johnny ducked his head down when I jumped in and started hooking over his head with both hands. We slugged it out there on the ropes. I could feel his punches but they didn't hurt me. And I could feel my gloves thudding against his face and body. I could hear shouts. My face was hot and my body was pouring sweat, moving like magic, without strain or fatigue, full of wind and endurance, punching, punching,

punching, with all thought of fear and anxiety long gone. Everything was pure intuition, automatic. My whole body was behind and in every punch with fluid, effortless motion, without thought or feeling, firing punch after punch after punch. It was thrilling.

Suddenly, the fight was over. There had been another round but I didn't even remember fighting it. I could hear the crowd shouting and cheering and clapping while the referee grabbed both Johnny's and my arms and turned us in a circle, calling it a draw. It was a draw. Al was in the ring, grinning, taking my mouthpiece out and throwing my robe over my shoulders. I felt a great sense of jubilation, with nervous skirmishes of fluctuating sound beating on my exposed, sweating face like quick blasts of wind. I couldn't think of anything to say. I couldn't speak. I just stepped through the ropes and down the aisle as if I were tip-toeing on air.

10

When I walked into the Knotty Pine from the side door, I saw Al sitting at the bar with a drink in his hand, talking to Curly and Al T. The highball glass shimmered with blue light from the glow of the crystal star in the low ceiling. He hadn't shown up at the gym for a week after my Santa Clara fight! It was as if I reached that exciting peak fighting Johnny in Santa Clara and then nothing else happened. I hadn't seen him at the house either. So instead of going straight to the gym when I got off from work at the library, I walked up from 14th and Grove to 18th, then cut down it a couple of blocks to the Knotty Pine, hoping he'd be there.

Al looked good, though, even with his receding hairline. He looked like a boxer. He had a powerful forehead, with a strong nosebridge and deeply set eyes. Even his lips looked puffy and pugnacious. When he saw me, he slid the drink behind his body, grinned and said, "Hi, Floyd! How's the champ?"

Curly and Al T. smiled at me, but I said, "What you got there, Al?"

"What? Me?" Al said, keeping a straight face. "I don't have anything. I'm just keeping my hand warm."

Then he grinned again and Al T. and Curly chuckled.

"It's okay," Al T. said.

"Al shouldn't be drinking. He's breaking training. He'll never make weight that way," I said.

"It's okay," Curly said. "I'm his manager and a little drink now and then won't hurt him. He needs to relax sometimes."

"But he hasn't been to the gym since I fought Johnny! Babe's mad!"

"Babe can go to hell," Al said, lifting his drink, holding it up so I could see it, then taking a sip.

"Me, too?" I said, and Al squinted at me over the glass, the thin scar on his lid showing.

"Naaaaw. You know better than that," Al said, and Curly said, "Al loves you like his own kid. You know that. And you'd jump off the bridge for him. I've never seen two brothers who liked each other so much. Not even me and my brothers."

Curly's thick black brows, his thin black mustache and black curly hair combed straight back from his forehead made him look serious, although he was still the ladies man in his expensive tan flannel sportshirt and matching flannel slacks.

"Al's been earning a living, Floyd," Al T. said, looking at me, but I couldn't see his eyes through the dark glasses in the low bar light. His face was puffy from all the scotch he drank. "I put him on the tail and he had to put the mooch on the bus."

"Mooch?" I said, still not sure what they meant by that. "And what-a-ya mean by tailing him? Following him?"

"It's a little game I earn my living at," Al T. said.

"Stealing?" I asked and looked at Al, who looked away.

"Naw, gamblin', not stealin', half-legit. Hustlin's a better word," Al T. said and took his glasses off, showing the deep, dark circles under his eyes.

"You can't beat them unless they try to beat you," my brother Al said as he faced me again and put his glass down on the bar. He pulled a folded wad of paper out of his front pocket. He spread the edges with his thumb so I could see about ten or fifteen twenty-dollar travelers checks.

"This is my cut for helping Al T. pull off a big score of almost two thousand dollars!"

He narrowed his eyes, waited until I said, "Wow! How? Gambling?"

"Yeah, gambling. And this is only twenty percent. I didn't do anything but hang out with the guy after he lost and then put him on the Greyhound bus. I didn't have anything to do with the play. Just put him on the bus afterwards, that's all. Spent some time with him until his bus came and that's why I didn't go to the gym today. Just earning some money, that's all." He said it with a drawl and spread the checks out so I could see how many there were.

"You make a buck an hour at that library as a page, a hundred and sixty a month. I just beat that in two hours."

"Your brother did all right for himself, Floyd," Big Press said, coming up behind me. He was dressed in a loafer jacket and slacks, like Al T. and Al. But at six-four and a good two hundred forty pounds, he looked huge, like some heavyweight bouncer with a baby face. He was only nineteen, Al said, but he'd been hustling and supporting himself on the streets since he was twelve.

"Al wouldn't let you down, son," Pix, the bartender, said from behind the bar, treating me like a little brother, making me feel a little better. "What about your job?" I asked.

Al's chin lifted. His upper lip got stiff. "I lost it," he said.

"When?" I asked, seeing my own face squinting up in the mirror behind the bar.

"Last week. The day after you fought Johnny in Santa Clara."

"How?" I asked.

"I got in a fight with a belligerent customer and punched him out when he threw at me. Remember when Dad talked to my boss to help me keep my job after that contributing charge?"

I nodded.

"I had to promise I wouldn't get into any more trouble and no more fights."

"Well, did he fire you?"

"Awww, I knew I was going to lose the job, soon's it happened. So I came down here and was telling the guys about it, and Al T. said not to worry about it, I could work with them."

He turned and looked at Al T., then back at me. "So, I been working with him."

"But you still could've come to the gym," I said.

"I don't have regular hours, Floyd!" He squinted that one eye. I could barely see the scar on the lid in the soft light now. "I've got to hang around and be ready to go all the time."

"All the time?" I asked and shook my head. "Come on down to the gym and train me. Babe's trying to get me to box like John L. Sullivan, like some musclebound body builder. Help me get ready for my next fight. I'm supposed to fight next week in Vallejo, remember?"

Al squinted his scarred eye at me.

"I almost knocked out Johnny Ortega last week, but I didn't know how to finish him. Show me, so I can stop the next guy!"

Curly chuckled. "Damn, this kid is great!"

Al grinned. "Trying to con me again, huh? You owe me a suit, already."

I looked right at him. "All right," I said. "Let's go buy you a sportcoat right now, for getting close to your weight, for getting down near one-forty."

"You'd do that even though I didn't make lightweight?"

"Yeah, let's go," I said.

"Maybe you ought to take him up on it," Curly said.

"Naaaw," Al said, "I've got too many other things on my mind. I got probation on that contributing to the delinquency of a minor charge. But I've got to earn some more money to pay off the fine. Money like this."

He ruffled the edges of the checks with his thumb and stuck them back in his pocket. "Good score and I want more," he said. "I ought-ta celebrate losing that job. Even if I was the highest earning driver there. Hey, Pix! Set up the bar! A round on me!" Al held up a finger for Pix.

It was cocktail hour and the bar was full. A few people clapped and a couple of guys near Al lifted their glasses to him. A woman stood up, went over to the jukebox and stared at the selections.

"You want a drink, too?" Al asked me. "You can celebrate with me."

"No," I said, thinking of all the money he was going to waste when he didn't even have a job.

"You sure?" Al asked. "He can have a drink, can't he, Curly?"

"Sure, anything he wants," Curly said.

"I don't want anything, Al. I don't want to drink. I want to go down to the gym and have you train me."

Al frowned, stared down at the bar as if he was trying to keep his temper, then looked up, smooth-browed, and in a hard voice said, "Listen, Floyd. I've got too much on my mind now. I wouldn't be able to concentrate on training you. I'm not in the mood for it. I've got things to do. I've got to pay off that fine. I tried to fight, but got tied up to that broad of mine, and it didn't work out. She doesn't support me. Right now ... " He stopped and looked past me at the front door and I turned and saw two men in suits and hats standing just inside the club, looking around.

"Vice squad," Al said under his breath, then spun around off the stool and stepped toward the back door.

"Hey, Al!" one of the men shouted and they both started running across the dance floor after him. Al spun to his right and took three bounding steps past the bar and into the toilet in the hall, slamming the door behind him.

The younger one reached the door first and jerked on the doorknob, shouting, "Open up, police!"

He was about Al's age, with an olive complexion and a brown mustache that made him look dapper in spite of the baggy suit he was wearing.

The other cop banged on the door and shouted, "Open up, Al, or we'll kick the door down." Then he kicked on the door. He was an older guy with pink, puffy cheeks, in a baggy suit, too, and a fuzzy, gray gangster hat, just like the bailbondsman's.

"Okay! Okay!" Al yelled and the cops waited, staring at the door, but when they heard the toilet flush, the younger one jerked on the door knob again.

"Goddamnit! Open up!"

But the door stayed closed and the only sound from inside was the sound of running water crashing down the toilet bowl.

"I'm going to kick your ass, if you don't open up, Al!" the older cop shouted, his pink cheeks puffing up. But the door didn't open until the water quit crashing. Then Al stepped out and with a stiff face asked, "What's the big rush, Mickey?"

The cop grabbed him and shoved him up against the wall, while the other cop threw the door open wide and stepped into the toilet.

"What're you salty about, Mickey?" Al said, and held his hands out in front of him, palms up.

"You know goddamn well what I'm salty about," the pink-faced cop said as he stuck his hand into Al's jacket pocket. He quickly shook him down, then said, "Turn around!"

When Al slowly dropped his hands and started to turn, the cop grabbed him by the shoulder and spun him around, saying, "Put your hands above your head and lean against the wall!"

"Hey, Mickey, relax! No problem!" Al said in a high, whining voice, as if it was all a big mistake.

Curly smiled. I glanced to see if Al T. was smiling, too, and saw that his bar stool was empty, his half-finished glass of scotch and water still sitting on the bar. Big Press picked up the scotch and poured it into his glass, then set the empty glass on the inner ledge of the bar, as if no one was drinking it. He just looked at me when I looked into his eyes.

I turned back to see Mickey pulling a comb and handkerchief out of one of Al's back pockets, his wallet from the other. He opened the wallet, spread it, looked inside, then slapped it closed and stuffed it back in Al's pocket.

"Turn around and drop your hands! And what'd you do with those travelers checks?"

"What travelers checks?" Al asked, lowering his arms just as the younger cop stepped out of the toilet and said, "He flushed 'um down the toilet."

"Al's been here all afternoon," Curly said, stepping into the back hall. "What's up?"

"Don't fuck around, Curly," the younger cop said.

Curley looked him full in the face and said, "I'm giving it to you straight, Joel. He's been here all day, since noon."

The young cop jabbed his finger at Curly, his mustache jerking as he talked. "The mooch he put on the bus got off in Richmond and called us, then came back. He said he met Al down on 13th and Broadway right after he lost his money. As soon as he described Al, I knew who he meant. Remember, I just busted Al for pandering? He looked at Al.

"I felt bad about busting you for that because you were working and trying to take care of your family. But you're not working anymore and you're out partying all the time. And if you hadn't flushed those checks down the toilet, I'd bust you right now."

Al spread his hands again and said, "I don't know what you're talking about, Joel," as if he were totally innocent, but barely able to keep from grinning.

The cop shook his head, slowly, a thin grin spreading on his face. "I'll get yuh next time, Al."

He slapped the other cop on the shoulder, turned away and walked back out of the short hall. Then he saw me and stopped.

"You Al's brother? The kid who works at the library a half a block from our office?"

I nodded, swallowing, afraid he'd say something about me being underage and in a bar.

"I'm Joel Taylor. Al's heading for big trouble if he keeps up this bunco shit. I felt sorry having to bust him for procuring when he was trying to earn a living and recommended the contributing charge for his record. But this is different. This is hurting people."

He lowered his head and eyed me for a second, then asked, "Don't you work out at Harry Fine's gym?"

I nodded, afraid to talk now, but he said, "Keep boxing and stay at that library." He looked at his older partner, jerked his head at the back door and said, "Let's go, Mickey. Al's got a pass on this one, but if he doesn't smarten up, he's going to end up doing some time."

Both of the cops stared at Al again. He squinted both his eyes as if they'd scared him, then spread both his hands and said, "I don't know wha'cher talkin' about."

"You will, if you keep messing around," Joel said and stepped out the back door.

The older cop started to follow him, but stopped and looked at me. His pink, puffy face was splayed with red and blue veins, as if he drank a lot.

"I'm Mickey Boise. I grew up in this neighborhood. You take Joel's advice and stay away from here."

I nodded, afraid to speak and watched him step out the back door.

Everyone was quiet for a moment, then Al pushed the door tight behind Mickey and, turning back around, said, "That was close!"

"Too damn close," Curly said, then grinned. "But that was pretty fast thinking, flushing those checks down like that. With reflexes like that, you could be champion of the world."

Al laughed. "I made 'em wait, didn't I?" Then he stuck his hand in his jacket pocket and pulled the lining out. "But I'm broke now."

"I'll cover that bar tab for you," Curly said and held up his finger at Pix, then pointed to himself. Then he asked me, "You want a drink, Floyd?"

I couldn't answer for a moment. I couldn't be disloyal to my brother, but I couldn't forget what both cops said. I looked at Al.

"You go on to the gym, Floyd," he said. Then he held up his hand, palm out, like a traffic cop, and before I could ask him to come with me, said, "I'll try to make it down to the gym, but I can't go with you now. I've got to get hold of Al T. and make some more money."

I dropped my head and looked down.

"But I'll come to your fight and bring Curly, too," he said. "How about that, Curly?"

"Sure thing. I wouldn't miss it," Curly said, smiling at me. I just turned around and walked out the back door, heading for the gym, alone, wondering if it was worth it.

11

A messy stream of blood and saliva drooling out of his open mouth and down his chin, puffy glazed eyes, his feet scraping the floor, a guy holding him up on each side, the black kid was dragged into the dressing room. I turned away and popped my boxing gloves together. I was next. My legs tingled. I had to piss, but my gloves were on and it was too late now. Al didn't show up once at the gym! Or at home either!

The stink of cigar smoke made me gag. I remember Al had vomited the night of his first fight. I turned back around. The black guy was down on a chair, head tilted back with checkered icepacks on his eyes. He looked like a mosquito.

How did I get here? In this room at this time? When Al wasn't with me? Some comeback!

I stood up and walked back and forth in front of the lockers so I wouldn't have to look at anybody. Maybe it was too late for Al to make a comeback. Maybe it was true that that hustling wasn't really stealing, but gambling. Even with the cops out to bust him? But I'd taken such a beating from Johnny before I could beat him and now Al wasn't here! He didn't go all out for me like I did for him. That hurt!

I stopped and stared at the black guy again, then heard "That guy never ran in the morning," and my heart leaped in my chest at the sound of Al's voice. I spun around, but couldn't smile.

"That's why he got hurt," Al said, standing behind me, squinting, in shirtsleeves, no coat, as if ready to work in my corner.

I still couldn't smile.

"You're in shape, Floyd! Nothing like him!" He poked his thumb at the black guy. "Don't worry!"

He spoke softly to keep the guy from hearing, but the guy was on Queer Street anyway and couldn't possibly care, even if he heard.

"You'll feel better once you get in the ring. Take my word for it."

I didn't know what to say. I was more unhappy than worried.

"He didn't have any class either, not half as much as you. All you gotta remember is to take your time, think and throw combinations. Then follow up if you hurt the guy. Stay right on him! Don't let him get away like you did Johnny and you'll stop him!"

He winked, but I saw him getting stopped, toppling over on his face in Sacramento and I felt a streak of fear split through me for the first time.

"Next fight!" a bald-headed guy yelled through the open doorway. Al slapped me on the shoulder and tightened my blue robe for me. Then he put his hands on my shoulders and said, "It's all up to you now, Floyd. You're the fighter, not me."

When I frowned, he said, "I gave it a shot! Don't think I didn't. It's just too late! I'm too old to start at the beginning again. Maybe, if I'd been a main-eventer already, a ten-round fighter, I could've done it. But you know, I never got any support from that old lady of mine."

His mouth stretched in a thin smile, but his eyes were sad. I tried to smile back, but my lips just quivered. Al turned and walked away without another word.

I followed, really depressed now, without will, as if caught in a current behind him, sucked around the blood-browned massage tables, by the battered green lockers, the knots of fighters ready to bust other fighters' faces in, and all the way to the door, where Johnny Ortega stepped in, his long robe streaming from his shoulders like a cape, hooded eyes slanted almost closed, grinning.

"Got him, Floyd," he said. "Dropped him in each one, too. Good luck, buddy." He slapped me on the shoulder and rocked by with that little short-stepped swagger of his to cries of "Good fight, Johnny!" "That's the way to do it!" "That a boy!"

I felt even worse when I stepped into the arena and saw the sheet of bright canvas. A crippling weakness shot through me, and I started shadowboxing like I did in Santa Clara to shake the sadness. I mockpunched down the aisle to show some spark, but felt weak, just arm, no shoulder nor upper body in my punches, no fire. Then I caught my breath when I stepped through the ropes and saw the canvas like a block of hot ice, polkadotted with blood.

Rows of faces looking up at me blurred into waves. I tried to fix my eyes on a ring post to steady myself, when Al pushed me out of the corner and pointed at the resin box on the other side of the ring. Sanding my leather soles in it, I noticed the boxing glove and the arm of the guy I was going to fight behind me. I felt a cold sense of dread, not so much of him, but of the whole spectacle, with everybody staring at me. I flexed my back like a cobra to steel myself and scare the guy, too, and then stepped back to my corner without even glancing at him, trying to get myself ready to fight.

Al took off my robe and nudged me into the center of the ring. The Mexican kid in front of me had black, curly hair and brown skin. That's all I could tell because I didn't look him in his eyes and didn't even listen to the referee's instructions. Al turned me around by the shoulders as if massaging them, and guided me back to the corner where Babe was standing on the ring apron. "You better wake up! It's time to fight!" he said. He pushed my mouthpiece into my mouth and slid through the ropes as the bell rang.

I put my arms up but the kid stayed in his corner halfway across the ring. Then, although I shuffled forward, he started circling around out of jab range even, his dark head drifting along the ropes, without coming after me, as if he'd heard that I'd fought the Gloves champ to a draw my first fight and was being careful.

I pivoted in one spot and waited for the guy to come back around from the other side, then faced him and waited for him to come in. But he didn't. He just danced back and forth looking for an opening and I just stood there waiting for him to take a chance. Finally someone yelled, "Fight!" and I heard Al mumble, then step up on the ring steps, crouch down and wave me in.

I skipped toward the guy and stopped, ducked in a feint, staying just out of range, trying to make the guy punch like Ortega would, but the guy skipped away, too, and somebody else yelled, "Fight!"

"Right hand, Floyd! Use your right!" Curly yelled and I saw him wave from ringside. Al T. shouted, too, and I shot out a right lead, which was short and got jabbed back in the face.

I jumped out again and skipped away, staying on my toes with a light-footed grace, close to the guy, but just out of range, like a moth caught just on the edge of the sucking heat of the ring lights. Al waved me in again and I leaped in but leaped back out when the guy jabbed again without coming close to hitting me. Someone shouted, "Let's have that step again, sonny!" A few others joined in and kept shouting as the Mexican kid and I skipped around each other without either of us striking a blow. There were lots of boos when the bell rang.

Al met me before I could get back to the corner, hooked my mouthpiece out with a barbed finger, then shoved me down on the stool and said, "Snap out if it, Floyd!" His voice was hot, impatient.

"Can't you see that this guy's scared of you? Don't follow him around like he's your Boy Scout leader. Go after him with a jab at least! Spear him with it until you catch him against the ropes, then cut loose with both hands! Try to stop him!"

I looked at him, but, instead of seeing his face, I saw him being stopped himself in Sacramento again. I could actually see him lying on the canvas under the ring lights. He tapped my cheek with his fingers, a tiny slap, to make me look at him. His jaw muscles flexed with tension. He tipped up the water bottle and poured some in my mouth, held up the bucket for me to spit and then jammed the mouthpiece back in with the buzzer and poured water over my head.

"Jab, Floyd! You can do that!" he said and pulled the stool out of the ring with him.

I stood up, but didn't move until Al said, "Fight!" Then I moved toward the guy as if shuffling in slow motion, as if underwater, each step pushing against the current. I was so slow that, even though I saw the guy lift his glove and stick it out, I still caught it right in the face. The guy then jumped back like he'd been burned and someone shouted, "Powder the other side of his face now," and people laughed.

But the guy took it seriously and pat-patted my face with two jabs, then backpedaled around the ring as if he'd touched a hot socket. Then, seeing that he got away with it, he danced in and stuck out another jab and scored again and the crowd yelled. But when he tried it again and again, I leaped back and made him miss. Still, I didn't jab myself. I didn't know why. I just didn't do it and somebody started stamping his feet and soon others joined in and then the whole hall was vibrating with the sound until the bell rang and the crowd booed both of us back to our corners.

Al was mad. He shoved me down on the stool, snatched the mouthpiece out, spilled water on it, and jammed it right back in to my mouth without saying one word or even offering me any water.

"I think he needs to breathe, Al," Babe said and reached into the corner from the apron and pulled out on my waistband. "Take deep breaths, Floyd."

"What the hell he need air for? There's not a spot of sweat on him," Al said. He took out the mouthpiece again and tilted the bottle up, held the bucket for me to spit, then blinked, his eyes sparking with every word. "What the hell's the matter with you? This guy can't touch a glove to you! Run out there and fight!"

I saw him lying on the canvas again and he stopped and stared into my eyes, as if he could read my face. "If I got knocked out, at least I got knocked out fighting!" he said. "You act scared. Fight, man! That's all I'm gonna say. Use your jab! Use your right hand! Use everything!"

He twisted the stool leg and tipped me off and slid out between the ropes as the buzzer sounded. I had to catch myself to keep from falling. Suddenly, I saw Curly and Al T. and Roy all staring at me, and I knew I looked bad, but I couldn't seem to get started.

"Right hand!" Curly shouted.

"Right, Floyd! Right!" Al T. shouted and Roy shouted, too, as the bell rang. I tried to dance after the guy and catch him, but every time I got near him, he seemed to float away. I couldn't touch him with my jab and couldn't see an opening for my right. Also, I didn't want to lead with my right and get hit again. I danced back when the guy came in.

"Fight!" somebody yelled and I stopped to fight, but caught a jab, then another, and when I jabbed, too, the guy was gone. I felt like a lumbering heavyweight, slow as a truck. I floated slowly through the whole round. Still, the guy couldn't really hit me either and nothing happened. The bell rang. Curly and Al T. and Roy got up and started moving away before I even reached my corner. Babe was standing outside the ropes, his glass lenses blind and glittering, and Al was rocking up the aisle with his back to me. My face burned with shame.

12

My bedroom door was closed but I could hear Dolores bitching at Dad in broken English in the kitchen.

"You . . . You always think your kids!"

She could speak clearly enough when she wanted to, otherwise she tried to make you speak, or *try* to speak to her, like I did, in her language, Spanish. She was so stuck up about her education and class, and she did have class. She thought everybody around her was less than her. But whether she liked it or not, she had to speak English, because we didn't speak Spanish at home. None of the Salas's had since my father's generation grew up in the first part of the century and inter-married with other, more recent European immigrants who didn't speak it.

I could see her giving it to my father, hissing through her gritted teeth, complaining about some money or attention that hadn't gone to her, with her fur coats and fancy dresses and big diamond rings. That familiar burn of resentment smoldered in my chest. She'd cashed in on her youth and class and his loneliness to snare him, with his big houses and apartments. But she had let me lie in bed with my burning, ulcerated eyes for days when I was sixteen, in '47, and hadn't even called a doctor. I wondered why I was letting it hurt me so much. Then I remembered that I'd lost last night! My face burned with a blush. I could actually feel my cheeks burn with shame. At least Al went down fighting! I didn't even fight and had lost! And Dad would want to know right away how I did!

I looked out the window, trying to distract myself, and saw a sky as clear and cold as a cop's badge. I threw back the covers and walked barefooted across the wood floor to the bathroom, dribbled piss into the bowl, flushed and then leaned down over the sink and splashed water over my face to erase that picture of myself, standing still in the center of the ring, getting jabbed in the face by that guy. When I raised up to dry, squinting with a headache, Dolores's voice rattled like a snaredrum in the distance. I combed my wavy hair back with only a couple of swipes, then stepped back into my bedroom.

I got dressed with a low feeling down in my stomach, put on a shirt and khakis, picked up my hanky, comb and wallet from the dresser, put them in my pockets and braced myself for a moment. I heard sounds on the floor upstairs from Al's kitchen, pictured him up there and blushed because I'd have to face him, too.

There was a lull in the fighting when I opened the door, yet I hesitated before stepping out into the dinning room to show myself. The dining room echoed with kitchen sounds: sliding drawer, jingle of spoons, clatter of a cup and saucer, tap of the coffee pot on an iron range, footsteps. Dolores must have come downstairs from her apartment to get something out of the house. Dorothy was probably shopping with the kids, since I couldn't hear her nor them. But in the back of my mind I was trying to think of a way to tell Dad I had lost, when I didn't have a mark of defeat on me, not one cut or bruise.

Dolores cut loose with a barrage of Spanish cusswords just as I turned into the dining room. Then she saw me looking into the kitchen at her and turned and walked out past me without saying hello. I saw my father bob his bald head with some gruff, but unconvincing reply in English to her. Then he saw me and asked, "Did you win?"

I ducked my head behind the refrigerator door, stalled by picking up the orange juice, stepping to the cupboard above the sink for a glass, then pouring the juice so slowly the kitchen filled with a gurgling sound for a few seconds. I didn't stop until I nearly spilled the juice, then jerked the bottle upright and put it down on the sink. "I lost by a decision, Dad," I said. "I didn't fight enough."

Dad blinked, looked down and smoothed his tie flat between his stomach and the back of the chair he was straddling. He rested his forearms on the backrest again, still without looking up. He then reached out and pushed back a chair with one hand and said, "Sit down and tell me about it."

I leaned over the glass and took a sip so I wouldn't spill it, still stalling, then straightened up again and said, "Dad! I lost!"

"Sit down and tell me about it. Then I'll tell you what I think."

"I lost, Dad. Don't you understand?"

"Aaaw, they probably robbed you. They ... "

"Dad, I lost! I lost!" I said, raising my voice, almost spilling the orange juice. "They didn't rob ... " I stopped as Dolores hurried back into kitchen in her high heels with an empty coffee cup and crossed to the stove to refill it. She didn't speak nor look once at me or my father. She just filled her cup, banged the pot down, leaned over the table for milk and sugar, and stirred her coffee as she left, striking her heels against the linoleum floor. Dad rubbed his hands together, waiting until her footsteps crossed through the dining room, then said, "You were sick, then. Something was wrong with you. Was it your brother Al? Didn't he help you?"

I thought a moment, looking down at my father, his one eyebrow raised just the way Eddy and I raised ours. I was struck for the first time by the idea that maybe Al had something to do with it. But when that brown, intelligent eye stared into mine, I didn't want to cop out. I said, "I wasn't sick, Dad, and no matter what Al did, I was the one who lost."

"All right, then!" Dad said, throwing his hands in the air. He then reached for his cup of black coffee.

I put the orange juice bottle back in the refrigerator, still tense but glad one of the worst parts was over, though I still had to face Al.

Tommy stepped out of the boxed-in stairwell with a baby bottle in one hand, holding her bright, yellow bathrobe together with the other. "I hear you lost, Floyd," she said. Her smirking mouth was smeared with lipstick. Mascara smudges made her eyes look lopsided, and the stubs of her shaved eyebrows stood up like insect antennaes.

I tried to ignore her by drinking my orange juice, but she waited, still smirking, cashing in on her complaints for the last few months, her resentment of every minute Al had spent training with me. She'd used everything from fighting to sulking to get him to stop. Now she gloated. Even when she turned around and stood up on her toes, she was so short, reaching into the cupboard for a pan and looking over her shoulder at me while she groped around and knocked a pan into the sink with a clatter that made her jump and Dad jerk his head around.

Tommy picked the pan up, held it under the water faucet and ran water in it, saying, "Al said that if you didn't win the Golden Gloves title, he'd quit fighting himself. What about that, Floyd?"

When I didn't answer, she clumsily twisted the faucet handle with the same hand she held the baby bottle in and, letting the water drip onto the floor from the bottom of the pan, put it on the stove and turned the gas on. She asked again, "What about it, Floyd?"

"I don't know," I said, not telling her that Al had already quit. "That's up to Al, and, besides, the fight wasn't for the Gloves. That's in November. This was just an amateur fight."

I thought of asking her why she wasn't heating the baby's bottle upstairs in her own apartment, but already I knew why—she wanted to torment me in front of my father. I kept quiet.

She went to the refrigerator and filled the bottle from the carton of milk instead of using the formula for the baby that was upstairs in her own refrigerator. She asked again, "What about it, Floyd? Now that you lost!"

"He might have lost, but he didn't get hurt," Dad said. "And neither of them has to stop fighting, either. He's still going to be as good a fighter as his brother."

"That's not saying much," Tommy said and put the carton back without closing its cap. She slammed the refrigerator door, stepped on a silver dollar-sized puddle of spilled milk and put the streaked bottle into the pan of water without washing it off. Then she suddenly stopped and smiled at me, smeared lipstick thickening her wide mouth. "I'm sorry you lost, Floyd," she said, a band of sunlight through the window electrifying the frizzy ends of her dyed auburn hair. She was trying to be nice, it seemed, sounding like she meant it.

I smiled and tried to thank her, ashamed of myself for resenting her, for not liking her, saying, "Thank ... " when she cut me off with, "Can you call me when the bottle's ready? I'll be upstairs. And maybe, if I'm busy or something, you can bring it up for me, okay?"

My face burned with hot anger at her. But when Al called down the stairwell, "Stay down there until the bottle's ready yourself, Tommy! And bring it up yourself!" I felt justified.

"Sonofabitch!" she whispered under her breath as his footsteps came down the stairs. She stayed by the stove until he came into the kitchen, then she stuck her pale, pointed nose up and looked out the back window. In a white T-shirt and gray plaid, sharkskin slacks, his body looked thick and muscular, no big belly on him since he'd been training. His jaw glistened with shaving lotion. A wave of tension swept over me.

Al ignored both her and me, although I had to move out of the way for him to get a cup and saucer out of the cupboard. He didn't talk to Dad either.

Finally Dad asked, "What's this about Floyd losing last night?"

I cringed inside as Al stalled, tilted the coffee pot, caught the bubbling stream in his cup and set the pot down on the stove again in two swift movements that took about three seconds.

"Well, answer me!" Dad said.

Al sipped from his cup and squinted at me through the coffee steam, concentration lines around his eyes.

I said in a rush of breath: "Couldn't move for some reason last night, Al. I couldn't think. I froze. I ... "

"Don't give me that shit, Floyd. We've been through all this scared stuff before. I told you how I lost in Sacramento! Win or lose, fight! I've told you a thousand times that it's just stage-fright, that all you needed was a few more fights, just a little seasoning would help, and that you'd be all right."

"I don't know if I was scared, Al. It's more like ... "

"What'll help you, Al?" Tommy interrupted, wrapping a dishtowel around the dripping bottle, leaving the gas on.

"I know what'll help you!" Al said, smacking his cup into the saucer and turning on her.

"Pop! Pop!" Tommy cried, cowering down between the stairwell and the stove.

"Leave her alone, Goddamnit!" Dad said. "Sit down and leave her alone!"

"That broad needs a good ass-kicking and she's gonna get it, too!" Al pulled a chair away from the table and sat down. When he picked up his cup and saucer again, they clattered in his hands.

Tommy ran up the back stairs. No one spoke. The bubbling sound of the coffee began to bother me, but trying to break the chilly silence in the kitchen, I asked, "Do you want another cup of coffee, Daddy?"

"I've already had two, son," Dad said. "Maybe Al wants some."

"Wanting some is what's got me in this mess," Al said.

"Watch your language," Dad said.

"I thought that she was a woman and that Floyd was a man, and I was wrong on both counts. I ended up with the shitty end of the stick." He glanced at me.

"Watch your ... " Dad started to say, but Al said, "I've had more fights with her over this guy than I've had in the ring. That's what I get for knocking up a broad when I've still got a kid brother to look out for."

"I told you to watch ... "

"I'm sorry, Al," I said. I hadn't fought, I knew. That was my fault, regardless of what Dad had said about trouble with Al.

"Sorryyyy?" Al said. "What the hell do I care about you being sorry? The one thing I don't want is an apology. All I wanted was a fighter! And all I got was a hound! You looked positively chickenshit. I'd rather have seen you get knocked out!"

He stopped, his elbows spread on the table around the coffee cup, his white T-shirt showing his husky body. His eyes glazed over as if he wasn't looking out but looking in, thinking of himself trying to get off the canvas in Sacramento. I felt ashamed for not being as brave.

"Al, Al, let me tell you ... " I started to say, but my voice sank down to a whisper when Tommy came down the stairs. Al's face seemed to slide under his big, shiny forehead.

"You said I could go shopping today," she said, stopping behind his chair.

"Do it, if you want. Don't bother me now," Al said, not turning around.

"You promised me," she said with a sour twist of her mouth.

"Don't ... bother ... me," he said, spacing his words, squinting out through the coffee steam, mouth stretched tight over the rim of his coffee cup.

"You said I could have a babysitter today."

"Get one and get away from me."

I held my breath, hoping she'd leave, but she stayed right where she was, her robe wrapped tightly around her small, slender body.

"I need some money," she said. "You haven't given me any since Monday."

"Didn't I give you a hundred dollars Monday?" Al said, his voice rising with exasperation.

"How should I know? I didn't count it!"

Al groaned and set his cup down in the saucer and braced his hands on the table, then asked her in a voice stiff with warning, "Why didn't you count it?"

"Why should I? You give it to me like a kid's allowance."

"And you spend it like a stupid kid! You're about as dependable as Floyd! Now get out of here and quit bothering me! I'm not in the mood for this shit!"

He still hadn't turned around to look at her, but when she took a breath as if she was going to say something else, he glanced over his shoulder at her, and said, "And if you don't have any money for a babysitter, don't go any place!"

"You stingy sonofabitch!" she said, and Al whipped his hand off the table and backhanded her across the cheek from his chair, knocking her sidewards against the stove and into the pan of still boiling water, spilling it onto her chest.

"Yi, Pop, I'm burned! Yi! Yi!" she screamed, jerking her robe away from her chest.

"You goddamned fool!" Dad yelled and leaped out of his chair and swiped at the steaming damp stain that streaked down her bright yellow robe.

She kept screaming. Al jumped up and knocked over his chair as I turned the gas off and picked up the hot pan. I batted it back and forth between my hands to keep from getting burned, then dropped it with a clatter in the sink as Dolores came running into the kitchen in her high heels, swearing and shrieking at Al.

"Stay out of this!" Dad yelled at her as Tommy started shouting at Al: "Bastard! Sonofabitch! Bastard!"

Al raised his hand at her again, but Dad shoved him back against the refrigerator so hard it rocked. "Leave her alone, Goddamnit!" he shouted.

13

"I don't care if you lost. You obviously didn't get hurt. There's not a mark on you," Velva said, standing on the other side of the MacFarland's Candy counter from me in the Payless Market. The tiny blue speck of the tattooed beauty mark on the tip of her high, pink cheekbone gave an hypnotic intensity to the fixed stare of her gorgeous blue eyes.

Payless was crowded on Saturday afternoons. There was a low rumble of noise rising up from all the food stands, the produce markets, the butcher shops and lunch counters. Telegraph Avenue outside was noisy and crowded with cars and shoppers, too.

"What does the whole thing prove anyway?" she said. "That you're tough? You've already proven that you're brave to me. I think it's mean, boxing. Fight, if you have to fight. I've seen you do that over me! But don't go beat somebody up just to get some glory, so a lot of people will know your name! I want you to be like Eddy, Floyd! Not Al! A washed-up has-been at twenty-six! Still trying to make a comeback, when he's never been anywhere to come back from!"

I had to smile and, although there was still a glare in her eye, she had to smile, too. I wished the counter wasn't between us so I could hug and kiss her. Then she tilted her head to one side, and her whole face softened. She looked really beautiful, with her slender, pointed nose, full, shapely lips, narrow, pointed chin, high, pink cheekbones and thick, golden bangs across her forehead.

"It's wanting to be like Al that's got you in trouble since your mother died. I know. I've been around you." She kept her voice down so that the other clerks and customers couldn't hear her. "You don't have to feel bad about losing last night. Al didn't even show up to train you, you said. I don't care what he thinks. I want you to go to college, like you planned. Go see Eddy, ask him what he thinks!"

"Eddy could fight, too," I said. "He beat Al up when they were in high school and Al was already a boxer. I saw him do it when I was a little boy. And Eddy boxed in naval college, too. He's not against boxing."

Velva's eyes widened with surprise, then she smiled and reached over the counter and cupped my cheek in her hand, holding her warm palm against it for a moment. I let her touch me and liked it, but said, "I've still got to

128

fight, Velva. Babe set up a rematch with that guy for the week after next. I went to the gym and asked him to do that today, though I didn't work out."

"Why?"

"I've got to prove myself to Al, for one thing."

"Just for Al, Floyd? When he doesn't fight for himself? It's not worth it. He got himself knocked out because he didn't train hard enough to win."

Those blue eyes drilled into my eyes again. They were filled with that will and sharpness that made her an honor student.

"It's not just for Al. It's for myself, too. I've been thinking about it all day. I'll never know if I was just scared last night, like Al thinks. I really don't know why I didn't fight. Al fought hard even losing. I looked liked a sissy next to him. I didn't have any spark. I just couldn't get going. I can't quit a loser. I just can't."

She reached over the counter again and put both her hands on my cheeks, looked deep into my eyes for a moment and said, "If it's for you, then it's worth it. Go ahead and do it. I understand."

Then, still holding my face, she leaned over the counter and pecked me on the lips. I grabbed her hands and squeezed them before she could pull them away. I didn't care if anybody looked.

"I better get back to work," she said, glancing around her.

I started to turn away when she asked, "Why aren't you at work? I thought you worked the twelve-to-nine shift on Saturdays?"

I shrugged my shoulders, then, not wanting to lie, said, "I do, but there was a big family fight in the kitchen this morning, and I just didn't feel like it."

She turned her head and looked at me out of her left eye for a moment, as if she might say something about it. But when I didn't explain, she asked, "Can you walk me home at nine tonight?"

"I'll be here," I said.

14

Eddy's voice was sharp *and* soft over the phone. All his words were spoken very clearly, yet there was a gentle tone to his voice that softened the edges and made me feel better right away. Eddy was a gentleman, ... a ... gentle ... man, I thought as I stared at the black, shiny phone box in the telephone booth at Walgreens Drugs on 13th and Broadway.

"I'm sorry you lost, and I'm sorry that Al's upset with you over it. But I'm sorrier that you're having such anxiety over it that you didn't go to work! That's what I'm really sorry about. That's self destructive behavior, a form of suicide."

"I need to talk to you, Eddy. About everything," I said.

"All right," he said.

"I mean, I'd like to go see you now."

There was silence on the line. Somebody opened and closed a phone booth next to mine with a clatter and swoosh of air.

"You mean, come here to the pharmacy?"

"Yes, I could catch the A train to San Francisco, then catch a streetcar to the pharmacy from the terminal."

There was silence on the line again. I looked at the dark, curling grain of the old-fashioned hardwood booth.

"Listen, you don't have to do that. I'll come by next week and see you at the house. I haven't seen Dorothy in a while, either."

"I work every day next week."

"After work. I could get there early and visit with Dorothy and talk to you when you get home."

"I go to the gym after work."

"After the gym, then. I'll wait for you."

"But I wanted to talk to you about the gym, Eddy."

"Floyd. I'm too busy to talk to you about something important here at work, that could take time!"

His words didn't allow any room to argue. I squeezed the phone receiver, then asked, "Soon?"

"Yes."

"What day?"

"Monday, if you like."

"Could it be tomorrow?"

"I work Sundays, too, Floyd."

I was silent this time, and he said, "It should hold until Monday, Floyd. There's no use you making such a long trip now, when I'm too busy, anyway!"

"I ... uh ... " I uttered, my stomach tightening, still needing to talk. "I don't know what to do, Eddy. I went down to the gym today and already told Babe, the manager of the team, to get me a rematch with that guy in two weeks! So, I've already said I'll fight!"

"Well, let me help you a little bit now, but just for a moment. What's bothering you the most?"

"Whether or not I should keep fighting! And what about school?"

"By all means, go to school! Go to San Francisco City College. Like I've told you before, Al is a good example of boxing talent, of real fighting ability, and what has it got him besides a little local glory? And knocked out and humiliated in front of a great champion like Joe Louis. You don't want that to happen to you! And didn't you say you planned to go to school in the fall, before Al got arrested and you decided to help him make a comeback?"

"Yes."

"Then, go! When's your entrance exam? August? September? It's already July. I'll get you workbooks on basic math and English so you can study for it. How's that? I'll get them from some bookstore and into the mail to you next week sometime."

I leaned my head against the black box of the phone. The fingertip holes of the dial loomed big as eyes to me.

"Can't I talk to you about it first, Eddy?" I said. When he didn't answer right away, I added: "It's too fast for me. I don't know what to do. That's why I need to talk to you. You tell me this on the phone, but it's too quick!"

There was silence on the line, then he said, "All right! I'll be there on Monday night to talk to you."

"Thanks, Eddy."

"See you Monday," he said.

I hung up the phone, stared at the box, but still felt down, because I still had to show up at the gym on Sunday, when I didn't know if I wanted to.

15

Velva was shutting all the drawers and candy cases, turning out the lights in them, covering all the candy with wax paper sheets. Her golden hair was tied back in a thick pony tail. She bent over out of sight behind the counter to put the bag full of money in the floor safe she'd once pointed out to me and, when she looked up, saw me outside on the sidewalk in my wraparound tweed jacket and gabardine slacks. I'd gone home to change, then had dinner by myself, glad no one was there, and then came back to town. She waved through the window, blew me a kiss with her full lips and held up one finger.

I smiled at her and pointed to the main entrance on the corner of Nineteenth and turned around and walked slowly toward it. I stopped just before reaching the entrance, took a deep breath, blew it out, then stepped up to the door just as the old security guard in his gray uniform let her out.

"Feeling better?" Velva said, reaching out for my hand and kissing me lightly on the lips.

I pulled her to me, pressed my cheek against hers, then leaned back. We started down Nineteenth Street toward San Pablo Avenue and her house a few blocks beyond it.

As we walked, she studied me without speaking, seeming to caress my face with her eyes. Her face was an oval of tenderness for me, soft and smooth, sweet as the love I felt for her.

"I'm really sorry you lost and had problems with Al, Floyd," she said. Although I walked in silence with her down the long, dark, windowless wall of the Payless building toward the lights of San Pablo Avenue, I knew she meant it and held tightly to her hand.

When we passed under a streetlight, I looked at her. "I called Eddy in San Francisco after I talked to you and he said I should go to City College in San Francisco. I'm all mixed up now. I don't know what to do. I've already got the rematch coming up next week with that guy, and now I don't even know if I want to fight! I feel pretty discouraged. Nothing seems to be working out."

She looked off down the narrow sidewalk of the long block and her eyes faded out in the shadow. She didn't say anything, she just held onto my hand until we got close to the darkened brick walls of the backs of the buildings facing San Pablo. Then when her face moved into the glow of a streetlight, she looked at me.

"I think you should do what your brother Eddy says. I don't think you should fight, if you don't really want to. I think you should go to college like you've always planned, like you promised your father when he was sick that time. Being a boxer takes a lot of sacrifice. I think you give up a lot, risk a lot for not very much."

Velva pulled on my hand when we passed the loud electric guitar and stomping beat of the Okie band in the 1902 Club. She didn't say anything more until we hurried across San Pablo, past the Doggie Diner hotdog stand with the big weenie with a daschhound's face and tail on top. I glanced down towards the Knotty Pine and thought of Curly and Al T. and Roy walking out of the fight in Vallejo without saying a word to me. When we reached the quiet sidewalk of the residential neighborhood on the next block, the noise of the avenue and its bright lights fell behind us.

"Eddy says I should think of my future now," I said.

"I agree with him," she said as we turned left and down a quarter block on Grove to Eighteenth, then turned to walk the three more blocks to her house.

"I'll be honest," she said. "I don't get to see you enough when you box, so I'm prejudiced and I'll admit it."

I looked away from her at the lawns and trees along the sidewalk and then, trying not to hurt her feelings, said, "Eddy's told me before not to get tied down and married like Al did before I made a career for myself. So, even if I went to school instead of boxing, I'd still be busy studying and that." Then seeing the hurt on her face, I put my arms around her and said, "But I love you, Velva."

She leaned against me as we walked and said, "I'd wait for you if you went to college, Floyd, no matter how long it took you. Four years isn't very long, if I get to go with you. We could get married after you graduated. I don't want to tie you down. I just want to be with you. I'll wait for you no matter how long it takes, Floyd."

I stopped and, after glancing around to make sure there was no one else on the dark street, slipped my arms around her gabardine coat and pressed her body to mine, kissed her open mouth, touched her tongue with mine, held her against me for a long time before releasing her. Then we walked the two blocks to her home without speaking, the memory of Al's contempt fading away a little, not hurting so much, and the doubt I had about still fighting not so pressing.

16

"It's a little late. Mom might say something," Velva said, standing out on the sidewalk in front of her house.

I winced at the idea of going back home, where there was nothing but the sadness I'd left. She seemed to read my face, glanced at the house again, then said, "But the lights are all on. If she's up, she won't mind. Come on in."

She stepped up the small, darkened stairway of the clapboard duplex, opened the door and peeked into the lamplit front room toward the light in the kitchen. I walked into the front room after her, wondering what kind of greeting I'd get. I stopped on the gray, old-fashioned rug next to the worn couch with the blanket thrown over it as her mother walked into the room from the kitchen in high heels and a silky dress. She was smiling, swaying slightly, her gray hair pulled back in a bun.

"Hello, Floyd," she said. "I thought you were in training and couldn't go out at night?"

"I get a day off because I fought last night," I said, pleased that she was so friendly, but afraid she'd ask me who won and I'd have to explain. I pointed at the small table radio next to the old couch and said, "That's a jumpy Charleston tune, isn't it?"

She tilted her head and listened to the pounding beat, the blare of the trumpet and said, "Yes! We used to dance the Charleston all the time when I was in my teens."

She grinned at me, then suddenly started hopping to the jumpy music, stepping back and forth in her high heels, kicking her feet out, tapping her toes on the floor in front of her, twisting her feet and fluttering her hands in perfect form, perfect rhythm and grace, her whole body vibrating in time to the catchy tune. She stared down at the floor as she danced. Her well-shaped calves swelled up out of her slender ankles. Her body was curving and graceful as she worked around the room on the gray carpet, over the worn spots, snapping back and forth in rhythmic steps, flapping her elbows.

I couldn't believe it! She was usually so solemn and polite! Yet, I could still see stiff lines in her face that etched down each cheek into her double chin and there was an intense stare in her blue eyes concentrating on the faded gray pattern of the thin carpet, as if it was hard work to dance around like that when you hit your forties. She was determined to stick it out, though, and looked proud as she danced, as if to say, sure, she was still beautiful, that even with age she was good to look at. Because I felt her need to be pretty for me, the physical strain she was now under made me feel uncomfortable. I wanted her to stop before she got too tired and was glad when the music ended. She stalked past Velva, out of the room and back through the dining room into the kitchen, her trim hips swaying.

"Wow, Mom!" Velva said, shaking her head at the dance and the sexy walk. She sat down on the couch and explained, "She's had a couple, I guess."

"She sure is good at it," I said, then said, "Oops!" and slapped my hand over my mouth at the comic slip and grinned, then said, " . . . the Charleston, I mean. The best I've seen outside of the movies. No college kids can dance that good and they're the only ones who dance the Charleston nowadays."

"Thanks," Velva said. "And she doesn't drink much, Floyd. Only a couple of drinks get her high. That's why she danced for us."

"I know. I don't care. She's being nice to me," I said softly.

Trying to make her feel better, I leaned her back against the couch and kissed her. I lingered with my lips on hers, cupping her moist mouth with mine, but jerked back away from her and wiped the lipstick off my mouth with my fingers when I heard her mother's footsteps in the dining room and saw her cross into the front room with her coat over her arm and a purse in hand.

"Velva always said how you'd make sure she got walked home from school dances, Floyd. So I wouldn't have to worry about her."

Her staring blue eyes glistened with light and I guessed she was saying she trusted me and was putting me on my honor.

"Have you signed up for San Francisco City College yet?"

"Not yet, Mrs. Harris, but I'm thinking of starting in September again now."

She smiled. She was a beautiful woman with the same classical features as her daughter. She the turned to Velva and said, "I'm going to meet Ron on Fourteenth Street. I'll be back in a couple of hours. Don't go out." She turned and swayed past us into the hall and out the front door.

"She still thinks I'm thirteen," Velva said when her mother's footsteps faded out on the sidewalk. "She probably won't even be back tonight and yet she wants to tell me what to do, as if she's still supporting me, when she's not! I even pay rent. I buy my own clothes and I buy a lot of the food. All the fruit and stuff like that in the house, I buy. She just goes out and leaves me alone and expects me to just sit here the way I used to when I was small."

Velva reached for the cigarette pack on the coffee table, picked it up, then put it back down. "In all fairness, she didn't start going out like this until last year when she didn't have to spend all her money just keeping a house for us."

She picked up the pack again, then threw it back down again, said, "Oh, I don't know!" and turned her head away.

I grabbed her shoulders, turned her back around to face me, then pushed her back against the couch again and stared at her beautiful face in the soft lamp light. I didn't want her to suffer. I wanted to help her, just like she tried to help me. Her eyes were too beautiful, too deep and sweet to have to suffer.

She wrapped her arms around me and pulled me to her, opened her mouth and cupped it against mine. Her lips were soft-soft, she twirled her tongue around my tongue. I wanted to drink the juice out of her mouth. I wanted to help her forget her problems and forget my own, too. I wanted to get as far inside her mouth with my lips as I could and still be kissing her. I pulled her toward me and twisted in a half-curl, slowly letting her down on the couch, still kissing her, until she was next to me and below me and I'd turned completely around. I was lying on my stomach next to her, my legs trailing off the couch, my torso over hers.

The swell of her left breast was under my right chest. I slid my hand up on her other breast and squeezed it slowly. She pressed hard on my back with her hands and the suction in our mouths drew us closer. Her tongue twirled into my mouth as I massaged her breast. It filled my whole hand with its softness. Her mouth! Her mouth! I loved her. I wanted her. I lifted my legs up on the couch so my whole body was against hers. I pressed my crotch against her hip, slid my hand down over her hips and butt and pressed her against me, crotch against crotch. The small hump of her box made me red hot. I pumped against her. She pushed her crotch against me. I pumped again and leaned over on her and, still kissing her, kept pumping on her.

She let me, thrusting her box out to me. I pumped again and again against it, my mouth still on hers, again and again and again, feeling the charge start to rise in me ... Afraid I was going to come, I rolled back off her and waited a moment until the thrill subsided.

Often, in the year we'd gone together, I'd pressed against her until I'd come in my shorts. I would then be glad that I hadn't touched her, that she was still a virgin, that she still had her cherry safely between her legs for the day we got married. But now I was too hot. I needed her too badly and, still kissing her, slid my hand off her butt and around her hips. I caressed the swell of her springy crotch under her skirt and panties.

She had let me once before, one night on the porch, when I'd slid my

hand down inside her panties. I stopped when I touched her curling pubic
hair, didn't try to go down any further, didn't try to stick my finger in it.

But now I did. I stroked it and stroked it until she turned over on her
back and, still kissing me, arched up to meet me. My fingers pressed down
into it through the skirt. I could feel the cleft down there, the slit in the V
down there. I put more of my hand over it, pressed my fingers into the soft
lips of her, pressed until her legs spread, then slid my hand down her leg to
the bottom of her long, shin-length skirt, below her knees and up her smooth
thigh, along the silken fabric of her dark hose, and for the first time I rested
my hand on the transparent, clinging material of her panties.

Feeling no resistance from her, I slipped my finger under the elastic edge
and between the moist lips of her vulva, then slid my finger up and down
until I found the soft hole, then slid my finger in until I hooked the membrane
of her hymen. Stroking it with the tip of my finger as she kept kissing me, I
worked my finger deeper and deeper in her until it was completely in. Then
I started pumping it back and forth in the moist, slippery groove, getting
hotter and hotter until it became so unbearable, I finally pulled my mouth
free and asked, "Do you love me? Do you?"

"Yes, yes," she whispered, her eyes nearly closed, and I pumped my
finger harder and harder in her until she started to pant.

I started pumping against her hip again and asked, "Do you want me to?
Do you?"

"Yes, yes. I love you. I want you to. I love you more than anything,"
she said and grabbed my head and forced my mouth down on hers, stuck her
curling tongue deep into my mouth. When she paused, I pulled back and
slid both my hands up her skirt and started pulling down her panties.

"The light! The light!" she said, and I reached up and snapped it off,
then reached back under her skirt as she lifted up to help me. She unsnapped
her garter belt and pulled her skirt up to her hips, then let me pull her pants
off.

She waited while I pulled back away from her, jerked off my jacket,
threw it over the back of the couch, then unhooked my belt, unzipped my
fly and slid my slacks and shorts quickly down to my ankles.

"Are you sure? Do you know what you're doing?" I asked.

"Yes," she said, softly, and spread her legs and let me see her body for
the first time.

But the sudden sight of her opened legs, the silken hose still on them,
the dark triangle of her crotch in the dim light in front of me shocked me. I
felt a wave of guilt sweep over me as if I was taking advantage of her and I
suddenly thought of Eddy warning me not to get tied down too soon.

"What's wrong?" she asked.

"Are you really sure?"

"Yes. I want you," she said. "You're the best thing in my life."

I knelt down between her legs and started to fit myself to her.

Not wanting to hurt her, I used my foreskin as a sleeve and only imbedded the head of my penis in her, then pressed oh so lightly against the thin skin of her cherry, pressed, pressed until she winced and her body jerked. Then I eased off and leaned down to kiss her. When I felt her body relax, I started pumping again, working the head slowly in.

I'd had some experience. I knew how to do it. I saw how soft her face looked, without fear or pain on it. I leaned down and kissed her again and pushed in a little further, then further, then further until I gave a sudden thrust and slid all the way into her and felt her stiffen under me with a slight, "Oh!"

I stopped, waited for her face to relax again, then hugged her to me and began to pump in her. I pumped all the way in, then pumped and pumped until we were rocking back and forth in rhythmic motion, rocking, rocking, rocking. I felt the thrill build up in me, but couldn't stop. I didn't want to pull it out. I didn't even try. I came in her with a jerking thrill that made my whole body quiver. Then I fell across her with a low groan, my back still tingling.

"I love you, Velva. I really love you," I said.

"I love you, Floyd," she said and stroked my hair. "I guess we did it now, didn't we?"

"I guess we did. Did I hurt you?"

"Just a little," she said. "Good thing there's a blanket on this couch. I'll have to clean it later. Don't leave me now. Stay close to me. Don't go yet."

I stared at her, saw the fine line of her nose, her high cheekbones in the dim light. She really let me go all the way. I'd broken her cherry, but loved her so much, I didn't care.

She studied my face, and, as if she could read my thoughts, said, "You love me, don't you?" And when I nodded, she said, "I really miss you when you train, Floyd. Since Al got out of jail, I've been so lonesome and unhappy thinking you didn't like me anymore that I've cried a lot."

She stopped stroking my hair and said, "Don't fight anymore, Floyd. You were doing it for Al, anyway, and now he's quit."

Her eyes had a moist glow, as if she might be crying.

"I can't stand it when you don't come over. Everything seems so futile, so useless. I go to school, then come home and do my homework, then eat and go to work, then come home, read a little bit, wait for you to call, cry if you don't, then go to bed. Go to school, like Eddy suggested, like you planned. Don't train anymore and we can spend more time together."

"I might not, the way things are working out," I said. "I really don't feel like training or fighting. I don't feel like doing anything. I feel like quitting everything."

She took my face in her hands and stared at me for a long time, then said, "I don't like to see you so discouraged and unhappy."

I stared at her in the soft light, thinking of what I'd just done to her and yet saw she was worried about me!

"We've both got problems, don't we?" I said.

"I don't care," she said. "Just as long as you love me and promise you won't let Al come between us. I know how much you care for him and how he hurts you. I don't want you so discouraged and confused you don't know what to do. Promise me you won't ever let him come between us! Promise, and I won't care what you do! College or boxing!"

I looked into her soft, beautiful face, thinking how much she loved me. Then I thought of my brother Al's contempt for me and I couldn't answer.

"Promise me that ... if you love me," she said and squeezed my face.

"All right," I said. "All right, I promise," but there was a strange feeling in me that made me doubt my own words.

17

With skin as colorless as her white hair, the assistant head librarian sat on the other side of her desk from me. Bony cheeks, long, bony nose, no lipstick, sunken eyes. Pale orbs of eyes that glistened through her glasses like dark stones at the bottom of a stream, not quite clear, not quite green, almost discolored by the current, sort of murky, as if troubled.

"You missed Saturday because you fought in Vallejo Friday night?" Her face was as somber as her voice.

"Yes," I said, hoping she wouldn't ask me who won. She looked like a ghost against the dark, old-fashioned wood-paneling behind her. I'd been in her office once before, after I was hired by the head pageboy and she had to pass on it. There was a closed-in smell of books and ink and paper, like some sterile embalming fluid.

"And two weeks ago you took off for a fight in Santa Clara?"

She leaned back and looked through her glasses at me. They magnified her eyes so much I could see the pink rims of her lids. I felt like an insect on a slide.

"Yes," I said in a small voice.

"Don't you think that's a little odd?"

I squirmed in my chair and fought the urge to tell her that I'd lost and felt bad because my brother was mad at me. "What do you mean?" I asked, stalling for time, struggling for a way out.

"What do I mean?" she asked and leaned back even more. She was very tall, even sitting down. "You weren't hired to box! This isn't a gym or even a high school! We serve the public with books not boxing gloves! You can't expect us to go short-handed while you pursue some sport!" Her mouth twisted with anger.

Feeling like I owed her an explanation, I said, "Sometimes we get back real late and I've been worried ... about ... " My voice sank because of the partial lie, I couldn't tell her the whole truth. It wasn't like I had to get up early. I started at noon on Saturdays. There was absolutely no real excuse. Yet, I couldn't tell her that my brother was mad at me because I didn't fight hard enough and that I cut work over it and then went and screwed my girl!

She blinked behind her glasses at me, then said, "Well ... I can excuse you this once. But I can't accept your being absent from work any more for

140

an extra-occupational activity. Do you understand?"

I stared into the pale eyes in the pale skin, noticing the blue veins that showed in her cheeks. I think she felt sorry for me.

"I understand."

"So you will not miss work anymore?"

"No, I won't."

"Fine, then," she said. "You may go back to work."

"Thank you," I said and got up, relieved that she had some pity on me, but I was still aching over Al.

18

"I wanted to inspire Al and do something good like you did for me, Eddy, when you told me I could be somebody if I studied in school. Al'd quit boxing and was just getting drunk and partying and I didn't know what to do." I gazed down at the thick, new maroon carpet beneath my feet. "I wanted to convince Al, like you convinced me. Now I've let him down."

"You don't have to get discouraged," Eddy said from the couch where he sat with Dorothy. "Al might have caused the whole thing by not supporting you in the first place, by hanging around the Knotty Pine and those racketeers, instead of going to the gym to train you."

He took a sip of coffee and held the cup to his full lips for a moment before setting it back in the saucer. Sitting down, the lapels of his gray plaid, double-breasted suit stuck out from his chest a little because of the thickness of his belly. He'd gained a little weight in the past year. But he did look like me. I'd heard it all my life and could see it now. The same, high-domed forehead and dark, wavy hair. He'd gotten a little puffy from the good life in Paris, where he'd been the past two years. His skin was fleshier and more pinkish and his face was round, now, not lean like it was during the war.

"You wanted to fight in order to inspire Al and keep him out of trouble? Is that why you didn't plan to enter school in September?"

He'd had a big, broken nose like mine once, too, that, though not as fist-battered, hooked just like mine over his upper lip. But the navy doctor had taken off the tip and his whole bridge in a nose operation he'd had just before he left the service. The doctor had left him with a low swelling prominence which now made his face round instead of aquiline. The beauty was gone. It shocked me when he had first come back from Europe.

"Yes. I decided to postpone junior college to February. I was going to try to win the Golden Gloves in the fall and get Al started on his comeback. But then he said he didn't want to fight anymore and that it all depended upon me and I went out and fought poorly last Friday, I mean, didn't fight much at all. Though I didn't get hurt. And now Al's mad at me."

Eddy was quiet for a moment, then said, "That's not fair to blame it all on you. But let's not lose the point." He paused. "I don't really know how I can help you change Al's mind about boxing. He's probably past his prime and knows it. But I don't think you should feel guilty for not fighting well."

"But I don't want him to get arrested anymore," I said.

"Get arrested anymore? I thought he got probation on that contributing to the delinquency-of-a-minor charge?"

"He did, but now he's hustling servicemen for their bonus money and I'm afraid he'll end up in jail again.

"What?" Eddy asked, and Dorothy frowned, her pretty dark eyes slanting.

"It's not really stealing. It's gambling. But it's against the law for sure, like selling bootleg booze and getting customers for girls."

"Well, men do gamble," Eddy said.

"I know, I know. It's not that, really, at all. Al says you can't beat the servicemen unless they want to cheat you. But I saw him getting booked in the county jail and it scared me! And now he's not boxing but hustling, and it doesn't seem worth it for me anymore."

Soft green eyes stared at me for a few moments, then Eddy said, "I admire your idealism, Floyd. It's like mine at your age!"

My cheeks got hot and Eddy said, "You don't have to get embarrassed for being young and idealistic."

Dorothy smiled, but I saw Eddy's eyes narrow with sadness. His eyes were usually so big and feminine with such long lashes, they reminded me of our mother's eyes. "Why didn't you become a doctor like you planned all your life, Eddy?" I suddenly asked. "Did it have something to do with Mom?"

Eddy leaned back against the couch and said, "That's very perceptive of you, Floyd." Then he twisted a little sidewards on the couch to face me. "You've got to have a lot of desire to do all that work, Floyd, and it helps to be young. I mean twenty-one, not a battle-scarred World War Two veteran, burned out from combat action. The war and Mother's death took it out of me. I got tired of being a witness to suffering! I wanted to live a little! Get some living in while there was still time! Be happy before I got killed!" He lowered his voice, uncrossed his legs. "And now that the war's over, I still want to live. I want to enjoy life more, become a rich business man, maybe, with my own pharmacy. I'm not as serious about life as I was when I was younger, growing up in the Depression years. I'm more cynical now, less committed, without your idealism any longer. Now that I've seen so much death, both slow like Mother's and sudden like in combat, I don't have the will to commit myself like you do anymore."

No blush stained my cheeks now. I listened.

"When Mother was alive and I had hope that she'd live, that her heart would hold up long enough to carry her into an old age, at least into deep middle age, I felt that I had to do as much as I possibly could, not just for her but for the whole world, like you now, trying to help Al. I wanted to save the whole world with my hands in order to save her, the most truly Christian person I'd ever known. Not pious, no, not pious, just Christian in the real meaning of the word."

He looked off into a corner of the front room as if thinking of her. His big green eyes looked so sad and pretty, I felt sorry for him and said, "In a way, I'm glad she's been dead so long, already."

"Why?" Dorothy said and Eddy's mouth opened.

"I'm glad my suffering over her death is over," I said.

"That's selfish, Floyd. She's been robbed of years of life."

"I didn't rob her, Eddy. And no matter how much I wish she would have lived, I'm still glad the big hurt inside me's not as bad as it used to be."

"I wish I could say that," Eddy said. "She left her influence on you, though. That's part of your love for Al, your idealism. Keep trying, but don't let yourself get depressed over it, nor so discouraged that it ruins your own life. That's what I worry about. Remember, you've got your own life to live. Don't let him influence you too much. And don't get disillusioned if it doesn't work out, like Mother's death disillusioned me."

"What do you mean, Eddy?" I asked and finally sat down on the couch, facing him.

"I mean, box, if you want to, and try to help Al, but go to college! Fulfill yourself intellectually, too, not just physically. Go to college in the fall as you planned. Choose a lifetime career! And train for it before you choose a mate, unlike Al. Don't follow his example there. Learn from him, love him, try to help him, but don't necessarily be like him!"

Eddy lifted up a long finger, like a teacher. One eyebrow arched up high on his forehead. "Do you realize I've only seen you about three times since I left for active duty four years ago, and you've kept studying like you promised?"

I nodded and he said, "You kept going in the right direction even when I wasn't around, no matter what Al did. Do that now. You have to make a real future for yourself, not just gamble everything on how many fights you win. Boxers' careers are short. Most of them are washed up by the time they're thirty, even if they're successful. Then it's too late to start another career and most end up in menial jobs and, if they're lucky, not punchdrunk and walking on their heels. Sometimes I wonder what's going to happen to Al, too."

As he sat there in his expensive suit, looking so much like the confident, successful professional, I couldn't help but remember Al in his khaki green, Eisenhower jacket getting fingerprinted in the county jail.

"I told Dorothy that it was fine that you box and that you have such a good friendship with Al, that you care so much for him. But don't make the same mistakes he did. Plan for the future after boxing, make sure you get to school and then choose a wife when you're ready."

Dorothy reached out and touched me from the big, stuffed sofa chair and said, "Floyd's doing good. He works at the library and keeps busy, trains every day and stays home every night during the week. And he has a nice, smart girlfriend."

"What kind of a girl is she? I'd like to meet her."

"You'd like her, Eddy," Dorothy said. "Velva's very sweet, intelligent and very mature for her age. When Floyd was in junior high school, she used to be the cutest little blond in the neighborhood, cute and plump. She's liked Floyd since she was eleven years old."

"Oh, you've known her that long?" Eddy asked, looking at me.

"I met her when I was twelve. She was cousin Marcella's best friend," I said.

"That can make for a good, strong relationship. But don't get tied down, yet! You're too young."

"But what about Al and me boxing?" I asked.

"Box, if you want to. But go to school, too. That's the most important thing for you now."

It made sense and I nodded to let him know I agreed. But I still felt that big hunk of doubt deep in my chest because I still had a fight coming up and didn't know how to train for it, and that couldn't wait until September.

19

I almost turned around at the top of the stairs when I saw all the people in the bleachers for the early Saturday morning workouts. Dorothy had winked at me in the kitchen and said, "I think Al's going to the gym, Floyd. Maybe you can catch him there and make things up between you." And I had hurried out of the house, because that meant, if I caught him, I could work out and finish in time to get to work by noon. My watch said it was only ten. But I didn't want to have to talk to Al in front of anybody. I just wanted to tell him I was ready to fight right then, do or die, and prove I wasn't scared, that's all.

Following the iron railing which fenced off the bleachers, stepping lightly on the hardwood floor, my gaze swooping over the gym for my brother in the blur of bodies and bags. I heard the pop-pop-pop of the speedbag as I walked, but didn't see Al. I started getting worried I might have come for nothing.

Then I spotted a reflection in a wall mirror on the other side of the ring, down by the locker room, and recognized the small, muscular body shadowboxing in front of it: Johnny, who'd run up another W on his record in Vallejo the night I lost.

Slipping under the railing and across the training area, trying to avoid anyone's stare, so I wouldn't have to make any clumsy explanations about where I'd been after losing for the first time, I dropped into a boxing crouch behind Johnny and waited for him to spin around and fake a punch.

He spun around, pivoting on his left toe, hands up, head down, crouched and ready to play, but suddenly froze, his heavy lids sliding down to slits over his eyes, and his lips twitching with a wry smile, as if he could barely keep from gloating over me for losing in Vallejo.

"Seen Al?" I asked, straightening up, the smile gone from my face.

"Back there," Johnny said, pointing to the locker room. Then, as if he couldn't restrain himself anymore, the total little fighter that he was, he said, "You stay away 'cause you lost last week?"

"Yeah," I said, toughing it out, but measuring the jaw of the little fighter who was spread-legged in front of me, taunting me, shoulders hunched, every muscle on his five-foot-three body so packed with power, it seemed about to split the skin. He'd broken my nose a dozen times, but whether I

146

lost or not, or didn't come to the gym for a week or more, he couldn't do it anymore and knew it. I stayed right there ready to fight, waiting for him to say something else, but when he didn't and I heard Al's voice, I turned away, stepped through the doorway of the partition which sectioned off the locker room and met Al's eyes.

Al looked away and slammed the locker door shut, then, heavy shoulders hunched, rocked to the far corner of the room along the row of lockers, past dressing fighters, as if trying to get away from me. He finally stopped and sat down on a bench by himself, sweating, his back to the partition. I waited for him to greet me and give me a chance to say how glad I was that he'd come back to the gym, that I could be ready to fight that guy next Friday night. Babe must have already told him about it.

But Al started unwrapping his hand without looking up, looping the white wrap off, following the contours of his hand from the wrist down, across the palm and through the fingers, back around the wrist and back through the fingers again, around the wrist and back through the fingers, back around the wrist and around the palm, curling around the thumb, reversing direction again, spinning the wrap down at his feet like yarn until he reached the loop at the thumb. Then he dropped the wrap off and looked up at me, wrinkling his forehead and popping his fist into his bare hand.

"Al, I ... "

His eyes were flat and coppery as pennies and, without speaking, he lifted up his other hand and began to unwrap it, too.

I caught myself with my hands up, trying to explain. I looked at my palms—they were damp with sweat—then looked around me, surprised so many fighters were stripping for their showers and getting dressed into street clothes when it was only mid-morning and the gym stayed open until three on Saturdays.

I looked back at Al, who stared at his handwrap, ignoring me. So I wiped my hands on my khakis, turned my back on him and went to my locker. There was still plenty of time for me to work out and still get to work on time at the library, which was only a half-dozen or so short blocks from the gym. I didn't want to leave while there was still a chance he'd train me.

I spun the dial of the combination lock, determined to get dressed and work out by myself, to at least prove to Al and all of them that I hadn't quit and that they hadn't heard the last of me. I guessed as I opened my locker that some of the amateurs had worked out light because they'd fought last night, and that, without sparring partners, most of the pros would work out light, too. I was probably too late to box, even if I did get dressed in my gym clothes. I reached into my locker, anyway, and pulled out my trunks, T-shirt, boxing shoes and socks, and started unbuttoning my sport shirt, determined to punch the bag by myself, if I had to. I couldn't pass up this chance to be in the gym with Al again.

The room crowded up quickly. Steam dampened the air. The water pounding on the metal shower wall forced the dressing, drying, chattering fighters to raise their voices. I kept on undressing and appreciated it when Big Press came in and, not seeming to notice the steamy heat of the room, nodded at me. He leaned against the side of a locker, buckling its side with his weight, and started cleaning his fingernails with a penknife. His large loafer jacket hung on his huge body like an overcoat. His slacks were well creased, shoes brightly polished, thick brown hair well-groomed, and not a drop of perspiration was on his brow.

"Did you see your brother Al sparring with Johnny?" he asked. "They put on a hell of a show, scrapped every minute of it."

"No," I answered and glanced over at Johnny, who was slipping his trunks off in front of his locker, then over at Al, who was stripping off his gray sweat pants, soaked with wet spots, dark as wet ash.

"Just a little grudge fight," Johnny said with a wry smile and glanced at me as if implying he was as tough as Al.

Al stepped to his locker, shoved his shoes and sweat clothes in and walked to the showers, his wedge-shaped back stippled with sweat. He glanced over at me as he stepped into the shower, as if finally noticing that I was getting ready to work out. That made me feel better. Big Press just kept cleaning his nails. The spray pounding on the shower walls kept up a steady noise.

Johnny stepped into the shower, too, stopping with one foot in and one foot out, glancing at me as I slid into my trunks. By the time I got my socks and boxing shoes on and was tightening the laces, Al was stepping out onto the damp rubber mat, grabbing his towel to dry himself. He wiped the water off the patch of hair on his chest, then glanced at me again as I tied my shoes. I felt a twinge of hope and a quiver of apprehension at the same time.

Johnny stepped out of the shower and started drying himself, glancing over at me as I wrapped my hands. I took my time, stalling so Al would say something to me. When I finally finished wrapping both hands, I started shadowboxing. I kept shadowboxing in the locker room instead of going into the gym. Al was finally dressed and standing in front of the mirror. He was combing the thin, damp strands of his hair down with quick swipes, pressing them down scalp-flat against his large, well-shaped head. His hair used to stand up and wave back only a couple of years earlier, I remembered, hoping for some kind of sign, a wink, a smile that he knew I was there and dressed to work out.

But Al picked up his damp towel from the bench and beckoned to Big Press with it, and Big Press leaned back off the locker with a pop as the metal snapped back into place. They started to walk out, leaving me standing by myself in the center of the room.

"Al!" I said in a high voice and waited for my brother to stop and turn slowly around, towel hanging from his fingers.

"What do I do? How do I work out today if I want to beat that guy in a rematch next week?"

Al tilted his head back and looked at me for a moment, as if to see if I really meant it. Finally he said, "You've gotta learn how to start the fight! How to go out there and beat that other guy! Knock him out! You gotta quit being a picture book boxer and learn how to hurt a guy and put him away, without fear! You gotta learn how to throw looping punches that really hurt! You gotta learn how to fight the big bag! Not box it! You gotta learn how to get tough! Get mean! How to charge out there and start the fight and kill 'im or get killed!"

"Okay," I said, waiting for him to tell me what to do, knowing that he fought that way himself.

"Get your bag gloves and come on out to the big bag and I'll show you," he said, smiling.

20

"That Flip kid and his manager think you're scared now," Al said as he slipped my robe off in the corner of the ring and pointed his nose at the opponent in the opposite corner. There were rows of faces behind him, clouds of stinking cigar smoke hanging in the air and a low mumble of voices back to the corners of the small auditorium. I wasn't going to fight the guy who beat me. He didn't show up and I didn't know why. I didn't even ask, because I didn't care. I was ready to fight anybody. I just wanted to fight.

"They were talking about you when I went over and filled the bottles. Why'd you go introduce yourself to the guy? They think you're a hound now. 'Your kid came over here,' he said, then smiled like you were chickenshit. Don't talk to a guy you're going to fight! How in hell can you want to hurt him after making friends? Make friends later, after you win. Now go on out there and slug him! Make a fight out of it!"

His voice twanged. I was sure everybody around the corner could hear him. I could sense Al was trying to get me mad at the guy so I'd want to beat him up. I looked across the ring at the tall, slender, brown-skinned Filipino kid. I held my hands up in front of my chest, tensed myself so I'd be ready, though I already knew I was going to run across the ring, throw an overhand right and try to take him out right away, just like Al said.

Face to face with him, listening to the referee give us instructions, I could see how his hair stood straight up in front in a crewcut, how wide his nose was and how black his eyes were. But most of all, I could see how his chin hung down and that I could hit it with an overhand right. The big problem was not getting hit leaping in. I had to watch myself or he'd get me with his longer arms. But I knew I could hit him with that right, because I'd practiced it on the big bag all week.

"Fight!" Al said when he slid out through the ring ropes.

I squinted my eyes at the guy to shut out the sight of everything but the brown face on the other side of the ring. When the bell rang, I ran across the ring and trapped him in his corner and looped an overhand right at him. But he threw up his arms, fell back against the ropes and I missed.

The next thing I knew, the guy cut loose with both hands, as if a bee had stung him: Bam-bam-bam-bam-bam! catching me glancing blows in the face and head, driving me back. I fell inside his arms, up against his body, hugging my arms to me, taking all the shots on the arms and head, pushing against the guy, but being driven back just the same.

My nose stung from one of the punches, as if I'd dived deep under water and couldn't breathe. One eye felt like it had been popped and puffed up and was running water. I kept trying to plant my feet and get set and hold my ground so I could punch back. But he was charged with adrenaline, just as if I had slapped and insulted him, and kept driving me back. He was the one who got mad, not me. I felt like I was suffocating. My arms were tired and weak. The crowd roared in my ears, yet I could hear the guy grunting with his punches. I couldn't hear Al, though I knew he must be shouting and I knew I was losing. I braced myself and shoved the guy, pushed against him, but couldn't stop him. I was winded and exhausted and didn't see how I could last.

Then, I sensed a slight lessening in the rain of blows, like a dropoff from a downpour to a dribble, and I managed to skip back clear of the punches for a moment. The guy was standing in front of me with his arms still for a second. "Jab!" Al shouted and I stuck out a weak arm and caught the guy in the face.

But it was so feeble, my arm was so tired, that the guy took the punch and charged again, throwing a flurry of punches, ringing my head like a gong, making my whole head hum. Throwing myself inside again, arms up, my head against the guy's chest, I stayed there until the hum went away. I knew I was losing, and when the bell rang, I turned away and wobbled back to my corner, my face feeling like a hot rubber water bottle.

Shoving me down on the stool, face waving in front of me, Al snatched my mouthpiece out, poured water in my mouth, held up the bucket so I could spit, then poured water over my head. Something stung in my nostrils and I jerked my head back from the strong smell and suddenly everything was clear. I could see the tiny scar on Al's eyelid, hear his voice come out strong and clear, no con in it: "Floyd! If you lose this fight, I'll never let you fight again!"

His eyes blinked sparks. "This guy can't touch a glove to you! Go get him! Move in with a jab! But keep the pressure on! He's punched out and tired! I don't care how you punch after you jab, but go after him and keep punching, wear him out, make him quit! You hear me?"

"Yes!" I said and stood up with the buzzer, popped my gloves together and, though my legs felt tired, I didn't feel weak, at all. I took a deep breath, felt air bubble in my chest, held the breath until it hurt, then blew it out.

Al was staring up at me from under the big dome of his forehead. Babe's glasses were circles of frosted light. He hadn't said a word in the corner, as if he knew it was between Al and me. I looked back across the ring at the guy and got set to charge out again. At the bell, I ran across the ring all over again and caught him by surprise this time, as if he never expected me to come and do it again. I caught him with a jab that straightened his head up, then hit him with an overhand right and a hard left hook. I felt the smash of my fist against his head, but then I stopped and waited to see what to do, and bang, bang, bang! he hit me back.

My head went numb. He got me good. He seemed to float in front of me, but I had enough sense to fall inside again when he cut loose with another barrage of punches. I got driven back again and wondered if Al was lying to me about him being punched out. I felt punched out. My punches seemed soft as marshmallows. But I hung inside the rain of blows and felt a space to breathe between the punches. Then a longer space. Then I realized the guy was just pressing on me with his body now, that he was just pushing on me with only an occasional punch. I heard Al shout, "Body! Underneath to the body!" I cut loose with two hooks to the stomach and heard him go "Whoof!" and fall back.

"Get 'im!" Al yelled and I jumped after him, punching with both hands, driving him back against the ropes, making him throw his arms around me and hold.

"Break! Break!" the referee shouted.

My arms were pinned. I looked at the referee and said, "Make him let go! He's the one holding!" Although it seemed to take all my strength just to say it and I felt exhausted, I kept struggling to break free, to get the room to punch.

The referee pried the guy's arms loose, jumped between us and pushed us apart. I saw that the guy's mouth was hanging open, that his arms were down and I jumped in with a jab, catching him good. I kept jabbing, knocking him back. I crossed with a quick right, felt it just graze his jaw, but still knock him back. Then I left-hooked and connected and jabbed again, three jabs in a row, connecting with all three of them, "Pop-pop-pop!" before the bell rang.

Not nearly as tired this time, I let Al push me down on the stool. Out with the mouthpiece. In with the water. Spit in the bucket. Cool water pouring over my head.

"That's the way to fight. Keep pressing him. I told you he was punched out. But he's gonna come back and try to take the last round. Whoever wins the last round wins the fight. He won the first big. You won the second, but he's got a plus on the strength of that big first round. So you gotta win the last round big to win. Go do it! Go win it!"

"My legs ache!" I said. It was because I'd gone to work instead of taking a day off to rest as I had with my first fight. He didn't say anything, but he let me sit on the stool with my arms hanging between my legs. The other kid sat facing me in the opposite corner, head down, his low forehead and heavy brows furrowed under his stiff hair, like he was worried. At the bell, I jumped up and ran across the ring after him again. He moved away at first, then stopped and met me, and we started slugging it out in the middle of the ring. Then the guy grabbed, then the referee broke us up, and I went after him again, determined to win it big.

I kept him backing up, but he kept fighting, too. Once in a while, we'd trade, but I felt the strength I had and kept after him with my popping jab, making it connect, making it hurt, jumping back when he tried to attack me, countering with a left and a right, catching him: Jab-jab, cross. Jab, cross, hook, jab again. Hook, cross. Jab. But he was tough and I couldn't knock him out. Yet, I knew what I was doing in the ring for the first time in my three fights. Moisture stood out all over my body. Still, I wasn't tired. I was only sweating, only warm, a fighter really for the first time. I was sure I could knock him out, if I could catch him. I felt bad when the bell rang, wishing I had another round. When the referee grabbed both our hands and turned in a circle with us, I knew I'd only gotten a draw. I still felt good, though, because I'd fought so hard.

21

"Whipped him a boy tonight, even if he only got a draw," Al T. said, standing in the hallway outside the dressing room, with his dark glasses, his rust-colored loafer jacket, slacks, and suede shoes. But Al said, "He fought. I'll say that for him, but he almost got stopped in that first round after missing that first right hand Sunday."

I blushed, not feeling like I had fought well anymore. Then, without even thinking about it, my mouth twisting with my hurt, I said, "Eddy said I should be thinking of something besides boxing. Maybe I better."

Al's chin went up. "Whatta ya mean? That you don't want to fight anymore?"

"Not that!" I said, not wanting him to think I was a quitter. "He just said that I could box and go to college, too, maybe get on the boxing team. That way I could do both, not put all my eggs in one basket."

Al's flat brown eyes met mine for a moment, then he said, "You don't really want to go to college. You're not a scholar like Eddy. You just read all those books so people will think that you're smart, that you're cool."

My whole head felt hot as an oven, and I was thankful that Al T.'s dark glasses hid his eyes. When I didn't answer, Al raised his eyebrows up on his forehead and said, "We'll talk about how to fight better tomorrow." Then he turned around, motioned to Al T. and started walking down the hall.

"Hey! Where you going?" I asked. "Take me with you! I wanna be with you tonight!"

Both of them stopped and Al turned slowly around.

"I thought you wanted to be like Eddy?" he said.

"Why should I have to choose between my brothers?" I asked.

Al T. said, "The kid fought good tonight, Al."

Al looked at him, nodded, then said to me, "You can't go with us, because you're in training and we're going down to Georgia Street to get some whores. Vallejo's a wide open whore town. You go back to Oakland with Babe and the fighters. I'll see you tomorrow."

"But I wanna go with you and talk about my fight," I said. Al held his hand up, glanced at Al T., then said, "We're gonna go see some whores. We can talk tomorrow, if you still want to be a fighter and not some sissy like Eddy.

154

22

"C'mere," Babe said as soon as I stepped out on the hardwood floor. "I wanna show you how to keep a guy off when he charges you. So you won't get in trouble like you did the first round of your last fight."

He stood in front of me, held his muscular arms almost straight out in front of him like an old-fashioned fighter of the nineteenth century, and said, "Stand straighter and hold out your arms like this, so you can hold the guy off and punch from there."

He stuck out two jabs, then held the left out and swung his shoulders and crossed with a right, then swung his shoulders back and hooked from there. He made it look fluid and simple, but I didn't like the stiff-armed way he did it, so I said, "Al said not to stand up straight like that. He said by holding my arms out from my body and standing straight up, I'm too easy a target for hooks and too slow, too."

I'd only seen Al once since I had fought over a week before. All Al had done was nod at me, as if he was jealous over my talking to Eddy about school. I still stung with resentment over him saying I only read books to act smart. Yet, I didn't really want to train unless he trained me.

Babe glared through his glasses at me, then dropped his arms and said, "You'd fight a lot better if Al didn't come around."

"Whatta ya mean?" I said, my face hot, all the feeling that was dammed up in me close to the skin, ready to explode.

"He distracts you. He gets you thinking about him instead of the guy you're fighting. He interferes with you. You'd be better off if you just fought for the team without him around. You could be a kayo artist. But he's always trying to get you to do what he wants you to do."

"He's my brother. He taught me how to fight. I should do what he says," I said, with a sense that I was kidding myself, since he hadn't been around since I'd fought.

"You'd still be a better fighter if he didn't come around."

"Why? He got me to fight that guy hard last week, and you said I fought good yourself," I said, noticing the white scar imbedded in Babe's eyebrow.

"If he wasn't around, you'd pay more attention to business. You'd be more of a fighter, like Johnny. You've got a lot of talent. You can box, place a punch and hit hard. And you showed you had guts last week, too. But you're always worried about what Al thinks or Al wants or what Al's doing, instead of just fighting."

I turned away without answering him, unable to say that the only reason I came back to the gym was to get Al to fight again. I saw Johnny Ortega shadowboxing in the ring, looping right hands and left hooks into the air at his imaginary opponent. His powerful body rippled with muscle. He snorted through his nose with each punch and fired away with both hands, punching, driving his man back, sounding like a train chugging up a hill, gathering steam, eyes narrowed, all business, all fighter. He wasn't like me, who needed his brother around.

"Where is Al, anyway? Why isn't he here to train you, if he doesn't like the way I do it? He hasn't been here since before you fought!" Babe said.

When I didn't answer, unable to tell him that I didn't even think Al wanted to train me, Babe added, "That's what I mean. You can't depend on him. You can't really get going and make yourself a champ, because you don't really have a trainer!"

When I still didn't answer, he said, "I bet he's in that nightclub with his pimp manager!"

I spun around and spotted his jaw, measured it, almost punched, but I knew he was right, that Al probably was there. I turned away and walked back across the gym to the locker room, determined to go to the Knotty Pine and tell Al what Babe said to get him to come back and train me.

23

"Naaaw," Al said, shaking his head in the low blue light of the bar. My heart sank.

"But before he said you'd be here, he said I'd be a better fighter if you didn't come around. And that's after he tried to get me to box like John L. Sullivan, like some musclebound bodybuilder. Come on down and show him, Al. He said I could be a fighter like Johnny, if you weren't around. Come with me and I'll challenge Johnny to a match just to show him, prove who's better, him and Johnny or you and me."

Al squinted his scarred eye at me, as if he didn't think I could beat Johnny, and I felt a quirk of fear. But I stuck it out.

"Come down and show me how to knock out Johnny. I'll give it a try, if you'll back me."

Curly laughed and his teeth looked blue. He slapped me on the back. "Damn! This kid is great!"

Al grinned and said, "You'd try to knock him out, if I went down there with you now?"

"Yes," I said, and felt fear tingle in me, as if I was putting my life on the line.

"That Gloves champ?"

"Yes."

"Maybe you ought to take him up on it, Al?" Curly said. "It'd be worth it just to see if he could do it. I'd bet a hundred bucks on him with that kind of guts. It'd be a great fight."

But Al shook his head again and said, "Naaw, too much trouble. Babe might have said it, all right, but I've got too many other things on my mind. I've got to earn some money. I'm waiting for Al T. Speedy's working the bus station right now. I've got to stick around. Anything could happen."

He spun around on his stool, faced me and said, "Go do it yourself! I helped you get started. Now go do it on your own!"

"Helped me?" I said. "After all I've tried to d ... "

"Or go read books, like Eddy," he said.

"Come on, Al!" I said.

"Yeah, Eddy!" he said. "He wants you to go to college. And you work in that library. Go do that! Since you like it so much!" His mouth was twisted to one side with his sarcasm.

24

Dolores was whispering to herself through grinding teeth, pacing back and forth from the kitchen to her bedroom. Her arms were wrapped around herself as tightly as a straightjacket, eyes bright and brittle as a nervous bird's, her fleshy nose pinked and running, mouth mumbling, mumbling that Annabelle wasn't home from school yet. It was one of the few times she was around to notice, I thought. But I didn't say anything. I just sat down at the table next to Dad, who sat at the kitchen table in his white shirt and tie. As soon as I got home from the Knotty Pine. I ran upstairs to his two-room apartment to tell him about Al quitting and to ask him what to do.

Dad gave me a quick stretch of his mouth for a smile, then looked straight ahead again. I didn't say anything about Al. It would only start Dolores complaining about all his kids, and get her started on me, too. I didn't want to make him feel worse than he already did. Through the line of windows that stretched across the room, I could see the backyard was now in deep shadow. It was after six and Annabelle should have been home already. But I wasn't about to say anything and get Dolores started on her again. That she showed any concern surprised me. She usually ignored us totally. But for some reason she and Dad were home and she'd noticed that Annabelle wasn't home yet. That gave her reason to complain. That's all I could figure out, because I knew she didn't really care what we did, as long as we stayed out of her hair.

Dolores kept mumbling and stalking back and forth between the two rooms. Dad said nothing, acting as if nothing was wrong.

My heart thumped in my chest when I heard Annabelle's footsteps come up the back stairs from Dorothy's kitchen. When the door opened and she smiled and said, "Hi, Dad! How come you're home?" I felt a little better.

She was almost fifteen now and looked cute in her green sweater, long skirt and bobby sox. Her light brown hair was cut into curls around her head, her round cheeks pinked with color.

"Hi, Floyd!" she said and crossed over to the table.

"Hi, Annabelle!" I said just as Dolores rushed in, bumped into her with her shoulder, grabbed a glass, filled it with water, then rushed back out of the room.

"I'm only a little late. What's wrong with her?" Annabelle said, dimples of exasperation in her chin.

"Sit down, Annabelle," I said and Annabelle pulled out a chair to sit down, while Dolores started grumbling in her bedroom again.

"Go tell her you're sorry for getting home late from school. Apologize, like a good girl."

Annabelle took a deep breath and let it out with a big sigh, her breasts bobbing up and down in the cashmere sweater. She was built slender, like me, and had the same long nose and wide jaws. She stood up, glanced at me for support, then pursed her mouth again, clenched her fists and went out of the kitchen and into the bedroom.

I could only hear Dolores's voice at first, a long lament on being misunderstood, punctuated at regular intervals by sniffles and sobs. I noticed Dad's bald head nodding in sympathy with her. But Annabelle defended herself, saying, "I was just a little late. You knew where I was. I haven't done anything wrong. I didn't know you were home, anyway!" The sniffles stopped and the unintelligible hissing began.

I noticed that Dad just stared at the wall and wouldn't look at me.

Annabelle shouted, "I'm not a whore! You are!"

Dolores's hissing exploded with a shriek and a slap that cracked through the apartment.

Annabelle moaned, "Ooooo, don't! I didn't do anything!"

Both Dad and I turned in our chairs. I waited for him to say something. But my big father just looked down at the table and wouldn't meet my gaze. He didn't speak at all until Annabelle cried, "Don't hit me! I haven't done anything! Daddy! Daddy!"

"You don't have to hit her!" he finally said.

"She is hitting me, Dad! She is!" Annabelle cried. Then there was a scuffle and another slap and I grabbed the edge of the table with both my hands, but Dad sat still in his chair.

"Stop! Stop!" Annabelle shouted.

A slap cracked twice like a ricochet. There was a sound of scuffling, of shoes sliding on the floor, a thump of bodies against a wall, the scrape of a chair, the clatter of something and mumbling, garbled threats rising to a hiss, dropping to a gutteral, animal cry, punctuated by Spanish curses and Annabelle's panting sobs. Long sobs without much hope, quick pants in which she tried to get her breath, then another hiss, a long sob, an unspoken cry for help, then the shout: "Don't dig your nails into me! Don't! Let go of my hair! Dad! Daaaad!"

Dad brought his fist down on the table like a hammer, but didn't move from his chair, didn't speak. The pants and the sobbing got louder as

Annabelle struggled from the bedroom toward the kitchen, making her way step by sliding step. Then there was another cry so close that I turned and saw my sister's fingers on the doorjamb, saw them slide off, then grab again, then blur with my tears. The fingers swam into the woodwork, the kitchen tilted, stove and sink and table and chair and my father all shifted in their places, ran into each other.

I stood up, hot tears pouring out of my eyes. With my eyes I begged the swimming figure to do something. But when he just sat there, I stepped across the room and grabbed for the fingers, gripped them tightly and pulled my sister free of Dolores grip and into the kitchen. I could see Dolores staring at me, astounded, her eyes wide. Then all I could see was my little sister, with her tear-smudged, pink-puffed face. I put my arm around her and helped her across the kitchen and out the door.

She cried, "Come on, Floyd!"

Dolores mimicked her in perfect English as we stepped out into the hall: "Come on, Floyd!"

I led Annabelle through the outside door of the house at the bottom of the stairs, without going through Dorothy's kitchen, and into the back yard, where I let her lean on my shoulder and cry. I cried, too, because that's all I could do.

But as we stood in the darkness of the yard, I watched Dolores arguing with my father. I could see her making gestures, holding her hands up in front of her like cat's claws as she shouted in English that she was leaving, that he could have his kids, that he could stay with them.

Then she started rushing around the two-room apartment, packing, coming out of the bedroom doorway with a suitcase, leaving it on the kitchen table, then filling it with her toiletry articles, her clothing, shoes. She kept arguing, now shouting at Dad in unintelligible Spanish, while he sat staring at the wall, speaking an occasional word, not telling her to go, but not asking her to stay either.

She finally appeared in the bedroom doorway with her coat on, shouted at Dad and left the kitchen, stomped back through the doorway and out of sight in the bedroom. Dad hid his face in his hands. All I could see of him was his bald head. I stared at him for a few moments, thinking that he sat like that after Mom died. He had sat like that for nights on end in the big front window with the lights off, suffering in the darkness. It tortured me then. It tortured me now. Suddenly, I knew what I had to do. There was nothing I or my father could do about Albert quitting training now. It was too late for that forever. I had to try and help my father. That's what I had to do. I had to be as true as the books I read on Jesus. I had to turn the other cheek.

"Wait here, Annabelle," I said and pushed her gently away from me. I pulled the streaks of hair away from my wet cheeks and wiped at the tears on her face with my fingers. "Wait," I said once more.

She nodded her full-cheeked face.

I left her in the dark yard and walked down the slope, around the back of the house and up the porch steps to the outside door and then up the stairs to the second floor.

Dad looked up when I walked into the kitchen, then dropped his face into his huge hands again. I walked past him and up to Dolores, who was coming out of the bedroom, dressed in one of her expensive suits.

Her face tightened with anger when she saw me. She was steeled to spit at me. I stopped and swallowed, tried to speak, opened my mouth, hesitated, and just as her lips curled back in a snarl, I said, "Don't go, Dolores. Dad needs you!"

The snarl vanished from her lips and her face seemed to melt with softness. She threw her arms around me and hugged me. I hugged her back, squeezed her hard, until I heard a chair scrape across the floor like a cough in the kitchen behind me. I turned to see my father standing in the room behind me with a pained smile lighting up his broad face.

PART FIVE

The Iron Crucifixion

1

The phone rang just as I was about to leave the house to go catch the bus downtown to the library for work. I felt a tingle of apprehension when I picked it up, since it rarely rang in the morning. Then when I heard Velva's voice say, "Hello, Floyd!" I knew something was wrong. She never called me in the morning.

"I've got to see you, Floyd," she said and I felt fear.

"What's wrong?"

"I can't talk on the phone. You've got to come by."

"But I've got to go to work now!" I said, scribbling her name on the memo pad next to the phone.

"Come by first!"

"But don't you have to go to school? I can just make it to work on time, if I leave now!"

"This is too important. I'll go late. You can go late, too. You've got to come by."

I shook my head, anxious to put the phone down and leave to catch the eight-twenty-five bus. I looked out through the lace curtain on the door window, then wrote "work" under "Velva" on the memo pad.

"Listen, Velva," I said. "I've been warned not to miss any more days. I got bawled out for missing work after my second fight, so I didn't even take any days off for my third fight a couple of months ago. I've got to be careful or I could get fired. Can't you tell me on the phone?"

"No, I can't. Mom's coming out of the bathroom now. I've got to hang up."

"Well, can't you ... "

"You missed work to box for Al, Floyd! I won't get another chance to talk to you today! You'll be at work when I get out of school and I'll be at work when you get off!"

"Well, can't it wait?"

"No! You've got to come by! I've got to see you!"

The phone was slippery in my sweating hand.

"Velva, I ... "

"Come by before work. I'll wait for you. I've got to talk to you today!"

"Velva ... "

"Mom's coming out," she said and I heard the phone click, then silence. I put the receiver back on the base and stared for a long time at her name and the word "work" scribbled beneath it. That feeling of fear was spreading through my body.

2

The door opened and swung back before I could knock on it. Velva stood next to it in the hall, frowning. I stepped into the front room and turned around to face her. Her eyes were dark blue and serious. The shades were still down. There was a soft orange glow in the room.

"Is your mother here?" I asked in a low voice. As soon as she shook her head, I asked, "What's wrong? Why did you insist I come over? I'm already late! I could get fired!"

But Velva just stood there in her long calf-length brown skirt and beige cashmere sweater, bobby socks and white buck shoes. She just stared at me.

"Tell me!" I said, barely able to keep from shouting.

"I'm pregnant, Floyd," she said. Then she reached down to the coffee table, knocked a cigarette out of a Lucky's pack, drew it out with her slender fingers, picked up the table lighter and snapped it into flame, squinting her eyes at me as shock hit me like a hot wave.

I wanted to say something, but couldn't. I just watched her pucker her lips, suck in the smoke and flutter her lashes to keep the smoke from the cigarette out of her eyes.

"So that's why you couldn't talk on the phone," I finally said.

"I wanted to see you, too. I had to see you," she said.

"Are you sure? You could be wrong!" I said.

"I've missed two periods already," she said and her words seemed to smoke as she spoke. "And I've gained weight. Mom even mentioned it last night and scared me. She said my waist looked bigger. And my skirts do feel tighter. It's been three weeks since I missed my last period and I'm never late. Floyd, I'm scared!"

She took another drag, squinting at me as she sucked the smoke in. I could hear her breath wheeze in through her open lips when she pulled the cigarette away. Her fingers were trembling. I remembered I promised her mother I'd try to get her to stop smoking.

"Sit down. Let's think about it," I said. I knew I didn't have time, that I should leave now and get to work, which was about six blocks away, and talk about it later. But she was so shook up, I couldn't just go away.

Velva took another drag and I said, "Sit down! You make me nervous!"

"How do you think I feel?" she said. But she sat down next to me.

Feeling sorry for her, I leaned over and kissed her, tasting the smoke on her breath. She let me kiss her, but didn't even pucker her lips. Her lipstick was a soft pastel pink that suited her fair coloring. She looked beautiful and I was almost proud that she was carrying my baby, because it meant she belonged to me. I felt a great tenderness for her.

"I care how you feel, Velva," I said. "Whatever happens to you, happens to me. We'll face it together. I want you to know that."

Her face softened. The frown went away. She touched my hand. "That's why I had to see you. I had to have your help. I had to see you say that. At first, I waited for my period to start. Then you had so much on your mind over your brother Al, I didn't want to worry you over maybe nothing. But when Mom mentioned it and looked at me so strangely, she made me feel guilty, and I knew I had to do something."

I turned away from Velva with a sense of despair, like that feeling I'd had after Al told me to go read books and that I'd never go back to the gym.

"What can we do?" I asked.

"Well, couldn't ... " She frowned again. "I don't know. I can't have the baby. I'd have to quit school and work and you couldn't go to junior college. Oh, I don't know!" she cried and covered her face with one hand and rocked back and forth.

I put my arms around her and hugged her to me, rocked her in my arms and patted her back as if she were a baby. I suddenly remembered a dream I'd had of her pregnant in my front room with my whole family and my sense of both pride and despair.

"No matter what happens, I'll stick by you! My family loves you, although Eddy doesn't really know you." I stared over her shoulder at nothing. "He was really hurt when Dorothy got married instead of going on to Cal with him. He might feel bad about it. And Al might not like it, either. He'll probably think we'll end up like him and Tommy, having kid after kid. But Dad knows you and likes you and he'll accept you, if we have to tell him. And Dorothy and Annabelle really like you.

"I'd rather we did something so we didn't have to tell them," she said, freeing her arm and taking another drag. "Can't you think of anything?"

"I'll try to get some pills or something. If I could only tell Eddy. He's got that pharmacy. He could give me something."

"Could he?" she asked, her eyes widening.

"But I don't want him to think bad of you," I said. "I don't want to ask him. He might not respect you. He won't say anything, but he just won't! He's real puritanical about sex. He didn't make it with a whore until he was nineteen when Al took him to one in Boomtown."

She flinched as if I'd hurt her and I quickly said, "I want them all to think well of you, Velva."

"Al?" she asked, lifting one eyebrow.

"I don't think so," I said. "He doesn't even think we've screwed. I wouldn't know how to approach him. He believes I've never screwed anybody. He think's I'm a virgin. I'd be ashamed. We should try and do it ourselves first. And if it doesn't work, if it gets desperate, I'll ask him. I don't want him to know, if we can help it."

"Maybe it's too late already," she said and fear leaped in me. "I hope not. I'll ask around," I said.

She reached out and grabbed my hand and said, "Stick by me, Floyd."

"Don't worry, Velva. We're in it together," I said and squeezed her hand just as a car pulled up outside.

"Uh-oh! That sounds like Unkie's car," she said and jerked her hand free and stepped quickly to the window. She bent back the shade and said, "It is! It is! And Mom's with him!" She spun around and said, "What'll we do? She probably thinks we're doing it."

"But we're not!" I said and jumped up. "Whatever you do, don't tell them what we're talking about! Just admit you're cutting school! That's all. It's no big thing. You cut school. Take the blame for that, but don't tell her."

I stayed by the couch, trying to control my trembling as her mother opened the front door and stepped into the front room in those low-heeled pumps that older women wear. Her blue eyes, shimmering with anger behind the rimless glasses, looked right through me. She looked all business: gray hair pulled back in a bun, a small round hat on her head and a short blue coat covering the bosom of a plain blue dress. She looked like a serious grandmother, older and grayer, no sexiness at all, like when she'd been drinking.

"Get your coat and come out to the car, Velva. We're going to school. And you, Floyd, you come, too," she said, acting like she'd caught us screwing.

I buttoned my coat, knowing that if I went with them, I might get fired. But I couldn't tell her I had to go to work or she'd ask why I came by first then.

"Get your coat," she said again, standing with her purse under her arm. Velva suddenly hid her face with her hands and started sobbing.

Sure she was going to give us away, I said, "Get your coat, Velva, and don't worry." She turned to the closet, still sobbing, and got out her long maroon coat, then followed her mother out the door and down the porch stairs to her uncle's green 1942 Pontiac sedan. I opened the back door for her and then got in myself, feeling like I was sitting on broken glass, afraid she'd give us away and just as scared I'd lose my job.

"Hello, Mr. Graves," I said to Velva's uncle, trying to be polite, at least. He was a thin man with straight, black hair combed down flat on his head. He glanced back from the driver's seat through his rimless glasses at me and nodded, but didn't say anything. He glanced at Velva and started the car when her mother got in. Then her uncle drove down Eighteenth Street, past Lafayette Grammar School and then left on Market Street, heading toward the high school four blocks down.

Her mother turned around and without even looking at me, acting as if I wasn't there, said, "How often have you done this, Velva?"

But Velva just hid her face in her hands and cried, her thick golden hair shimmering with her quivering sobs. Soft and persistent, they filled the car. I wanted to hug her and console her, but didn't dare try in front of her mother, whose blue eyes focused like microscopes on us behind her rimless glasses. She finally turned back around to face the front, giving me a chance to reach out and pat Velva's knee. But Velva didn't look up. She just kept crying, making me really fear she'd break down in the school office and tell on us. Between her being pregnant and me in danger of losing my job, her cutting school wasn't so serious, especially for somebody like her, who'd never been in trouble before. I just didn't want her to tell on us. I squeezed her hand again to keep her spirit up while her uncle parked the car across the small side street from the Mac High office.

I got out, opened the door for her, walked her across the street, and held a door open for all of them at the entrance. I followed them into the office of the school I had attended for a year once, where I had gotten into all kinds of trouble for cutting school myself.

"The Girls' Dean, please," Mrs. Harris said, standing very proper and businesslike in front of the counter.

"I'm the Girls' Dean," said the woman, her brown hair cut off straight and level with her ears and trimmed in back like a boy's. I couldn't tell if she was young or old. "I'm Miss Shirley. What's wrong with Velva? Come into my office, please."

She led us into her office, closed the door, stepped around her desk and glanced at me as she sat down opposite us. I knew I was in for it and that it could take a while, making it that much worse for me at work. I was afraid to look at my watch and see how late I was.

"We caught Velva cutting school. She was alone in the house with Floyd, here, her boyfriend. We want her to know how serious it is. We do not want her staying at home with her boyfriend and cutting school," Mrs. Harris said and glared at me as if she knew what we'd been doing.

Miss Shirley looked at Velva, who was sobbing in her chair. Then she looked at me with pale eyes that almost made me shiver. She asked, "Where do you go to school?"

"I don't," I said, wanting to get it over with and get to work. Suddenly, I was conscious of how quiet it was. Velva had stopped sniffling to listen. She was looking at me with reddened eyes. "I graduated from Alameda High School last June."

Miss Shirley studied me for a moment with her pale eyes, as if surprised. Her face was plain, hard, almost manly. "How old are you?" she asked.

"Seventeen," I said, aware of the implication that I was smart for graduating so young. But I was glad she couldn't get me in trouble for cutting now. I was in enough trouble already over Velva and my chances of keeping my job were getting slimmer and slimmer.

"Since you've already graduated from high school, you can be put in the city jail and charged with contributing to the delinquency of a minor," Miss Shirley said, trying to frighten me.

I thought of Al and his contributing charge for working with an underage whore. How ironic it was for her to mention that when I loved Velva so much. I knew it was untrue, anyway, since I was a legal minor. But I could be put in juvenile hall for screwing her, for delinquency, even if it wasn't statutory rape. I didn't argue. I wanted to get it over with and try to save my job. I met the stare of the pale eyes behind the rimless glasses to show I was listening.

"As for Velva ... " Miss Shirley said and looked at her, " ... she's an honor student and a class counselor and, as far as I know, has never cut school nor been in trouble at any time in her entire life. We can let this one go. She's only missed two classes. There's no need to punish her for it. You don't have to cry, Velva. Just don't cut anymore."

But Velva covered her face with her hands and started sobbing again, really hard.

"Stop it! Stop it, now, Velva!" her mother said. "I think you should go to class now."

"No! Oh, no!" Velva cried and lifted her face up from her hands. Her eyes were red and swollen. Her nose was pink. She snapped open her purse and pulled out a hankie. "Not now! I don't want to go to class now! Let me go home! I want to go home!"

She broke out in a little cry and sniffled and wiped at her nose, then started sobbing again. Big tears ran down from her blue eyes. I felt really sorry for her, yet scared she was going to tell.

Her uncle suddenly said, "There's more to it than that."

Velva looked up at him with her swollen eyes, still sobbing, but watching him. I braced myself. I knew how much she admired her uncle, how smart she thought he was. He'd acted like a father to her since her mother'd gotten divorced. She really respected him.

"They've been seeing a lot of each other. Maybe too much," he said and clasped his bony hands together.

I froze, guessing that he might break Velva down, but Velva said, "What do you mean? I don't get to see him enough."

She sobbed and wiped her nose again and said, "With his boxing and job at the library, I only get to see him on weekends. That's one reason why I wanted to see him today."

She closed her eyes with another wave of tears and I cringed, sure her uncle would ask what the other reason was.

"That's not what I mean," he said. "I mean, you two, you act, well ... " He swallowed and his Adam's apple bobbed. "You lean on him too much. You depend upon him too much. Like, well, like ... " He looked at her mother, then at Miss Shirley, then at me and said, "Well, like you're married. You're too young for that. It's ... It's dangerous."

I stiffened with fear, feeling all eyes upon me, like they'd caught me between Velva's legs, and I blushed.

Her eyes slanted with tears, Velva said, "Can't I love him? Can't I have a boyfriend? Somebody who cares for me? Who watches out for me? Mom's always gone. What am I supposed to do?"

"I am not always gone, Velva!" her mother said and leaned back, tucking her tiny chin into her wrinkled neck and, blushing, glanced at Miss Shirley. "And what about your studies? Don't you still want to be a doctor? Don't you want to go to college? You're too young to fall in love. It's too serious.

"Why is it too serious to want someone to love me?" Velva asked. Her mouth puffed out with another sob and she covered her eyes with her hanky.

I blushed as all three adults looked at me, as if I were responsible, as if I were the guilty person. I wanted to tell them to leave her alone, that I'd take care of her, that I'd even marry her if I had to. I'd even marry her. But first ... I had to keep my job.

3

"Hey, Rich! Sorry I'm late. My alarm clock didn't work," I said, rushing up to the head page boy, Richard Brown, who was sitting at his tiny desk in a dark corner of the library office. A small cone of light shone down on a timesheet on a clipboard with my name on it, where his dark hand rested. "It's only an hour," I said, fibbing again, trying to save my job, knowing it was an hour and a half. I'd jogged the five blocks from Miss Shirley's office to the library.

But Rich's dark brown eyes looked two different ways behind his horn-rimmed glasses and I couldn't pick which eye to focus on. I couldn't tell if Rich was trying to avoid looking at me or if it was because one of his eyes looked off.

"You've already been fired, Floyd," Rich said in a voice as soft as suede.

My whole body sagged. The words hurt like a kayo punch to the chest. I'd really tried to make it.

"It's only ten-thirty, Richard," I said, holding my hands out.

Rich turned to the timesheet on his desk as if he couldn't look at me, twisting his head so the fold at the back of his neck showed, his kinky hair cut close to his scalp and his little ears. He stared at the time sheet for a moment, his dark skin, black under the eyes where the shadows were, then said, "The Assistant Head Librarian said she saw you get off the bus at the ice rink at nine o'five this morning and noticed that you were late. She buzzed you five minutes later to reprimand you, and when she found out you hadn't signed in yet, she got very angry. When an hour went by and you hadn't signed in yet, she told me you were fired and to set up some interviews with the employment office. She wouldn't even let me look for you."

His words were as hard as a slap in the face. Stunned, I tried to focus on his right eye, which was bloodshot from working as a page and studying for his degree in history at Cal.

"I argued with her, Floyd. I felt that she was being too punitive and should give you a chance to come in and explain. I was sure something was really wrong, that you weren't just being irresponsible. It was too odd you not signing right in. And you hadn't missed a day in three months. You deserved a chance to explain, at least. But she's an older woman and rigid. She'll be retiring next year.

173

Richard was trying to be nice to me, I knew, but it didn't do any good. My whole life was ruined now. Al had quit fighting and training me. Velva was pregnant and her family was getting wise. And now, I'd been fired. There wasn't much even Rich could do to make me feel better.

"Did you get off the bus across the street a little after nine this morning, Floyd?" Rich asked.

Grabbing at the chance to be honest and save some face, I said, "Yes! But I had to go somewhere!"

Richard shook his head and looked at me, wrinkling his forehead, and almost smiled, but then he said, "Had to go somewhere? You were supposed to be at work at nine, not be late and then go somewhere. Was it so important you'd risk your job over it?"

I didn't know how to answer, got confused and lost focus on Rich's right eye and stared at the left eye, which looked off to the side of me.

"It was an emergency," I said and jumped as the buzzer sounded once from the literature desk. My call, if I still had my job, to go get a pamphlet or some magazines.

Rich nodded and his voice went soft as suede again with its educated and sincere tone. "Couldn't you have signed in and then asked me, Floyd? I would have let you go! I think you used poor judgment. You could have taken care of it and come back to work."

"I had to, Rich, so I could get back to work quick. Then it got more involved and I couldn't get back." I stopped, about to tell him about Velva, wondering if it would help.

"Couldn't you have come in and told me and given me the opportunity to help you?" Richard said and lifted his face so the light from the lamp glowed in his eyes, soft brown like his voice.

"I wish I had, Rich," I said.

"I wish you had, too, Floyd," Richard said. "But why? Why did you get off the bus right across the street so she could see you? It was so self-destructive! Though knowing you, I'd guess it was just inexperience. I'm sorry, Floyd. I'm really sorry."

4

I could hear something frying in the kitchen when I stepped in the front door about five. It was sputtering like steak or hamburger. I didn't hear any voices. I'd spent the day walking the streets by myself and didn't come home until I got tired. I closed the door quietly behind me and stood in the hall a moment, dreading having to say I got fired.

No lights were on, at least. I walked into the shadows of the front room and looked through the open doors clear to the kitchen. Al, bare-armed in a T-shirt, was standing next to the stove, holding a knife and fork over a frying pan. For a moment, I resented those hands. I'd missed work to fight for his benefit and now I'd gotten fired over it, at least indirectly. I knew what happened today was my fault, yet it all started with my trying to help him. Still, blaming him wouldn't help me, I knew that. I walked like a school kid with bad grades around the big stuffed chair through the dining room and into the kitchen, ready for more trouble.

"What're you doing home so early?" Al asked, leaning back from the stove and putting me right on the spot. "Don't you go to the gym anymore?"

A steak was sizzling in the frying pan and the aroma made me hungry.

"I got fired," I said and Al froze with his fork in the air.

"What for?"

"For being late to work this morning, after I'd missed two days a couple of months ago, boxing. Remember, I told you about that and you made me go to work the last fight?"

Al turned back to the stove, speared his steak, turned it over, and then, as if he hadn't heard the last part, asked, "Why were you late?"

"I had to see Velva," I said.

"Couldn't it wait? Did it have to be before work?"

"She thought so," I said and then asked, "How come you're down here cooking your own food? Where's Tommy?"

"There was no food upstairs and she's out shopping at the last minute. Her usual story. Claims she wasn't feeling well because she's pregnant again. Both kids are taking a nap," Al said, then asked, "What're you gonna do now?"

"I really don't know," I said and opened the refrigerator door and pulled out a slab of beef from the meat compartment. My father had bought it wholesale and brought it over from the restaurant.

"Maybe you ought to start going to the gym again?"

"That's the least of my problems," I said and closed the refrigerator door. I stepped to the sink, pulled out the cutting board and put the meat on it, keeping my back to Al, not about to tell him why I really had gotten fired.

"You should have gone to work, you've got plenty of time to go see your girl at night."

"I work when she's free and she works when I'm free," I said, driving the knife down through the cold red meat and cutting off a thick slice. "Unless I go over there late and stay late and then don't get enough sleep for work the next morning."

"You still shouldn't have lost your job," Al said. He turned the gas off under the frying pan, picked up his plate, speared his steak, dropped it in the plate, turned to the table and sat down to eat.

"You lost yours," I said, rinsing off the butcher knife and putting it in the dishwrack to dry.

"I lost it trying to earn money, not visiting my girlfriend! And I got another job right away!"

Putting the slab of meat back in the refrigerator without answering, I dropped my steak in the hot pan with a sputter and turned the gas on. I stared at the red steak and didn't know whether to say it or not, but then did: "Hustling? That's almost like stealing!"

Tension sputtered like my sizzling steak. I watched Al cut himself a bite, stick it in his mouth and chew, waiting for him to say something. His jaw muscles swelled and relaxed, swelled and relaxed. Finally, he swallowed and said, "Hustling's just like being in business, like Dad and Uncle John and Cousin Chris and Eddy with his new pharmacy. I get the mooches to gamble, to try and beat me, then try to fix the odds. I try to control the game, just like a businessman. I have to use my brain and take my chances, and so do they. There's no stealing to it. It's just clever business, the gambling business."

"Crooked business," Tommy said, stepping in the back door with a shopping bag hanging from one hand. "Hustling booze and women when he was supposed to be driving cab, and now he's hustling servicemen."

"Hustling was part of my cabdriver's job," Al said. "And I notice that you catch cabs everywhere you go. You like that five hundred a week I bring home, even now without a regular job."

She skirted past his chair and when she was safely on the stairs, said, "What little of it you'll trust me with, Big Fighter!" Then she turned and started running up the steps in her high heels as Al spun around and threw his arm over the chair back and puffed out his bicep muscle.

"Do *your* job right sometime!" he shouted up at her. "I still go to work! I still take care of business! Get that, Floyd!" he said, turning with the ring of the phone, pointing toward the front hall. I turned the gas off under the frying pan and hurried through the dark, polished walls of the dining room, the front room and into the front hall, where I picked up the phone.

"Hello!"

"Hello, Floyd?"

"Yes, Eddy?" I said, my stomach sinking again.

"I've sent you a folder on simple arithmetic to help you with your entrance exams for junior college. You're still planning to go in the Spring now, right?"

"Well, I ... " I stopped.

"You sound hesistant. Are you going to school in the Spring or not? I thought you postponed going in the Fall, but said you were going in the Spring?"

"I ... I've thought about it, Eddy, but I don't know if I can now," I said, squirming like a fish on a line, trying to be honest, but trying not to tell on Velva either.

"Why not?" Eddy asked and I heard my own breath in the silence. I wanted to ask him for help, maybe for some abortion pills from his pharmacy, but couldn't let him think poorly of her. There was no way I could go to school and forsake her.

"I don't ... I can't ... I've got too many ... " I couldn't finish. I couldn't tell him that I screwed Velva before we were married. I couldn't do that to her. Finally, I said, "I'm not sure, Eddy."

"All right," he finally said. "The booklet's in the mail. It's up to you. But I want you to know that if you make up your mind to go, I'll help you." He stopped, then said in a tight voice, "Remember that," and hung up without saying goodbye.

The click hurt. He thought I was a quitter. If I could only tell him the truth without making him think badly of Velva, I would. But I couldn't get that picture of her with reddened eyes in the school office out of my mind. Then tell him I got fired!

I put the phone receiver back down on the base and stared out the front door window at the weeping willow tree in the front yard. Sunlight filtered through the branches that hung over the porch and stairs, and I felt like weeping. I hesitated, dreading having to go back into the kitchen and talk to Al again, when the phone rang under my hand and made me jump.

"Yes?"

"Floyd, it's Velva."

"Yesss?" I asked, afraid of what she'd say.

"What am I going to tell Mom? What am I going to do?"

Her voice was high, quavering, almost hysterical. I could tell she'd been crying. I hadn't talked to her all day, afraid to call. I could see her reddened eyes, her puffy lids.

"I'm starting to get fat, Floyd. I'm going to have to quit school after this Fall semester. I can't get fat at school! I talked to a girlfriend on the phone and she said that it's already too late, that only an abortion would get rid of it now. What am I going to do?"

"Tell me!" I said. "I wish I knew. Eddy's mad at me for not going to school and Al's mad at me for getting fired! I forgot to tell you that."

She caught her breath. I could hear it over the phone.

"What? Why?" she asked.

"For being late this morning after missing those two days when I fought a couple of months ago. The Assistant Head Librarian saw me get off the bus this morning and not sign in right away."

"Ooooh, noooo," she said. "I'm sorry, Floyd. I would never have insisted you come over, if I'd even dreamed of this happening. But I had to talk to you. I was going crazy."

I ached for a moment, without answering, then said, "I'm sorry, too."

"Oh, what are we going to do?" she said.

"I guess we'll have to get married," I said.

"Married?"

Her voice was high, hopeful now.

"Yes," I said. "We wanted to some day, anyway. It's the only thing I can think of. At least we can be together then."

She was so quiet I wondered if I was wrong about it. Then she said, "I love you for saying that, Floyd. It makes me see that you really do love me. But will that help? Won't they still know we did it first?"

I thought a moment, then said, "I could get ink erasure and change the date back like I did on that fake draft card. So they'll think we got married before we did it. That way they'll respect you. We can lie about our ages in Reno. I've got my draft card, like I say, that says I'm twenty-one. That's the only thing I can think to do. And try to get another job right away."

I felt like I was both saving us and sinking down at the same time.

"I love you, Floyd," she said and caught her breath, then started sobbing.

"I love you, too, Velva," I said with a tight gut.

5

When the Reno cabdriver leaned across the front seat of his yellow cab and looked at us, I knew we were going to get hustled. I turned on the wide concrete stairs of the courthouse toward the hotel to avoid the guy. But he pulled the cab up and stopped next to me on the sidewalk and, poking his head over the roof of the cab, shouted, "Hey! Going to get married?"

"Yes," Velva answered before I could say anything.

"I can take you to a nice place," the cabbie said.

Irritated, I said, "We haven't decided yet," and saw the guy frown. Thinking I'd gotten him, I kept on walking when Velva said, "Oh, let's go with him and get it over with, Floyd."

"He might try to hustle us," I said in a low voice, noticing the cold sore on her lip again. I'd first seen it when we caught the Greyhound Bus at ten in the morning on San Pablo in Oakland, only four blocks from her house. It reminded me of the sore on my mother's lip in the coffin. Velva turned her face slightly away and said, "What can he do? He's got a meter in there. Let's ask him to take us straight to a minister. Come on, Floyd!" She tugged on my arm.

"How much to a place to get married?" I asked, playing it safe, and the cabby stared at me for a moment with light, glittering eyes. He had no hat, sandy hair, a hard, lined face, and was probably in his thirties. Then he grinned as if he thought it was funny that I didn't trust him and said, "Two bucks round trip."

Velva nodded at me and I said, "Okay," and opened the door of the cab for her. But as soon as the driver made a u-turn, crossed the bridge and turned up the first street next to the river and started heading up into the low hills of the residential section, I said, "My brother drives cab in Oakland." I didn't want the guy to think he could take advantage of me just because he thought I was a kid. I'd made enough mistakes already.

"Oh, yeah," the cabby said and glanced back at me, but didn't grin this time. He flicked his thumb at the row of big houses on the low hills on the other side of the river, and said, "Every house is owned by a millionaire. Reno's got more of them than any other city its size in the world." I began to relax a little, confident he wouldn't try to get more than the two bucks.

"How would you like to move into one of those, Floyd?" Velva asked and smiled at me. She was so beautiful with her huge blue eyes and golden hair curling in a page boy over the rich burgundy of her coat, I squeezed her hand.

"You look good enough to be a millionaire's wife," I said, not caring if the cabby heard. She was dressed like a high school student in a cashmere sweater, long, woolen skirt and flats under her expensive maroon coat. She hadn't dressed up so her mother wouldn't get wise. Velva had told her she was just spending the night with a girlfriend. Her heels and dress suit were home, but she still looked like a millionaire's wife to me. I leaned over and kissed her lightly.

"It just popped up this morning. Nerves, I guess," she said and pointed at the cold sore.

"That's okay," I said. "That's nothing compared to ... " I leaned back.

"Compared to what?" she asked, leaning over in front of my face. "Tell me! Compared to what?"

Her face was right next to mine. I could see deep into her eyes and didn't know how to tell her without making her feel bad.

"I like marrying you. That's not it. I like the idea of everybody knowing that this gorgeous girl belongs to me, that you're my woman forever."

She tilted her head as I talked, as if really touched by what I was saying, and though I could tell the cabby was listening by the way his head was cocked, I spoke anyway, but in a low voice, almost a whisper.

"What's wrong is that I'm fired and I can't even support you yet, let alone be a millionaire. It makes me wish I'd told Eddy and asked for some pills and we tried them at least or that I'd told Al and asked him. He's always bragging that he can get anything he wants. That's what makes me feel bad. Then I wouldn't have to worry about supporting you and a baby. They're going to know we did it, anyway, even if we did get married first."

"But that's okay, then," she said. "Remember your dream? About me pregnant in front of your family? It'll be all right. They'll accept it and you'll get a job. I'll help you."

Velva's lips almost touched mine as she talked, but she still seemed hesitant, as if she saw something else. Instead of kissing me, she asked, "Is that all?"

"Not all. What really depresses me even more than losing the job is how I lost it. And that every time I really love somebody like you and Al and try to do something for them, it turns out bad."

"What do you mean?" she asked and leaned back, frowning.

"Oh, everything, like I told you before." My chest ached with a tense feeling. "Wanting to fight for Al and then him not wanting to be with me afterwards, and then getting jealous about Eddy talking to me about going to school, not caring that I had fought so hard for him.

"I know, I know," she said and patted my hand.

"Then with you. I love you and really care for you and I get you in trouble. Then, trying to help Al and you, I get fired. That's what really hurts."

I clasped my hands between my knees, looked down at the dirty floor of the cab, at the ashes spilling out of the cigarette tray, and paid no attention to the pretty houses we were passing.

"I kept thinking everything was going to turn out roses. That Al would be a world champion, that I'd win the Golden Gloves, then go to college and marry you, but marry you last, after I'd done those things, not marry you first because I had to. It's all turning out backwards, like in *Of Mice and Men* by John Steinbeck."

She squeezed my hand.

"You probably saw the movie, it's just like the book. The migrant field-workers kept thinking they were going to get a farm, and kept kidding themselves about it, until they were destroyed. That's the way I feel, like some stupid kid. 'Out of a good tree comes good fruit. Out of a bad tree, bad fruit,' Jesus said. Well, I guess my tree was bad, because it's only putting out bad fruit."

"Oh, Floyd," she said and leaned over and kissed me this time. "I love you for caring enough to try and help Al and me, even if it did turn out bad with Al. I ... I ... " She looked out the window past me and said, "I'm sorry I got the way I am and you had to marry me. But I love you for it! I love you for sticking by me and I'll stick by you. I'll be true to you all my life. I'll prove that what you did for me was right. I'll pay you back with my love, my loyalty. I'll die for you. I love you more ... than myself. I really love you, Floyd." Her voice faded out and her nose wrinkled up as if she might cry.

I pulled her to me, kissed her on the lips, cold sore or not.

"This is it!" the cabby said, pulling up in front of a brick house with a tree in the front yard. I saw a small sign in the window, which read, "Reverend Love, marriages performed," and felt the tension rise in me again. But I wasn't sad anymore.

"Want me to be a witness?" the cabbie asked, staring at me as if he'd heard our conversation.

"Sure," I said and smiled, guessing I'd have to tip him for it. I cracked my knuckles after I got out, then closed the cab door and followed Velva up the walk. When I pressed the doorbell, it buzzed like the ten-second warning signal in the ring. This was it! Ten seconds to go before the fight! The same tension gripped me! My life was changing forever, right now, and I knew it! I grabbed Velva's hand and held it tightly. When she smiled at me and I saw how calm she was, I turned with a smile to the small, bald man who opened the door.

"Wedding?" he said. "Come in, please."

Reverend Love smiled when we stepped in, his pink cheeks flushed with the heat of the room. He asked us to sign a register at a small table in the hall when I handed him the marriage permit. Then he motioned to us to follow him into the front room. He stopped us with his hand almost as soon as we stepped in and, after saying that the cabby and his own wife could serve as witnesses, he started reading the wedding vows.

I looked at the girl now becoming my wife, at her lovely face. I couldn't see the sore from this side. A strange feeling filled me. I was almost sad, the event was so important, yet I felt really happy. When the reverend asked, "Promise to love and cherish until death do you part?" I looked into Velva's beautiful eyes and my voice cracked a little as I answered, "I do."

"And do you, Velva Harris, promise to love and obey until death do you part?"

"I do," she said in a calm voice, and the whole thing hit me and my hands trembled as I slipped the small gold wedding band on her slim white finger. I realized then that she was going to have to quit school and her job and go live with me, when I didn't have a job to support her. I also was going to have to quit worrying about Al or about going to school or even boxing. I felt a great love for her fill me. I really didn't know what our families were going to say. But, she was finally and completely mine, and there was nothing anybody could do about it. We were together. I wasn't whipped. I'd only been dropped and lost a couple of rounds. I could still win a decision, maybe even a kayo, because I had Velva.

6

Under the fluorescent light of the State Employment Office, wrinkles pinched the edges of her lips, even under the pink lipstick and the white powder on her cheeks.

"You have only a high school diploma and no experience but this library job. And you don't have the background for a clerical position."

There were about ten other women in the big office that looked like her: gray hair and rimless glasses. Some stood at the counter talking to long lines of unemployed people. There was a dry smell of paper and pencils. A young woman was typing in a corner.

"At your age, the best thing you could do would be to get some education, some training in a junior college, then try to get a clerical job. Or get an apprenticeship in the trades somewhere."

"But I've got to get a job now!" I said, leaning toward her in my chair. "I'm married and my wife's ... " My cheeks got warm ... "going to have a baby!"

"A baby?" She leaned back, made a double-chin and stared at me with round, whited eyes, like she'd caught me doing something dirty. But I stared right back at her and she looked down at her lap and said, "You're almost a baby yourself!"

I blushed again.

"Why did you leave your library job?"

"I missed two days in three months. My supervisor, the Head Page, objected to the Assistant Head Librarian for letting me go over it!"

"Well ... "

"He said it was too punitive and that she was too rigid."

"Well ... you would have been better off to have stayed on it. There's nothing I can really offer you. There's a beginner's job in a hat company ... but it's only for fifty cents an hour and I notice you were earning a dollar an hour at the library ... and they say they want experience of some kind, too. I'm afraid that working in a library doesn't prepare you for warehouse work."

"I could try it," I said, going for anything. She shook her head and said, "No. I wouldn't want you to get it and quit right away because it wasn't

183

enough money for a married man. And I really don't think they'd hire you. They want a taller man. You have to have reach up in a warehouse."

She picked up my application and said, "Right now, you should be in training of some kind. You're just too young to be married with a baby on the way. Sorry." She dropped it in a flat, wire basket.

Twelfth Street was a long line of store fronts on my side, dismal and bare-looking under a layer of clouds all the way to Broadway, six blocks away. For the first time since I had gotten married, I felt sorry for myself. I turned my back on the Employment Office and started walking west, toward downtown, when I heard, "They tried to tell us we're too young/ too young to reeee-alllly be in luuuuv," and stopped in the doorway of a bar next door to the Employment Office and listened. Nat King Cole's soft voice sang from a jukebox pulsating with rainbow colors, filling me with a sweet feeling.

"They saaaay that luuuuv's a worrrd / a word we've never heard / and can't beee-giiinnn to know the mea-ninnng uuuuuv. / And yet we're not toooo yuuuuung to knooooooow / this luuuuuv wiiiill live though years may gooooo / And thennnnn sommmmmeday they mayyyy recalllll / We we're notttt / tooooo yunnnnnng / aaaat aaaaaaalllllllll."

My body tingled with sweetness. I saw Velva's beautiful face in front of me as I turned and headed down Twelfth Street again, not so sorry anymore. I'd keep my eyes open. I wasn't too young. I'd get a job right away. And just as I reached the corner, I saw the signs of a private employment office in the doorway of a storefront building with venetian blinds on the windows. Job listings were written on small blackboards hung outside and others were printed on big sheets of white cardboard attached to the glass doors. I stopped to read them.

"Cook, short order, $1.50."

"Maid, references required, live-in."

When I saw "Kitchen Helper, $1.00 per hour," I stepped into the doorway and peeked through the glass doors. I could see a lot of black women inside, sitting on benches, a couple at the counter, at desks, and one white man. There was a sign on a counter saying, "Applications. Get in line." I pushed the door open, went inside, got an application, sat down and filled it out quickly. In "Position Wanted," I wrote "Kitchen Helper," checked "Married" under "Marital Status," and for "Reason For Leaving Last Job" wrote "personal." I then got in line behind a plump black lady, who turned around and looked at me.

Wearing a tan sport coat, tan gabardine slacks, a sport shirt and suede loafers with crepe soles, I was dressed to look as mature as possible, as Dorothy had suggested, without wearing a white shirt and tie.

The black lady in front of me turned away from the counter and sat down on a bench to wait for an interview. A thin man with glasses and graying hair, hollows in his gray cheeks, took my application, scanned it quickly and said, "You've got no experience in kitchen work?"

"No," I said, "but I have a high school diploma and can learn quickly."

But the man shook his head and said, "We just sent an older man out there with good references. I don't think you'd have much chance."

"I could try," I said.

But the man shook his head again, said, "We don't like to waste their time. I really don't think they'd hire you. Sorry," and pushed my application back at me.

"Sure," I said, picking it up. I turned away, avoided the stares of the black ladies, dropped the application in a waste basket and walked out onto the sidewalk again. It had only taken about ten minutes, I could see by the tall City Hall clock. It didn't look like anything good was happening today, I thought, fighting the bitter feeling rising in me, wishing I hadn't lost my library job, remembering what Eddy had said about not getting married until I'd chosen a career.

Crossing the street, I walked another block, my whole chest tight with tense unhappiness. I saw another employment agency and my heart quickened.

"Summer Cannery Jobs," it said, but underneath, "Experienced Only."

I slowed down, ambled by it, but kept walking, saw a paper rack on the next corner and thought that I ought to buy a paper and go through the want-ads. But then I saw another sign saying, "Salesmen wanted. No experience necessary," and, my heart pounding, I turned into the store.

There were a couple of women at desks and an Asian girl with a pretty face who got up and walked over to me.

"Can I help you?"

"I want to apply for a salesman's job," I said, and stood very straight and serious. She looked at me through heavy-lidded eyes with just the hint of a smile on her lips, then turned and walked back to a man sitting at a desk. He was young, with curly blond hair and a narrow face. He looked very Southern, like a transplanted Okie, probably a World War II veteran. He glanced over at me, said something to her. I held my breath when she came back, then breathed again, when she said, "He'll see you."

"Do you have any experience?" the man asked as soon as I told him I wanted a salesman's job.

"No, but it says no experience necessary," I said.

"How old are you?"

"I just turned eighteen, but I'm married and my wife's going to have a baby and I need a job. I can do it, just give me a chance! I've got a high school diploma and received good grades in school," I said, stretching the truth a little bit. I'd gotten great grades in grammar school and the first year of junior high, but poor, then finally fair grades the rest of my school years. But I was a heavy reader on my own, so I wasn't really lying. And, besides, I knew I could do it, whatever it was.

"Married, huh? You want to sell, huh?"

"Yes, I need a job," I said. "Right away. I'll start today."

The man smiled. He was a good-looking, wiry guy in a white shirt and tie. With his lanky build, I could see him in a sailor's uniform.

"Sit down," the man said. When I did, he added, "I'm Bob Holcolmb, the sales manager. We have crews that go to the suburbs mainly, like Vallejo. That's where we're working now. They sell door to door, housewares like lamps, ashtrays, blankets, etcetera, to housewives."

"It sounds good. I can do it," I said. "I get along well with people."

"I'm sure you do," the man said and smiled again. "But it's strictly commission. You get from a dollar to five dollars apiece for each article you sell, and if you sell nothing, you get nothing." His eyebrows went up. "Still interested?" he asked.

I looked right back at him and said, "Sure. When do I start?"

The man grinned.

7

They'd liked me from the first day. I was one of the best salesman and the youngest by ten years, though I walked and sweated from door to door to make ten bucks a day, on a good day, if I was lucky.

I held up the crucifix to show it off. It was a gaudy, cast-iron table model a foot high with an iron plate for a candle and an ashtray at its base with bits of red, green, blue and white glass chips imbedded all over its gray body. No Christ on it, just the iron metal cross. I actually liked it myself. It reminded me of the jeweled hilt of a dagger or a jewel-encrusted scabbard, like a knight might carry. I knew that neither my mother nor my sister would ever allow it in their houses, not with their furniture. It was too vulgar. I knew that! But I liked its sense of massive strength, rugged, like the real cross. I talked about it as if I liked it and women bought it from me.

With each house, I was getting better, too, learning how to convince them. At first, I didn't know what to do. The young housewives would stare out the window at me, then invite me in, listen to me for a while, then buy the crucifix. I usually sold five a day for the first month, down in the poor homes by Mare Island, the navy base. Just guessing did it. Trying to be nice. But in the newer homes, I didn't do so well. I tried harder then because I wanted to talk them into it. I had to get better at talking them into it. I had to become more persuasive and make more money. I had to learn how to lie better, in a legal way, if I was going to take care of Velva and the baby.

The iron crucifix felt slippery in my hand, even before Bob Holcomb's station wagon reached the paved road and the dust settled behind it, leaving me on the dirt lane on the outskirts of Vallejo near a cluster of old houses surrounded by fields of weeds. Sweating hands! Just like before a fight! Like here in Vallejo where I'd fought twice just a few months ago. Selling was like laying my life on the line, though I should have been used to it by then, after three months.

I blew breath out between my lips, buttoned my gray flannel sportcoat, patted the order pad inside my breast pocket to make sure it was there, then tried to press the curls on my head down to make sure they weren't too wild. I started down the dirt lane toward the houses, determined to sell some crucifixes.

I had to sell some crucifixes, at least three a day for six days to make eighteen dollars a week, which came to seventy-two dollars a month, which—added to Velva's forty-five a week or one-eighty a month—came to two hundred and, and ... let's see ...

I squinted my eyes in the bright winter sunlight.

One seventy-five to round hers off and seventy-five of mine came to one-fifty, no two-fifty, minus three from mine, for seventy-two, came to one ... no, two forty-seven, but hers was really one-eighty, which, add five more for ... two fifty-two or ... close enough.

Staring at the houses as I drew closer, I could see that two of them were on the same property. A long, brown, two-story, weathered house, looking more like a hotel than a house, with shaky-looking outside stairs on both ends leading to the second floor. The other building was low and flat, a one-story house with the same old, unpainted wood, just as rickety-looking and not too promising. My stomach tightened. They might not have much money. They might not buy anything at all.

I started figuring again. I still had about a half a block to go. If I made the three today and every day for the whole week, for the whole month, and if we then had one-fifty, no two-fifty, then thirty dollars for the rent, left one, no two-twenty-two, then food, about fifteen a week, for four weeks or sixty dollars from two-twenty-two comes to, let's see ... ? From two-twenty would be forty from two, or one-sixty plus two, one-sixty-two.

Out of that one-sixty-two we had to pay for the milk delivery, about fifteen a month, that's one-forty-seven. Then we had to have money to go out, and money to pay on her old clothing bill at Goldman's—about ten dollars. She still owed about ninety. That ... let's see ... that's one-thirty-seven.

So, we should put maybe fifty dollars in the bank to add to the two-hundred we already had in there, and in a couple of months, we'd have three-hundred and could pay for the hospital bill for the baby, including the doctor. That would give us about eighty dollars left or twenty dollars a week for bus money and lunch money and going to the show. Wow! It was driving me crazy. Being single on that library job never looked better.

Getting closer now, I could see a black lady looking out an upstairs window at me. An old Model-A Ford, parked in the dirt yard, stuck out between the buildings. Looked like there was some life around. I just might be able to get my self-imposed quota here. Maybe? Just maybe? I had fifty cents in my pocket for a hamburger and a coke somewhere for lunch and that was it. It was strange not to have money all the time. Dad had always given me a big allowance when I went to high school, saying he always wanted me to have money so I'd never ask or never borrow from anyone. And before I married Velva, I always had money, lots for a seventeen year old. I only had

to pay Dorothy ten a week for room and board, and the rest of my one-ten a
month clear after taxes was to do whatever I wanted with it. It was no fun
having to worry about money.

Velva got more unhappy over it than me. She was used to having as
much money as me, even as a high school girl, and now that she was getting
a belly, she'd throw fits for almost nothing. Like she'd suddenly shout at
me for closing the door too hard or pressing up too tight against her when
we'd squeeze with my sister and brother-in-law Frank in the front seat of the
company truck that Frank got to drive as superintendent of Best Fertilizer
Company. I didn't shout back because I knew how she felt. I got stomach
cramps and threw up almost every day as soon as her stomach began to swell.
I even thought I had ulcers at first, until Dorothy laughed when I told her
and said I had morning sickness and sympathy pains. I wondered if it was
because I felt guilty, and then it stopped. There was nothing I could do about
Velva getting a big belly but try to earn more money so she could buy herself
something, so we wouldn't be so pinched for cash, so she'd feel better. I had
to sell some crucifixes. I was going to sell some crucifixes.

I was almost there now. I could see there was a dirt lane up to the paved
road a couple of blocks away across the fields on the other side of the two-
story apartment house. The woman was not in the window anymore. There
was a line of five or six houses on the other side of the apartment house, too,
widely spaced on separate lanes to the paved road. I could hit them all, but
it was going to be a lot of walking, going up and down those lanes, unless I
could find a way to cut across the fields. Moving over to the side of the dirt
road, near the ditch and the dry weeds, I tried to see if there were any fences
between the houses. There weren't, and I felt better. I just might sell some
crucifixes.

"Hi!" I said and waved my hand, then crossed the clearing, past the front
end of the old Model-A and over to a young black man.

"How do you like this?" I asked and showed him the crucifix.

He squinted one eye and looked up, a gold tooth showing under his lifted
lip.

"Looks fiiiine," he said and I handed it to him and waited until he turned
it around. Then I held up one finger and said, "You can have it for only one
buck! ... down!" I swung my hand down with the word and added, "And a
dollar a week for four more weeks, that's all. Only a dollar now."

The young black guy looked up at me, squinted again, his upper lip
lifting, showing his gold tooth.

I pointed at the crucifix and switched his attention to the cross again.
"See! You've got a cross around to remind you of Jesus without having just
a cross."

I guessed he liked Jesus. All colored people liked Jesus.

"It actually serves a religious purpose in your house, besides being an ashtray. Easter's almost here and this is all about his crucifixion."

I wondered for a brief fraction of a second what Jesus would think about that, and almost had to snort at the thought. Well, I didn't make the crucifix. I was only selling it.

The young guy squinted up at me again. He had smooth, black skin and couldn't have been over twenty-five at best.

"Some women put candles in the bottom, like a shrine, and keep them in their bedrooms and pray to them."

I stopped a second to let that sink in. The guy looked back at the crucifix as if to see if that made sense, how they might do it.

"And other people, men like you, put them on their coffee tables and use them for ashtrays. At night, it looks pretty when the low lamp lights or the candle flame makes the iron shine and the jewels glitter. Like campfires around Jesus's cross, glittering off it. See it?"

He nodded his head as he stared at the cross, and I said, "And it's only a buck. Whatta ya say?"

The guy looked up with widened eyes, then looked down again and shook his head very slowly and said, "Seems like I'm always gettin' in debt."

"Pretty, though, isn't it?" I said, getting him off the money and back on the crucifix, then grinned at him.

He was a big, rangy man, dressed in blue dungarees, and skin so black it shined. He grinned back. His gold tooth showed. "It sure is," he said.

"It'd be nice if all the Easter presents you bought only cost you a dollar a week for four more weeks," I said. When the guy nodded, I said, "Give me a buck and I'll have the sales manager drop one off this afternoon, so you won't even have to wait a week for it. By the time Easter comes around, you'll not only have enjoyed having the crucifix around for a month or so, you'll have it paid for."

I held one hand out and waited. He was still holding onto the crucifix, still looking at it, when he said again, "Seems like I'm always goin' in debt."

I held up my finger and said, "Just a dollar!" Then I breathed a little when the guy stuck out his long leg without saying anything and started reaching into his front pocket.

I watched carefully until he pulled a crumpled dollar out and handed it to me. Then I quickly put it in my slack pocket, filled out a credit form, got the man's name and address, had him sign it, then gave him back a yellow copy.

I was warmed up now, confident, sure I could do it again, only two more to go to get my quota. I looked up at the second story window next to the stairs on this end and saw a soft, light brown face with big dark eyes like a doe looking down at me. I hurried up the old wooden stairs and knocked on the screen door, holding up the crucifix.

"I'm selling these crucifixes for Easter," I said, then smiled when a pretty face appeared on the other side of the screen and smiled at me.

"Oh, come in," she said and opened the door for me. I felt my heart start beating when I stepped in, knowing from experience that just one foot in the door could lead to a sale.

"Like some coffee?" she asked, pulling out a chair for me, her big doe eyes all soft and pretty. Then I saw the lump under her apron and thought of Velva, who had one now, too, and I felt a little sorry for her.

"I don't drink coffee, but I'll have some water," I said and sat down.

She got me a glass off the old wooden drain board and turned on a leaky faucet. Everything was old and worn, from the sink to the gas stove, the gray, unpainted walls, the table and unmatched wooden chairs, the bare wooden floor. But everything clean and brown like her. And she certainly wasn't worn. She was soft and smooth and tan, with her hair shimmering in curly waves down close to her head and tied in neat braids in the back. She showed pretty white teeth, between large, soft lips which turned a dark pink color when she smiled.

"They sure are pretty crosses," she said.

"They only cost a dollar ... " I held up one finger, " ... down! And then only a dollar a week for four more weeks."

When she frowned, I said, "But you can have it right away! Today! This afternoon! For only one dollar! You don't even have to wait for Easter."

When she still didn't say anything, I said, "My sales manager's got his station wagon full of them and will deliver it today. Then a collector will come around once a week until it's paid. You won't even have to leave your house, this very kitchen, and have it paid for in a month! It's a service we offer to all our customers."

"One month?" she asked. When I nodded, she said, "Okay," and reached for her purse on the icebox. It was the first icebox I'd seen since the war, when people couldn't buy new refrigerators. She took a dollar out and gave it to me. I saw a wad of bills in her pocketbook before she could close it.

"Would you like to buy a table lamp, too? See this pretty picture?" I asked.

I pulled a brochure out of my pocket and showed her the picture of the lamp, with its frilly edges. It was just right for Dorothy's front room, but too fancy for this poor kitchen or this whole house. But I'd get five bucks if I sold her the lamp.

"Isn't it pretty!" I said.

"Sure is," she said, staring at it with her soft eyes.

"Would you like to have it? It's only a dollar a week for nineteen more weeks and you can have that today, too. My boss's got some in his station wagon and can drop it by in a couple hours."

She turned and looked into my eyes, then up to the waves curling onto my forehead and said, "Aaall riiight," and smiled, spreading her full pink lips.

Seeing that she liked me, I said, "How about one of our new synthetic blankets? It's a new material they developed during the war for soldiers. It's really good stuff. The government uses it."

I made it sound important. She stopped smiling and her big, luminous eyes seemed to quit staring to look at me as if she were really listening.

"The same way: a dollar down and a dollar a week ... " I didn't add that it was for nineteen weeks more, too, but said instead: "It's got a real satiny surface to keep it from itching. See how it shines?"

She nodded.

"Just a dollar."

She turned her big, pretty doe eyes on me again. Her skin was a smooth tan and I felt an urge to kiss her, but thought of Velva and the money. The purse was still open in her lap. I glanced at the money, then held out my hand. She gave me two dollars. I could barely believe it! My mouth was all smiling teeth. She grinned, too. We grinned at each other across the table.

"Look!" I said and turned the brochure over, saying, "A pot and pan set," showing her the picture of a neat descending row of pots, from big to small.

"Oh, yes!" she said. "I could use 'um. Don't have any good pans. Just got married."

She looked down at her belly.

"Congratulations!" I said, pretending not to notice her belly. "It's perfect for you. A dollar down and a dollar a week, the same way, without having to even step out of your house."

I didn't add it up for her. I didn't want her to think about the total.

"Okay?"

"Okay," she said and pulled another dollar off her wad. I tried to think of something else to sell her as I took the dollar, when a big black woman stepped into the kitchen doorway from another room. She had big, full breasts like melons and smiled when she saw me.

"He's cute as a doll. Where'd you get 'im?"

The pretty tan woman giggled and said, "He jus' come up the back door, sellin' these crosses. So I bought one."

"Would you like to buy one?" I asked, tingling again, trying once more. "One dollar."

"Only a dollar?" the big woman asked and cocked her head as if she didn't believe me.

"A dollar down and a dollar a week for four more weeks, that's all," I said. "You can have it delivered today. And the collector will come around once a week like a paper boy and you can have an Easter present right now for only a dollar."

She bent down and examined the cross on the table, leaned over so the top of her dress hung open and her full breasts showed in all their swelling and aroused me. She looked up and caught me looking at them and grinned.

"Okay?" I asked.

"Okay," she said and sat down at the table, reached across it and patted my hand.

I wrote quickly, filling out the order pad, but before I asked her to sign it, I asked, "Would you like to buy a lamp, and a blanket, and a pot and pan set like her? The ones in the pictures?"

She didn't answer. She just stared at me, then winked and grinned and said, "Cute as a bug," and looked down and said, "These?"

"Yes. Just a buck a week, that's all, and the sales manager will deliver them and a collector will come around every week. You won't even have to bother over it."

"You sure are cute," she said, and when I smiled at her, she said, "I'll go get my purse," and stood up and left the kitchen.

"Your name?" I asked the pretty woman. I wrote, "Emmy Lou Jones," almost as quickly as she said it, then her address, too, and checked off the items she'd ordered and filled in the amount of the deposit, all mine. I guessed I'd sold them a hundred and twenty dollars worth of merchandise. I was doing great in a poor apartment house. The big lady came in and handed me four dollars and I got her to sign, ripped out their receipts, handed the slips to them, put the order pad back inside my coat pocket and said, "The sales manager will be by this afternoon. He's driving around Vallejo right now delivering. You won't have to wait."

I waited for them to answer so I could leave, but the big woman said, "He has pretty hair like Tony."

"Prettier than Tony's," the pretty woman said.

I reached up and patted my curls down and didn't know what to say, thinking that they liked me and wondering if there was anything else I could sell them.

"Wouldn't you like to have a boyfriend as cute as him?" the big woman said.

"I wouldn' mind at all," the pretty woman said and I smiled. Then, not knowing what to do, I took a step back. They acted like they really liked me, but what could I do? With two of them? And what about Velva?

I reached over and grabbed my crucifix ashtray, stepped back to the kitchen door, stopped, couldn't think of anything else to sell them and pushed open the screen door and stepped out onto the porch. I waved as the door closed, then ran down the old wooden stairs, trying to get away before they could change their minds, feeling like a thief.

8

Velva surprised me by looking up from her ironing and over her shoulder at me as I stepped into Dorothy's kitchen. I was on my way down to Foothill Boulevard to catch the bus to work at the sales office. I thought she was supposed to leave for her job at the candy store at eight. She looked back down at the shirt she was ironing without saying anything. It was my pale blue sports shirt, which she said went well with my dark wavy hair. Her beautiful face was soft in the high-ceilinged light, but silent, closed in. Dorothy looked over at me from the sink, where she was washing dishes. Neither of them spoke.

I didn't feel like talking either. Though dressed neatly in my dark-blue sportcoat and blue slacks, a white sportshirt open at the neck, I dreaded walking around all day again, going door to door, talking at a high pitch, trying to sell crosses. I'd sold five the day before and made five dollars, the most on my sales crew, but I had gotten tired. I'd never again had a great day as when I had earned the thirty-two dollars at that one house in Vallejo—beginners luck! The warm weather helped some, but it was hard trying to talk one person after another into giving me their money. That's what it added up to, whether I wanted to admit it or not. I was hustling for a buck, just like Al and Al T. and Curly and my father and Eddy. I hadn't been to the gym since I walked out months before on Babe. Al's hustle looked better and better to me now. He made real money, not just pocket change like me. Survival of the fittest, they called it.

Starting around the table to go catch my bus, it dawned on me that no one had spoken a word since I came into the kitchen and both women were staring at me.

"What's up?" I asked, getting worried when they both looked at each other.

"She got laid off, Floyd," Dorothy said.

I looked from her to Velva, who was holding the iron up in her hand. She had on a short smock that pregnant women wear. She wore it all the time.

"My boss said I'm too heavy to work in public, Floyd." She looked down at her stomach and grimaced and I wondered how we'd get the money for the baby now.

"She said that after I had the baby, she'd give me the first opening, full or part-time. She was trying to be nice." She looked down at her stomach again.

"She couldn't help it, Floyd," Dorothy said, wiping her cheek with the back of a soapy hand, pushing the dark lock out of her big, soft eye.

"She's getting heavy, all right. That's the way it is," I said, holding up my hands, trying to be a good husband. Then I cocked my head to one side. "The only problem is that I can't earn enough money on my job to really support us, let alone save money for the baby." I dropped my hands. "Maybe I should turn pro and try to earn some money that way?"

"No!" they both said at once.

"But what else can I do?" I said. "I don't have any college education and no work experience. At least, there's a chance to earn money that way."

"Boxing hasn't done Al any good," Dorothy said, looking really sweet and pretty. "I don't want you to be like him. He thinks he fooled the Army into discharging him, but he might really have something wrong with his head. I worry about him. He's done some crazy things in his life. Go see Dad, instead. He might be able to help you find a job."

"But Dolores won't like me coming around, not even to talk to him! She's forgotten that I'm the one who asked her to stay when she was leaving."

"Go talk to Eddy, then," Velva said. "He's got a new drugstore." "But last time I talked to him, it wasn't too ... "

"Go see him," Velva insisted.

"Yes, go see him," Dorothy added. "He's your brother and he cares about you. He said he'd help you go to school. He knows you're married now."

"Yeah, but the last ... "

"Go see him," Velva said again and Dorothy nodded.

"Okay," I said and stepped over to Velva, kissing her on her soft lips and hugging her shoulders as Dorothy smiled.

"We'll make it," I said.

Velva put the iron down on end and put her arms around me, hugging me back, pressing her stomach against me.

9

The big red and green globes in the wide pharmacy window above the sidewalk looked impressive from the street. The five-story medical building in downtown San Francisco looked impressive, too, making me proud of my brother. It gave me hope that I could get a job working for him. But when I walked up the marble stairs and saw how professional the pure white pharmacy looked through the glass door with "Salas Pharmacy" printed on the glass, I got a little worried. I might not be good enough to work there. I tingled with fear when the bell tinkled as the door opened and I saw Eddy in the back room behind the cash register.

He looked up, one eyebrow raised, to see who was entering, then frowned. I knew I had made a mistake by not calling first. I should have warned him I was coming, but I didn't want him to put me off the way he had the last time I tried to go see him. If he hadn't, I might not even be married now. Still, I was starting off wrong.

Eddy smiled when he got up, as if he'd seen the doubt on my face and was trying to make me feel better. His face looked round above the white pharmacist's smock and his body looked bloated, too.

"Can I talk to you, Eddy?" I asked. I saw him stop, then glance back at a blond man standing in the room behind him. He stepped past the cash register and pointed to two white wicker chairs next to a small wicker table by the big front window.

"Sure. We can sit there," he said.

As I was stepping toward the table, I saw the blond man in the sport coat staring at me. "Am I interrupting you?" I asked.

"No! Sit down!" Eddy said quickly and stepped over and pulled out a chair for himself, out of the blond man's sight. "It's okay," he said as I sat down, then reached out and shook my hand with the same firm handshake he taught me when I was a little boy. He smiled again.

From the window, I could see down the busy street with the hotels and bars lining it.

"What is it, Floyd?"

His first frown still bothered me. I glanced out the window at the hotel across the street. In a small voice, I said, "I came over ... " I stopped, swallowed, then came out with it: "I got fired from my library job, Eddy, and I've been selling door to door and not earning very much. But Velva had a job, too, and we were making it. But she's too big now and got laid off, and I can't support us or save any money for the baby on what I'm earning. The baby's due in June, too!"

I stopped with the narrowing of Eddy's green eyes, and my heart dropped when Eddy said, "I can't afford full time help, Floyd. Certainly not enough money for a married man with a pregnant wife."

"But don't you have twenty-four hour emergency delivery?"

"Yes, but I've got two part-time college students working for me now and I couldn't fire two men just to make room for you. That wouldn't be fair now, would it?"

"I guess not," I said and shrugged my shoulders.

"And you don't have a driver's license, do you?"

"No, but I could learn fast, then get one."

Eddy smiled and in a soft voice said, "I'm just starting out, Floyd. I really couldn't afford to pay you enough money to support your wife. I pay my two students only fifty cents an hour. They use the money for entertainment. They're both on the GI Bill. I couldn't afford them otherwise."

"All right," I said.

When I shoved my chair back, the blond man came out from behind the counter. "Your younger brother, Eddy?" he asked. "He looks like you."

"Yes, he was just leaving," Eddy said and I stood up, hurt by the hint for me to leave. The man was short with blue-toned cheeks and soft, long-lashed eyes. Eddy didn't introduce us.

"He's handsome," the guy said and winked at me, but Eddy stood up, too, and said, "Well, Floyd. I'll see you!"

"Oh, your younger brother?" another voice said. I turned and saw a dark-haired man with a smooth, pink face and dark eyes step out from behind the cash register. He crossed over to us with short, almost feminine steps.

"Yesss, he is handsome," he said and blinked his eyes at me. Eddy stepped between them, went to the door and opened it with the tinkle of the bell.

"You better get going, Floyd, to beat the bridge commute traffic." Before I could answer that I was riding the A train and didn't have to worry about the traffic, he said, "If something comes up, I'll call you. But don't count on it. You should ask Dad to let you work in the restaurant, if you want to earn enough money to support your family."

"Oh, he has a wife and baby?" the dark-haired guy said.

"Yes," Eddy said. "See you soon, Floyd."

"Sure, Eddy," I said and stepped out.

10

I took Velva's hand and helped her off the bus at the brightly lighted intersection of Fourteenth and Broadway in the center of downtown Oakland. We were going to see my father at the restaurant in the evening, after dinner hours, when I hoped there wouldn't be many people around and I could talk to him without interruptions. When I got back from San Francisco, I told Velva what happened at Eddy's pharmacy. She said I shouldn't get discouraged, but we should go see my dad after we ate. So there we were.

Still in my dark blue sportcoat and blue slacks, white sportshirt, I hunched my shoulders at the chilled air that swept up over the city. I looked down Fourteenth Street to see if I could spot the library where I'd worked only a few months before. I felt a twinge of regret that I'd lost my job there. I knew now how valuable it was, how it made my life work.

But it was too late now, I thought, and I grabbed Velva's hand and started heading north up Broadway for Nineteenth and my father's restaurant, El Patio, in the middle of the business district.

As I walked on the outside with her on the inner, higher slope of the sidewalk, she looked taller than me, though we were exactly the same size. I still felt uncomfortable walking with a pregnant woman because everybody looked at us and thought I looked too young to be an expectant father. But when she turned her face to me and smiled, her eyes such deep blue wells of beauty, my heart turned with feeling for her.

Here she was with me, trying to help me earn money for us. For all the work and suffering, I was lucky to have her and knew it. I wasn't lonely for the love of a woman, anymore, like I'd been lonely for the five long years since my mother had died. But I didn't want her to be disappointed, if nothing came of it. I almost wished she weren't with me for that reason. Still, I had to try and get a job.

Once past Fourteenth Street, I could see a good half mile down the wide, bright street of Broadway, with its fancy stores, theaters and broad sidewalks busy with people. I started to hurry so I could talk to my father right away. It had gotten chillier, too, and I wished I'd worn an overcoat. But we walked fast and soon covered the five short blocks to Nineteenth, where we stopped in front of the all-night drugstore and looked across the street, down a half a block to Dad's restaurant. I felt a surge of pride.

200   ⊖   ⊖   ⊖   ⊖   ⊖   ⊖   ⊖   *Floyd Salas*

The El Patio was a fancy place right across the street from the Mardis Gras, a big nightclub owned by one of Al's acquaintances. It was only a half block from the Leamington Hotel, the most expensive downtown hotel, where Al T. stayed. All the best men's and women's stores were in this neighborhood. My father was well-known among the business people in the area and was once written up in an entertainment sheet that came out monthly. On weekends, he'd wear a red cummerbund and black tuxedo trousers and would charm all the customers. Dolores, although she looked pretty in her Mexican folk costume, stayed in the back mostly, running the kitchen. I hoped she was back there now.

Velva squeezed my hand when we crossed Nineteenth Street. We walked past the front of the restaurant and saw that there were only a couple of customers still eating this late at night, after nine. I couldn't see my father. I opened the door and stepped in. I didn't see Dolores, either. That helped a little bit. Marguerite, the waitress, looked up from behind the counter at us with her green eyes and smiled. I nodded hello, pleased that we'd timed it just right, at the end of the dinner hour.

"Is Dad around?" I asked.

"He went to speak with some businessman about opening another restaurant. But he said he'd be right back. He's been gone a half hour already. Sit down and wait for him."

"Okay. How about a couple of 7UPs?"

"Sure," she said and slid the cover of a Coke box cooler back, plucked two 7UP bottles out and opened them. Then she took two glasses from a shelf and walked down the counter and slid them across to us. I thanked her and went to sit at an empty table by the window, with my back to the counter and the kitchen and facing Nineteenth and Broadway so I could see my father coming. Velva sat on the inside of the table next to me. Then I remembered that I should pay, so Dolores wouldn't get angry. I stood up, went back to the cash register and left thirty cents on the rubber mat next to it. I caught Marguerite's eye and pointed at the coins.

She smiled and nodded her head, but didn't bother to stop wiping glasses, so they could close by ten. I went back to the table and sat next to Velva to wait. I poured the 7UP into my glass and watched it fizz, then took a sip and set the glass down, swallowing the sweet liquid very slowly, turning the glass in circles, feeling like I was turning in circles, wondering what to do next, wondering if I could get along with Dolores, if my father would let me work there. I knew she'd do nothing but find fault, and I might end up causing trouble between my father and her. I took another sip of liquid, put the glass down and said, "Maybe I should just ask Dad for help finding a job someplace else, Velva? That way I wouldn't interfere with his life. He's got connections. He could help me."

She started to answer me, but when I sat up, thinking I saw him in the crowd across the street from the drugstore, she turned to look out the window, too.

A streetcar, whining and clanging across Nineteenth Street, blocked the view. I twisted in my seat to see better after it passed, when I glimpsed a flash of something flying up at my side. I turned and saw Dolores smashing a broom down on my head with a thud, just as the streetcar clanged noisily down Broadway out of sight.

I was so startled, I didn't even duck when she lifted the broom and brought it down again, hitting me right in the middle of the head this time, stunning me, making everything blur in front of me for a moment. But, as if in a dream, I reached up and knocked the next blow away, and saw her standing there with gritted teeth, a mumble of Mexican curses hissing out of her mouth so fast that I could only guess what she was saying, but knew that she hated me and wanted me out.

I stood up and, trying to keep my dignity, batted down another awkward blow with my right hand. Then, checking to see if Velva was following me, turned toward the door and walked with my left hand held up to ward off any more blows.

Dolores kept following me, still holding up the broom, still cursing at me. I held open the door for Velva, then backed out to her hisses, and saw Marguerite staring at me with her mouth open and her hand half-raised, holding an empty glass.

11

"Don't do it! Don't do it! I don't want you to fight pro!" Velva said, trying to grab my hand as I started across San Pablo at Eighteenth, heading for the Knotty Pine. But though the thump on my head from Dolores' broom still hurt a little, it didn't hurt near as much as my feelings. I saw Al in the streetlight just walking toward the side door of the Knotty Pine on Eighteenth Street and I ran to catch him before he went in, dashing in front of a big, fancy black Buick, clearing it with plenty of room and skipping up onto the sidewalk. "Al! Hey, Al!" I called.

Al stopped outside the door to wait for me, but I had to wait on the corner for Velva to cross San Pablo, too. When I finally walked up to him, he had a tight, peeved mouth as if he didn't want to be bothered.

"What's up?" he asked, standing just outside the door. I could see blue light shining through the narrow foot-high window.

"Dolores just hit me on the head with a broom!" I said, making it sound dramatic to justify bothering him.

"What?" Al said and looked at Velva.

"She did," Velva said.

"Just now," I said.

"What'd Dad say?" Al asked, leaning forward as if to hear better.

"He wasn't there. I was waiting for him to ... "

"Awww, that's why she did it. What'd you go there for, anyway? You know she doesn't like us around. You gave her a chance to take it out on you."

"I went there to get a job. I went to ask him to help me, maybe hire me at the restaurant." I waited for that to sink in, then said, "I went to see Eddy, too, today ... "

Al's eyes went hard and glassy in the streetlight at the mention of Eddy's name, and I said, "I need a job. I don't earn enough money on that salesman's job to support Velva and me."

"Get it, then," Al said and turned and reached out to grab the door knob.

"I've been trying. But I need help. That's why I went to see Dad. That's why I'm here to see you."

"How can I help you?" he said, still holding onto the door knob.

Glancing at Velva, I said, "Turn me pro, Al. Make a fighter out of me and we'll earn some big money together. I need to earn good money to be able to take care of Velva and the baby."

Al looked at Velva, but she shook her head from side to side.

"How about it, Al?" I said.

He shook his head, too, but let go of the door knob.

"Fighting pro is a hard life, Floyd. You gotta have a lot of drive. You gotta really want it. I must have never really wanted it or I would've kept driving. If I'd have kept it up, you probably would've, too. But I don't think you really want to fight as much as find a way out of your problems. And it takes years to make money at boxing. I've never made it." His mouth was thin and tight.

"And I don't want to train you, either. I'm not into it. I've got to earn money right away, too. Right now! Go call up the Old Man on the phone and ask him that way."

"I could never work in the restaurant with Dolores there, now, Al!"

"Go work with Eddy, then," he said and turned and reached out for the door knob again.

"I already tried that, today! He said he can't afford to pay me enough to take care of Velva," I said and didn't mention the two gay-looking guys.

He looked over his shoulder at me. "Well, then, tell Dad to help you get a job with Uncle Johnny out in Hayward. He's got a big construction company going. It's a long way every morning, but it's a job."

"Aaaaw, Al. I don't have a car and it's forty-miles round trip, not like catching an A train for a half hour to San Francisco. It's impractical."

Al sucked air in through his tight lips again and said, "I don't know what to do for you, then. That's all I can say."

He pushed open the side door to the Knotty Pine and stepped in, leaving the door open behind him just as the band began to play. I stood there in the doorway and watched as he stepped up to the bar. Velva stepped next to me to look in, too, just as the blue wail of Johnny Cappolo's trumpet seemed to vibrate the very air inside.

I was transfixed and couldn't move away. The sheer high cry seemed to ripple with a blue glow through every cocktail glass on the bar. Pink Lady, the bartender's wife, lifted her face to watch Cappolo. Sequins scaled her white, form-fitting dress. She looked beautiful in the blue light. Al's brow looked bullet-shaped and burned a sullen blue in the light from the stars on the ceiling. His thick upper lip curled like a cupid's bow. Al T. sat with a satisfied smile on his fat cheeks, his skin sleek and oily, the dark shadows under his eyes giving him a sage's look, like a round Buddha. I saw Curly look over at me with tweezer-tip points to his thick mustache and devil tufts to his thick eyebrows. Only the thickness of his face, the residue of alcohol in the cheeks, filling up the hollows under the high cheekbones, kept the look of Lucifer off it. Big Press stood at the bar on the other side of Al, his loafer jacket looking a mile wide across the chest and shoulders, his big face shaped short and clean.

Keeping my foot in the door so nobody would close it, I pulled Velva close and felt a thrill fill me when Johnny Cappolo blew redhot quick and high with the first short riff of "Gin for Christmas" by Lionel Hampton. The belled lip of his silver horn shimmered quicksilver as he raised up, frog-cheeked with puffed air, and blew for a short riff, then slid his horn away. He seemed to hum with his cherry-red lips, then unbuttoned his double-breasted suit coat and let it flap open as the tenor sax came growling in.

Gutty Walt Lowe, a handsome guy, lean like a track star, came on with a funky solo. He was a white boy who could play boll-weevil blues by way of Chi and Fifty-Second Street, Bop City in San Francisco. Then Johnny Marabuto tinkled down the keyboard of his piano like a mountain stream and Tall Keith hummed up high on his bass and handed it over to Happy Van Sickle, who thump-thump-thumped a pop-pop-popping melody in percussive phrase, until the whole band picked it up and blew into a final chorus. When they stopped with a "Da-da, da-da, da-da, dum!" and the nightclub burst into a crescendo of clapping. I felt so good I pulled Velva into the club and up to Al.

Then, as soon as the clapping died down, I said, "Al! Let me work with you and Al T. Turn me out on the strap with you. It's the same as selling, just like I've been doing, except you can make good money, which I can't do door to door."

"Turn you out with me?" Al said, facing me. But he stopped with his mouth open when Velva spun around and ran out the door.

"Velva!" I called, running after her. "Velva!"

But she hurried down Eighteenth Street toward her mother's house without turning around.

12

There was a thump of footsteps down the carpeted stairs when I pressed the doorbell of Velva's mother's house again. I held my breath until the doorknob turned. Then the lock clicked and I breathed again when Velva stuck her head around the edge of the door and said, "It's almost eleven, Floyd. Don't wake Mom up."

"Why did you leave me? Just because I asked to work with Al?" In the faint glow of the high street light at the corner I was barely able to make out her features with her face still back in the shadow of the darkened hall. I could see she had on a silken robe.

"Shhhh," she said, putting a finger to her lips. "Don't wake Mom. She's been drinking and she might cause a scene."

"All I wanted to do was make some money and take care of us."

"Not so loud," she said. "Mom's been drinking."

"Get your clothes on and come home with me."

"Why'd you take so long to come and get me?"

"I still have to earn money, even if you don't like it. So, I asked Al if I could work with him."

"It seemed more like you liked the fancy place and the pretty woman at the bar," she said.

"Yeeeah, I liked the scene. It's better than pounding those sidewalks for pennies. And Eddy and Dad let me down. Why shouldn't I ask Al? He's my brother, too," I said, still angry at her. But then I lowered my voice, "Come home with me, Velva."

"I can't." Her face was an ashen mask in the shadow.

"Why not?" I asked, my voice tight again as I stood stiffly on the porch in front of her.

"We're not happy together," she said and stopped with her mouth still open, as if she wanted to say more.

"It's only because I don't have a good job. Because you're pregnant and we don't have enough money. That's why I wanted to work with Al and have enough money to have some fun on, too. Why shouldn't we be able to have some fun?"

"Shhhh," she said and touched her lips with her finger again, then stepped outside on the porch and shut the door nearly closed behind her. I slipped my arms around her in the silken robe and pulled her to me, felt her swollen belly against me, and tried to kiss her. But she turned her head away and held onto the doorknob.

"Don't, Floyd," she said and pushed me back with one hand. "I left because I don't like what they might make of you. I don't care how much money they've got, whether they drive Cadillacs or own nightclubs. I don't want you to be that way. I don't want you to be like Al. I see only trouble ahead, if you work with him. Whether they call it gambling or stealing, whether it's legal or not, whether they get away with it or not, I don't like their slick life." She shook her head at me as if she couldn't believe I couldn't see it.

"I want you to be like Eddy and your father, somebody people can respect."

"Come home with me, Velva," I said, really wanting her now.

"I can't."

"I've worked hard, Velva, I've really tried."

She nodded just once, slightly, and my hopes rose. But she said, "I'm too unhappy right now, Floyd. I'm going to stay here and have my baby and raise it myself. I want something worthwhile in life. I don't want to end up like Tommy, having kids all the time, always unhappy because you're uptown running around with Al. And I don't want to end up like my mother, either, divorced and still trying to have a good time while she's still even a little bit young. She played around a lot and now she's older and doesn't have anything, not even a husband. Ronnie's left her. That's why she's on a drinking binge again."

She looked off toward the light pole on the corner to avoid my eyes. I thought of how I revered the memory of my mother and I suddenly felt sorry for Velva.

"They, her and her sister, my aunt and her husband, my uncle, didn't stop drinking until my aunt got sick with TB. And now that she's an invalid, my mother goes out and gets drunk with somebody else, like she's still a young girl. Then tries to act like a respectable mother when she's home with me. She goes on periodical drunks every time her boyfriend leaves her, and I have to nurse her back to health, like right now. You haven't seen that. She already needs my help. So, it's that, too."

She turned full face to me, looking sad but beautiful.

"And my uncle wouldn't go to college and be a doctor like his father when he was young and ended up traveling from town to town, working in restaurants during the Depression, and didn't settle down until my aunt got sick. And now he coughs and coughs all day from all the running around they did, the drinking and smoking ... I don't want that, Floyd. That's the kind of life they lead at that Knotty Pine. I don't want it for you, either. That's why I walked off."

"But I can't work with Eddy and I can't work with Dad."

"Keep selling, then," she said.

"It's like digging a hole for my grave. I can't even support myself on the money I earn, let alone you and a baby. And I don't like it, either. I'll try to get another job," I said, leaning back from her, but still keeping her belly pressed against me. "And I'll go see Dad again tomorrow and ask him if he can help me get a job. If he does, will you come back to me?"

"We'll see, Floyd."

"Don't you believe me?"

"I believe you can do anything you want. You're the smartest boy I know. But I don't want to live with you now. We're too unhappy. It's too hard. I'm going to stay here with Mom until I have the baby. Then I'll go back to work full-time."

I winced. She had just said no.

"I don't know if I can depend upon you right now. You're too upset over everything that's happened. And you admire Al so much. He's changing for the worst, and I'm afraid you will, too. I don't want you to be flashy like that Knotty Pine crowd."

Shaking my head, my chest tight with my bitterness, I said, "Don't you love me, anymore?"

My stomach tightened into a fist when she answered, "I don't know."

I dropped my hands and turned and stepped down the short stairway, wanting her to call me back. She didn't, and I started walking up the sidewalk toward the Knotty Pine until I heard her call, "Floyd!" I stopped and turned around to see her standing out on the edge of the porch.

Stepping back, I stopped at the foot of the stairs and kept my hands at my sides, my chest swelling with the urge to cry. I wanted her to say she loved me and wanted to go with me.

"I need time, Floyd," she said. "I got pregnant, then you got fired, then I got laid off and ... you can't take care of us and now my mother's drunk. She'll keep drinking and maybe kill herself, unless I stay with her."

Suddenly, she threw her hands up so the sleeves of the silken robe billowed down from her elbows in big, hollow folds. "When I came home, a man was laying on the couch and ... " She shook her head, then squinted as if she might cry. "He wouldn't leave until I told Mom I was going to call Unkie. Then she had to drag him out the door by his arm!"

Her eyes glistened with tears. "I'm really confused. I've got to help her now, and then help myself. I need time away from you to think. I can't go with you. I've got to stay here."

"Could I stay with you?" I asked. She shook her head. "I don't think it would be good if you stayed. You couldn't stand it. The front room is littered with beer cans. I'll have to clean them up tomorrow. She already looks like a hag. She'll look like a zombie by the time it's over. No, you can't stay."

I stepped up the stairs and reached out for her, but she pulled her hands away from me. I asked again, "Do you love me?"

She made me catch my breath when she lowered her eyes, hid them with her wide, creamy lids, and didn't answer. Finally, she said, "I need time, Floyd. If I tell you I love you, you'll want me to go home with you, and I can't. I need time, Floyd. Give me some time."

"You don't love me, then," I said.

"I need time, Floyd."

13

"So this is where you hang out, huh?" Dad said, eyeing me from under the brim of his beige Stetson, a cowboy dress hat which, with his brown, doublebreasted suit, shirt and tie, made him look like a Texas oil millionaire. He turned his head in a wide scan of the Broadway Bowl pool room. The bright green tables stood out new and clean under the bright fluorescent lights on the ceiling. Men and women played at the tables. The cocktail waitress swayed into the big room from the bar in her black slacks. The muffled crash of falling pins carried into the room from the bowling alley.

"For a while, Dad," I said, guessing he came to see me because Marguerite had told him that Dolores hit me on the head with a broom and that Velva told him where he could find me. I couldn't suppress a tight feeling of resentment that I couldn't work with him because of that crazy bitch Dolores.

I'd been hanging out at the Bowl since I saw Jack Fernandes at the Doggie Diner that same night I left Velva at her mother's. He brought me down to the Bowl to teach me how to play pool. I hadn't gone to see Dad again or gone back to my sales job. I was tired of being rejected by everybody. I wasn't going to kiss anybody's ass anymore. Yet, I missed Velva.

"Play a game of pool? Can you play pool?"

"A little. I just started learning this last month after I quit selling crucifixes."

"You quit that?" he said and took a cue stick down from the wall. He smiled and nodded hello to the small group of guys seated in chairs against the wall, then switched the cue stick to his left hand and reached out and shook hands with Jack Fernandes.

Jack looked like he stepped out of a magazine ad in his white shirt and knit tie, perfectly pressed sport coat, creased slacks and highly polished shoes. His smooth, sallow Portuguese-American face didn't have a bristle on it.

"Yeah, I quit. I couldn't make enough money, so I quit," I said and paused, swallowed and tried to keep the resentment out of my voice, but didn't tell him why.

"I see, Sonny Boy," he said and chalked his cue. I rolled the cue ball down to the other end so he could break, then took the rack off the balls and waited. I had to smile when he squinted one eye under the hat brim to take aim, made a snappy draw and a good, smashing break and knocked in a striped ball.

"You've done a little hanging around pool halls, too, huh, Dad?" I said, and all the guys against the wall grinned.

"I've played a little on my wanderings," he said and smiled as he leaned down to aim again. "Been in every state in the Union, buddy. After my father died in the 1918 flu epidemic, I walked off the farm and traveled all over America, working in mines in the twenties and in tunnels and dams in the thirties. I always had a dollar in my pocket."

He stopped talking, concentrated, with his belly resting against the edge of the table, then shot and made another striped ball, the thirteen into a side pocket. He then stood and chalked his stick and said, "I used to keep a twenty dollar bill hidden on the inside of my shoes when I hit the rails in the Depression. That's when you were a little boy, not too long ago. I couldn't take my family with me anymore, like I used to when I was making big money mine-contracting in the twenties."

He leaned down to aim, but lifted his head and said, "I came out to California to see if there was any work. Me and a couple of guys hadn't eaten in two days once because we didn't want to get off until the train reached California. Then it stopped in Southern California and hooked some new cars on. We smelled some oranges on a fruit car and took a whole day to break into it only to find that there weren't any oranges in there at all, only lemons. But we were so damn hungry, we ate all the lemons we could stand and then had stomach aches and the runs for two more days."

He leaned down and squinted as all the guys laughed. I was really proud of him. He looked handsome and successful in his Texas hat and double-breasted suit. But before he shot, he straightened up and said, "Here! Before I forget!" and took his wallet out of his back pocket, opened it and pulled out a ten dollar bill and handed it to me. He then winked at Jack and the other guys, who were all staring. He put the wallet back, then leaned down to aim again. But he glanced up at me, past the brim of his Stetson, and said, "I'll help you out if you need it. Maybe I can get you a job with your Uncle John or your brother Eddy. And if you need money until then, come and see me for a couple of bucks on the side, but call first! So I can be sure and be there!"

My chest ached inside. I knew then for sure that he knew she'd hit me. "Thanks, Dad," I said.

"One more thing! I'm buying a house for you and Al and your wives! You can live in it together!"

He grinned at me. I thought of Velva leaving me and that it was too late already, way too late. Everything he was offering me was too late, but I made myself grin back to thank him and really chuckled when he made another ball. All the guys against the wall snorted and laughed at the way he was running the table. Then, when he lifted up, still grinning, his smile bright and winning with his mustache and white teeth, I knew I wouldn't bring up Dolores, either—ever. I wouldn't ask him any embarrassing questions about a job, at all. And maybe I would and maybe I wouldn't tell him that Velva had left me, that she didn't plan to come back to me. How could I move into that house for me and my wife when I didn't have a wife?

14

Jack Fernandes suddenly stepped across the sidewalk from Compton's Donut Shop, out of the bright glow of the window, and almost sprinted across the sidewalk to the tree in the planter box by the curb. I couldn't believe it. We'd rehearsed the whole thing twice. He was supposed to stay where he was and approach the mooch and me out in the open, so the mooch wouldn't get suspicious.

The mooch was an old guy in his thirties, for sure, lines around his sunken eyes from drinking, like an enlisted man. He was a country boy. I could tell by his plain-toed black shoes and the sailor way he wore a wide-collared sport shirt open over the lapel of a dressy, double-breasted, shiny gray suit that called for a tie. I'd picked him up just after nightfall at the Greyhound Bus Station on Twentieth and San Pablo. I told him I was a merchant seaman from New Orleans, since the guy said he came from Louisiana, and asked him if he wanted to walk around town and pass the time till his bus came. We stopped at Spaghetti Joe's on Seventeenth and San Pablo. I had a Coke and the guy had a beer next to the steam-misted front window. We talked about getting girls. I'd told him how I got one from a guy downtown the night before and the mooch said he could go for one tonight himself. He said that, if I wanted, we could get a room in the hotel across the street from the Greyhound and he'd pay for it.

I didn't know now how to take that, and I looked quickly into the guy's eyes, but he didn't flinch. Then, on my suggestion, we walked down dark San Pablo Avenue to Thirteenth and Broadway, where Jack was waiting for us.

I'd invented the whole game after Dad told me about buying Al and me a house. I got the idea that if I could make enough money to carry Velva and me for a while, I might be able to talk her into coming back to live in the house Dad had bought for us. I still had money in the bank, six hundred dollars, but that was to pay for the baby and I couldn't touch it. But if I doubled this ten, then I could double that and double that twenty and double that, too. I would work at hustling every day, the same way I had worked at selling door to door, until I earned enough money to get her back. That's what I wanted to do.

That's what made me think up this game. It was "survival of the fittest" and I was going to survive, my way, without anybody's help, not Al's, nor Eddy's, nor Dad's.

I gave myself a mental kick in the butt, though, for not telling Jack exactly where to stand. Yet, he could still approach us from the curbside of the wide sidewalk as well as from Compton's, so it wasn't too bad. But we didn't get more than ten feet closer to him, when Jack turned and hurried down to the corner and stopped, as if waiting for a traffic light. I figured he was going to wait and approach us on the corner there. But we barely got to the corner, when Jack took off across the dark street again.

"Goddammit!" I cursed under my breath.

"What?" the mooch said, wrinkling his high forehead.

"I think that's the guy," I said, and pointed at Jack's back as he hurried across Thirteenth Street and stopped on the corner by the blind man's news stand and glanced back at us.

He looked slick with his stiff hair pomaded down, his sallow, almost yellow complexion and his nearly slanted eyes and smooth face. But he wasn't slick. As soon as we got halfway across Thirteenth, he took off again across Broadway, against a red light, cutting from the corner in front of the Walgreens towards Foster's Cafeteria, with windows all around it all lit up like a fishbowl, the worst possible place to approach us.

"He must not have seen you," the mooch said.

"I guess not," I said. I stopped on the corner next to the blind man's newstand and waited to see what Jack was going to do. I hoped I wouldn't see anybody else I knew, for fear they'd say hello to me and I'd just have to snub them.

Jack stopped on the busy corner under the corner street light in front of Foster's. He looked back at me and the mooch and then, as if afraid we'd seen him, turned and pushed through the glass doors of Foster's and headed back through the tables next to the wall of windows which looked out onto Thirteenth Street and the line of yellow cabs there. I lost sight of him in the flow of people inside. I hoped to God he'd headed down to the men's room in the basement at the bottom of the stairs that were set in the back wall of the cafeteria.

"Come on, let's see if we can get him," I said and cut across Broadway before the light turned green. I was afraid I'd lose Jack for sure if he didn't go into the men's room, wondering when the mooch was going to get wise. I couldn't believe what Jack was doing. We'd gone over the whole thing in detail. It was a version of the old Murphy Game that Big Press had told me the colored guys did down in West Oakland: get a guy who wants a girl, then put the rest of his money in an envelope and hold it for him, then take

off. But that's for the guys who go down there already looking for a girl. I
was going to go get a guy and talk him into looking for a girl. I'd talked this
guy into getting a girl and was going to use the ten dollar bill my father had
given me that afternoon to pay Jack for getting us a girl and get the guy to
pay him for one, too. Double my money that way, and split the difference
with Jack. I told Jack my plan after all the other guys at the Broadway Bowl
went home to eat. We bought a Doggie Diner hamburger and a root beer
apiece.

I pushed the glass door back and stepped into Foster's, then headed for
the stairs in the back wall. "I think he went back there," I said and walked
quickly past the tables, filled with people eating, to the clatter of trays, the
ring of the cash register, the hum of the traffic from the downtown streets.
I remembered that Velva said she was afraid I'd go to jail if I hung around
with Al. How shocked she'd be to see me now, as I led the mooch down the
cement stairs to the men's room, totally lined in yellow enamel tile. I spotted
Jack at the long floor urinal. I held my breath, afraid of what he might do
now.

"Say," I said and stopped at the long urinal next to him and unzipped my
pants. "Aren't you the guy who got the girl for me last night?"

"Yeah," Jack said, looking sidewards at me as he pissed into the urinal,
pretending he didn't see the mooch, who was on the other side of me using
the urinal, too. I waited for him to act like a pimp and ask if I wanted another
girl, but he just looked at me. Up close, I could see the faint imprint of dark
freckles across his nose. But he just shook his dick, stuffed it back in his
pants and started to turn away without saying anything.

"Can you get us a girl?" I asked, stopping my piss and zipping up.

Jack stopped, looked at me, then at the mooch, and finally said, "Sure."
But he just stood there staring at me without saying anything else.

"How much?" I asked, putting my hand in my front pocket.

"Uh ... "

"Ten dollars apiece?" I said, afraid I was pushing too hard and worried
that the mooch was going to get wise now. I had slightly over ten dollars in
my pocket and should have bought some fake money at Kress's, like Press
said Al T. did, so I could pretend I was giving Jack more money and he could
ask for more money.

"Uh ... " Jack uttered, and I stuck the bill out in front of him to make
him take it while we still had a chance to pull it off.

"Yeah, ten dollars," he said and finally reached out to take the bill. When
I held onto it and stared at him, he added, "Each!"

I let go and he then held out his hand to the mooch, who stuck his hand
in his pocket and pulled out a small wad of bills. He gave Jack a ten spot,

too.

We both waited as Jack put the bills in his pocket and stared at us without saying anything again.

"Should we go to the St. Mark's hotel like last night and take the elevator to room 505 again? One at a time?" I finally said.

"Yeah," Jack said and, finally getting into the act, added, "You come up first, then he comes up five minutes later. I'll have a girl for each of you. Give me five minutes to get up there and tell the girls you're coming."

"Okay, we'll be there," I said, able to breathe freely again. Jack headed out the door with the money. I nodded at the mooch and smiled, but caught my breath when Al and Big Press walked in the door.

15

"He was going to school, is all, Al," Al T. said, rattling the ice in his scotch as he sat on the edge of the big Hollywood bed in the bedroom above the club. "Your little brother's a natural, from what Big Press says."

"He did okay for a pure novice," Al said and nodded. His big shoulders seemed hunched as if to cradle his big head.

Everyone but me and Jack was drinking scotch from a bottle sitting on the small bar in front of the green drapes. Downstairs the club was dark, the neon sign outside turned off.

"He proved he's got some hustler in him, that's for sure. He made up his own game and had the guts to go pick up a guy on his own like that." Al turned to me. "Bet you learned that by being a door to door salesman!"

"Maybe." I shrugged my shoulders. "Probably."

The narrow scar under Al's eyebrow was as transparent as a fishscale, making it look like he was squinting. He nodded, but said, "Press saw you walk by with the mooch and we followed you. It looked more like Jack was playing hide and seek with you at first."

"No matter what the other kid there did," Al T. said, tipping his glass at me, "Floyd did damn good for a beginner, Al. How many guys you know, without any hustling experience at all, can make up their own game, huh?"

"Not many," Curly said. "The kid could be a highclass pimp with that kind of imagination."

"You want to be a pimp, Floyd?" Al said.

I looked at my brother, then at Curly, who sat there in an expensive brown suede coat. "I wouldn't mind being a pimp, if I could make lots of money and have my wife, too."

"See!" Curley said. "The guy's got sense. That's class, see! He could be a highroller, a first-class conman, end up with his own joint, too. Sooner than me, maybe in a couple of years when he's only twenty-one and barely old enough to even go into a bar. That's what I mean."

"The kid's got more class than me," Al T. said.

"Al said *you've* got a lot of class, Al T.," I said.

"What I mean is, you're conservative, like Curly," Al T. said. "You'll end up with something in the bank, like Curly. He's only thirty-four and he lives like a rich man and has his own nightclub and belongs to the Chamber of Commerce. But he still has a whole stable of whores he never risks his freedom for. Because he saves his gold, he doesn't just party like me!" He jabbed his thumb at himself.

"I make about a grand a week, when the average wage is only fifty bucks. But I blow it week after week. I have to start some days without the price of a cup of coffee. That's how I met Al. He lent me five bucks one hungover morning I came into the Knotty Pine without enough money for a beer. And sometimes I get into real rumbles, too. They busted me for vagrancy at the Leamington when I had a couple grand in my pocket. Got me as a transient without any visible means of support. Kept me seventy-two hours, too. And if the mooch hadn't gotten cold feet and caught the bus out, they'd of had a case against me."

Staring at him sitting there in an expensive blue loafer jacket and slacks, blue silk sport shirt, gold watch, dark circles under his eyes from too much scotch and easy living, it didn't seem like it could be true.

"I can barely write my name," Al T. continued. "Did you know that? If I had an education, I wouldn't be conning at all. Or, if I did, it would be on a real high level, like a big businessman, and I wouldn't be risking any long stretches in the can for it, either," he said.

Curly nodded and said, "If there's one thing I hate, it's when some straight sonofabitch looks down on me in some bank just because of the bar business I'm in. ... When it's those really big businessmen like Kaiser and Knowland who are the really big thieves in this town."

I thought of how I didn't like the slick way he dressed the first time I met him. I felt badly about it when he said, "The only thing that saved me is I had a chance to earn all that money during the war, when it was all around to grab, and then I put it into something solid, my nightclub."

"You made it and saved it, though," I said. "I could do the same. Then I could take care of my wife and kid, without having to worry. That's what I want."

"I bet you could do both, save it and take care of them, too," Curly said. He took a sip of his scotch and said. "You know why this street San Pablo is great? Because it's a debarkation point for all the discharged servicemen coming back with war bonuses from Japan. All landing on this street before they head home. It's loaded with bus and train depots, from Fortieth and San Pablo down to Third and Broadway. And all the hustlers come from all over the country to work it and hang out right here in this bar. There's great bunco men here, with Al T. at the top of the list. There's Earl and Speedy, my brother. My brother, Roy, and his stable of whores. Bob Monzo and his brother. Top petty thieves like Big Press. There must be twenty guys working this street and hanging out here. I bet more than a few grand a day gets taken off the street, counting all the different kinds of hustle that I personally know of. This is a great place to turn out for a young guy with talent like you, Floyd. Take advantage of it. When the occupation ends in Japan, the street will dry up. Don't pass up any chances to turn out with sharp guys."

I looked from him to Al T., then my brother caught my eye. He was sipping a highball of scotch and water. There was a blue glow on his cheekbones from the low lamp and a tremor of emotion in his voice when he said, "I'm going to turn my brother out on the strap game myself, with Big Press and me, since you've got a full team already, Al T. That way I can keep my eye on him."

He winked at me and I smiled and so did everybody else in the room but Jack.

16

Nearly all the benches of the Greyhound Bus Station were filled, bags and bundles were everywhere. The hum of bus motors filled the bus station like background music. I put my hands in my pockets and looked around, making the neat shape of the gray flannel sportcoat pockets bulge out a little. It was the only flaw in the clean, quiet, tasteful appearance of my dark gray flannel slacks, dark blue gaucho and wing-tipped cordovan shoes.

There had to be somebody I could make money from in the place. Now was my chance to make big money. I needed money, money I could go and get Velva back with. If I could show her some money and tell her about the house Dad was going to buy for us, she might come back. I had to do it, just like I had to sell crucifixes and lamps. I had to do it. Yet I was proud, too. I'd done my own thing and made Al respect me. And now I was getting a chance to work with him and make some good money. It was now going to pay off.

I stopped by a rag-snapping shoeshine boy. Black, bald and bespectacled, he was wisecracking with a couple of white sailors. I heard him say, "So you boys at Treasure Island!" and I moved off into the waiting room with the long lines of travelers stretching back from the loading doors. Al said it had to be a stranger just passing through on his way out of town.

I walked through the center of the waiting room, past the baggage check, almost kicking the long legs of a black guy in sun glasses who was stretched out on a bench with his eyes closed, sleeping. I stopped to let a lame girl come sliding by me in leg braces and metal canes, "Shhhhh, shhhhh, shhhhh."

I looked over a long line of bus riders, all burdened with suitcases and boxes. There were lots of servicemen, pea-coated sailors with sea bags, four or five soldiers and a ten-gallon hatted cowboy with brand new, fancy-stitched boots of yellow hide. But they were already in line and ready to leave. No chance there.

The electric burr of the dispatcher's voice sounded: "Bus 407 from San Jose arriving at Door One!" The roar of a bus engine and the sigh of airbrakes obliterated the faint tune from a jukebox in the bar. I moved over to the pinball machine, where I saw two sailors playing, and caught a strain of Nat Cole singing, "They tried / to tell uuus / we're tooo younnnnng."

219

The sailor and his buddy laughed. Their skinned heads both bobbed around to glance at me, then turned back to their game. They changed places and one put a nickel in the machine and it lit up again. The ball rattled and the score started popping on the board. They stared up at it, much too occupied to cut in on. I stepped past, then stopped at the sight of a big marine standing by a magazine rack with his skin-bumped head stuck in the pages of a magazine with orange-tinted nudes on its cover. His sandy-colored sideburns prickled down from his olive green military cap. Alone and wasting time. Perfect. I moved past a couple of people in front of the bright paper covers and stopped next to the Marine and said, "Those are some wild shots there!" and stared the guy in the face.

He was a big, clumsy, red-faced, clodhopper kid, built heavy as a full-back, with a bull-sized neck like a middle-aged man, puffy cheeks and wiry hairs on his puffy hands, and dimples where his knuckles were.

"You bet!" he said and poked a blunt finger into the crotch of the girl with the spread legs on the page. His voice trickled out of his mouth in spurts, "Haven't had ... any stuff ... that wasn't ... sideways ... in the three years I been in Japan."

Perfect. I grinned because I felt so good but he grinned because he thought I thought it was funny. I was a salesman again, doing what I did with those crucifixes. Ready to sell him my game.

"I got some last night, after I got in," I said. "Just got off a merchant ship with seven-fifty. Going home. What's your name?"

"Ev-vurt," he said. "Yeaah, I got three-hun'red in traveler's checks and ... a hun'red dollars in cash, plus ... mah bus ticket home."

"Where to?" I asked, right away, closing in.

"I-o-way," the Marine said, then cocked his head back and stared at me from pink-rimmed eyes and clamped his mouth shut and stared back at the nude. There was something stubborn in his thin, tight lips.

"I'm George from Denver. I ship out in the Merchant Marines," I said, changing the subject. "I've got a couple of hours to kill. When's your bus come? Like to take a walk downtown and get a cup of coffee?"

The Marine glanced at me from between the pink rims of his little eyes, then blinked, slapped the magazine shut, dropped it onto a crooked stack of them and said, "Sure, buddy. I got an hour or so. Let's go."

I felt like I might make a sale finally and led him out of the wide lobby into the hallway where they sold tickets, past two lines of people waiting to buy tickets and out onto the street. I hesitated at the sight of Big Press standing right outside by the cab stand in his big brown loafer jacket and slacks.

"Hi, George! Good to see you!" he said.

I said hi back, just in case, but I wondered if Al had changed the plan and didn't want to take any chances with me because I was so new at the game. Big Press was supposed to tail, not get into the play.

"He got drunk with me last night. We got some girls," I said to the Marine, meeting his pink-rimmed little eyes, and kept walking down the avenue with Big Press on the other side of the Marine as if just enjoying the walk. I tried to keep the talk going, but not talk too much myself. When we walked right past the Knotty Pine, I was sure Al was watching from inside. I kept in step with the big men, even skipping a couple of times to do it, until I spotted a Chinese restaurant with high-paneled booths that would give us privacy. It was across the street from City Hall. I pointed. "That looks like a good spot for a cup of coffee. How about it?"

"Sure," Everett said, without even looking at me. We crossed San Pablo and went into the restaurant.

I led him into a booth with drapes in a corner by the window, where Al could see us and the cashier couldn't hear us.

"How'd you like the way that Big Spender put a whole hundred dollar bill on the bar and let it stay until he'd blown it all buying rounds for the house last night, George?" Big Press said.

"Yeah, fun!" Then I turned to Everett and said, "Then he took us to a whorehouse and paid our way. Wish I could see him again. The guy was a lot of fun."

But Everett just turned and stared at Big Press next to him from between his pink-tinted lids and kept his mouth clamped shut. I was glad Press wore his hair short and didn't dress flashy. In his loafer jacket and slacks he looked like a well-dressed sailor on leave.

"Great guy!" Press said with a stiff smile, then turned to the thin Chinese waiter in the white jacket who, pencil and pad in his hands, asked, "What you like?"

"Coffee," Everett mumbled, without looking up.

"What?" the waiter asked, smooth skin crinkling up at the eyes as if he didn't like what he heard.

"Coffee!" Everett repeated, still without looking up. The waiter pinched his pencil in his small hand and scribbled on the pad.

"Coke," I said, remembering what Al said about running up a bill with only a little bit of money to work with, no coin to waste on frills. Still, the waiter made me feel cheap the way he wrinkled up one eye and stared down at the pad, then scribbled the order down. But when Big Press said, "A cheeseburger and a chocolate shake," the waiter started scribbling really fast. He almost grinned when Big Press picked up the menu and said, "Hmmmmmm," and ran his finger down it.

I tapped Press's leg with my toe and made him look up and meet my eyes.

"Uuh ... " Press said, glancing at me, and told the waiter, "That's it ... for now."

I didn't miss those last two words, but there was nothing I could do about it. I said, "Be nice if we could see that guy again."

"Sure would," Press said, slanting his eyes nearly closed with his smile at me, trying to make up. The Marine looked at him, then back at me, then snorted and picked up the sugar shaker and shook it back and forth in his big hand. I wondered where Al was. I was never going to earn the money to get Velva back this way. The seconds dragged by like minutes. I could hear the blare of a car horn, the roar of an engine, the ring of a traffic signal.

Big Press didn't say anything either, and the Marine just stared at the sugar shaker and shook it back and forth. Yet, I had to respect the guy. Al said you couldn't beat them unless they tried to beat you. And this guy was either too dumb or too smart or too honest to get sucked in.

I was just about to start a conversation about something, a great big lie about anything, when the jingle of doorbells made me look up and almost sigh with relief.

"There he is. That's the guy we've been talking about. Hey, John! Come over here!" I said and waved at Al with a genuinely happy smile on my face. The Marine quit shaking the sugar shaker and looked up.

Al waved from the doorway, his upper lip curled in a smile, then he walked over to us and sat down on the bench next to me. He reached over, slid the drapes closed and said, "Glad to see you guys. You ready to party again today?" Then he reached out to shake hands with the mooch, saying, "John."

The Marine put the shaker down and stared at Al as if he couldn't believe the Big Spender was there. Then he shook hands and I felt for the second time since I'd picked him up that the guy might, just might, get it on. Al went right to work.

"Do you know what happened to me last night with that little whore? After I fucked her, she wanted to bet me twenty dollars against a free piece of ass that I couldn't put a hairpin in the center of her garter strap."

Al reached into his sportcoat for the strap as the waiter slid the drape back, set the tray down on the edge of the table, put the coffee in front of the Marine and the Coke in front of me. Al froze with his hand still in his pocket when the waiter put the cheeseburger and shake in front of Press. He looked at the cheeseburger, then at Press, then at the milkshake, then at Press again, and with a straight, expressionless face said, "No, thanks, nothin'," to the waiter in such short syllables that the waiter didn't even frown. He just skidded the drape back along the chrome bar and walked away.

Al stared at Press as if daring him to pick up the cheeseburger, but the Marine stared at Al as he poured sugar into his coffee. "What happened with the garter?" I asked. I was afraid I'd never get the money to get Velva back.

"Yeeaaah, like to know how you did with her. Pretty girl from what I saw. Bet she had beautiful legs," Press said with a big smile.

Al stared at him for just a moment, enough to make him look down, then smiled at the mooch and said, "About this round and milky white." He took his hand out of his pocket and circled both hands for size and met the hard, staring, pink-rimmed eyes of the marine. Then he leaned quickly over the table and said, "She pulled her garter off her leg after I came and snapped it at me for fun, then bet me I couldn't put the prick in the poke. And, me, ha-ha, I think she wants me to twirl her hoop again, and I say, 'The hell I can't!' and she says, 'How much?' And I say, 'Twenty dollars!' And she cuts the garter with some scissors and folds it and winds it up in a circle ... like ... Hell, I'll show you! She gave me the goddamned garter after I lost."

He started to feel in his coat pockets, first one, then the other, slapping the breast pocket of his loafer jacket, then stretching his leg out and digging into his pants pocket. He glanced at me, giving me the tiniest flicker of an eyeball to be ready, and I leaned forward, ready to play as he pulled the garter out and laid it on the table.

But he'd just bought it for ten cents at Kress's and it looked a little too clean, too white, with a thin blue thread on the outside edge. He rubbed it between his fingers and wrinkled it a little, but when he opened his mouth to speak, Big Press tore open the potato chip bag with a loud, ripping sound.

He stopped and stared at Press, his upper lip curled in a snarl. Press only grinned at him as if nothing was wrong, put the top of the bag in his plate and waited. Then, just as Al started to speak again, he reached into the cellophane bag with a crackle!

Al stopped and glared at him again, and he stopped with his hand still in the bag, then grinned again, as if everything was okay. But just as Al turned to the mooch again, holding out the strap to show it to him, Big Press stuffed the chips into his mouth and started chewing with loud, crunching bites.

Al snapped his head around and stared at him, making him stop in the middle of a bite.

"How'd she roll it, John? Show us," I said.

Al turned his head back toward the Marine and, managing to keep his lips spread in a stiff, sour smile, said, "Like this."

He folded the garter once in half, then rolled it up from the folded end, making a neat circle of wrinkles with two tight loops in the center. He made a face and raised his voice to a falsetto, trying to mimic the girl, "She says,

'Pretend this here hairpin's the bull's prick, see?' "

But he couldn't hold his breath and he dropped down to a low speaking voice and said, " 'Try to poke it right in the cow hole in the middle, if you can.' And I bet her twenty against her snatch and put the hairpin in this hole, right here!"

He touched the toothpick to one of the twin folds in the center of the tightly rolled strap, waited a moment with the toothpick still touching the fold, until Press finished chewing his chips, then said, "She unrolled it real slow after that, but I lost. I still think I'm right, though! And I'll bet you the price of the check that I'm right!"

He pushed the strap toward the Marine, and, looking up, wrinkling his brow, waited for the guy to bet.

But Big Press took a bite of his cheeseburger and mustard squirted out over the table and onto the Marine's sleeve. The Marine jerked his arm back and said, "Goddamn, boy! What chew doin'?"

I snapped my napkin up from the table and reached across to wipe the Marine's sleeve and said, "Sorry about that," trying to save the play.

But the Marine took the napkin, dabbed at the green woolen sleeve and said, "Why'nt we get outta here?"

"We have to wait for Mister Big Eater, that's why!" Al said and poked his thumb at Press.

"I'll take the bet," I said, still trying to save the play.

Turning the strap to me right away, Al then handed me the toothpick.

I reached out and touched the toothpick to the strap, but couldn't stop my hand from trembling and, looking up at the Marine, I said, "I'm a little hung over from that booze last night."

Then I looked down at the strap again and said, "That's not the hole. This is the one. No, this one."

I waved the shaky toothpick back and forth between the two tight folds in the center as if I couldn't make up my mind. Then I looked at the Marine and said, "Which one do you think it is, Everett?"

"Yeah, Jyreen! Which one do you think it is?" Al said.

The Marine squinted down at the strap and the tiny eyelets in the center, stared for a second, then looked up at me and snorted, "Huh!" and switched his eyes away. Then he looked back at Al with a raw, pink edge to his eyelids, and said, "This here one might be it, buddy. But I'm not betting any money on it, not even for the check or even for the price of your toothpick. This looks like some kind of a carney game to me. We had some guys that acted noisy like you come and visit our town with shells when I was a kid and cheat everybody in it, too. Nothin' doin'!"

Nobody moved. I could hear the clatter of dishes in the kitchen, the splash of a water faucet, the high-pitched shrieks of someone giving a bawling out in Chinese, the ring of the cash register. I was never going to make enough money to get Velva back this way.

17

"One more play like that and we'll end up in jail without money for bail," Al said and looked at me as if it were my fault. His hot breath seemed to blow hard across the booth table at the back of the bar, near the back door, the toilets and the stairs up to Curly's place. Curly and Al T. and Big Press sat around a table with us in the dim blue light.

Al took a sip of scotch. Curly had given us a round on the house. I drank Coke. Nobody spoke.

"And this goddamn Press here knew we only had a few bucks for scuffling money and ordered himself a lunch with our coffee money. Then he chomps away on those goddamn potato chips when I'm trying to talk the mooch into playing. I can do without that!" Al said and glared at Press, who sat next to the aisle with his head towering above everyone.

"That doesn't seem to be what was really wrong, though, Al," I said in a mild tone, trying not to get him mad. "He was a stubborn guy and he didn't trust you or me, either! He told me so when I walked him back to the bus. And how come Big Press didn't just play tail like we planned? Then he wouldn't have been around to mess up. You said we always had to have a tail!"

"Oh! So now you're going to blame it on me!" Al said. "I wanted to make sure you didn't get messed up, pick up a cop, maybe. To keep you out of jail until you learned how to protect yourself, wise guy!"

"Sorry," I said, but didn't look away.

Al T. said, "Take it easy, Al. Just going to school is all."

He sat like a Buddha in the booth with his dark glasses on, lips puckering up with the word "school," waving his puffy diamond-studded hand.

"Going to jail, you mean!" Al answered.

"But Floyd didn't do nothin' wrong," Al T. said. "Did you make a spread with some big bills to suck the mooch in?"

"No," Al said. "Didn't have any big bills, just twenty dollars, scuffling money."

"Then, that's what's wrong! You didn't tempt him! You have to make a spread and get 'im greedy! Let him win the check bet so he then wants to bet again and win your big money."

"He wouldn't even bet for the check," I said.

"That's right," Al said.

Then Curly said, "Al T.'s right. You gotta make a spread and get him going. And the kid's gotta learn, too."

Al looked down at his drink, his bullet-shaped forehead glowing. I started to say, "Al, we can all learn how to . . . " when I saw my father come walking in the side door, his wide body in a blue dress suit taking up the whole doorway.

He stopped and looked around the club, over at Pix, the bartender. Then he saw Press, Al, then me. He stepped up next to the table, his dark eyebrows nearly touching over his large, dark eyes.

"What're you doing taking Floyd around this place with you, Albert?"

We all froze. Nobody moved. Nobody spoke.

He glanced at me, but looked right back at Al again and said, "I just bought you boys a house on upper Twenty-third Avenue. I'm giving you a chance. But I'm warning you, buddy. If you take your little brother to jail with you, I'll kill you! I promise you, I'll kill you!"

18

"Dad thinks you're a man, Eddy," I said, and checked an urge to reach out and touch my brother, afraid it would make him feel unmanly.

His white smock buttoned up to his neck, Eddy's round pink face glowed in the bright light coming in through the front window and reflecting off the glass jars and vials of the glass-enclosed prescription booth. He stared past me out the window, with its red and green crystal balls hanging in the upper corners. His slightly protruding eyes were dreamy and moist, as if seeing nothing but the inner sights of his mind.

"You are a man, more of a man than either Al or me. I'll never be as much of a man as you," I finally said.

I sat up on the high druggist's stool in my clerk's white jacket, my wavy hair falling in curls over my forehead. After Eddy finally gave me a job, Velva came back to me without saying a word. She was just there one evening, beautiful in her silken pink robe, talking to my sister Annabelle in the kitchen of the house Dad had bought Al and me. A few days later, she had our baby boy Greg.

"Oh yes, you will," Eddy said. "I'm eleven years older than you, Floyd, but you're already more of a man. You're more of a man to Dad. You're a man's man, and I'm a bisexual. Even if Dad doesn't know that, he feels that I'm not manly enough. He's always felt I wasn't manly enough. I used to embarrass him because I wasn't rugged enough as a boy."

He turned full face to me and looked at me with his yellow-flecked green eyes, pausing as if to pull his mind back from his mother and father to his younger brother. He said, "I used to say, 'I hate him! I hate him!' And Mother would say, 'Don't say that!' and look through her glasses at me with those really quick eyes. But her face would get soft and pink and her voice would be both kind and stern at the same time. She'd say, 'You've got to become man enough to love him with his faults, even if he never thinks of how other people feel. You've got to see that he's good and kind, that he never means anything wrong. You've got to see the good in him and not just his faults, or you'll never be a man.' "

Eddy looked off through the window again. He looked round and bloated to me with those protruding eyes and soft, pinkish skin, almost as if he were decaying. He should exercise, I thought, as Eddy looked out the corners of his large eyes at me.

"I've never become a man, Floyd. Because I'm still not man enough not to hate him, though I do love him."

"But, Eddy, you were always brave," I said. "One of my early memories is of you knocking Al flat with a bloody nose when he tried to sneak out one night when Mom and Dad weren't home."

A quick smile crossed Eddy's full mouth and he nodded, then said, "But you'll surpass me. You'll achieve more."

I spread my hands and, avoiding any mention of our father, said, "Oh, no! At my age, you were already a sophomore at Cal and had proved to the world that you were brilliant. You won the best scholarship a public school could give! Even if you're not a pro boxer, like Al, or had a couple of amateur fights like me, you've been a naval officer in war time and have been decorated for it. You're more of a man than either Al or me because you've done more in a man's world."

"Not to Dad," Eddy said. He looked around at the shelves neatly stacked with vials and jars and boxes of medication, no sundry goods. "This is a professional drug store, not a supermarket," he always said. His round face got pink and animated as if a quick glance around his own store had reassured him. But then his hazel eyes became hazy and dreamy again, soft with an inner ache.

Still trying to convince him, I said, "You've succeeded at everything. You've gone to Cal and Harvard, studied medicine, published articles and short stories, and now have your own successful pharmacy, and you're only thirty! You've really lived and accomplished as much as a man in his fifties. You've proved you're a man to the whole world. You're an exceptional man, Eddy."

He stared at me, but he still didn't say anything, and I said, "I don't see how I could possibly surpass you. I haven't even started school yet. Got myself all tied down ... How could you say that?"

"Because you're more manly, Floyd. I'm not just feeling sorry for myself. I tend to pat myself on the back too much as it is. But you see, men will feel your manliness and they'll give you more respect. They'll open a bigger world for you."

"I don't see it," I said, shaking my head. "I'm so far behind you, I'll never even be near you at your age."

"I may not be around when you're my age," Eddy said and turned away again and looked off through the window.

"What do you mean?" I asked and sat up stiff-backed on the high stool.

"Because I might kill myself, Floyd," Eddy said and faced me again with his heavy lips pursed.

"Oh, no, don't say that!" I said. "You have everything to live for. Nobody has done as well as you."

"Dad doesn't seem to think so," Eddy said, looking off through the window again. Suddenly he said, "Mother died this month, in June, seven years ago."

19

The conversation bothered me badly the rest of the day. I'd go about my deliveries, mopping the floor, laundering the smocks, tending the store, with a depressing vision of Eddy in the same casket with Mother. I'd then come back and look closely at my brother, seeing the horrible vision inside my head while my living brother in his pinkish, living flesh was there in front of me. There was a glow to him in his white pharmacist's smock, his face broad now. The large, hooked craggy nose he had when he joined the Navy was now gone, cut off by a naval doctor. The nose job had been so poorly done that a decaying hole appeared in the bridge and Eddy now wore a flesh-colored band-aid over it. Yet, even this evidence of dying flesh couldn't make me believe that my brother standing in front of me would ever be dead.

20

The pharmacy window was dark when I got to work in the morning. There was hardly a shimmer of reflection on it and the wooden frame which it enclosed like a picture, with the red and green crystal balls in its upper corners, held a shadowy still-life of the pharmacy inside. The glass front door which opened out onto the stone porch of the small medical building was closed and locked, too. Pressing my face against the cool glass, I could tell that not even the back room lights were on. It was after nine in the morning and Eddy never opened late, no matter how little sleep he had the night before. He'd drop the pink heart of a dexie pill, wash his face, make coffee and get to work. Yet, the green Chevrolet I used to deliver prescriptions was parked in front of the store in the reserved white zone. It confused me, because it meant Eddy was inside.

I walked down the stairs and crossed the wide sidewalk to the car to try the door. It was unlocked. So, I sat down inside with the door ajar to wait for Eddy to appear, expecting him to come down the sidewalk from either direction or out of the medical building where the dentist-owner had his office. The dentist was bisexual, too, and jealous of Eddy over his lover Bill, who came from a wealthy family.

I stared down the street of the Tenderloin section of San Francisco. It was a lonely deserted neighborhood on a quiet, sunny morning. The nightclubs and girly shows with their neon signs and dusty showcase windows looked a little shabby by daylight and depressed me. I began to worry over Eddy's words about killing himself the day before and, though I continued to sit in the car after the meaning of the conversation first occurred to me, I couldn't get it out of mind. Finally, I got out of the car, slammed the door and went up the stairs to the pharmacy door again.

I tried it once more, then looked past the lettering on the glass, SALAS PHARMACY, MEDICAL PRESCRIPTIONS ONLY, and into the interior at the glass-enclosed prescription booth with its chin-high counter, the cash register next to it, the small passageway between them that led to the back room and the stairway up to the sleeping alcove where two camp cots sat between walls of books.

He must be upstairs asleep, I thought, but tried the door again. I shook the knob, then turned and hopped down the stone steps to the sidewalk. Taking

long steps, arms swinging, my wiry torso straight-backed in a sportshirt and
sweater, I hurried past the front window and down the basement stairs of
the building into the Turkish Bath below the pharmacy, through the long
hallway with the lush, bright, tropical flowers painted on its walls and into
the big steamy massage room at the back of the building. I tried the door to
the back stairs of the pharmacy, then told the small, foreign masseur with the
rapier mustache and flour-white skin that I was going to climb through a bath
window in the airshaft into the supply room window a floor above. Propping
the masseur's ladder against the building, I climbed up to the window, which
I knew was unlocked.

I had to lean back at the top of the ladder to open the window, which
opened out like a door, then stuck my head and shoulders into the darkened
room and stepped over the sill into the sink. I stopped there when I saw my
brother wrapped in an army blanket on the floor with his head to me, and I
smiled, thinking, "Poor guy, he's wiped out." I then pulled my other leg in
and let myself quietly down to the floor so as not to scare Eddy. I tip-toed
past him through the room, past the passageway with the stairs leading up
to the alcove, and out into the front room where I turned on the lights and
opened the front door to get ready for business, then stopped with my hand
still on the knob of the open door.

I saw the reflection of my whole body in the glass of the open door. My
right eyebrow was arched, my face scared as I listened for sounds of Eddy
waking up, getting off the floor, saying something. I only heard total silence.

Turning to stare back into the darkness of the back room, I could hear
or see nothing. I let go of the knob and stepped quickly back past the cash
register, through the passageway and into the room where I switched on
the light above the desk. My brother was lying on the floor with deep blue
circles under his eyes and his full lips cracked open and dry.

"Eddy! Eddy!" I screamed and jerked the phone off the base and, hands
trembling, dialed the operator. I seemed to wait minutes for the mechanism
to click and the line to buzz, for the operator to finally answer while staring
at my brother lying motionless on the floor across from me.

"Send an ambulance, please! My brother is dying! 231 Ellis Street!
Hurry! Hurry!" I cried and slammed the receiver down, ran past my brother,
down the back stairs and out the back door into the Turkish Bath where,
my face stiff and contorted, my mouth and eyes wide, I shouted, "Masseur!
Masseur! Come quick! Eddy's dying!"

Running back into the pharmacy, the door slammed shut behind me. I
jumped back and held the door open for the little man, who ran in his slacks
and undershirt past me and up the short flight of stairs into the back room.
He dropped on one knee, threw the army blanket back and pressed down and

up on Eddy's stomach, making his cracked lips part with a moaning groan, "Uuuuuuuuuuuh!" Then he did it again and again with smaller groans each time. My hopes, which had risen with the first groan, sank with my sagging face on each of the following, failing tries.

Finally, I heard a siren and ran back up to the front of the store, down the stone steps and out onto the sidewalk, where I waved at the ambulance, stopped it right out in front and motioned for the attendants to follow me. I led them at a run into the store and straight to the back room where they lifted Eddy, blanket and all, onto the stretcher, carried him out to the ambulance, let me jump in, then shot down the street to the corner.

The driver turned right down Mason for two blocks, then turned right up Market Street, siren wailing, the back doors flying open as the ambulance zigzagged in and out of traffic, around cars, over the streetcar tracks, through red lights, while one attendant kept an oxygen mask over Eddy's face and I sat facing the back, my hand touching the cold hand of my brother.

Eyes dry, chest aching, the siren screaming in my ears, I watched the wide street waving away from me, the marquees and automobiles, the shiny streetcar tracks, the people on the crowded sidewalks turning to stare. I knew that I'd never forget, that what I saw and could not stop to think about now would stick in my mind forever. I had the presence of mind, though, to jump out first when the ambulance stopped to hold the doors open for the dark-haired driver, who ran around from the cab and said, "Good boy!" as he pulled out the stretcher. He took the front end and another attendant carried the back end and they hurried into the emergency ward with my brother.

I followed them down the white-tiled corridor to the emergency room, where a nurse closed the door in my face and made me stop. I turned and paced back and forth, back and forth, back and forth in the corridor, my hands in my pockets, head down, my hair falling over my forehead, my eyes on the small, shiny white squares which stretched endlessly before me, suppressing sobs in my throat, needing, wanting to cry, but unable to while there was still hope my brother would live. I relived over and over again the moaning grunt that came from Eddy's mouth, counting on it, needing to count on it, though still unable to forget those words of suicide, the talk about our father and mother. As I paced back and forth, back and forth, I stared at the frosted window of the emergency room door.

I had gone halfway down the hall for what seemed the hundreth time when I finally heard the door open behind me. I spun around to see the young blond doctor step out and walk slowly down the white tile floor toward me like some white apparition: white hair, white skin, white smock, white floor, white walls, white door behind him. His head was lowered, his tall body slack, but his eyes were on me, sizing me up as he approached. His mouth came half-open when he stopped a couple of feet from me, as if afraid to speak. I looked into his light eyes for a moment, then said, "He's dead, isn't he?"

He nodded.

"I hope he chose it," I said. "I hope he did it on purpose."

He nodded again.

"I better call my father," I said, but couldn't find a dime in my pocket, no change at all. The doctor said, "Let me get a dime from the change in your brother's pocket," and he seemed to materialize right in front of me again with a thin silver dime in his hand.

"Thanks," I said and stepped into a phone booth in the hall. I dropped the dime in the coin slot, dialed Dad's restaurant number and waited in the thick, wire-glass enclosure until Dad answered the phone.

"Dad," I said. "Eddy's dead.

"Whaaaaaa? Whaaaaaaaat!"

"Eddy's dead, Dad! Eddy's dead!" I said, my voice breaking with a sob, and I smashed my fist against the wire-glass wall, tearing big, gaping, painful holes in my hand.

21

Eddy's moon face, with its deep blue circles under his eyes, cracked lips puffing apart with that final breath, "Uuuuuuuuuuh!" woke me to a bedroom that was a heavy blanket of smothering darkness. Horror. Hopelessness. I was afraid to go back to sleep, afraid the face would come back and haunt me again, haunt me because I had gotten my father's love and not him. And that's why he killed himself.

But the face stayed with me when I woke in the morning unrested, feeling light in the brain, as if I hadn't slept enough or had slept too much. I thought of my brother on the floor wrapped in that army blanket and fought the guilty feeling that came over me for not realizing sooner that something was wrong and for not going through the back window right away, maybe getting in there in time to save Eddy's life, maybe ...

Still tortured by the vision, I was packing Eddy's books into cardboard boxes in the alcove upstairs, when I saw a small, green, bound notebook with "PRIVATE / Lieutenant JG John Edward Salas" written in black letters on the thick green cover. I jerked it open and read on the first page: "Mother died June 25th, 1943."

"Each person has a life potential," it said in thin, flowing script on the first page. I had to stop and wait until the picture of Eddy dead on the floor passed, then I swallowed and began to read.

"Each person has a life potential. Each person has a purpose for being here—good or bad. Each person is a minute cog in the wheel of life. The length of this potential may be influenced by the activities of one's life, environment and friends. Everybody has to work. Always while on earth a person must work—see physics definition (i.e. a transference of energy from one body to another.) The idea to approach is a state where one is content with the work one does. The real way to live is to live today! Upon passing on, there are no regrets for oneself. Life may have been full and the purpose served—but was he happy? Define word happiness. When one passes on, the dirt claims you. When one suffers a major death—as of mother—if one doesn't believe, the suffering is harder. There is no faith, no belief, no beautiful talk of that great day to heal or ease the suffering or tightening within one's rib cage. When life has ceased, it has ceased to be forever. You become part of the hillside. Hope my hillside is green. But after death—what matters? A body should be laid to rest if circumstances are such; otherwise the spirit of the individual will be allowed to infect the bereaved, even if only in a minute degree. Then life goes on—the sun still shines, the surf still roars and women still continue to have babies.

"One rule—be happy, it's infectious. Remember that with each disaster suffered and each hardship endured, new strength emerges to cope with other stones or pebbles that may rise to hurt one's feet while treading the path of life.

"Won't say life is boring!"

I took the diary with me. I read it often, but I couldn't shake off my brother's suicide.

One night, as I waited alone for the bus in front of the terminal building on Mission Street, I paced back and forth by the bench, depressed by the inability of my brother to be happy, to love our father, and by the dead-end his brilliance and goodness had come to.

The frustrating pain built up with such great pressure that I suddenly stopped, glanced around and saw that there was no one anywhere on the narrow sidewalk. I lifted my head to the dark, clouded sky and words burst out of my lips, poured out of me in a flood.

"I love you, Eddy," I said. "I swear by your memory and my love for you that I'll try to live up to the image you had of me! I swear I'll do good on this earth and that I'll try and achieve happiness in the here and now."

As I spoke, I didn't think. I listened, rather, to each emotion-laden word that rose out of me, each word that somehow helped to clear my mind and ease the constriction in my throat, the tightening in my rib cage, the ache in my heart.

"I'll work at something which will bring me personal contentment and will help others, too. Something, not law—which is too dry, too unsatisfying—something in the arts, writing or painting. Something like what you wanted for yourself, like the novels you wanted to write, after Mother's death killed your will to be a doctor, killed the reason you worked so hard, killed the driving impulse to save her and everyone like her, which grew so large during her long years of heart trouble, from the day I was born."

I looked around again, but there was still no one on the whole block this late at night. I raised my voice and my fist and said, "I swear that I'll work as you believed. Not for subsistence but for self-fulfillment. That I'll seek the freedom of the artist, the free man! Do significant, meaningful work! Work, Eddy, that would have kept you from committing suicide, if you had only followed your own advice."

Then I started sobbing. I stayed on the corner, sobbing for a long time.

PART SIX

Bleed Me Down
to Serum for His Veins

1

"Say, listen, Floyd," Al said, his small brown eyes narrowing at the sound of the word "money." He was really looking into my eyes for the first time since he'd come home from the county jail in the late morning.

He looked good, a little heavy, with a full round face, thinning wavy hair he combed straight back, as we walked down Broadway in the warm Oakland sunshine. I was trying to get him to go to the employment office and look for a job.

He'd just done ten months in Santa Rita Prison Farm for two counts of petty theft, six months each, with two months off for good behavior. He didn't look like a junky anymore, as he had before going in, skinny and rundown with hollows under his eyes and yellow skin. I was going to do my best to keep him off junk forever. That's why I was with him, cutting my classes at art college today. I had told him he could collect unemployment, too, and have some money to move around with.

"I do need to get some money," Al said, stopping on the sidewalk in front of the State theater.

"If we go down to the employment office and register you, you can probably draw on those years you drove a cab and get money coming in every week."

"How long will that take?"

"Couple of weeks. There's a waiting period of one week and then another week before your first check reaches you."

"I'm flat broke. I need it now," he said.

"I only have a couple of bucks, Al," I said. "I only earn thirty-two dollars a week and I give that to Velva to buy food for us. Dad lets us have the basement apartment rent-free or I couldn't even go to school. That's why I gave him the cottage back. I had to work full time to pay the mortgage and couldn't study enough. She's working at that women's clothing store on Seventeenth Street. We don't have any spare cash, Al."

"I know," he said. "I've got an idea."

"What?" I asked.

He turned away and looked across the street at the Kress dime store. When I looked over there, too, seeing the windows shimmering with reflections of the street, he said, "All you gotta do is go in and ask the clerk in there to look down inside the glass counter."

"What'a ya talking about?" I said. I could feel my face get warm with quick anger.

He looked back across the street and stuck his nose up, pointing at the Kress. "It's no big thing, Floyd. I'm not asking you for money. I know you don't have any money to lend. I wouldn't bum ya for money when you're broke, you know that. But I can't go around town without a damn dollar in my pocket. You wouldn't want that!" He squinted that left eye at me. The faint line of the old cut scar on his lid still barely showed.

"I guess not," I finally answered.

He squeezed my arm and said, "You don't want me to feel like some bum, brother!" He squeezed my arm again. "You know how I'm used to having money on me all the time."

I nodded my head a couple of times, feeling sorry for him, wishing I had a five-spot I could lend him.

"You know how generous I am with everybody," he said.

"Yeah," I said, feeling cheap.

"All you gotta do is go in and talk to the salesgirl and I'll tap the till of the cash register."

"That's all?" I asked, narrowing my eyes at him now.

"That's all," he said. "I'll give you half of it."

I shook my head, remembering what Dad said to him about teaching me to steal four years ago.

"I don't want any," I said.

"Do it for me, then," he said.

I looked across the street. Broadway was the busiest street in Oakland. Streetcars and busses and cars moved past in both directions. People moved up and down the wide sidewalks. I turned back to him and started to shake my head, saying, "I don ... "

"Just this once, Floyd. For me, for your brother, who took care of you during the war when you were a little kid. Remember? After Mama died?"

I nodded.

"All you gotta do is get her to bend down and look on the bottom shelf of the display case."

When I didn't answer, he said, "Let's go," and turned to walk back to the corner of Fourteenth, forcing me to follow him.

I felt a deep sense of fear and fatalism, remembering how I got caught stealing that pen at Payless when I was only nine and what a lousy, failed bunco man I turned out to be, too.

After we crossed Broadway and reached the front door of the Kress, he said, "See that girl behind the counter down there, on the other side of the cash register?"

I nodded again, knowing it was a mistake, but feeling unable to back out without being disloyal to him.

"All you gotta do is go down and talk to her. Get her to take something out of the glass counter and show it to you."

"That's all?" I asked, not believing him.

"That's all," he said.

"Why don't we go ask Dad if he can ... "

"Aw, co me on, Floyd. You know how Dad is."

I thought of how much money Dad had already given to Al and knew he wouldn't lend him any just to run around town on.

"Just this once," I said and walked down the counter, which ran parallel to the big glass windows on Broadway. I wondered how in the hell Al was going to be able to open the cash register without being seen and heard. When the young woman clerk asked, "Can I help you?" I looked down inside the glass case and pointed at some shaving kits and said, "Can I see that one on the bottom shelf there?"

"Sure," she said and stepped back, bent over, slid the glass door back, reached in and stretched to take the box out of the front part of the glass case, then stood up and put the kit on top of the counter.

I looked it over, touching the can of shaving powder, the bottle of after-shave lotion, feeling like a cheap liar. I asked, "How much?"

She picked up the kit, turned it over, looked at the back, and said, "Two ninety-five!"

I shook my head and said, "I don't think so." I paused, wondering how in the hell I found myself standing next to this counter, lying to some young woman so my brother could steal money from the store.

"Maybe I better look at that other one there," I said and pointed down at another shaving kit on the bottom shelf. She bent down to put the first kit back and lift up the other one, when I heard a tap on the big window and looked up to see Al standing outside the store. The sun was shining through his thin hair, he was holding a coin up to the window to tap gain.

2

"I don't want to go to Emeryville and see Val Silva and Danny Wood," I said. "I want to go to the employment office like we planned."

We were standing right next to Velva's old gray Plymouth on Thirteenth Street, just between Washington and Broadway. People moved up and down the street. It wasn't nearly as crowded as Broadway, but still busy. I could see the clock on the tower of the Oakland Tribune a block and half down in the direction of the employment office. It said three o'clock.

"Ah, Floyd. It's too late now."

"No, it's not," I said.

He shook his head, then stuck his chin up and said, "How about first thing tomorrow?"

"I gotta go to school tomorrow. I can't take off another day."

He stuck his hand in his pocket, pulled out a wad of bills and tried to peel off a five and hand it to me.

"I don't want it, Al," I said, shaking my head.

"Come on, Floyd, take me up to Emeryville to see Val and Danny and I promise you, you can drop me off at the employment office tomorrow morning on your way to school."

I squinted my eyes at him this time, but he stared right back at me with wide open eyes, his eyebrows peaked in the center of his forehead.

"You promise?" I asked, getting tired of all the hassle now. When he said, "I promise," I said, "Let's go."

But as soon as we drove up San Pablo Avenue to Emeryville, and talked to Val and Danny outside Val's father's apartment house, the first thing Al did was ask, "Where can I get some smack, Val?"

"There's a couple of places. You got the money?" Val asked, his narrow, olive-complected face suddenly tight and tense.

"Yeah," Al said.

I shook my head and said, "This is the beginning of the end, Al."

"You don't have to get so dramatic about it," Al said.

"You go with them, I'm going home. This is a waste of time," I said.

"Oh, Floyd never messes with that bad-ass dope," Danny said, in a deep, bass, mocking tone, looking down on me with his blue eyes. "Mister Lord Fauntleroy himself."

244

I looked up at that big, six-foot, lanky frame with wide shoulders. He was really tough, but so was Val and Al, and I could fight a little bit myself, too. I wasn't the least bit afraid of him.

"You never said a truer word in your life," I said.

3

Dad's face got long in the mouth and he said, "You've got a good job at that freight company. You're a junior executive, a gentleman. A lot of young men would consider themselves successful to have a position like yours."

He was standing in front of me in a business suit and tie in my new apartment three years after Al came home and tapped the till.

I shrugged my shoulders and said, "Maybe I'm just too intellectual, Dad? I feel like I'm wasting my life! Every morning when I take a shower I get this terrible sense of futility! I've got to try and write, do something that has meaning to me. I haven't felt good about myself since I quit art school to earn enough money to pay our bills. I've paid them off now. I don't want to end up making a lot of money but feeling so dissatisfied and miserable that I'd kill myself like Eddy did!"

He looked down at the hardwood floor and shook his bald head.

"I need more academic education, more polish. I need to go back to school! I'm going to do it one way or the other, Dad." He looked up at me again and said, "Okay. If you really want it that bad, I'll buy an apartment house so you can have your own place and you can quit that office job and go back to school, too, like you want."

I grinned and threw my arms around the wide chest of my big father, hugged him and said, "Thanks, Dad. I'll keep myself on the honor roll. I promise."

"I know you will, son," he said, then leaned back away from me and added, "but your brother gets to live there, too."

I frowned, and Dad said, "He's got six kids now. I can't just leave him out. He's nothing but trouble, but he's my son, too."

I stared at him, looking so neat in his suit, his big belly covered by the gray herringbone material. His face was so lean, his shaved head so perfectly round, eyes so soft, yet so alert.

"I know, Dad. But it'll be hard. You know he won't help out."

Light gleamed on his bald head when he said, "You've got to do it. It's the best I can do. This way you've each got your own apartment and you won't have to work full time to pay the mortgage and can go to school. I can't buy two houses."

I stared at the hardwood floor in the Spanish style stucco apartment house Velva and I now lived in. She was a bookkeeper for the Grodins Mens Stores buyer. We were doing really well financially for the first time in our young married life together.

"Okay, Dad. I'll do my best."

He grinned at me, his black mustache making the white teeth of his wide smile look bright. I grinned back, but knew I was going to regret being around Al all the time again.

4

The house had thumped with running feet like a school gym when we first moved in. Six wild untrained kids, ranging from eleven down to four. They'd shout and yell and take turns knocking out the steps on the back porch with a two by four board, or tear the wallpaper off the walls, just for something to do when it rained outside. I'd line them up when one of them did something really wrong and—so they wouldn't have to tell on each other—I'd kick each one on the butt with the side of my foot so I wouldn't hurt them, then have to kick my son, too, not to show favoritism, though I knew he hadn't done anything.

And I'd tell them stories at night when I got a break from my studies and part time job. And finally, they began to behave fairly well, without any help from Al, who'd only showed interest in running the house once, when I had collected the rents.

5

He'd come up to my small two-room front apartment from his big apartment downstairs and sat like a thin, junky shadow on the chesterfield and asked how much money I collected.

"Not enough to make the mortgage payment without my rent, too, Al," I said.

"There's nothing left over?" he asked, being careful not to offend me when he'd done nothing to help me paint the halls nor the rooms of the three other apartments besides his. When I used a hose to wash the dust off the outside of the big, two-story house, he'd lain on the lawn and watched me instead of helping saying, "There's no use both of us working."

Now he wouldn't look me in the eyes because he knew I'd been going since seven in the morning, with classes and studying all day until four, when I went to work in the billing department of a trucking company in Emeryville. I usually got off at nine and came home, then studied until midnight, tried to get to sleep by one, then got up at seven to start all over again.

"No, there's nothing left over, and we're going to have to figure out a way to pay the taxes when they come due, too," I said. "All the rents just pay the mortgage."

He kept his narrow face turned away, the shadows under his eyes dark like Al T.'s. He finally stood up and left without saying another word, not even goodbye.

6

I'd barely taken off my suit coat and hung it up when I heard a knock on the door. "Come in," I said.

Al stepped in, but didn't speak. I wondered what was up. He'd seen me walk in the front door, then go upstairs to my apartment.

"You get a job?" he asked, tilting his head back and sticking out his chin.

I had gotten laid off the trucking company job. When June came around, and school was out I was desperate for a full-time summer job—anywhere, doing anything. I needed to bring some money in while I still had a chance to work forty-hour weeks before school started again. I'd gone to a different employment office every day, but had been turned down for unemployment insurance because I was going to school. I had no money coming in at all.

I just shook my head, not wanting to talk about it.

"You need money?" he asked.

"Sure, I need money," I said. "If I don't earn enough during these summer months, it'll be hard on us during the school months."

He stayed by the door as if he planned on walking right back out, but said, "I know how you can earn some good money, fast."

"How?" I asked, paying close attention to him now.

"Remember how you talked to that salesclerk at the Kress when I first got out of Santa Rita that time?"

"Naaaw, Aaalll," I said, shaking my head, dropping down on the big sofa chair by my son Greg's small, blond wood piano.

"It's not much. You did it before and it was nothing. All you gotta do is talk to a clerk and I'll take care of everything else like I did before. And you could get some real money. I'll split it with you this time."

I thought of how easy it was, talking to that woman like that, but shook my head again. Still, he must have seen the look in my eyes because he said, "Floyd! In two hours, you could have a couple hundred bucks as your share."

Two hundred bucks. I stared right into his eyes and realized for the first time how much money he'd stolen from the Kress when he offered me that five bucks. He stared right back at me.

"Two hours and two hundred bucks, Floyd. You worked a month, four thirty-hour weeks for that at that trucking company last fall."

Sitting in the big chair, knowing how easily he could do it, tempted me. But I thought of how hard I'd worked for really good grades and how I was president pro-tem of the Oakland Junior College honor society, with a 3.54 gradepoint average, and how proud Eddy would be of me for it. I shook my head again.

"Be so easy, Floyd," he said, and this time I stood up.

"What's the matter with you, man?" I said. "You see how hard I work. What if I got busted with you? What about everything that Velva and I have worked for? And what if we both go to jail and lose this house? After Dad made such a big down payment on it for us? How can I be a writer, if I steal?"

He looked past me. The towers of the Golden Gate Bridge on the edge of the ocean were visible from the bay windows in the corner of the second floor room.

"And what good is it going to do my son, if I steal? When I teach him to be honest? And what about your kids? What about them? You going out and stealing all the time? A month ago, you left me standing in the middle of the sidewalk with Kathy as soon as Val Silva showed up! So you could go hustle some heroin! What's going to happen to them, if you keep this up?"

He turned to face me with a tight mouth. "They've got their life and I've got mine," he said.

"How can you say that? You made them! You're responsible for them until they grow up! What are you, anyway?"

He stepped toward me and stuck out his chest. "A thief!" he said.

"A petty thief," I said, and he turned around and jerked open the door and slammed it behind him.

7

"Wanna smoke a joint, Floyd?" Al asked at Auntie Dolly's party on Encinal Avenue in Alameda. Her house was full of friends and family. My cousin John, a senior in Electrical Engineering at Cal, had just finished playing a classical piece on the piano. Dolly was my favorite aunt and reminded me most of mother. She had the same big heart and sharp mind. The whole family, all the cousins and uncles and aunts were there, plus a lot of our friends, too. It was a happy evening, and I felt like celebrating because I'd gotten a good job as a paymaster for a big construction company. I was making good money, enough to think of putting school off for a year, until I earned enough to pay the house taxes and saved some money for another year at school. We wouldn't be so poor that way. They wouldn't have hired me if they thought I was going back to school in September, anyway.

"Sure," I said, willing to be my brother's friend, but still unwilling to go steal with him and still not liking the way he cheated his kids. Bob Fields, a husky, blond Portuguese-American guy who lived in one of our apartments, walked down to Eddy's old Chevrolet with us. Dad had given it to me after Velva's old Plymouth had broken down. Bob got in back and I sat in the driver's seat and waited for Al in the passenger seat to pull out a joint and turn us on. It was a quiet, old residential neighborhood in east Alameda, with the bay at the dead end of the block and lawns and hedges on both sides of the street.

But instead of taking out a joint, Al said, "What-a ya been picking on my kids for?"

"What?" I said, my mouth hanging open. "Picking on your kids?"

"Yeah, you've been beatin' 'um up for nothin', and all the time!" Al said.

I shook my head, but he was so transparent. I said, "Just because I wouldn't go steal with you, Al, is no reason to start trouble."

"You been puttin' me down, too. You think you're better than me because you go to school like that Eddy."

I snorted and rocked back. "It's not a matter of personal superiority, Al. It's acting like a grown up and accepting responsibility for your kids and that house."

"Grown up, huh?" he said and swung his body around and smashed me in the eye.

I saw stars, but tucked my chin down to my chest and wouldn't duck nor put my arms in front of my face. I looked at his hollowed eyes in his skull-shaped head and said, "I'm not going to fight you, Al! You're not going to slug your way out of this. You've still got to take care of your kids." And he slugged me again and again, solid shots to my mouth and nose. But they didn't stun me and I still wouldn't lift my arms.

"This is going to hurt you more than me, brother!" I said and he stopped and glared at me. His lips twisted in a snarl, then he held his fist out to hook me again. I looked at the fist, then at him and said, "Go ahead, man! We'll see how much good it does your kids!" He twisted around, threw open the door, jumped out and disappeared in the darkness toward the house. When I got out of the car, I could see the lights on the porch and a couple of people standing on the steps. Bob got out the back door.

When I walked into the front room and everybody saw my face, the women all cried out. I saw Al motion to Tommy, his wife. She nodded at him, then came over and took my arm and said, "Oh! What's wrong, Floyd? Let me help you, honey!"

She'd always been jealous of Al's love for me since I'd known her. She had never been affectionate to me, ever. But I wasn't surprised at her words, since I knew she was as deceitful as Al. Though one eye was puffed shut, I stared at her for a moment out of the good eye, without answering, to let her know I'd seen through her. She let go of my arm and turned away without saying anything more. Then I let my cousin Hope, a nurse, lead me into the bathroom, where she sat me down on a high, white stool and started wiping the blood off my face, saying, "He's been like this his whole life, Floyd. He's always been a rat!"

Tears moistened my eyes for the first time since he hit me, but I didn't sob. A moment later, my Aunt Dolly stepped into the bathroom, her blue eyes glittering behind her glasses, and said, "Why didn't you just beat him up, Floyd? You could beat him up! You should have beaten him up!"

Bob Fields, built like a football player, had followed us into the bathroom. He shook his head at Dolly's words and said, "Floyd wouldn't hit his brother. He's a Biblical character."

8

Walter Soots, his face flushed pink under the brown freckles, slapped me on the back and shook my hand, saying, "Floyd! Floyd!" then pushed a bottle of cheap sweet wine in my face. "Drink! Have a drink!" he said.

I pulled my hand free of his, glancing up into his pale brown eyes, the same brown color as his hair and freckles. Then, when he pushed the bottle at me again, I blocked it with my left hand and asked, "What's up, man? I've never seen you so zipped up. You on a benny? Something wrong?"

I was surprised to see him at the liquor store where our mutual friend Pete worked nights and went to art school days. We'd been childhood friends. Walter'd been the most promising young musician I'd ever known in school, period. But he was married now, settled down with two kids, and only playing in combos on weekends.

Peter was our bandy-legged buddy from Alameda High School, five-six and muscular, with wide fishlike eyes and a big, beaked nose. After he closed the store, he was going to turn me on to a cheap pound of pot that would last me years.

A couple of months after Al had punched me, I came home and found a rolled-up boxing scholarship tied to my apartment doorknob. For the first time in University of California boxing history, they'd given scholarships and only two, at that. My cousin John, who was a six-two light heavyweight on the team, had taken me up to Cal in the spring to spar in front of the coach when he heard they were going to give the first scholarships out. I'd won one for the fall semester. Al had won a one-to-ten-year sentence to San Quentin for grand theft. He came out in the hall and smiled at me the night before he got sent away in September, 1956. I said hello, but I couldn't smile back. But I was going to school now and that was behind me.

"Just glad to see my old friend Floyd," Walter said, then took another sip of wine, squinting to keep from looking in my eyes. I was alert because Pete had shown me the pound of pot he was going to sell me in the back room in front of Walter. I felt a quick tremor of anxiety in my chest. Just the big size of the paper bag package scared me. I handed Pete back the pound, saying I'd wait until he got off work and would look it over with him then. Now, I suddenly remembered that Pete's roommate had dropped a plastic vial of grass in a mailbox on sighting a plainclothes cop in their hotel lobby a couple of weeks ago and they'd had to move out that night.

Pete could be hot. I wondered if I could be hot, too, over Norman, one of our buddies, an African-American painter, crippled by polio, who lived in Berkeley. He'd been busted with two buddies in graduate school, one at Cal and the other at Stanford, over thirty-one pounds of pot in the ceiling of their flat. Had the tentacles of the narcotics police already spread out through the artistic, bohemian crowd of Berkeley to me?

Back in 1949, Pete had been the first kid from a good home busted for pot in Alameda County. Braumeller, the state narcotics agent—who was himself later sent to prison for trading heroin to addicts for stolen goods—had sworn to get him if he ever messed around with dealing again. Now, I realized that it was soon after Pete told me about the vial in the mailbox that he'd told me about a guy holding pounds and pounds of dope and that he could let me have one cheap. All of it made me uneasy inside.

"I'll wait outside in the car while you count up, Pete," I said. But Walter grabbed my arm, pushed the bottle in front of my face and said, "Stay here and drink with an old buddy. Have some wine! Just like old times!"

Now, I'd never drunk wine with Walter, ever! We'd smoked a few joints in high school together, that's all! He was the first guy to turn me on to pot. I didn't even start smoking pot regularly until after Eddy had died.

I pulled my arm free and opened the liquor store door, which was exactly on the corner of Thirty-eighth Avenue and MacArthur Boulevard, facing the corner where the two streets met. Walter stepped in front of me and said, "Okay. You stay inside and I'll go out and wait."

"What?" I said and leaned back to look at him. Walter swayed a little as if he were drunk, then tried to beat me out the glass door and close it on me. Though I couldn't understand why he was acting so strange, I didn't think it was cute. I pushed by him and went out and got in my car, which was parked in the first space next to the red zone on the north side of MacArthur facing the liquor store. Walter got in the passenger seat.

The boulevard was brightly lit, although traffic was light so late on a week night. All the stores except for the liquor were closed. I was turning down a sip of the wine for the second time, when I saw a man drive slowly by in a cream colored coupe. He had receding blond hair on a bullet-shaped head. He stared really hard at me with pale eyes, then looked closely into the liquor store as he turned off the boulevard and down the side street into a residential neighborhood.

I sat there, wondering if the guy was the big kilo dealer coming by to deliver or maybe a dealer for Pete, although he looked too old for that. Or maybe he was an armed robber casing the store? He was so suspicious looking, I said, "That's a strange-acting guy."

"Oh, don't worry about it! It's nuthin'!" Walter said and handed me the bottle. I pushed it away, hoping Pete would hurry up, when I saw the guy in the cream-colored coupe reappear off the side street of Thirty-eighth Avenue, which dead-ended on MacArthur. He pulled up to the stop sign on the corner, peeked at the store, then started backing his car into the red zone.

"Hey! That guy just came back!" I said and sat up.

"He's probably a customer," Walter said. "Here!"

I pushed the bottle away again and said, "I better go tell Pete."

"Stay here! It's okay! Everything's all right!" Walter said.

"I'm not so sure. Pete's got a pound of pot in there," I said and opened my door, pulling my arm out of Walter's grip. I got out as the man got out of his car, too.

For a couple of seconds we walked straight toward each other, him crossing the small street, me walking toward the corner. Then I suddenly saw him lengthen his step as if trying to beat me to the liquor store door. I picked up my pace, took big, quick steps, barely able to keep myself from running, and reached the corner first, where I turned into the store, snapped the lock on the door as I closed it, and shouted, "Hey, Pete! Some strange man's coming across the street!"

"What?" Pete said, stepping out of the back room. Then his bulbous eyes popped open at a big thud behind me. I spun around to see a big cop in a blue plain clothes suit, not the small blond man in a sport shirt and khakis. He hit the glass door hard, rammed it with his shoulder and tried to jerk it open. He hit it again, shook it and rattled it as another big cop in plainclothes came running across the boulevard from a double-parked blue cop car without markings.

"Don't let them in, Pete!" I yelled and ran past him into the storeroom, grabbed the paper bag out of the whiskey case Pete had put it in and, with the sound of Pete arguing with the men who were banging on the door and shouting, "Open up! Open up!" I ran into the toilet.

With shaking hands, I dumped the weed into the toilet bowl and flushed it, shouting over the rushing water, "Don't let 'em in! Don't let 'em in!"

"The store's closed," I heard Pete shout as the water ran down and a layer of wet grass floated to the top. I flushed the toilet again, but there wasn't enough water left to carry the layer of grass down. It swirled a little but stayed on top, a good two lid's worth. I jerked the handle again to make sure there wasn't more water. Then sure I was going to get caught and go to jail, I started scooping the wet grass up and stuffing it into the paper bag. With shaky hands, I got all I could out of the water, then jammed the bag back into the whiskey case, pushed the case behind some others and then flushed the toilet again.

But a thin layer of grass still stayed on the top and I picked up what was left with trembling fingers and washed it down the sink. Then, hands still shaking, legs weak and wobbly, I stepped back into the display room where Pete was shaking his head and saying no to a single cop in a plain blue suit still outside at the door. The big cop stared at me, just for a moment, then turned and recrossed the boulevard to his unmarked dark blue car, got in and drove off with the other cop.

Hurrying to Pete, who was still at the door, I looked across the side street to find the cream-colored coupe now gone. I started to explain what I'd seen when Walter stepped in front of the glass door and said, "What's taking you guys so long? Let me in."

"Don't open the door, Pete!" I said. "The cops might still be around."

"Open up, Pete," Walter insisted.

"Don't do it, Pete!" I said. "Those were narcs! You almost got busted! You weren't sitting outside and didn't see what I saw. Walter kept ... "

"Hey! Open up!" Walter said. When Pete unlocked the door, Walter took one step in and stopped with his foot in the door, staying outside, keeping the door open.

"Make him come in, Pete!" I said.

Walter shook his head as if he couldn't figure out why I was acting so strangely. I grabbed his arm and pulled him inside, then locked the door behind him again.

"What's the matter with you guys?" he said.

"Didn't you see those guys just try to break in here?" I asked, unable to believe he couldn't have seen them fifty feet in front of his face. I stared into his eyes. He looked away and I suddenly understood it all and shouted, "You finked, Walter!"

His eyes popped open. All the color went out of his face. Freckles seemed to stand out like blackheads on his pale skin.

I caught him with an overhand right to the cheek, knocked him against a display shelf of wine jugs and dropped him flat on his face on the floor, breaking a jug of burgundy. He rolled into a ball and covered his head, but I kept pounding on his back with both fists, shouting, "Fink! Fink! Fink! Fink!"

9

When I woke up the next morning, I looked around the room at the walls, the ceiling, the familiar pictures, the open closet with Velva's and my clothing in it. My stomach quivered with fear. I rubbed my sweating palms on the bedspread. My mind churned.

The room was like a vacuum, a temporarily suspended space in which my past life and future were balanced just outside of me and my living sphere. The past, the good, the familiar, the very room and bed in which I lay were in danger. And the future was a threat, a chance to get put behind bars, to wake up in the morning to the clang of cell doors, the jingle of keys, a cop marching past my cell to count me, dark steel and dull concrete all around me, prisoners on the make, no privacy, being lonely but never alone, only boredom and monotony and emptiness.

I remembered the suffering of jail, seven years ago, when I'd done four months in a cell waiting for trial for punching a plainclothes cop I thought was going to jump me. I never knew what was going to happen to me and sweated it out from day to day, my hands shaking whenever anyone came to see me. I remember my father saying in a voice close to hysteria, "What are you shaking for?" As if it were my fault I was shaking. Big fat man, he stared at the shaking hands with fear on his own face. Unable to reach out and touch me, he said, "I've got to go! I've got to get out of here!"

Soon after the near bust at the liquor store, I'd see this soft-faced blond guy with glasses staring at me through the book stacks at school. At night, when I left the campus, I'd see an older man with a gray hat and overcoat standing near my car. He had a thin, tweezer-tip mustache and looked at me slyly out of the corners of his eyes, as if he were trying to unnerve me. I wondered about him.

Then a guy who looked like Jack Dempsey started appearing around me a lot at school. He had a square face and black hair growing straight back from down low on his forehead, close to his thick eyebrows. He wore a brown, suede jacket and didn't look like anyone associated with the university, but more like a truck driver, a garbage man or a cop. A boxer tailing a boxer.

He'd appear between the shelves of the library and his eyes were all I could see of him. Or he'd sit at the next table in the cafeteria and sip from a cup of black coffee. When he got wise that I was on to him, he'd come walking slowly by me in the library, heels clicking, then suddenly spin around a few feet from me, meet my eyes and slowly back away, staring all the while, trying to scare me. I was no longer the college student, but the hunted outlaw.

I had barely escaped that night by springing the trap too soon, by insisting on going outside, by refusing to let Walter manipulate me and keep me inside where I couldn't see the trap spring shut. Now, they were after me in more ways than one, I thought, and it suddenly hit me. Cop-out: inform to the cops. I thought about that word with the hyphen in the middle.

Walter was a stool pigeon. There was no question of that. He was working for Braumeller, the state narc who had busted Pete. They probably picked up Pete's trail with that vial of pot in the mailbox and picked up my trail through my painter buddy Norman and the Berkeley bohemian crowd, to which Pete also belonged. They must have tried to kill two jail birds with one stone through a mutual friend, Walter.

That was as close as I could get to logic, which was guess and assumption when it came to the undercover men. Only a court of inquiry could prove anything and maybe not then. But I did know that I almost went to jail and that my life was now in a tailspin. I thought it was ironic that I wouldn't help Albert steal, but I still had to worry about cops.

I was, whether I liked it or not, on Al's side, made an outlaw by the law, put outside the law and classified with thieves and murderers. I now saw him in a different light. We were brothers in more ways than one: both outlaws, him for shooting dope and stealing for it and me for smoking pot. They were both classified as narcotics, both were felonies! I now saw him as a victim!

The next day after class, when I went into the library, I saw Jack Dempsey standing in his suede coat by the door of the big room where I usually studied in the afternoon. He stood with his big shouldered back to me, looking at the bulletin board. I knew he'd go sit down near me after I found a seat. So instead of just finding an empty seat, I walked through the room and out the back door, then quickly went down the stairs to the bottom floor and out the back door of the main library and across the wide walk into Wheeler Hall and through Wheeler and out the other doors. I then cut down to Strawberry Creek so I was below the pavement and out of sight, hidden by the giant redwoods and thick shrubbery. I followed the creek until I got to a bridge parallel with the Campanile tower, crossed it into Faculty Glade, then quickly walked across the glade and around the faculty building and headed straight toward the law library. I looked back as I walked without once catching sight of Jack Dempsey hulking broad-shouldered along behind me.

I walked up to the reference desk and told a red haired student that I was doing a paper on marijuana and wanted to research the laws on it. I then sat down and waited, hoping that Jack Dempsey wouldn't show up until after I got what I wanted. Or better yet, didn't show up at all. I already knew a lot about the effects of marijuana because I'd researched it when I worked at the Oakland Public Library. I read everything there was on the subject, on all drugs from alcohol to heroin, opium, morphine and amphetamines. And through my research, I saw that it was only a mild stimulant with the least harm to mind and body, personality and mood. Alcohol, the socially accepted drug, was the worst.

I kept looking around me for Jack Dempsey, but he didn't appear. The student appeared with a slip of paper and handed it to me. He pointed to the law books where I was supposed to look, then turned to wait on someone else.

I looked around me again. No Jack Dempsey. I went to the book shelves and finally found the big, thick law book, took it out and set it down on a table and, pulling my notebook out, searched for the marijuana law until I found it.

My heart pounded as I read it, then re-read it and copied it, verbatim, so I'd know exactly what it said. As long as the pot wasn't in my possession, I couldn't be convicted of possessing it. I didn't even think of selling it. Friends sold to friends, but they didn't become dealers. So I had no fear there, but I also couldn't give it away, that was a felony, too. That scared me, because I had given friends a joint or a roach. I was vulnerable there. And they could set me up like they had Peter. They'd try again and they could make my life miserable in the meantime. They *were* making it miserable.

I looked around the wide floor of the law library. There must have been a hundred students bent over their law books, preparing to become officers of the court, and here I was preparing to get busted! It hurt. I slammed the big law book closed and started to go ask for anything else he might have that could help me plot a course of protection, when a guy in a blue and gold Cal jacket walked onto the floor and looked at me. I recognized Knute, a student I'd taken a night U.S. History class with a couple of years before. He'd brought a small slab of hashish to class one night and we'd gotten high on it next to the Snow Museum on Webster Street. He'd never brought it again and I'd completely lost track of him since.

I stared at him and nodded. He was a good-looking kid, who looked like Mediterranean stock of some kind. He nodded back at me and waited for me to say something, but I walked past him and out the door onto Bancroft Way, guessing that they'd sent him and they now knew where I'd gone. There was nothing to do but study for my finals, whether they watched me or not, and I did. I had three As going into my philosophy test, where we were asked to write an essay on liberty, in a huge auditorium in Wheeler Hall. There must have been a thousand students there, but I could see Jack Dempsey's head sticking up in the very last row at the back.

He looked at me and I glanced back, then began to write. I wrote with passion and anger. I attacked Plato and his Republic on the grounds that his ideal society wouldn't fall, as he so superstitiously predicted, because of the number nine multiplied a thousand times or so, coming up and causing its downfall. It would fall because he limited the society to three types only: the workers, the soldiers and the philosopher kings. And by doing that, he violated John Stewart Mill's statement that a society that cannot tolerate eccentricity shall not have liberty and, without liberty, the genius to solve the problems of the society would not develop. This would cause its downfall. Any society that banned poets because poets stirred up the people emotionally was fascistic and deserved to fall. It was based on intellect only, not the feeling of love, not the spirit which leads to the deepest and ultimately unexplainable thought. It was a rigid society that lacked compassion. This failing applied to our own society, which made outlaws of poets, because they insisted on eccentricity and refused to sit or spit or shit like their neighbors or get drunk or smoke cigarettes or join fraternities and salute a military president, Eisenhower.

As a poet, I wasn't going to let them kill me! I believed that because I was a moral person and gave to society, that my stand for individual liberty— "the right to seek happiness as long as I didn't interfere with the happiness of others," a la John Stewart Mill—made me a patriot. In the end, my battle to be able to smoke, on occasion, the least harmful, passive stimulant on earth, marijuana, made me a patriot! I didn't smoke nicotine for the quick rush, a processed chemically treated drug that killed you for the benefit of corporate profit, or drink the most harmful of all drugs, alcohol, which contributed to people not only killing themselves and others in cars, but also committing such savage crimes as murder. I was a patriot like Thomas Paine! Like Socrates and other great rebels for freedom and beauty, like all kinds of artists. I didn't choose it. Society thrust it upon me through its rigid rules, but I would do my best to be true to those ideals, plumbed and polished in this philosophy class.

When I finished after a long two hours, I walked down to the stage and handed my examination blue book to my teaching assistant, a refugee from East Germany.

"How'd you do, Mr. Salas?" he asked. He kept his head nearly shaved like a Prussian.

"I wrote about liberty and the freedom of the artist in a dogmatic, conventional society," I said. He stopped and stared at me, and I knew I'd get an A.

The next morning at five a.m. I said goodby to my wife and hitched a ride on my brother-in-law Frank's truck to Los Angeles to write my poems and my stories and, eventually, novels that would make the society respect me for what I was. I may not have liked Plato's *Republic*, but I understood Socrates' stand, and even why he died for the principle of the thing. But I felt that he'd given in to the fascists, who did not respect the very idea of democracy he was willing to die for. They killed him when he could have continued to exert a liberating influence on the populace of Athens and possibly have saved it from its demise only fifty years later. The other Athenian citizens bought and sold votes and supplanted the democracy he believed in. He *shouldn't* have let them kill him with hemlock. He should have fought them and saved Athens. I wasn't going to let the cops kill me, if I could help it. If that meant running to get the liberty to write, about them, too, then I'd run. And I did, and won a Rockefeller Foundation Creative Writing Scholarship to Mexico City with my first series of short stories.

10

"If you want to train me for the Golden Gloves, I'll fight, Al," I said. "I know they're only three weeks away, late January, and there's not much time, but that way you can keep busy and stay off junk."

He eyed me from the front room of his apartment, in the house on Thirty-sixth that we still owned together. I never moved back after I went to L.A. to write. I was living at Dad's house on Foothill Boulevard since Dad moved to the Mojave Desert.

Al looked thinner and older now. Fifteen months behind bars in the big house had aged him. He was in good shape, though, down to one-forty without sweating it for the first time since he left the Army. He'd fought for the lightweight title of San Quentin and lost a decision because he got tired in the last round. But his body never looked slimmer and stronger.

Tommy stared at me, too, with her plain brown eyes. Her skin was very white and smooth, because she scarcely left the house, day or night. She had a lovely complexion for a thirty-year-old woman. I hadn't seen her or Al since I'd gone to L.A. to write for six months. Velva and Greg had finally followed me down. It was a lonely time, and I worked hard bussing tables by day and writing at night. But it was the first time I'd produced some really solid short stories and poems.

"Why didn't you write or come and see me at San Quentin?" he asked.

"Because you carefully told Frank I wasn't supposed to write anything about our problems, only say hello and how are you, and above all not mention anything about how you punched on me for calling you a thief and refusing to steal with you."

He smacked his lips and asked, "Then why the big change now? You wouldn't even hug me when I got sent away."

"I've paid a few dues since you've been gone myself, over pot. I can see now that it wasn't all your fault. If they'd legalize drugs, you wouldn't have to steal. The only real difference between us is the kind of drug we use. Mine's mild and yours is hard and costs you more in body wear and addiction. I can do with or without mine. You can't when you're using and it makes you commit crimes."

He showed his teeth as if he might either smile or snarl, but did neither. I said, "You also tried hard and got out of there in fifteen months, which must be some kind of record for a one-to-ten on grand theft. I respect that, and I'll help you because you tried to help yourself." I smiled at him and then said, "You got out of San Quentin on December 7th, 1957, Pearl Harbor Day, a day of catastrophe for our nation. I figure the country needs my help, too."

He didn't grin back, but said, "Try it again, huh?"

"Yeah, but this time you don't have to train, just train me, and you'll have something to do with your free time."

He eyed me again, then looked at Velva, who was standing next to me in his front room.

She seemed to anticipate the question in his eyes and said, "If he wants to try and help you, Al, it's okay with me."

He nodded slowly, without saying anything, but Tommy said, "Humph!" and looked away with a puffed, sullen mouth.

11

Sweat ran into my eyes, dripped in damp spots on the floor below me. "Uuuunnnnh!" I groaned and, with my feet on the bench next to the ring in Babe Figuera's gym, I pushed myself up for the eighteenth pushup, doing my exercises last after working out for two hours already. I had to stop and rest and try to get the strength to try for the nineteenth and twentieth pushups. It was torture getting in shape again for the first time in ten years. The Golden Gloves were starting at the end of the month and I only had three weeks to lose twelve pounds and get in shape. I now weighed one-thirty-one, not the one-nineteen of the natural bantamweight I'd been for years or the one-twenty-six at Cal when I'd gotten the boxing scholarship in '56.

"Two more," Al said, standing over me. I could only see his legs in slacks and his black dress shoes to my side, nothing more. I took a deep breath and dropped slowly down, then pushed and grunted again and got the nineteenth one. I took a deep breath and dropped down again for the twentieth, but couldn't push up. I had to wait there until I got the strength and then almost caved in on my left elbow pushing up again, but did it! I put my feet down and stood up, sweat running down my face.

The gym was in an old ballroom, where I'd come with Walter Soots, who was one of my buddies then, before he turned fink. He used to come out and practice clarinet in the amateur vaudeville show here during the war. Now, guys were punching bags back by the showers. Guys were boxing in the ring. Guys were shadowboxing and skipping rope. It was all very familiar, except for the excruciating physical exertion I was going through. That was painfully unfamiliar. I could barely punch the fast bag, my arms were so weak. I'd keep missing it or hitting it wrong and having to start over again. It was killing me, but I was determined.

"Let's box," he said. "You need to box today."

"The first day?" I said.

"Yeah," he said.

For the first time since I could remember, he looked wiry, he'd gotten in such good shape in the fifteen months at San Quentin. I realized now why he had gotten tired fighting those big guys over a hundred-and-forty pounds. He was too small. They used their weight on him. He should have been wiry, not husky as a fighter. But he was in shape now and wanted to hit me. I could see it.

"Okay," I said. I had absolutely no fear. He had never been able to hurt me with his punches, even when he picked his best shot. And sure enough, as soon as he got in the ring, he came out jabbing and punched on me, trying to hurt me. I danced away out of his range, but got tired quickly. I was so tired that I had to stand flat-footed and catch the punches on the headgear and the arms and the shoulders. He was in shape after fifteen months of no dissipation and rest and sleep and daily training in the joint. I could barely lift my arms, let alone punch back.

I could see his face, determined to hurt me in the most mechanical way as he came in leading with a jab and then throwing right crosses and left hooks. They bounced off my arms and my gloves and my headgear. Small thumps that made me cover up. I couldn't even punch back, I was so tired. I could see hard San Quentin Prison in his bony face.

I knew then how lucky I'd been as a teenager who'd been active all his life and didn't drink nor smoke. I had never smoked and still barely drank—a couple of beers on Saturday night, no more—but I wasn't a seventeen-year-old kid in natural shape anymore, either. I was twenty-seven and exhausted and I was in the ring and my brother was pounding on me, hitting me with eveything he had.

I had to go three rounds, though, even if I just stood out in the middle of the ring, trying to keep from catching any good shots to my face. I made it. I accepted the punishment, because you have to be driven and pushed and punched and made tough and hard just to box, let alone win the Gloves. That was part of the territory. But when the final bell rang, I was exhausted and felt like lying on the canvas.

Al got out of the ring, then sneered back over the top rope. "Shadow-box three rounds."

I made myself shadow-box around the ring. Some heavyweight kid with dark hair kept staring at me, as if he couldn't figure out why it didn't bother me. But I was tough and I knew what I could do when I was in shape, which included handling my brother, too.

The next morning, I was running around Lake Merritt in the wet, dark drizzle with three other fighters. I led the first mile and a half, but when we got to the small hills of lover's lane, the trainer was waiting for us and had us run quick spurts up and down the hills and around trees, which totally drained me. When he said, "You really picked those legs up there," I was really surprised, because I thought I'd run myself out already.

I sunk down into the bathtub in my father's house when I got home. It was only eight o'clock and just turning light. I lay there sweating for an hour, too tired to even get out of the tub, drained of all energy.

For breakfast, one cup of jello and a glass of skim milk, no coffee, no food at all, so I could lose eleven pounds in two weeks.

I was so weak, when I went to my desk to write on one of half a dozen short stories I had going, I had to lean back in the chair with a pillow behind me and write with a pencil in a notebook. The first words of my first novel were scrawled across the page like the scribblings of a suicide note. I was so weak, I had to rest in the chair. It took me six hours to handwrite six pages about a little boy in a reform school, a story inspired by Peter Gambarini.

I was amazed when Peter knocked on the door about three hours later. He'd come up from L.A. in his new red convertible to see his son, who lived with his ex-wife Joan in one of Dad's apartments downstairs. He was very proud because he expected to win a painting scholarship to Pomona College in L.A. He looked at the scrawled first pages of the new story I was writing based on his life and said, "You ought to give up writing and get a degree."

"Did I hear you right?" I said.

He answered, "I uh ... uh ... Oh, I think you have talent, Floyd, don't misunderstand me."

I forced myself down to the gym that afternoon, knowing I had to do it for Al, like Dorothy had told me years before. By the end of the first week, I was down to one-twenty-four already and really strong now, but I still could barely move at night after training was over. I was strong enough, okay, and when Babe Figuera asked if I wanted to box Johnny Ortega, I said sure, which I would've answered no matter who it was.

I looked over at Johnny in the opposite corner. He was still fighting ten-round main events and had been a world title contender for nine years now. He was a real pro, the fighter personified. He was wearing a sweatshirt instead of exposing his muscular body in the gym the way he used to as a teenager. I didn't give it much thought, though. He looked a little bigger, but all fighters put on muscular weight as they grow older. Most guys go up one weight class at least and lots go up more than one.

I'd seen Johnny lose a ten round fight at an arena on 10th Street in San Francisco two years before, but still I expected the same battle I'd always gotten from him ten years before when I was seventeen. So when I moved out into the center of the ring, I came to fight. I thought he was going to come and try to kill me the way he always did. I'd only fought Al once so far this comeback, and he'd tried to kill me, so I went out to fight to kill without even thinking about it. I didn't sweat it, just went out to do my best and get in shape for the Gloves, which was not much more than a week away. I was a natural bantamweight at one-nineteen and Johnny was a hundred-and-twelve-pound flyweight in good shape, but he looked heavier, too. We were both overweight by one weight class. But I was bigger and was going to use my height and weight on him.

I came out and stuck him with a stiff jab. Popped him with it a couple more times. When he jabbed, I slipped it and hit him with a quick straight counter right over his jab. I expected him to charge me and he did, but I danced away and jumped right back in and hit him with another jab and then a quick right hand. Then I did that three more times, until he caught me against the ropes and tried to maul me. I grabbed his arms and hugged him, using my height and weight on him. But Johnny flipped his left hand behind his back and hit me in the nose with a cute little shot. Everybody laughed and Babe called out, he was so pleased that Johnny got a shot in. I continued to dominate the round with jabs and one-twos and counter right hands over his jab, sometimes dropping in and sinking a right hand to his body under his jab. I felt really good. After boxing a guy as big as Al, who was naturally twenty pounds heavier, it was easy handling a little guy, even a famous fighter like Johnny.

When I went back to the corner after the first round, Al said, "You better lighten up on Johnny or you're gonna knock him out. You're killing him with that straight right hand to the head!"

After the third round, Al was really excited because I had almost knocked out a ten-round main event fighter, even if his best years were now behind him.

"Did you see how he knocked Johnny around!" he said, but the other managers in the gym weren't impressed, or at least they didn't answer back.

In the shower room, Johnny said, "You want a new sweatshirt, Floyd?" and he handed me a thick, blue sweatshirt.

"Come and have dinner with me, Johnny," I said.

In our kitchen, he didn't see the chicken breast on his plate and jerked back when I pointed it out to him. He was losing his sight! The years of ring wars had taken their toll on him; his body was used up from fighting and boozing. I hadn't done more than a little amateur boxing, had never boozed nor burned myself out like him, and still had the vigor of my youth, once I had gotten past that first painful week. He was over the hill, even if he was still good enough to fight main events.

The next day, Al didn't show up. The following morning I ran with the other fighters and he didn't show up then, either. There was only a week to go before the Gloves and I needed to be trained. He didn't show up again on the third day, but I nodded when Babe asked me to box Johnny again.

I didn't use my right hand on Johnny. Just jabbed around and stayed away and didn't punch on him. When Babe was taking our gloves off, he said, "What was the matter with you today?"

"I didn't want to use my right hand," I said, and Johnny said, "Or you might hurt me."

When I got home and Al hadn't called, I told Velva, "He let me down like this when I was seventeen. As soon as I did well, he quit showing up at the gym, just like he's doing now. But I'm not seventeen, I'm twenty-seven, and I don't want to be a fighter, I want to be a writer. And there's only one week to go, and I weigh one-twenty one, not one-nineteen, and that's after my work-out, not before, like I have to weigh before a fight. I'm not going to kill myself when he doesn't even show up!"

She'd just come home from work, where she was assistant credit manager at a downtown woman's department store and looked pretty with her beautiful blue eyes and strawberry blond hair.

"I've had enough, Velva," I said. "I kill myself and he hasn't shown up again. Who knows what he's doing? He could be high on junk right now! And the Gloves are next week."

"I want you to do what you want to do," she said.

"Let's go see him, then."

When we found Al, he said, "It's okay with me, I just couldn't make it the last few days." He glanced at Tommy and added, "Been looking for a job." She stared right back at him and didn't say anything.

12

Al took off his hat. He had shaved his head bald, the way they did to humble him in reform school. "I need you, Floyd," he said.

The last time I'd seen him was at my sister Dorothy's house, where he snubbed me because I hadn't fought in the Gloves like we planned, blaming me for it now. I then snubbed him and when he saw my reaction, he tried to be friendly again. He came up and said, "Some little bantamweight you would have knocked out for sure won the Gloves."

I didn't argue the point with him. He'd gotten hooked and thrown in jail again when I was gone, didn't pay on the mortgage for eighteen months, not a penny on the taxes, and wound up losing the apartment house. But I worked hard on my stories and entered the Rockefeller Foundation contest and won a scholarship to a writing center in Mexico City. Dorothy had told me he wanted to see me when I got back from Mexico.

When I saw him, I hugged him and said, "I'll help you, Al. I promise."

I did more than that. I took him up into the hills to Redwood Park, where I'd camped out as a kid and showed him the pound of pot I'd brought back from Mexico and buried in the ground.

"I'll share it with you," I said.

I was working as an assistant to a foreman in a cannery that summer. I got Al hired on with me, too. But just a few days after I'd shown Al the pot, when I was relieving some guy on a canning machine, a guy I'd seen around stopped to talk to me. He had a muscular body that he showed all the time by stripping to the waist because of the heat of the machines. He said, "Rudy Archuleta went to your house to get a lid of pot for twenty bucks today."

I looked into the smug, wise-guy face with his pencil-thin mustache and, without a word, dropped in low to my right and looped a sweeping left hook right into the middle of his gut.

"Uuuuuuuuuu," he groaned and doubled over as if he were doing a jack-knife dive.

Gilbert Sierra, a pretty, pale-skinned guy who looked ten years younger than his thirty-odd years, was standing near me. He had seen it all and watched when I stepped up to the guy, still bent over, and told him, "If you fight back, man, you'll lose."

"IIIII'm hiiiiiiip," the guy groaned, still gripping his belly.

"Did you tell your cousin-in-law that I had some pot to sell, Al?" I asked, facing him off in my writing room.

"I just mentioned we had it," Al said. He kept his face turned away from mine.

"He's got a reputation as a fink."

When Al didn't say anything, I said, "You could have gotten me busted. Now they know I have it. You put me on the spot. They're going to keep trying. You put pressure on me. Don't ever go up to that pound without me and don't ever tell anybody you've got any of my pot to sell.

He turned and faced me. "All right," he said, then walked out of the room.

Al kept his cannery job until I gave him my next temporary job as busboy that fall at Mitch's, a first-class restaurant in downtown Oakland. I quit so I could sell shoes at night and on weekends part-time and go to school and write during the day. I'd been so good on the job the two weeks I'd been there, they'd said I'd be a top waiter if I kept at it. I didn't. I brought Al in on a Saturday night when they couldn't get another busboy from the union hall. I told them I was quitting, but that my brother could take my place.

I used to go by and pick up Al sometimes. One night, when I was waiting in the bar for him, the maître d' came over and told me that being in prison had made Al a little slow. He needed to get some more hustle into him. After Al got off, I told him what the maître d' said. He went home and beat up Tommy, then came back and became such an excellent bus boy that they trained him to be a waiter.

He stayed at the waiter's job, making good money, and chippying with junk, but not getting hooked until his parole was up. Then he quit his job, started stealing and got hooked again. I'd done what I could. The rest was up to him.

13

"GeeGee got busted with a police inspector's son on a burglary charge, Floyd. You gotta help me," Al said.

I found myself sitting that day in a juvenile probation officer's office trying to save Al's thirteen-year-old son, saying, "I'll take the boy to live with me, if it'll keep him from being sent away."

GeeGee's eyes got wild that first night in my house when I told him he was starting school the very next day, his first order. He started screaming like a wild ape. It shocked me. My whole body tingled with a weak fear at the gutteral cries and the wild, blazing eyes. But I caught myself, suddenly understanding that he had willed it, that he knew what he was doing. I pulled my belt off my pants right then and whipped him with it for five or so whacks until the madness went out of his eyes and he started sobbing. Then I stopped and took him for a very long walk around the neighborhood and told him I would never touch him again, and he never threw another fit again, either. I do believe I kept him from forming a habit of flipping out and going crazy when he wanted to control adults, which would have led him to the nuthouse, for sure.

He could draw, I knew, from having lived in the same house with him on Thirty-sixth Street. His first drawings were sharp with jagged lines, spear points, knives and monsters with fanged teeth in hard, dull colors, full of anger and suffering. So, I took him and Greg out on Saturdays to sketch boats on the estuary. By the time he left us six months later, he was drawing pastel-colored hills with round, flowing lines that looked like festive balloons rising up into pale blue skies. Sweet instead of sinister. I matted all of them, glued them to black cardboard with a border. He took them all when he left, without giving me one, and they were soon thrown away at his mother's house. But I still have one he drew on Thirty-sixth Street when he was only eight.

I had made one big mistake. Al came over one day and I overhead him talking to GeeGee in the tiny room he shared with Greg. I was in the kitchen sitting at the table, waiting for Al to come back in the room.

"I wouldn't hang around with a kid like that when I was your age. I hung around with cool guys," Al was telling GeeGee. He was talking about a cute, little, cleancut, pudgy kid about nine years old who lived down the block and was Greg's friend. His mother was a fair-haired English woman his father had met and married overseas during World War II.

I stood up to say something, but didn't want to interfere between a father and his son. I wanted to ask him if he wanted GeeGee to be like him, and what had happened to all those cool dudes he hung around with. Every single one of them went to prison, probably. But I didn't say anything, and I lived to regret it.

While playing darts in the house, GeeGee stuck Greg with one. I knew it was deliberate. While playing basketball, he hit Gregory in the face with it and broke his nose. I loved GeeGee and felt sorry for him, but he was just like his father. Al's son was doing to my son what Al had done to me. Cain and Abel.

We went to court and the judge tried to get me to keep GeeGee with me after I showed the court the difference in his crayon drawings. I told them that he never had a chance to make it because, no matter what Velva and I did to help him, his mother and father undercut our efforts. Al wanted to be admired as a tough guy and Tommy wanted the child assistance check. Neither of them cared much about the boy. They lived off the welfare checks they got for those nine kids. That's why they didn't care if they had more.

14

When I drove away from my apartment, I was usually followed by a man in a station wagon. Every time I crossed the Bay Bridge on the way to San Francisco State, where I was now working toward a degree in Creative Writing, a car full of sailors would drive alongside me, two with their backs to me, two facing me, as if they were talking to each other.

A green sedan with a long antenna and a license plate with the call numbers of a shortwave radio station would come by the house on Carrington Street at least once a day. It was driven by a thick-necked, middle-aged, black-haired man. He would slow down on the hill outside the house, stare up at the big bay window where I sat at my desk, then drive slowly by.

A firetruck started coming by once or twice a week, too. The truck would turn the corner from the side street and cruise past the front of the house with all the firemen on the truck staring up at me! It was unnerving, but I got the point: I was hot! They'd never stopped, but now they were putting the pressure on me again.

Al showed up soon after that. I told him, "I've got cops on my tail."

"Naaaaaaw," Al said out of the side of his mouth, squinting one eye, pushing his snap-brimmed hat back on his high forehead. But his dark, hollowed eyes never met mine.

"Nobody's after you. You're too respectable. But if you need to get some money to work on your book, why don't you help me plan a big job? You're supposed to be a big brain. We could make a lot of money. You could go off to the mountains like you want to and write your book, quit breaking your ass on a job, too."

The idea was tempting. It was just a matter of time before the cops set me up at the shoe store on Fillmore, where I worked nights and Saturdays. With some money, I'd be able to go away and write a novel, get it published and come back a big enough success that they'd have to leave me alone. But I'd been through that crime thing with Al before and I didn't like it. What would Eddy think of it? I said, "No. Not ever again. We've gone through this already."

He squinted at me, didn't speak for a moment, then said, "How about some weed? You could use some weed. You always need weed. I know where you can get a pound quick."

I straightened up and nodded. "Yeah. If you know where I can get it, I'd like some weed. It helps me write. It'll keep me from going out on the streets and getting set up."

We were smoking a joint as we drove along the big boulevard to the dealer's place, when I spotted a station wagon with four big, beefy men inside. It was coming up fast behind us, as if trying to pull alongside my car. "Cup that joint, Al. There's a car full of cops coming up on us," I said. Without speeding up too quickly, I changed lanes and slowly out-sped the station wagon, then turned off the boulevard and went around a block and came back up on the boulevard. I didn't see them again. I waited in the car while Al went inside a big gray apartment house on Twenty-seventh Avenue and Foothill Boulevard. I noticed a car with a conventional looking man and woman in it parked a couple of cars behind me. They looked too old to be sitting around in cars necking. I waited for a half an hour and, wondering what was happening, finally rang the bell of the dealer. I was let in to find Al and the connection, a tall, gray-haired man who tended bar, with two full hypos of methedrine ready for use on a coffee table. As soon as I stepped in, Al tied his bicep muscle, bent his arm and shot into the big vein of his forearm. He wiped off the blood and set the hypo down. I waited for the tall guy to shoot up, too, but he said, "I don't want it. You can have it," and pointed at the hypo.

"Not me," I said.

"I guess I'll have to take it, then," Al said and picked up the needle and looked at me. "Make you feel better," he said. But I just stared back at him as he tied up his other arm and put the needle to the forearm. Then he looked at me again and I just shook my head.

He plunged it in and the second jolt seemed to lift him up on his toes and turn him into a zombie with bulging eyes and stiff limbs. He was so comic that a wave of love swept over me at my crazy, crazy brother. I reached over, wrapped my arms around his waist and lifted him up in the air, saying, "You're crazy, Al!" But I put him down again and asked, "Where's the pound?"

He pointed at the bartender, but didn't speak. The bartender came back out with a paper bag about the size of a pound of coffee. I took it, looked inside and paid the guy a hundred dollars. Then I said, "Let's get out of here."

But Al only dropped down in the sofa chair and stared with glazed eyes at the ceiling.

"Let's go," I said, again.

Al only waved his hand and said, "Take it home. I'll see you there."

The couple was still sitting in the car like twin shadows in the twilight. I had no coat to hide the brown paper bag. I knew they'd see it and that I was in danger. I put the car in gear and drove toward the stop sign on the corner only a hundred feet away just as a pickup truck parked on the boulevard with two men in it suddenly pulled across the street and parked in the crosswalk in front of me, completely blocking my lane.

I stopped and glanced in the rearview mirror, the car with the man and woman in it had now pulled out from the curb and were coming right up behind me. Fear shot through me, but I swerved my car to the right, bounced up a curb, and sped across the corner of a service station and out onto Foothill Boulevard, out of the trap between the two cars. The truck chased me and I sped up and made a right turn on the next corner, shot down a side street to the next corner and turned left. But the truck was still on me and I zigzagged from one street to the next, my lights off in the twilight, increasing my distance from the truck until I lost it. Then I shot up into the Oakland hills to Joaquin Miller Park, where I hid the bag in a bush behind the dead poet's little white cottage. I'd get it later, when it was safe.

When I got home, I stepped to my desk, turned off the lights and watched a cop get out of his patrol car. He shined his flashlight on both sides of the front hedge and along the plants just under my big bay window, where I sometimes hid my pot. He wasn't going to find that pot, but one thing I knew: I could never trust my brother Al again. The thought tortured me. When the cop drove away, I drove back up into the hills, got the pot, drove back down and hid it in the backyard of my father's house.

Two days later, I went over to see Dad and to check to see if the ground had been disturbed. Al was there with Dad. I went into the kitchen.

Dad said, "Al, show your brother what you've got. Don't keep anything from your brother."

Al went out on the back porch and came back into the kitchen, carrying a black pistol. I knew as soon as I saw it that he was now going to try and get me to commit an armed robbery. Without saying a word, I stomped out of the kitchen, grabbed the oil painting of Eddy from above the fireplace and stalked out with tears in my eyes. When I got home, I started writing. I knew I had to write. And I would never speak to my brother again.

> A man stands by my bed
> and squeezes the top of my head
> with his hand

black hand color of the night
shade of the dark
black hand like its brother
that holds my chest down

I try to yell to scream out
but can only cough
We wander from room to room
taking our little blue bags with us
searching for an empty bed
There is no place in this house for me
I have lost my bag
the shape of my heart
muscle of my love
hid like a corpse there

My father is dead
I walk with his ghost
a scar on his neck
to cover up a boil
We walk into prison
to search for my brother
my lost brother
brother with a gun
and a dick in his hand
He shoves it up against the bars
through the stripes of his pants

There is no honor among thieves
He will bleed me down to serum for his vein
and pop me into his arm
He will sell me to the fence
at the corner grocery store
He will sell me to the rag sheeny
who trots his bony horse
through the alleys
swishing at flies
blinders on his eyes
He will sell me for a gun
to kill my father and we'll all die in the end

I walk with my lost brother
in a strange city
He has been drinking
I try to find a place for him to rest
I ask people
old men
girls
They shake their heads
There is no room in this house for the dead
We stand alone in the street
my brother and I
and cry.

PART SEVEN

Blood Money

1

I was crying for him, for Al. The day was gray, overcast, with a stormy-dark sky. I think I was by a train station, a gray depot, as gray almost as the sky. And my big sister Dorothy was with me. She was a shadowy silhouette next to me. Something was really wrong, but when I woke up I couldn't remember what it was. But I knew I was supposed to pray like I did when I was a kid and Al got put in jail. Whatever it was, something was really wrong.

I was worried. The dream was too sad. I had just come back from a year in Europe where I had gone after the publication of my first novel, which had earned me a writing prize, The Joseph Henry Jackson Award of 1964, a Eugene F. Saxton Fellowship in 1965, a few dollars and a lot of critical acclaim.

> "Without peer . . . a work of genius, but because of its subject matter a classic without a genre." Andrew Vachss, best selling detective novel writer, in *Justice Department Magazine*.
> "One of the best and certainly one of the most important first novels published in the last ten years." Michael Curtis, editor of the *Atlantic Monthly*, in the *Saturday Review of Literature*.
> "A Classical first novel!" *New American Review*.
> "A masterwork." *Forgotten Pages of American Literature*.
> "A natural talent of tremendous strength." *Kirkus Reviews*.
> "A work of art." Walter Van Tilburg Clark.

Finally my writing had established me as a worthwhile citizen, not a criminal. My long battle, my political and artistic dissent against conformity was finally justified.

By now, I'd spent all of the money and was living with my lady, Ginny, in a studio apartment of two rooms and a bathroom at the back of a redwood-shingled house on Josephine Street in Berkeley. Velva and I had broken up a year and a half before, after she had begun to make big money and I had begun to feel unneeded. I cried, but I left her and kept on writing.

I got on the phone and called my sister, Annabelle, and asked her if she had a number for Al. She didn't, but said she'd tell him to call me if she saw him. I called my sister, Dorothy, and asked her, and she didn't either but would tell him I wanted to talk to him. That night, the dream came back to me: A sky full of dark clouds and streaks of pale light hung over me like a damp blanket. I felt both hot and chilled, sweat prickling my whole body. I woke with dark circles under my eyes, feeling tired and weak. I snatched at the phone when it rang.

"I hear you want to talk to me," Al said.

"Yeah," I said. "I had a nightmare I was crying for you. I think we better start working on that book about your life."

Silence. He had asked me to write a book about his life as a notorious dopefiend after he'd heard me speak on a half-hour TV interview. I'd talked on the show about how Al had taught me as a young boy never to lie or cheat or steal, and he'd liked that.

"It was a nightmare and ... "

"What are you, Floyd, a *brujo*?"

"What's that?" I asked.

"A witch," he said.

"No," I said. "But I'm a poet and in touch with my emotions. I pay attention to them, and I better pay attention to this."

Silence.

"Why don't you give me your ... "

"Call this number," he said before I could finish the sentence. He gave me the number. I wrote it down.

"Tomorrow, I have to go appear on a library radio show in San Francisco to talk about my new novel. The main branch. So, I can't call you till it's over."

"Call me in a couple days and we'll figure out how to get together," he said.

"Okay," I said. "It was a sad dre ... "

He hung up.

I could see the librarian interviewer through the glass. He was a round-faced guy with a strand of straight hair falling into his eyes. He wore a salt-and-pepper tweed jacket that he couldn't button across his puffy belly when he sat down.

I'd had my ex-wife Velva sell my MG when I was in Europe, so I had to hitchhike to San Francisco to be interviewed on the publication of my second novel, *What Now My Love*. Getting there took longer than I thought.

I had missed entering the radio booth by two minutes and they wouldn't let me in.

When the librarian came out, he said, "I didn't like your second book. The attitude's too anti-social for me. Dope smokers deserve what they get."

I didn't argue. The book would get great reviews in the *New York Times*, the *Boston Globe* and the *Los Angeles Times*, among many others. But I didn't feel good. I didn't feel good when I caught the Berkeley bus in front of the Terminal Building on Mission Street either. Not just because he didn't like the book, but because I'd missed the interview, too. I went to sit in the very middle of the long back seat as I usually do. Sitting by the back door was a pretty Catholic high school girl in her white blouse and blue skirt. She looked at me when I walked by, then turned on the seat and put one arm across the back of it and looked at me again.

She had pale blue eyes that shimmered beautifully with the color of her curly, naturally red hair—a soft red, not the harsh brightness of the bottle redhead—and a slightly freckled complexion. She must have been seventeen and was about five-seven or eight, a hundred and thirty-five pounds, with full breasts that stretched her white blouse. I didn't mind her looking at me. I just minded my own business and didn't stare back at her, although I did look at her when she turned back around in her seat. She faced the front most of the way across the Oakland Bay Bridge, glancing back once in a while. That's when I noticed the book in her other arm. I could read the title from my seat.

Suicide, it said.

That bothered me. I could never forget finding the dead body of my brother, Eddy, even if it had happened nineteen years earlier. Then I thought about crying for Al in the dream again. I didn't stare back or smile at her when she glanced over at me as she got off in Berkeley. Her book had depressed me. When the bus got to Shattuck and University, I decided to get off and walk from there. As I stepped down from the back door steps, I saw a slender young black man sitting on the bus-stop bench. His hand was resting on a book on the seat next to him.

Suicide, it said.

When I got home to my two-room apartment, Ginny had already come home from her job at the State Public Health Building on Shattuck. She was busy cooking dinner.

She smiled and kissed me, wrinkling her blue-green eyes at me. She had slightly red hair, too, and a slightly freckled skin, like the girl on the bus. But Ginny was petite, about five-three, a hundred-and-fifteen pounds.

She asked me how the interview went and I told her I missed it, that the interviewer, whom she'd met a couple of years past when my first novel came out, didn't like the book.

She made a face and curled her lips in a sign of displeasure.

"But that's not what really bothered me," I said. "What really bothered me was this girl on the bus with a book about suicide under her arm. I could read the word in block letters in the title. Then when I got off the bus, this black guy, who looked like a Cal student, was resting his long fingers on another book with suicide in the title, too."

"What?" she said.

"Yes," I said, and she leaned back and put her hand in front of her mouth.

"What's the matter?"

"Today, three times I got reminders about death. When it happened the third time, I thought of you and how I would have told you you were just imagining it, if you'd told me about the death signs."

"What were they?" I asked, leaning over the kitchen table.

She turned her long-lashed eyes on me. "My boss told me to go look up the death statistics on Latins in California and I saw your name Salas in the statistics. And I never see it. It's not a common name like your mother's maiden name, Sanchez. But then I saw Sanchez, too."

"Wow!" I said.

"Then, I went back up to the fourth floor and gave my boss the statistics. When I went to take my break in the cafeteria, the first thing the girls at the table talked about was how one of the women at the office, who'd missed work for three days, had been found dead in her house. It's the third death in a week of people in the health department building."

"Damn!" I said, shaking my head. "And I had that dream about Al two nights in a row. I better call that number right now."

"Go do it," she said. "I know how you sense things. Go do it. Call him and make us both feel better."

I hurried into the next room where the phone was and called the number Al had given me. It rang six times before somebody answered it. As it rang, I got more and more anxious, seeing Ginny's face watching me from the kitchen. Finally, someone picked up the phone in the middle of the seventh ring.

"Hullo," a woman with a black accent said.

"Is Al Salas there? Can I talk to him?"

"Ain't no Al Salus here."

"There's no Al Salas there?"

"No," she said.

"Are you sure? This is pretty important."

I waited in the moment of silence, hoping I'd swayed her, but she said, "No Al Salus here," and hung up.

"The dumb bastard gave me a phony number," I said.

Ginny shook her head. We didn't talk about it anymore, but I couldn't shake the bad feeling. That night, I had the bad dream again. This time when I started crying, the tears splattered on my face like a rain squall. I woke up with the ringing of the phone. I jumped out of bed and ran across the floor bare-footed to pick it up.

"Floyd," Annabelle said. Her voice was high and urgent. I could picture my round-faced little sister. I knew something was wrong.

"Yes," I said.

"Randy, Al's son, hung himself in a jail cell last night.

2

"I've come to see the body of my son, Randy Salas," Al said, holding his hat in his hand. There was a long bruise, a track of junk spikes, snaking right up the main vein of his forehead and into the thinning hair of his slowly balding skull, which was wrinkled and sweating and had the pallor of a sick man. He was forty-seven years old.

A slender clerk, a son of the shanty Irish, came swiftly out of the back of the office in a white shirt, tie and suitpants. He met Al's eyes with his pale ones, which were nearly the same tone as his silvery hair and stark with his long red wino nose. "I'll have to get it ready," he said.

"Put your hat back on, Al," I said as the man walked away, so Al would cover the junk track up the lifeline of his forehead. It looked like a bad bruise at a distance, but up close it was a clear trail of spikes—a lifeline he had to use if he wanted to get high, now that scar tissue from nineteen years of shooting junk had covered up all the veins of his body.

Al, the father of nine kids ranging in age from twenty down to ten, all raised on welfare, had a false ID in his pocket for cashing fraudulent checks. He was a three-time loser, had eight years of parole to do yet for Washington State and his sweetest son was supposed to have committed suicide in a jail cell. Randy had hung himself because he thought that his best friend had died from an overdose of reds they both had taken. They had staggered down the streets and had been arrested for being drunk.

The clerk came out a side door and held it open for us. Al hesitated, so I went first and walked down to the end of the hall, where I could just see the head of a dead man through the window of a door in an adjoining hall.

"That might be him there," I said to Al.

Al stood up on his toes and answered, "That's him, all right."

"Step in there," the thin clerk said, pointing, and we stepped into the icy hall. The all white tile floors and white tile walls, the windows and hard edges were cold and impersonal.

"Yes, that's him," my brother said.

I could see it myself through the window, although I hadn't seen the boy in ten years. I had forced my brother to come and see the body to make sure that he hadn't been beaten to death, then strung up, like some cops will do.

But the boy's face was unmarked. He had been beautiful, with arched eyebrows, large eyes with long curling lashes, a truly fine nose and perfectly shaped lips. He was beautiful even now with a deep, browned, blood-red, almost orange complexion.

"We'd like to see the body, please," I said to the clerk standing next to us.

"You won't like it," he said.

"We want to see if there are any marks on him," I said.

He swiftly stepped back into the other hall and reappeared in seconds inside the glassed room with the body of Randy. He lowered the sheet and showed us Randy's neck. A deep, dark, wine-red bruise disappeared under his chin, was caught by the chin, pressed down to his chest.

My brother shifted his weight from one foot to the other, then turned to look at me as if he wanted to go. But I said through the glass, "Let us see the whole body." The man lowered the sheet down to the slim waist of the dead boy, revealing the slight but well-proportioned torso. He lowered it enough for us to see the coroner's knife cut, now crudely stitched up, that crossed his chest like an X, from just below each bare shoulder down to each hip bone, both lines meeting in the very middle of his solar plexus. It was all stitched together like soft, crude leather.

"Show us the rest of him," I said.

The man turned to look at me, stared, but then put a towel over Randy's genitals and pulled the sheet all the way down to his feet, showing how one hand had twisted up stiffly in front of the body. It was as if it had been up against the bars and Randy might have been trying to save himself at the last minute or trying to push off the bars and tighten the noose and strangle himself faster.

"Are those bruises on his back?" I asked.

"No, that's blood," the man said.

"It's settling on the bottom of him, then, huh?" I said, and he nodded.

"Let us see the other side of him now," I said. The man cocked his head and glanced at me with his pale eyes, but turned the gurney around and drew the sheet all the way off the body this time.

"It's okay, isn't it?" my brother asked me.

But I said, "Let us see the back of his head, too," without answering Al. The man hooked his fingers in Randy's coarse brown hair, lifted his head off the block and turned the gurney around with his free hand so we could see the entire back of the head, which was just thick, pressed down hair.

"Thank you," I said.

Al and I turned around and stepped back into the main hall, walked back down the icy tile walkway to the office and started to walk out the front door when the man called out.

"Say! You'll have to sign a statement that you saw the body!"

"We had to make sure there was no foul play," I explained to the man as my brother signed. "Our brother died under mysterious circumstances nineteen years ago, and we never found out what really happened."

Al then put the pen down and, looking up from under the brim of his hat, said, "Does Mister Skiles still run the office?" Skiles had been a lieutenant of the county jail farm where my brother knew him.

The man nodded, without looking up, busy with the statement.

"Mister Skiles is a really fine man. Yes, Mister Skiles is a really fine man," my brother said, his waxy dopefiend's skin wrinkling up with a smile.

But the clerk just kept writing on the statement.

"Mister Skiles is about one of the finest men I know," my brother finally said, trying to make sure the cops wouldn't hold this against him the next time he got busted.

The clerk lifted up his face at last, smiled and murmured something.

3

When GeeGee got out of the car in the lighted parking lot of the funeral home in San Leandro about eight at night, my heart turned. Randy's older brother by a year or so, he had the same fine, sensitive features, but an olive complexion, not the pinkish tinge of Randy.

He waved to me, then turned and met the rush of a young, slender woman with a dark complexion and dark hair who threw her arms around him. I watched them hug each other. It was touching. I guessed who she was, his wife, although I wasn't sure they were legally married. They were mates, though, and she'd had his kid.

He was out of Santa Rita Prison Farm on a pass for the funeral of his brother. I think he was in on a drug charge, but I didn't know the details and didn't ask. I waited for him to finish greeting her before I stepped up to them.

"Hi, Uncle Floyd," he said in his tiny voice, which was so out of character with the thin, black line of the tough guy mustache over his upper lip.

"Hi, GeeGee," I said and then looked at her. She had a tiny cross tattooed between her eyebrows. She was as finely featured as he. But the cross marked her as an outcast and bothered me. I'd written my first novel about reform school kids who tattooed themselves like that and called it *Tattoo the Wicked Cross*.

I hadn't seen GeeGee in two years, since Thanksgiving, 1967, at my big, modern cabin by Big Basin State Park, when I'd invited the family up as an attempt at reconciliation with them. I had stopped seeing any of them in 1962 when I felt they were cooperating with the narcotics cops to bust me for pot. After the success of my first novel, I was trying to trust them again by inviting them all to Thanksgiving. Al had brought GeeGee up to the redwood ranch. Both of them were high on heroin. GeeGee looked so slender and pretty then, it was hard to guess that he was loaded. But at the funeral he was straight.

I shook his hand and hugged him. He turned and said hello to Ginny and introduced us to his woman, Rosemary.

I looked into her eyes. She met my eyes and blushed. She was dark and petite, just as delicately built as GeeGee.

I was really surprised to see my Aunt Mattie get out of a car and greet me. A redheaded lady, her complexion was as creamy white and pink as GeeGee's wife's was brown. With her was my cousin Marcella, a plump, married matron in her late thirties now, and her son, David, a slender boy with a fair complexion and brown, wavy hair. Aunty Mattie hadn't attended our family gatherings since my mother, her sister, died. So, to see her in 1969 at the funeral of a nephew's son she didn't know was a surprise to me. She smiled and greeted me, introduced me to her grandson and was gracious in meeting Ginny, whom I introduced as my fiancee.

Family gathered at marriages, baptisms and funerals. There was some consolation in that. Inside the funeral home, I saw Tommy. Still a tiny woman, under five feet, with fine, narrow features and pale skin. Age had claimed her. She was soft and a little puffy now.

I felt sorry for her, losing her son to hanging that way. But Randy had tried to commit suicide for the first time at nine, when Tommy had taken off for her brother's funeral in Denver when he'd committed suicide. She had left the kids untended with no food and hadn't told anybody about the suicide of her brother. Finally, my two sisters went to their house and fed Al's six children.

They cleaned the house—the first time it'd been scrubbed in years— washed the dirty, stinking clothes that had been stacked as tall as a man on the back porch for months, washed the children and put clean clothes on them. They then took turns staying there with the children until Tommy finally came back a couple of weeks later and made sour faces at them for showing her up as a mother.

I pushed that out of my mind as I walked down to the coffin in front of the pews, where the glow of smoky candles and the heavy smell of gardenias gave a soft, warm ambience to the harsh reality of the body in the coffin. Al's oldest daughter, Anita, stood by the head of the coffin, staring down at her dead brother. She had the same fine features of her mother's family.

I watched her shake her head and moan a little, then tears fill her eyes.

"Don't cry, Anita," I said and stood next to her, put my arm around her full shoulders and squeezed. "Don't suffer too much. Look how beautiful he is," I said. "Look at his slender nose, those beautiful eyes, beautiful even now. His perfect lips. How sweet he appears."

She looked at me with teary brown eyes and nodded, caught her breath and said, "He was cocky, too, though, Uncle Floyd. Just like ... "

"Don't cry, Anita," my sister Dorothy said in her husky voice. "It's all for the best."

I looked at her. In her forties now, she was still a lovely woman with the beautiful eyes that Randy had, the same brown color and brown hair.

She didn't notice me. She was looking down at Randy and trying to console Anita. But I shook my head and barely kept myself from saying, "How in the world, even through your sentimental, optimistic, rose-colored glasses, your brave effort to make the best of everything, Dorothy, could the death by hanging of a nineteen-year-old boy be for the best?" Then I thought of Anita's unfinished sentence and knew who Randy was cocky like, who he got it from: his father, my brother.

4

"Hung himself in a jail cell?" the lawyer said, his voice rising high with shock over the phone. It seemed I did nothing but talk to people about death and suffering over the phone. I'd never met the guy, didn't have the slightest idea what he looked like. He was my lawyer Robert Treuhaft's assistant.

"Yes, a jail cell in San Leandro," I said. "My problem is, though I checked the body with his father and found no marks, I was later told that he asked the jailor how his friend was and when the guy said he died, Randy committed suicide. But his friend didn't die! The jailor lied and caused Randy to kill himself. So I think they're at fault. I just don't want them causing his death and nothing coming of it."

I didn't tell him that I thought they were all victims of drugs, the whole family, including Al. He died like a ghetto kid, but they were so uneducated, they didn't know it.

"Tell me the details," the voice said.

"Mainly, it's what I heard from the buddy he got busted with for being drunk in public. They got locked in jail while a third friend who was with them was sent to the hospital when he passed out. They were afraid he'd o.d.'d, over-dosed."

"Yes?" he said in a skeptical tone.

"Well, according to his buddy, Randy asked the cop in the San Leandro jail how his buddy was in the hospital and the cop said his buddy had died. And that night, Randy hung himself with a strip of blanket."

"How do you know this?" the voice asked.

"I talked to the guy in jail with him," I said.

"Give me Randy's whole name and the date he was in jail," the lawyer said. "I'll check into it and see what I can do."

I gave him the name and hung up, feeling pretty good.

I told Ginny about calling the lawyer when she came home and she felt better about it, too. I didn't try to call Al or Tommy because nothing might come of it. The next day I was glad I hadn't because when I answered the phone, the lawyer said, "Do you have any proof at all that the cop told him his friend died?"

His voice was harsh, punitive, not the least bit sympathetic.

"No, I don't," I said.

"Can you tell me the name of the person who told you the cop said that?"

"No, I can't right now, but I could find that out for you."

The soft Indian summer weather filled the room with a sunny glow, so different from the tone of voice of the lawyer. It depressed me. But I didn't lie when he said, "Do you know of any other witnesses?"

"No, I don't," I said.

"Is it true that this boy had been put in a juvenile camp only a year or so ago?"

"I think so. He wrote me a letter from some juvenile camp when my first novel came out and I autographed a copy of the book for him."

"And isn't it true that other members of his family have been involved with drugs?"

"Ye ... "

"Including his father?"

"Yes," I said, guessing it was all lost now.

"I'm going to ask you once more. Do you know of any witnesses to anything that occurred related to this suicide of Randolph Salas?"

"Only hearsay from that one guy and other members of my family. That's all, and I can't tell you if the other guy is credible or lying. I'm not trying to get blood money, I just ... "

"All right," he said. That's all, nothing more. He never called back and I never heard from him on that subject again. And I didn't try to call him on it.

But a couple of months later, I saw Al.

"Tommy lucked out," he said.

He was dressed nicely in slacks and a soft cream-colored alpaca sweater and short-brimmed, gray hat that covered his bruised forehead. His face looked slender and sensitive. I could tell that he was high on smack and was hooked, just because he was so slender. Still, if he had to be a dopefiend, he didn't look dirty or rundown.

"How?" I asked.

"She got ten thousand dollars!"

"Wow!" I said. "Then my efforts paid off!"

"What-a you mean your efforts?" he said.

"I called Treuhaft's office and told one of his lawyers all about it."

"When?" he said, squinting his left eye as if he still didn't believe me.

"Right after Randy died. But the lawyer was so mean to me when he called me back on it, acted so much like I'd made it all up, then never called back again, I thought that was the end of it."

He was looking at me now with his head up so I could see his whole face, his small, brown eyes open and clear. He did look better than when I'd last seen him and wondered if I was wrong about him being high. But just then he took off his hat and I could see the strands of thin hair he'd combed across his balding skull. His head was all sweaty. The spike tracks were still there. He *was* high.

"What's she doing with it?" I asked, when he didn't thank me. "Why doesn't she put a down payment on a house with it?"

"Aaaa! She's blowing it! She won't give me any, but Sonny made so much of a stink, she gave him a couple thousand."

"What-a ya mean?" I asked. Sonny was the nickname of his oldest son, named Albert after him.

"He came over and threw a fit, screamed at her, stayed on her so long, she gave him some and he went out and blew it on junk, too."

That made me blink. I didn't know Sonny used smack, too. "How about you?" I asked.

"You think she'd give me any?" he said and put his hat back on and still didn't thank me for my efforts.

I had tried to help him and his family and he didn't appreciate it. He hadn't always been that way, I thought, trying to keep my bitterness down because he'd been good to me once. Still, I said, "It's blood money."

5

"How did it happen, GeeGee?" I asked. "I'd really like to know. It's hard to believe it could happen so soon after Randy's suicide."

I could see the calm expression on GeeGee's face as he talked and I drove, shifting down the Volkswagen gears at a red light on Mission Street in Hayward. It was a sunny January day, but it was cool enough to wear a coat. GeeGee had on a brown loafer jacket and slacks as he looked straight through the windshield ahead of us. I wouldn't have thought by his face that he was describing anything important, at all, let alone the suicide of his wife, Rosemary.

"She wrote a goodbye letter to her father and put it on the kitchen table so he'd see it when he got up to go to work in the morning."

I felt my face blush with guilt. She had read my expression, seen the critical attitude in my eyes when I saw that cross on her forehead at Randy's funeral.

GeeGee stared through the window for a long time and I held back other questions I wanted to ask him, but now didn't dare. Like, what was in the note? Was she despondent over Randy? Was that why she killed herself? Were Randy and she lovers, as my sister Dorothy had told me?

From the side I could see the bubble of transparency in front of GeeGee's iris. He had the most limpid and lovely dark eyes I'd ever seen on a man. They were large and moist with long lashes, but they weren't feminine. They were just as deep and gentle as I'd remembered them when I had taken him into my home at the age of thirteen.

He glanced at me now when the light turned green and I shifted into first and gunned the motor. Volkswagens make a lot of noise for such little cars. I shifted into second and raced the engine enough to get the speed up to thirty, then shifted into third and looked at him again.

"What'd her father do?"

"He read the note and went to work, anyway, without going upstairs ... "

"Jeeesuuus Christ!" I said and still marveled at the calm way GeeGee was talking about it.

GeeGee looked sidewards at me with the first facial expression I'd seen on his face since I met him at the house. I realized then that he'd taken me away from the house, as if I wasn't wanted. I had gone to see Randy at the funeral home, but didn't go to the funeral the next morning. I didn't have a car then and didn't want to borrow Ginny's mother's car again, after already using it to go to the coroner's office and the funeral home three days in a row. Maybe they felt I slighted them? Or maybe they thought I didn't like Rosemary? Or it could have been because I'd caused trouble by insisting we go look at Randy's body. Or maybe they were embarrassed. I'd never know.

GeeGee turned and stared through the windshield again, stared for quite a few seconds, then said, "He called up his wife at noon and told her to go check on Rosemary."

He turned and looked at me again. His eyes were so dark brown they were almost black. "When his wife went upstairs, Rosemary was already dead."

"Goddamn!"

He looked at me, but didn't seem to see me at all.

I let the speed drop down to twenty-five and stayed in the right lane. We were on that two- or three-mile stretch after you leave San Leandro and enter Hayward proper, surrounded by flat residences and the occasional restaurant here, gas station there. Wide Mission Boulevard stretched out ahead of us, flat and banal.

I glanced at him again. He was looking through the window again.

"How'd she do it?" I asked, trying to keep the anger out of my voice.

"She took a vial of reds," he said, with expressionless calm.

"They're sleeping pills, aren't they? The same kind of pills Randy took to get high?"

He nodded at the windshield. His profile was so neat and fine, so clean until I got to that narrow black line of mustache on his upper lip, which looked so ugly against such clean features.

"He might have been able to save her life, if he'd gone up right away," I said, my voice rising again. I was more upset than he was. Maybe GeeGee didn't really love Rosemary? Maybe heroin use had made him cold and unfeeling already, like his father? Maybe she really did kill herself over Randy?

"Her dad didn't care or didn't believe her or what?"

GeeGee stared straight ahead again, didn't speak for a long time, then, still without looking at me, he finally said, in that same flat tone, "They didn't get along."

I suddenly knew he was high on smack.
"They fought a lot. He didn't like the way she lived.

6

Something was up, I could tell right away by the cocky look on GeeGee's face. He was smoking a cigarette and was very high, very cold and above it all, so different than yesterday when I'd suggested going to the Economic Opportunity Office, hoping I could do him some good and make up a little for looking down on Rosemary—even if I hadn't said anything about her.

"Let's go in and register," I said. I could see all the young men crowded into the EOO lobby inside.

"What for?" GeeGee said, staring into my eyes.

I thought a moment before answering. Joe, GeeGee's sister Kathy's boyfriend, was standing at my side. GeeGee had gotten a ride to the EOO office with him. Our eyes met. There was the tiniest smile on his mouth. His fair hair was combed back from his forehead. I realized at that moment that he had the same fair coloring as Kathy and they probably made a cute couple.

"To try and get a job or, maybe, even a scholarship to California College of Arts and Crafts, like we talked about. They said they want to provide opportunity. This is an opportunity." I didn't tell him that I didn't want him to kill himself like his wife and brother and that I was trying to keep it from happening.

GeeGee dropped his cigarette on the sidewalk, ground it out with his shoe sole, then turned around and stepped through the open glass doors ahead of me. I followed him in through the crowd of young men who all seemed to be wearing working men's clothes. None of them were wearing slacks and a sportcoat like GeeGee. I pointed to a desk just opposite the doors. He glanced back at me with just the slightest smirk on his mouth, but stepped ahead of me to the desk.

As he signed the register, I asked the desk clerk, "Is it possible to try and get a college scholarship as well as a job?"

The woman looked up at me. She had to be in her forties, plump and nicely dressed in a brown silken blouse and a brown skirt.

"I don't know. We've been trying to get jobs for the Latins in this community. Nobody's asked that question yet."

"I read in the paper that they were providing economic opportunities for Latins and other minorities. I know they give scholarships at Cal to Latins.

They've got a whole scholarship program going there."

She waited until I was through speaking, then said, "Talk to the interviewer about it."

"How soon can we see one?"

She looked down at her list, then counted some names on different lines and said, "About fifteen minutes. They'll call his name," she said, pointing at GeeGee with her pen.

"Thanks," I said, but GeeGee turned around and walked through the crowd of men and back out onto the sidewalk.

I glanced at Joe, who shook his head, then walked outside with me again.

"What's up, GeeGee?" I asked.

"I don't want to have to wait any fifteen minutes."

Yesterday, when I'd seen him, he had a shocked face, almost vacant of feeling. Now there was a demonic, angry glare in his bright eyes. They looked absolutely black and intense. His mouth was tight and ready to spread into an instant smirk.

"What else do you have to do?" I asked.

I took GeeGee back fifteen minutes later and the lady, a fair woman with thick, plastic glasses, wrote down everything I said and listened carefully to me when I explained that I was a former professor at San Francisco State College and had gone to California College of Arts and Crafts myself. She glanced over at GeeGee when I said that they'd let a person in, in spite of his grades, if he showed artistic talent, as he had shown in his childhood drawings.

She finally said, "I'm going to see if I can get someone to look at this and get back to Gerald, not you, because you're not the one requesting the scholarship. He's got to show that he can do it himself. But he can notify you and you can go to the college with him for the interview, if you like."

"All right, thank you," I said, smiling. When GeeGee stood up and started to walk away, I said, "Forget something, GeeGee?" He turned and said, "Huh?" then looked down at the lady and said, "Oh, yeah . . . thanks!"

7

Hickies big as bites showed on both sides of GeeGee's neck, under his chin and even on the jugular vein, darkening his olive skin into brown spots. At first sight, I wondered if he was shooting up in his neck! His father still had a bruise up the lifeline of his forehead!

"Did the lady ever call you from the EOO?" I asked.

He stood by my table next to the pool at my ex-wife Velva's home in the hills of Orinda. Velva was still very much a part of my family and attended family functions as much or more than I did, even though I left her back in September, 1966.

"No," GeeGee said and glanced over at the flickering waves in the pool.

Younger teenage nieces and nephews splashed in the water, taking turns diving from the board. Ginny played pool at the table in the family room, off the patio with my son Greg.

Velva's handsome fancy man cooked steaks in an alcove of the patio just outside the family room, his sun-bronzed muscles rippling as he turned the steaks over. The delicious smell of broiling meat wafted over the table.

I guessed GeeGee was lying. I could tell he wasn't high, but I was unhappy with him for not appreciating how I had tried to help him.

Still trying, I said, "Call her up, then. You heard her say that they wouldn't call me. Now get her moving, prove you want the scholarship. Give her a prod! They give those scholarships to Latin students at Cal. You can't get in Cal, but you can get in Arts and Crafts! I know. I did. But you have to show a little hustle. Show them that you want it!"

He just stood there and shook his head. He seemed sweet and warm, the beautiful boy that Velva and I had liked the most of Al's children when we'd lived in the apartment house my father bought us back in 1955. But he also seemed so weak, so inept. The back of his head was a little flat from not being lifted out of his crib as a baby. He'd screamed with a curdling gurgle when I walked past the head of his crib once and it scared me. That's when Al had first deserted them and, I guess, Tommy had rejected the new baby over it. She'd told me that Sonny was her favorite. That's why she didn't pay much attention to GeeGee, as if admitting it excused it.

"All right, Uncle," he said in the softest voice.

I said, "You know, GeeGee, when you speak like that in your soft, high voice, your mustache seems all out of character. It makes you look like a wanna-be tough guy, when you're not."

"You don't like it?"

"It's not that I don't like mustaches. I just don't like it on you. It's out of character. You're not a tough guy. You don't have that kind of personality."

His face was soft and full of vulnerability again.

Al nodded as if he really liked what I'd said, which surprised me, since he always projected a cocky veneer. He sat next to me, at one of the half-dozen tables on the shady side of the pool, under the porch roof. I kept myself from looking at him. I wanted to try and reach GeeGee, talk to him, help him, not pay attention to Al. But Al suddenly said, loud, "Floyd!"

"What?" I asked, trying to keep the hostility from ringing in my voice.

"Go to my car and get a package out of it for me!"

"What?" I said. I couldn't believe he'd have the guts to ask me to do his errands after GeeGee and I had just talked about GeeGee doing his own work. Even GeeGee stared at him.

"Yeah! Here's the keys." He held the keys out in his hand. It was an Oldsmobile or something like that, sportsman model.

He had half a smile on his mouth, but his small eyes were appraising me. I sensed something immediately. I could see calculation in them. Along with the straightforward stare in his brown eyes and the pallor of his sweating, balding skull, the bruise up the lifeline of his forehead gave a demonic touch to his expression.

I looked into those eyes, so different in their plain brownness from the limpid beauty of his son's nearly innocent, deep-brown eyes.

"No, man! Go out and do your own running around," I said and looked up at GeeGee. "Look at your father trying to hustle me, GeeGee! He's always manipulating somebody. Jail habits! Look at him! That's why you act like you do!"

I said it with a small grin, in a joking way, trying to keep it friendly. But GeeGee didn't smile and I turned back to Al and said, "No, Al. You go do your own thing. Don't order me around."

Al looked away and didn't say anything else. A sadness suddenly swept over me like a cold chill: I couldn't do my own brother a favor for fear it was some kind of trick.

"You like it?" Al asked the next evening.

I turned to face him at the back of the driveway, where my rear apartment was. There was only a hundred-watt porchlight to see by in the dark. Yet I could see the dark, lustrous glow of the walnut colored wood of the stereo set in the trunk of his car.

He'd pulled his brown, sports coupe Oldsmobile up into the end of the driveway, right next to the small lawn, which wasn't much bigger than the car. Kathy, his eighteen year old daughter, stood next to him as he opened the trunk of his car. He'd called me outside without even saying hello when I answered the door. He didn't even wait for me to greet Kathy before stepping to his trunk.

I could see Kathy looking at me with large, dark eyes, under thin, arching eyebrows. The creamy skin of her high cheekbones glowed in the soft porchlight.

"It looks nice," I said looking at a stereo set, and, wondering if it was a trick, asked, "What's up?"

"It's yours," he said.

I slanted my eyes at him. "What for?" I asked, the old resentment about being used rising up in me, tightening my stomach muscles.

"I would've given it to you sooner for helping GeeGee, if you'd gone out to the car at Velva's barbecue yesterday when I told you to."

He had his head raised with his hat tipped back on his high forehead. His face was narrow from not eating when he was high on smack, his mouth twisted in a smirk of contempt at me for being so dumb as to miss out on the stereo set for not doing what he'd told me to do. He still had the nice features of his youth and, in the darkness of the driveway, the hollows of his cheeks were softened by the night.

"I could use the stereo, man," I said to him. "But the set's probably stolen and belongs to somebody else, not you. So I can't take it for that reason alone."

His mouth dropped open. I could see his wide false teeth. I was right. He hadn't paid for it.

"But also, I don't like it that you'd endanger me with your present. And I mean receiving stolen goods, a felony! Why don't you give to me the way I give to you?"

His mouth closed.

"I helped GeeGee with the EOO the same way I helped him when he got in trouble as a kid and helped you when you got out of prison and I came back from Mexico. Got you jobs, put myself out for you, without risking you. You make my taking of your gift an immoral act! Why don't you spend your own money for a change and buy me a present? The same way I bought a drum set for your son Frankie for Christmas? I borrowed the money to buy that drum set! He said it was the only Christmas present he'd ever had in his whole life!"

Kathy's eyes widened, shocked that anybody would dare talk to her father that way.

"And why do you have to make it a trick? Why can't you do something honest and straight-forward? I didn't put any strings on my present!" I said. "I didn't make it a trick!"

Al's mouth came open again, the first sign that I'd somehow reached inside that veneer of dopefiend smugness. He slammed the lid of the trunk down, glancing at Kathy next to him, then stood with his feet spread and his head down and his arms at his sides, eyes staring up under the hat brim at me, as if he were getting set to throw a punch.

I went on, "And what about GeeGee? Did he follow up and call the EOO office yesterday? Why didn't you help him do that?"

"Why should I?" he said. "You know what that guy did to me last night?" Before I could answer, he said, "He tried to burn me, his own father!"

He took a step toward me and I tightened up.

"So I punched him out."

"You hit your son?" I said, thinking of GeeGee's sweet face. "Why?"

"He shot the dope I gave him to sell and then said he got burned."

His mouth was twisted in a sneer he'd picked up in some prison to protect himself from the other psychopathic cons. "Can you imagine burning his own father? I'd never have done that to my father!" He glanced at Kathy again, playing his big man role.

I said, "Your father didn't teach you how to shoot dope or steal, either!"

His head spun around toward me, eyes narrow, shoulders sloped forward, fists closed. I could see he was ready to punch. I slipped my left foot forward, my right foot back and my weight balanced so I could either take a punch or give one.

He feinted forward in a quick jerk of his body as if he was going to punch me. I waited for him. Once he threw, I'd move to slip it or block it, then hit him back. I was faster and stronger and could hit much harder than he could. For all his boxing experience, he'd never regained the power of his boxing days after he got hooked and had starved all the muscle off his body on his first long junk run. I could even take his best shot and put him away with a single punch. He knew it and I knew it. I'd saved him from big, tough gangsters—Louie Benavidez and big Boo-Boo—twice already and dumped each of them with one punch, too. Louie Benavidez didn't wake up for eighteen hours and when he did, it was in a hospital.

When I didn't go for the feint or act the slightest bit scared, he straightened up again. I noticed that he didn't look back at Kathy this time. I could see a shocked look in Kathy's eyes.

"Whatever happened with GeeGee, you caused," I said.

8

WARD 5413

Form 301–AB–39   Date of issue 10–10–70

ON ACCOUNT OF THE
SERIOUS CONDITION
of
Mr. Gerald Salas   Ward 5413
The bearer, a member of the patient's
immediate family, is authorized
to visit at any time.

As soon as I looked from the white card up to the white door to check the number, and saw the number 13 on the door in the hallway of Highland Hospital, even if it said 54 first and 54 was part of the number, I stopped, feeling like it was all preordained. I felt like they were telling me GeeGee was going to die. I wondered why I hadn't noticed the number on the card until I saw it on the door. Thirteen was ominous. Thirteen meant death.

I waited outside the half-open door and tried to get up the nerve to step in. I could feel my pulse throbbing on the outer muscle of my thigh, a quick, nervous flickering just under the leather of my bell-bottomed leather pants.

Ginny stood next to me, her face open and expectant, the blue-green of her eyes serious, her small mouth on the verge of trembling. She could feel my fear.

I put the card in the wide pocket of my leather dress jacket and stepped into the room. It was a big room with half a dozen beds spaced in a half circle around the door, each bed separated by high, hanging drapes. I glanced around me, then saw him: a thatch of black hair at the back of his head against a white pillow, face turned away toward the window. I started toward him. I could hear Ginny's high heels on the tile floor just behind me.

He didn't even move his head to look at me when I stepped up next to him. He just kept the left side of his face against the white starched pillowcase. He looked so sad, so downcast. His eyes had the transparency

305

of a fawn. With his head down, I saw how long his lashes were, how deep and soulful the dark brown color of his eyes was against the pure white of the eyeballs. How smooth his skin was, how unblemished and healthy looking. If it weren't for the sad look in his eyes on his unsmiling face, he looked in perfect, beautiful health. It didn't look possible that he could die.

"GeeGee," I said and his eyes went into the corners to look at me. He didn't move his head, as if he were too weak to even do that, and I quickly pulled a chair over and sat next to the bed, right in front of him, so I could see his face. It was a high bed, and, propped up as he was on the white pillow, I could see his face well, even on the side that leaned against the pillow.

"How are you, son?" I asked, but he continued to stare straight at my shoulder, as if even the effort to turn his eyes was too hard for him.

I ran my hand through his thick, short hair, saw how his eyes went up with the discomfort it caused him, and jerked my hand free. It hurt because I wanted to touch him and show him I loved him, make him feel better so I'd feel better. I suddenly remembered what was wrong with him. Heroin had eaten away his heart valves, but it was a new thing and they didn't know how to treat it. He was dying and they didn't, and I didn't, know what to do.

"What can I do for you?" I asked, still unable to believe that such a handsome, healthy-looking person could possibly die. I felt deep guilt for not taking him back to the EOO counselor, for not following up. "Tell me what I can do."

For the first time, his eyes turned in his face to look into mine.

"Bring my father! Tell my father I want to see him! My father, bring him here!"

His eyes were intense balls of need. Brown orbs glistened against the bright white balls. The long lashes seemed to stick up like rays. The eyes were almost as insane as they'd been that first night as a child when he'd thrown that crazy, raging fit.

My heart seemed to sink into my stomach. He wanted smack! What was killing him he had to have! I felt Ginny grab my arm and squeeze it hard, even through the thick, leather jacket. She kept squeezing it because she understood, too.

9

Annabelle stared at me from the other side of her round marble coffee table. In the bright light through the windows, I could see my mother's face in hers: the pink, oval shape, the eyebrows that slanted down at the corners, the round cheeks. Her brown hair, pulled back close to her head and bunched in a bun in the back in a stylish way gave her face class and sophistication. But there was a hard glaze to her brown eyes.

"Why can't you go to GeeGee's funeral?"

"The last one I went to, for GeeGee's wife Rosemary, they didn't want me there. They got GeeGee to drive around with me and keep me out of the way." I could hear bitterness in the tight edge of my voice.

"Didn't you notice I wasn't around at the burial or the gathering later? I went to that funeral out of respect for the family, even if they didn't deserve respect, even if they didn't respect me. Well, I don't want to go to this one because I don't respect them, neither Al nor Tommy. This time I'll save them the trouble of trying to keep me away."

I turned my head away from her, looked at the gleaming hardwood floors, crystal chandeliers, the wrought-iron staircase curling around the tower in the front corner of the expansive, two-story stucco house. Beautiful drapes framed the picture window that looked out onto a redwood tree, a green patch of lawn and some of the other beautiful homes in the tiny enclave of Veterans Street in the Diamond District at the foot of the Oakland hills.

"What about our family? Don't you respect our family? You owe it to the family to go to the funeral of your brother's son."

Her little son, Freddy, about ten years old, came into the room. He was olive-skinned like his father, Fred, with straight black hair that fell across his eyes and with a solid build, wide shoulders like his father. I saw him stare at me with dark brown eyes, then sit down on the couch and listen.

"Listen, Annabelle. Al never gave a thought to our family, not even to his own family. He killed that kid as surely as if he shot him up with an overdose himself. He got him hooked. And he didn't care if he did. He didn't care what happened to him."

"Prove it!" she said.

"Remember when Dad bought us that apartment house on Thirty-sixth Street in 1955? The second house he bought us? Al got himself good and hooked on heroin and spent all the rent money and didn't pay the mortgage!"

She stared at me with that opaque brown glare.

"I was going to college and killing myself working thirty hours a week and carrying fourteen units and running the house, too. I told him, 'Can't you see what you're doing to your kids?' And he said, 'They've got their own life, I've got mine!' That's when he was spending all their welfare money on dope! That's why he let himself have kids! Kids gave him an income! Kids meant big welfare checks! Plenty enough to get by on, if you feed them weenies and canned beans!"

Annabelle turned to her son and with her smooth cheek to me said, "Why don't you go out and play, Freddy?" But Freddy just sat there, his small legs not touching the hardwood floor.

She turned back to me and said, "Can't you do this favor for him this time? GeeGee's dead!"

I stood up from the couch and walked over to the window, looked out at the fancy houses in the cul-de-sac. Annabelle had made something of her life through hard work and character, by not doing harm to other people. I didn't want to hurt her, but I turned and said, "It's always do something for Al, never Al do anything for anybody else. Do you know how much I've done for him? He didn't pay the mortgage for eighteen months after I moved out, so he lost the house, which is worth a hundred thousand now. And now he's caused the death of the boy I took into my house, trying to save him from reform school. Now, he'll cry a little in front of everybody and get ready to kill the next kid. I'd like to bust him in the mouth for what he's done to those kids. I'm not going."

She lifted her chin to speak, but I poked my right index finger up.

"Dorothy told me once that I was the only person who could save Al. I took her at her word. When he got out of jail—Twice! Twice!—I tried to keep him off heroin by getting him to hang around with me. I took him to college parties. I took him around my college buddies. But by the time it was over, he even had me helping him steal, supposedly to keep him off heroin."

She shook her head as if she could never believe that.

"He conned me and used me and took advantage of my wanting to help him to corrupt me, just so he could get some dope as soon as possible. Then, as soon as he bought it, which was as soon as he got some money, I quit trying to help him and went back to school."

She turned to her son again and said, "Why don't you go outside, Freddy?" He stood up and glanced over his shoulder as he went up the curving stairs to the second floor toward his room. Then she turned to me again and said, "This is the second son that's died, Floyd! Can't you get that into your head?"

I could see little Freddy's legs in his green cords showing at the top of the stairs, as if he were still listening. I knew she didn't want him to hear what we were talking about, but it was too late now.

"Get it into my head!" I said, jabbing my finger at her like a prosecutor. "Al killed GeeGee as surely as if he put a gun to his head."

Her round face turned back and forth in one slow disbelieving shake. Then our eyes locked.

"I overheard Al in the tiny bedroom GeeGee shared with Greg, when I was taking care of GeeGee. He was telling GeeGee not to hang around with a clean cut, nine-year-old kid who lived down the block, that he wouldn't hang around with a little punk like that when he was his age. He only hung around with 'cool dudes,' and every goddamn one of them ended up in reform school and prison!"

Annabelle didn't flinch when my voice rose with the strong feeling in me.

"I was in the next room when he said it, and I wish I'd said something then like I wanted to, and GeeGee might be alive today! But GeeGee's dead and you want me to go to his funeral!"

She flinched this time and looked down at the shiny, hardwood floor. Her mouth puffed as if she might cry, but she kept her eyes down as if she couldn't bear to look at me. I could still see the green corduroy of Freddy's legs at the top of the stairs. She looked up at me and said, "I still think you should go to the funeral."

"How can you say that? After everything I just told you?" I shouted.

She jumped up and screamed, "I don't care! There's still the family! I want you to go-ooo!"

Her cheeks puffed and her face turned red. Little Freddy started down the stairs. I could see a frown on his face. When he looked at me, he glared.

"Annabelle. Listen to me," I said. "Al didn't shoot GeeGee with a gun, but he caused his death and the death of Randy. He the same as led GeeGee to commit suicide, like Randy. GeeGee killed himself with that heroin because he didn't want to live anymore. He surrendered because he felt his life was hopeless. He lost the will to survive. He quit fighting to live and just took an easy suicide out! Instead of hanging himself like Randy or taking an overdose of pills like his wife! Don't you understand that?"

"No!" she shouted. "I don't understand that! He did not commit suicide! He died from using dirty heroin! The valves of his heart collapsed!"

I lowered my voice this time, trying to keep the whole thing even a little bit sane. "Since Randy's suicide, and then GeeGee's wife's suicide, plus our brother's suicide, twenty years ago, plus Tommy's brother's suicide, about eleven years ago, I've researched suicide. I've read a stack of books, laid flat, a desk high!" I held my hand up to my thigh. "A life style of self-destructive behavior can be a form of subconscious suicide. Don't you realize that Kathy's next? Don't you know that? Don't you know that Kathy's going to die next?"

It was as if the steam went out of her body. Her face seemed to lengthen, the frown came back over it.

"I took her shopping with me last week," she said in a high, squeaking voice, "and she had a convulsion in the middle of the department store!"

10

The ringing of the phone sent an electric shock through me. I stopped writing in my bound journal and sat up, then dropped my pen with the second ring and, with a tingling sense of apprehension in me, stood up from the kitchen table.

On the third ring, still tense, I stepped into the hallway, where the phone sat in a wall nook. I picked it up on the fourth ring and hesitated a moment, heard the tense silence on the line, and then said, "Hello?"

"Floyd! Kathy killed herself last night!" my father said. I fell against the wall, ducked my head, and put one hand over it.

"Oh, noooooo!"

"Yeee-es," he said in a quavering voice and then told me where the memorial service and funeral were going to be. I didn't listen. I knew I couldn't go, ever!

I kept seeing her up at Big Basin Ranch at Thanksgiving in 1967—years ago—beautiful with her fair, tawny complexion and slender figure, full of fun and the joy and vigor of being sixteen.

I couldn't help but think that my near fight with Al over the hot stereo had a disillusioning influence on her. He took her around with him because she was pretty and he couldn't get a girl, let alone a pretty young one anymore. He needed someone to show off in front of. When I refused his hot present and called his bluff, I might have made her see what he really was. I had taken away what little she had to believe in, which depressed her, made her feel hopeless. It could have helped kill her. That thought hung in my head.

Nobody pressed me this time to go to her funeral. They knew I wouldn't go. I guessed that Annabelle had Dad call me about Kathy because she couldn't after our argument and my prediction that Kathy would die next.

The next day I got a copy of the *Daily Review* from Hayward, December 9, 1970, and read what happened.

"Hayward Family
"3RD CHILD LOST TO 'DRUGS'
"Hayward – The Albert Salas family, 1210 Highland Blvd.
lost its third child in a death related to drugs or alcohol when

Kathleen Salas, 19, hung herself last night at Fairmont Hospital, the county coroner's office reported.

"The coroner's report said Miss Salas, despondent over the deaths of two brothers within the last 14 months, slashed her left wrist and took a deadly combination of Seconal (a barbiturate sleeping pill) and champagne.

"She was taken to the hospital at 3:50 p.m. yesterday and placed in one of the two special detention rooms used for attempted suicide victims. At 10:15 p.m. she was pronounced dead after being discovered hanging from a sheet she had tied to the bed and looped over an inward-opening window, the coroner said.

"Hayward police records show that one brother, Randolph R. Salas, also 19, was booked into the city jail on Oct. 17, 1969, on a charge of being drunk in public and that he hung himself the following night in his cell, using a strip torn from a blanket.

"Gerald Mark Salas, 21, the other brother, was admitted to Fairmont Hospital on Oct. 8, suffering from vomiting and jaundice, was transferred to Highland General Hospital, and died there Oct. 10, the coroner said. An autopsy uncovered narcotic vegetations (ulceration) of the heart valves and morphine (heroin) in his bloodstream.

"The coroner's office said that in retrospect it was clear he was suffering from necrotizing angitis, a disease associated with heavy drug use, first reported by a group of Los Angeles doctors last month.

"Records at Fairmont and elsewhere indicate all three Salas children had used heroin, the coroner's office said.

"Dr. Anton Tratar, the director of clinical services at Fairmont, said the handling of Miss Salas' case is being reviewed to determine, among other things, how long she was left alone in the detention room. The hospital has no specific guidelines for surveillance of suicidal patients but in each case a doctor decides how often a nurse should check the patient, Tratar said."

A short time later, I heard from Annabelle that Kathy's boyfriend, Joe Pacheco, had hung himself in a back shed, leaving a suicide note that said he couldn't live without her. He died with her picture right in front of him. "P.S. I'm straight," he added.

11

The phone rang again. It was about six and dark outside already. Ginny and I had already eaten dinner. I was afraid to answer the phone now. Kathy's death had put that fear in me. And sure enough when I picked it up, Annabelle said, "Floyd, Dad's in a coma at Merritt Hospital. He's been there for three days."

When we walked around the edge of a high building, heading toward the main office at Merritt, a woman passing by in the opposite direction, as if she'd just finished a visit, said to the man with her, "People have to die and you have to adjust to it."

Upstairs, the nurse told us the room number. But when I got to the door, there was a note on it that said, "Have a good time and go out with lots of girls."

Inside, a thirtiesh black man lay on a bed, grinning at some other guy in another bed. Ginny and I walked up to a narrow gurney with high slats on the sides like an infant's bed. My father lay straight and still on his back inside it, his eyes closed as if he were already dead.

All the wasted years I could've loved him hit me as I stood there looking down at his strong face with its aquiline nose, perfect lips, the shiny, perfectly shaped skull. For all his weight, it had never shown in his face. He'd never had fat cheeks nor jowls and, even now at 76, the skin around his eyes was smooth. There wasn't even a crease on his brow. He looked good, just asleep. But the eyelids stayed closed and I reached inside and touched his face. Tears started running out of my eyes and down my cheeks.

I could see the young black man watching me, but I didn't care.

"Daddy, Daddy, Daddy," I sobbed, then suddenly bent down next to his ear and shouted, "Daddyyyyyyy! It's Floyyyyyyyyyyyyd!"

Just as I straighted up, one eye opened and from under an arched eyebrow looked right into my eyes.

The next day, my father had been moved to a regular-sized bed in a regular room. He had one hand tied to a sidebar so he wouldn't pull the IV out. I stepped up next to him and leaned down over him again. I sniffed his cheek, loving the warm smell of his skin, sniffed his ear, where the white hairs curled out, then sniffed up his bald temple to his balding head, across the top of it to the other side of his face, taking in the warm, living smell, loving it, loving my father alive. I sniffed down his face to the open collar of his nightgown, sniffed at his wrinkled neck, then down his arm, outside the blankets to his right hand which was tied to the bed frame, sniffed the palm, loving the warm, living smell, and, loving my father. I turned my head and laid my cheek in my father's palm and saw his eyes suddenly widen with wonder at my love for him. Then, a slight smile spread across his lips and his whole face glowed with light.

I pressed his palm against my cheek and held it there, looking into my father's eyes, loving the glowing love in my father's face. I held it there for a long moment, never moving from his hand, never looking away. Eye to eye, face to face, close to my father, really, for the first time in a long time, tears of happiness rose up inside me.

"How's Dad?" I asked when I stepped into the hospital room and saw everyone standing around the bed looking down at him. My sister Dorothy's daughter Lydia, Annabelle, Fred, Annabelle's husband, and Dorothy and Frank were there. Al was there, too, with his son Sonny.

Then I saw Dad propped up on several pillows, his eyes closed, taking deep breaths, nearly grunting for each one. His eyelids were closed, his strong nose curving down toward his upper lip. His arching brows seemed beautiful but, with his eyes closed, they were deeply sad. His big belly stuck up. He didn't move.

"Daddy! Daddy!" I said, then started sobbing, seeing through my tears my brother and sisters, my niece, my nephew Sonny standing blurrily around the bed, watching me.

"Daddy! Daddy!" I cried again, but when he lay there, his big belly rising up and down with his gasping breaths, just lay there as if dead, all gray and bloodless, with gray stubbled hair at the sides of his bald head, I sobbed, "Daddy! Daddy! Daddy!" Then I reached up and started stroking his head, stroking his head, stroking his head, and kept sobbing and crying, "Daddy! Daddy!"

"You better touch him. You'll never touch him again. You better touch him now!" I said and reached out with both hands and squeezed his shoulders.

And, still sobbing, I squeezed his big chest and his arms again, and stroked his smooth, bald head, kissed his cheeks and kept squeezing him.

"You shouldn't do that!" Dolores said, stepping into the room, frowning. "That's sacrilegious!"

"Touch him, if you want, Floyd!" Al said, and Dolores turned and walked out of the room. I looked at Al to thank him for once, but noticed his son Sonnyboy standing next to him, staring at Dad with a frown of dislike on his pale face. I knew he'd been taught by his mother to dislike him. I turned and looked down at Dad in the big, soft bed, still gasping for breath. A sob burst out of me again.

12

Sonny led me into the house somewhere in North Oakland, a little cottage that didn't look big enough to be a shelter for addicts. Yet, sure enough, a beautiful girl lay sound asleep on a mattress right in the middle of the front-room floor, in the middle of the day. There were haunting hollows in her slender cheeks, her dark hair was sprayed across the wrinkled white pillow. Her lips swelled in a sensual puff. Her nose made an exquisite point. She was gorgeous to look at, making me long for her. Yet the word *dopefiend* rang in my head and frightened me, made her tragic, made me hurt for her.

"They said we could stay here a week, my wife and I, then we have to find another place," Sonny said. I hadn't seen him since Dad had died the year before and I'd never forgotten that look of dislike on his face.

"You can come and see me, if you need help," I said. "I'll try to help you."

"Thanks, Uncle Floyd," he said and reached out to shake my hand.

I took it and looked into his eyes. He had pale skin and very fine features, like all his brothers and sister. I had known him since he was a baby, had seen him living in rat holes when his father was hooked or in jail. We'd all lived together in the apartment house my father bought us. Al's kids were wild animals. Sonny, dying for love and attention, willing to kill to get it, would go around the house destroying it methodically, ripping the wallpaper off, taking a broom and knocking out the steps of the back staircase. Once he even smashed with a ballpeen hammer a big, soft clay sculpture I had been working on for months. He'd scream and start fights with strangers at family picnics to attract attention, like his father, for his father, so his father would look at him. It took everything I had to like him, but I tried, and though I never loved him like I loved GeeGee, I learned to like him and care for him when he got older and he quit acting like a brat. He tried to behave around me.

"I have to go to Mendocino to teach poetry for a week, but call me the following week and let me know how you're doing."

"Okay, Uncle," he said and shook my hand again, hard.

When I got back from Mendocino a week later, Ginny told me that he had called up and asked for forty bucks or so and told her that I said he could have it. So I didn't call him. I didn't want to support his habit.

316

I didn't hear from Sonny for two years after that.

In January of 1973, I found my own son Greg shivering with the DTs in the flat he'd rented to go to Laney College. I fell on the bed and hugged him. "Not you, too," I thought, wondering if there was a curse on the family. I got him to move to Sacramento with Ginny and me and go to school. I couldn't take the chance of leaving him alone. A couple of months later, the phone rang. I was sitting writing at an old PG & E utility cable roller that I'd made into a table.

"Uncle Floyd! This is Sonny! I'm in a drug program at Contra Costa County Hospital."

"I'm glad to hear it, Sonny."

"We're having a talent program this Friday and I'm going to be in it. I wondered if I could borrow your conga and bongo drums?"

"Sonny," I said, "I don't have a car. Ginny's still working in Berkeley for a couple more weeks and living with her father and mother in Pinole. She uses her car to drive to work in Berkeley from there and only brings it down here to Sacramento on weekends. I just can't get up there next Thursday to lend them to you or to see you."

"Okay, Uncle Floyd," he said, and I quickly added, "Also, I've got Greg in junior college down here. He's doing well. I've got to be here when he comes home and cook dinner for him and support him, give him some companionship. He's still got his drinking problem. I'm sorry, Sonny."

The line hummed with silence. A few months later, he was in Santa Rita Prison Farm on a drug charge and Greg went to see him. A week after the visit, Greg's face was sallow and intent as he stared out the window of our Sacramento cottage.

"I went to see Sonnyboy at Santa Rita Prison Farm, like he asked me to and like you told me to, Dad. And I told him to get his act together, get out, get a job and stay clean, because I didn't want to go to his funeral, too!"

He turned and looked at me. His big, sloping brown eyes were nearly gray, they were so pale. They seemed to glisten as if he might cry.

"Sonny said he was going to do what I said! He was glad to see me! I told you, remember? Remember I told you?"

"Yes," I said, wanting to reach out and touch him, but didn't, not wanting to stop him from getting it out of him. He looked right at me with wide, round eyes.

"And then he goes and hangs himself in the hole!"

"I'm really sorry about Sonnyboy, Al," I said the next time I saw him at a family picnic, feeling a little guilty about not taking those bongo drums to Sonny. Nobody called me with details about the funeral.

"Sonnyboy didn't like jail. He should have never been in there," Al said, a softball glove hanging from his hand. He was walking out onto the grassy field to play. He'd learned to play games to help do time, a form of extended boyhood that all convicts have. "It's his own fault."

I couldn't believe the coldness, even if he was a junky. I narrowed my eyes at him. He was older now, still had the hollows in his junky cheeks, but he also had crows feet wrinkling out from his eyes, and wrinkles creasing his brow. He was bald, except for a tiny trickle of hair down the middle of his well-shaped skull.

I was staring into the wrinkled face of a vampire! This guy had lived off the bodies of his kids! He'd used them for welfare income. The fourth one had just killed himself. How could he stand to live? "I don't like jail, either," I said.

"But you stayed out of jail and he didn't," Al said.

Eight suicides, if you counted Kathy's boyfriend and GeeGee's girl-friend, my brother Eddy and Tommy's brother. I feared suicide. I had read a stack of books as high as me on suicide by then. Yet I still heard the clarion call to end all my troubles, like Al's kids did, even while I tried to keep my own son from killing himself through drink and carelessness. I had never had problems with my son until we lived around Al and his kids. But my battle over pot had hurt my son, too, although to a lesser degree than Al's addiction to heroin, because I didn't steal and I maintained moral standards. Al's antisocial acts killed his children, but my rebellious acts had seriously hurt my son by bringing great stress upon him. My being hunted for pot had ruined his life, and that was my great guilt. We were both honest, though, and contributed to society. We didn't just take like Al did. But, I was partly guilty for my son's alcoholism, too, and I knew it. Although I tried to do my best, I wasn't so successful either. What scared me was who was next? Not my son, I hoped. Maybe me?

PART EIGHT

Each Tear Is a Crystal Heart

1

Tears streamed out of Al's wrinkled eyes, just under the short brim of the gray hat pulled down low on his head. We stood at a counter facing the outside window of the bar on the suburban Napa street corner a couple of miles from the wide grounds of the mental hospital where he was in a drug program. Small trees lined the sidewalk on that gray, cloudy day.

"It's when Kathy died that I cried," he said and sniffled a couple of times. "That's the one that got to me. Finally, a couple of months ago, I woke up one morning after a long run on junk and decided to either overload and go all the way out, get it over with, or clean up. I couldn't go on the way I was."

"Good move, Al," I said.

He was a little heavy, about a hundred and fifty or so, because he wasn't shooting junk. His face was round and full-cheeked, his body a little thick and soft. But seeing the weight on him was better than seeing him walking around like a cadaver. We were the same size, but I only weighed a hundred and twenty-six and was in fair shape because I ran three times a week and did calisthenics every day. My wavy hair curled over the back of my turtleneck shirt. I dressed younger with a leather vest, brown cords and polished half-boots.

"It's the first step, brother. President Kennedy quoted the Chinese proverb: 'The journey of a thousand miles begins with a single step.' You've taken that. It's a very big step, all the rest follows from that."

He squinted at me, a bright, brown glare between the wrinkled lids.

"But how did this happen?" I asked. "What made you do it? Twenty-five years as a dopefiend, four dead kids, without you even showing the slightest regret. What brought this change on? Something brought it on. You were cold as ice when Sonny died. And you told me you still hated Dad after he died."

"It was Kathy," he said.

"But Kathy died in 1970. This is 1975. Sonnyboy's died since then."

"I got to the end of my rope," he said.

"Then where did you go?"

"George Perry. Remember him?" he said.

"The Safeway burglar you were in San Quentin with?"

"Yeah," he said. "Perry's been clean. He cleaned himself up."

"All right," I said. "Peer group pressure. You knew he could do it, so could you. A role model."

That right little eye stared at me again. "Yeah," he said, then started sobbing again.

I let him cry. I didn't try to stop him. I wouldn't have believed he still had it in him to feel anything deep enough to cry over after twenty-five years on junk. He'd been hooked since Eddy committed suicide, the fall of 1950. I thought the crying was a little practiced, a little easy, as if he had learned it in therapy groups, but he certainly had cause to cry.

When he sniffled to a stop, I said, "If you want me to help you, I will, Al. As long as you care, I'll help you."

He faced sidewards and looked at me out of one eye, which was still squinting and wrinkled from crying.

"This could be the turning point I told you about back in the fifties when I read in the *Archives of Criminal Dynamics* that middle-aged career criminals often changed for good. Remember I told you about it?"

He turned to face me now, a small smile coming over his lips.

"This could be the beginning act of a climactic event. If you stick to it, I'll help you. I promise you."

That small smile still played on his lips.

"Right in front of me is what I'd hoped would happen all these years! What I hoped I'd see some day! When you told me Sonny asked for what he got, I swore that I'd never talk to you again. So believe me, I'll follow through!"

"Thanks, brother," he said and put his arms around me and squeezed me against his chest.

"You want another drink?" I asked when he let go.

"Naaaw," he said. "I better get back for dinner, but ... "

That eye was on me again.

"What's the problem?" I said. "Let's go."

"I wanna buy a bottle to take back with me."

Now, he was really squinting, as if he wanted to look at me to gauge my reaction, but didn't want me to look into his eyes. I didn't answer back, but the decision was his. I wasn't a cop. He would or he wouldn't. The decision was up to him. But the booze was better than heroin. He didn't hum with angry hatred while drinking, the way he did when hooked. Most of all, he didn't have to steal and break the law and go to prison to buy booze. Three big pluses, even if he was still getting high.

"All right," I said. Before leaving I let him buy himself two pint-bottles of vodka and stuff them into the belt of his slacks to smuggle back into the hospital.

2

Two cop cars with yellow roof lights flashing were parked in front of Annabelle's house when I drove up at dusk. As I got out, I could see that my brother Al was handcuffed in the dark back seat of one of the cars and that my nephew Freddy, Annabelle's sixteen-year-old son, was handcuffed in the back seat of the other, which was parked fifty feet in front of the first one.

Al had called me on the phone, saying some cop was going to arrest him for lying about Freddy hiding inside Annabelle's big fancy house. Supposedly, Freddy had snitched a car for a joyride and had been trailed home by a helicopter.

"Come now," he had said, "or they'll take me away."

I'd jumped in my car and taken the freeway to her house in the Diamond District of Oakland, intending to do what I had promised him I'd do. There were still five kids left. I had to put myself out, if I didn't want another suicide like Sonny.

I walked over to the cop sitting in the front seat of the car where Freddy was handcuffed. The policeman turned his head to look up at me and rolled his window down.

"That guy in that car back there raised himself out of the gutter," I said. "He hasn't had a drink in eighteen months."

The cop didn't say a word, just listened to me as I told him how Al was trying to save his life and had quit getting high and quit stealing and going to jail after twenty-five years of shooting junk. By the time I finished, without saying one word, he got out of his car, went over, took Al out of the back seat of the other cop car and unlocked the handcuffs. He gave Al a citation to appear in court for interfering with a police officer in the performance of his duty.

"Thank you, officer," I said and he nodded, then said, "But the kid's going to juvenile hall for joyriding."

"Why didn't you tell him Freddy was in the house, Al?" I asked when the cop walked over to drive off with Freddy.

"I couldn't tell on the kid," he said. Then he turned and walked into the house without saying another word to me, not even thanks.

3

Al stood in my office doorway with a slip of paper in his hand. He had a quiet, serious look on his face, his brown eyes sizing me up as I sat at my desk typing. I hadn't seen him since I had gotten the cop to let him go in front of Annabelle's house.

"What's up?" I asked, knowing it was another favor.

"Ronnie's gonna get sentenced in a week and a half on two counts of assault with a deadly weapon."

"What?" I said and pushed back away from my typewriter.

Al had walked in the front door, which I kept open on warm days, since the house was set far back from the street. It was exactly the wrong kind of news on such a beautiful day.

"Yeah," he said, speaking out of one side of his mouth and twisting his face like a crook, a habit he'd picked up in Walla Walla Prison.

"Well, what happened?" I asked.

"Frankie's been living in an apartment complex on Southshore in Alameda. They were having a poolside party and wouldn't let Frankie and his guest in."

"Oh, no, and he lives there?"

"Yeah. If they wouldn't let him in, you can guess what they think of him there."

I shook my head, but kept my mouth shut.

"When they tried to throw them out, Ronnie pulled a knife and stabbed the security guard and then ran off."

"Ooooh, noooo!" I moaned. "I thought he was such a good fighter! And could hit so hard! What the hell is he doing using a knife?"

Al hunched his shoulders, then let them drop.

I didn't say anything more about it. It wouldn't have done any good, but I asked, "So what do you want me to do?"

Al stepped up to my desk, into the bright light from the big window behind me. His face had a tight-mouthed intensity to it. He leaned over the desk and put the slip of paper down. "Write a letter to the judge for me now. Here's his name and address."

"I'm working on a book right now, man! You want me to stop what I'm doing right now?"

"He goes to court in eleven days and I've got to get the letter to the judge before he sentences him."

I stared up at him. "Why didn't you tell me sooner? So I could fit it into my schedule?"

He hesitated a moment, thinking up an answer, then said, "I didn't think of it before today."

I shook my head again, knowing he was manipulating me to suit his exact purposes, but I thought of Ronnie and didn't want to make the mistake of Sonnyboy again and help kill another of his kids. "All right. I'll do it now so I can get it over with. But you've got to get it re-typed and give me back the original and a copy of the clean letter."

He leaned back away from the desk, as if surprised he had to do any of the work.

"I'm not a clean typist and I always have to re-write to get good copy. It's a hard job. You do that, if I write the letter," I said.

"Okay," he said.

"I'm stopping my work and doing it now, Al, because you're trying to help him, and because I told myself I would, if you tried to do good. I'm doing it because it's a lot better than going to see Ronnie in some funeral home."

He stared into my eyes and I was sure he was thinking of Randy's body in that coroner's morgue, too, or maybe all of them.

I pulled the page of the novel I was writing out of the typewriter and slipped another clean page in. "All right!" I said again. "Let's get the good points, first. So I know what I'm doing."

"Whatta ya mean?"

"Tell me good things about Ronnie that I can use in the letter to counteract the bad fact that he stabbed a man. Twice I guess, if there's two counts against him." I kept myself from shaking my head again.

"I got him to turn himself in!" Al said.

"Good!" I said and typed in "Good Points," and under it:

"1- Father got himself to turn himself in."

Then as Al spoke, I typed in the other good points.

"2- Was released on OR (Own Recognizance) and has not committed another crime.

"3- Held a job until he was laid off— "

"How long did he keep working?"

"Three months," Al said and I typed in three months.

"4- Now has another job.

"5- Father has rehabilitated himself through AA and NA, Veterans Administration, Napa, Board and Care home for SSI.

"6- Steps he is taking to rehabilitate himself. Father wants him to go into the drug program because drugs are at the root of his behavior."

I looked up at Al and added: "a drug addiction that he developed from his father's lifestyle."

Al looked over my shoulder and then down at me.

"Don't think of your own vanity, Al. Think of saving him. And tell the truth."

I stared up at him until he finally nodded, although he didn't speak, and while he waited, I typed out the letter.

Judge Stanley Gold
Alameda Superior Court
1225 Fallon St.
Oakland, Calif.

Al Salas
9/25/78

Dear Judge Gold:

This letter concerning the case of Ronald Salas, my son, who will appear before you on October 6, 1978, in Alameda County Superior Court, for sentencing on two counts of Assault With A Deadly Weapon. I am writing this letter to you in the hope that you will send my son to a drug program rather than to state prison.

I base my hopes on this for several reasons. First of all, through my urging, my son, Ronald Salas, turned himself into the authorities rather than try to escape. I convinced him that it would be better for him to face the consequences of his acts rather than run and ruin his life. Because he trusted me, he followed my advice.

Secondly, he was released on his own recognizance and didn't run away and has not committed any crimes since.

Thirdly, almost ten months ago I helped him get a job at Triple A Shipyards at Hunter's Point in San Francisco. He was never late and missed only one day when he was sick. He did a good job. They told him they would call him back in November of this year when the next big ship, "The Mitchell," comes in. That job will last eighteen months to two years. He is a member of the Plumbers & Steamfitters Union, Local 38, in good standing. In the meantime, while waiting for the job in November, he has been doing landscaping work in Montclair with his cousin, who lives there.

And lastly, and just as importantly, he has been attending Alcoholics Anonymous and Narcotics Anonymous meetings with me in the attempt to learn about the reasons for his own behavior and thereby to rehabilitate himself and prove to the court that he intends to improve himself, make himself a worthwhile citizen and not be a threat to society.

"Good!" Al said, reading over my shoulder.

I looked up at him. "Now, we've got to say something about how you accept part of the responsibility for this crime, Al."

He frowned and started to shake his head, but caught himself, then nodded again when I said, "And how the drug program helped you change, so the judge will believe you set a good example that Ronnie can follow, and that he'll change, too."

"Judge Gold was a lawyer for my crime partner nine years ago and knows me through that bust."

"Let's go!" I said and started typing as he spoke again.

Your Honor, I came from a life of crime. You yourself were the lawyer for a crime partner of mine, Larry Schubert, back in 1969 when he was charged with possession of narcotics, heroin. You may have known my involvement in that crime. You know my reputation as a criminal in this county. I was a heroin addict for twenty-five years, beginning in 1950. My last fix was on Thanksgiving Day, 1975. Since that day I have not used any mind-altering drugs, including alcohol, pills or marijuana. The reason I have not used any of these drugs is because I entered myself into a drug program in the veterans hospital in Palo Alto, where I stayed for seven months, learning about myself, my motivations, my psychological needs and feelings, and built a base of understanding which allowed me to reenter society and make myself a worthwhile citizen.

Since that time I have been an active member in NA and AA and, though I no longer go to two and three meetings a day, I still attend these meetings at least three times a week or any time I feel the need. So, instead of getting a heroin jolt I get a spiritual jolt. My belief in a Higher Power has developed and become all important in sustaining me in my battle to stay clean and alive in harmony with my society. I have been a drug counselor, helping myself through helping others, and now I am often asked to speak at NA and AA meetings, to share my experiences, strength and hope.

I want to do that with my son. I know he has committed a violent crime and I know that he has committed such a crime that you feel he must be put away to protect society. What I am asking you to do is help him and help society by entering him in a drug program which will teach him about himself, as I learned about myself, so he will not repeat this behavior or any behavior like it.

I want my son to improve himself and save his life.

Al was leaning down close to my shoulder now, our eyes level.

"That's a lot already, Al, but now you've got to really tell on yourself."

"Whatta ya' mean?" he said and straightened up.

"I mean, tell how you failed to be a good father." He started to shake his bald head again, but I said, "So he'll see you're being really honest and will trust your word."

He looked up at the ceiling. From below him in my chair, his eyes looked like white slits. Then he looked down again and said, "I was in San Quentin for grand theft when he was born."

"Now you're talking," I said and wrote the rest of the letter out, giving my own interpretation of his role as a father without denigrating him, slanting it in a favorable light.

When he was born I was in San Quentin and since he was born I have been absent from my family either through heroin addiction or incarceration for his whole life, except for small periods of time. He has never had a real chance because I have not been a real father. I have only learned how to be a real person through the drug program the last three years, and only now when I am strong enough myself am I learning how to be a real father. That is why I asked him to turn himself in. I did not want him to repeat my unhappy life. I did not want him to follow in my footsteps.

I couldn't help but stop and think of Al telling GeeGee not to hang around with a cleancut little kid he considered a punk, but to be like him and hang around with big, tough guys, who all ended up in prison. When he glanced at me, I focused my eyes on the page and finished off the letter.

I ask your honor to consider this plea from me because I tried to help society myself by getting him to turn himself in.

Thank you, your honor, sincerely and hopefully,

Albert Salas

He brought me back the original letter and a clean copy. I saw his eyes narrow when he handed them to me, then open to natural size again when I put them in an envelope without bothering to read them. I knew he'd changed that last paragraph. But I didn't care, he'd already mailed the letter to the judge, anyway. I just wanted him to live up to what I'd written in the letter. But it didn't turn out that way.

4

"Ronnie's in a minimum security camp in the mountains."

"Good!" I said.

"Yeah, the judge liked that letter I sent him," Al said in my office on my new property in Berkeley. He didn't thank me for my help and acted as if he had done it all without me to impress the young woman with him.

"This is Reggie's daughter, Marian. Remember Reggie? You used to be friends with him back in the fifties."

She was a plump, fairly pretty brunette in her twenties.

"Hello," she said, smiling. She actually did resemble Reggie.

"Reggie used to be a pretty handsome guy," I said.

"He still is," she said.

"Glad to hear it," I said. "What's he do ... "

"Saw your name in the paper. The sports page of the *Tribune*," Al interrupted, looking up at me with his head down. "About the re-publishing of your first novel. How you were a boxing coach at Cal and boxed like a Leonard and fought like a Duran, fine boxer but a fighter, too. Reggie saw it, too." Al glanced at Marian. "He said he wasn't surprised you made it as a writer because your room was always filled with books when you were a teenager." Al stood there looking at me as if he saw now that I really was that writer I wanted to be—I was publicly acknowledged.

"Al, that's probably the nicest thing you ever said to me!" I said. "Thanks for liking it. It makes me feel ... "

"Never made any money, though," Al said, interrupting me, his full upper lip curled with contempt. "Floyd's never made any money."

He stood on the other side of my desk in my corner office. He was showing off for her.

I looked into his eyes, then down at the yellow note pad in my hand where I had the names and numbers of our relatives in Colorado, which he'd come to get from me. He was going to Colorado. He didn't invite me, although he knew I wanted to go do more research on a novel based on our family ancestors who had been prominent pioneers there. He'd come to ask me for another favor, hadn't thanked me for the last favor, or any of the favors, and, smug because he had a girl with him, was putting me down for being poor. He was implying that it was too bad I wasn't cool like him, because he made more money and had a fancy, unpaid sports car outside. This, despite the fact that he was standing on *my* multi-unit property.

"Doesn't even have a woman anymore," he said and shook his head. But she looked at me with her light-blue eyes and said, "I write poetry, too," then turned and looked at Al and said, "People have different values, Al."

5

The phone rang while I sat writing at my desk on an overcast January day in 1980. I finished the sentence before I stopped so I wouldn't forget it, then picked up the phone.

"Ronnie got out!" Al said without introducing himself.

"Is this Al?" I asked, wondering what he wanted now, trying to keep myself from getting annoyed.

"Yeaaah," he said. "Isn't that great!"

"Sure is," I said. "How long did he do?"

"Fifteen months in a forestry camp in the Sierras."

"Not bad for stabbing a security guard twice," I said, waiting for him to acknowledge my part in the light sentence, feeling good about it myself.

But Al said, "You know that party you're giving? Make it in honor of Ronnie for getting out!"

I rocked back in my chair. I gave a big birthday party every year for friends and family. My friends included writers and fighters, since I was an assistant boxing coach at Cal and had been for six, going on seven years. Now, he wanted me to give it up for him. The gray sky out my window looked oppressive.

"You know I give a birthday party every year, Al. And this year it's special since Ginny and I got married in Reno last summer!" We'd gotten married on the anniversary of my mother's death day, June 25th, it turned out. Not a good omen. "Her mother and father and a lot of her relatives will be here to congratulate us!"

There was silence on the line for a moment, then he said, "He just got out, Floyd! Why don't you do it for him? Wouldn't hurt chou?"

My face got hot, but I kept my temper. My voice tight, I said, "Why don't you give him a party at your house? Then he can go to two parties: one for Ginny and me and one for him."

It wasn't really Al's house, but our sister Dorothy's, and he got to live there almost free. She let him stay there because she liked having a man around the house now that she was divorced again. "Our house is too small, Floyd," he said.

"Al," I said, "Dorothy's house has six rooms and my house only has four. You can ... "

He hung up. I held the phone for a moment, then put it slowly down. He never gave Ronnie a party.

6

"She ought to be able to go, if she wants to," Al said, sticking his nose into my business at my niece Dotty's house, where we were having an Easter dinner barbecue. His face was an unsmiling frown under his short-brimmed hat.

"But I want Ginny to wait until summer when school's over. I won't be teaching and I can go on vacation, too," I said. "It's only a couple of months. Annabelle can go with us then, too."

I noticed that Annabelle hadn't shown up for the barbecue because she didn't want to have to face me. She and Ginny had made plans to fly to Hawaii and visit Ginny's sister Joan there, and she knew I didn't want Ginny to go. Annabelle was having problems with her husband and wanted to get away from him. He went to whores for sex. She really didn't like him, but felt stuck with him in her middle age, seeing how her divorced girlfriends, spoiled and pampered all their married lives, now had to work for a living.

"Let her go now," my ex-brother-in-law Frank said, sitting on the couch, his heavy belly stretching his sportshirt. He'd been divorced from my sister Dorothy for almost twenty years now, but was still part of the family, just like Velva. Dotty, my niece, was his second daughter by Dorothy.

"Yeah, her and Annabelle deserve a little fun on their own," Al said again. Again, there was no hint of a smile on his face. He was still mad about my birthday party and because he'd lost his girl and now I had Ginny back.

"But Annabelle and me already have the plane tickets for Hawaii," Ginny said. She was standing in Dotty's front room, where a huge abstract oil painting took up a large part of one wall. I liked the painting, warm blues and reds with a patched quilt look to it.

"Let her go!" Frank said again.

I shook my head, saying, "All this hostile advice and not a woman between the two of you."

"Not because I can't get one," Frank said, his thinning, silvery hair still thick enough to wave on top of his handsome head.

"What makes you think I can't get a girl?" Al said, twisting his mouth down to one side.

"I know this: if you keep messing with mine, you're gonna have to pay for it," I said.

He stuck his lower lip out and sneered, but turned away without saying another word about it.

7

At the Thanksgiving dinner at Annabelle's house, I wondered why Al came up to shake my hand again, after he'd already said hello with a sullen mouth and cold, staring eyes. He came in from the TV room, where he was watching sports with the other family men.

Now he was really friendly, all shaved head and smiling false teeth, as if we were great buddies again. I couldn't figure it out, but I turned and introduced him to my new mate, Claire, who was standing next to me. She looked gorgeous with her beautiful hazel eyes, fine line of a nose, pink lips without lipstick spread back revealing her straight white teeth, and her long, lustrous hair.

I'd shut Al up at Easter, but he'd done his evil. I'd asked Ginny for a divorce when she came back from Hawaii, knowing he'd contributed his share to it, even if he wasn't mainly responsible. When my sister Annabelle had tried to apologize to me for going off with my wife, I'd said, "I don't blame you for it!" and let it drop. She hadn't tried to hurt me like Al had.

I noticed that Al walked with us into the dining room for dinner. He pushed himself in between Claire and me at the table and sat down next to her so I moved around to the other side. I watched him leer out the side of his eye at her, as if she were a piece of sex meat. He looked like a caricature of a scheming villain in a melodrama. His designs were so transparent it was pitiful. I couldn't believe it. I saw her trying to be polite but keep her distance. She'd answer when he said something to her, but kept trying to start a conversation across the table with me. Finally, he shut up and ate his dinner with a sullen mouth.

8

"Naaaaaw!" Al said again. "I'm not wearing any headmask."

He looked trim in a gray sweatshirt and sweatpants. I could tell that he'd been training at the YMCA. His face looked slender and I knew he wasn't shooting dope, so it had to be good shape. I hadn't heard from him since Thanksgiving. Now, here we were a couple of months later. He just showed up at my house and dragged me down to the Cal gym to box. I was really surprised. I guessed he was out for revenge because I'd threatened him about interfering with my estranged wife Ginny, and now I had a new girl.

At the gym I remembered how he never used a headgear in the professional gym when he was a pro to prove how tough he was. So I told him, "I won't box you unless you wear the headmask, Al. You've got false teeth, you don't have a mouthpiece, and I'm not going to take any chances on cutting your mouth. I want to be able to throw some punches without having to worry about cutting you."

He squinted at me for a moment, then gave in and put the headmask on. Claire tied it tightly behind his head.

The headmask looked like a headgear. But unlike the headgear, which has padding to protect the head but has an uncovered face, the headmask has a padded mask on an iron frame that fits over the whole face and tucks under the chin. It had an iron bar running from the forehead over the nose and mouth and down to the chin, somewhat like a catcher's mask, that cushions all blows and protects the face from getting marked. It's used when a fighter has a face injury but still needs to spar. There's an open space over the mouth, under the padded frame so the boxer can breathe.

I always brought my own gloves, which were twelve-ouncers and shaped in a small ball over the fist so I could throw neat, clean punches, rather than the sloppy punches of the loose-fitting, big-balled twelve-ouncers the Cal team used.

"Here! Wear mine," I said and handed him my gloves. He looked out of the side of his eyes at me as Claire tied them on him, as if trying to size me up without letting me know about it, as if something was up. But I didn't sweat it. I was in good shape and had been for six years. I could go a good, hard, three rounds with anybody any day, including good professional fighters. I'd box six college boxers in a row without getting out of the ring.

It was a college ring and our primitive bell rang every minute instead of two and one—or the three and one minutes of pro bells. I told Al the round didn't end until the second bell and then put on my own headgear, which protected the head, but didn't have a mask. My face was exposed, though the padding over my forehead would protect me some from getting cut and lessen the chance of getting black eyes. I handed the loose-fitting twelve-ounce gym gloves with elastic wrist bands to Claire to pull on my hands. After getting those on me, she put in my mouthpiece.

I turned to meet Al when the bell rang. It had been over twenty years since we'd been in the ring together, since 1958, when he had gotten out of San Quentin in good shape and tried to beat me up for not going to see him in the joint. We'd boxed once at my ranch house in Big Basin in 1968 when I had a puffed right thumb from breaking branches for firewood over a tree stump and couldn't punch with it. He'd tried to get me to box then because he knew I couldn't throw my right. I'd had to box him one-handed.

Now, I moved out toward him. I could see his little eyes through the mask holes on both sides of the big iron bar in front of his face. He was intent. Though he'd taught me to box, in part, I had a different style from his. I'd learned a lot by myself and just by watching other boxers. He had always been short for his weight and had to bob and weave and get in close to punch. I was a natural bantamweight of average size, even taller than some opponents. So I'd learned how to box from a stand up style. But I'd also learned to hook in the streets with bare fists where I usually fought taller men. He'd seen me box three times at the New Oakland Boxing Club when I was forty-five and forty-six years old. One time, with one overhand right in the second round, I'd knocked out a six-foot amateur welterweight who'd tried to punch on me. Another time, I gave a short amateur lightweight and former national collegiate junior lightweight champ a boxing lesson and even Al had said I boxed like an old pro.

The last time, he'd shouted at me to run and jab another amateur welterweight, who thought he could knock me out, because he outweighed me twenty-five pounds. But I'd refused and out-boxed and out-punched the guy without having to throw weak, little pitty-pat punches that didn't even hurt because I was running away. I retired that guy. He quit coming to the gym after telling Art Garcia, the coach of the club I worked out with, "That little guy hits!"

I'd never drank much nor smoked at all, had always run at least a couple of times a week since my thirties, done daily morning calisthenics for muscle tone and I'd never really lost my shape. I looked young in that ring and felt young. I felt good now.

I was used to boxing with college boys and, combined with my good

shape, my pro style was too much for them. I hadn't had the draining effect
on the body of a lot of fights and I had a lot of gym experience over the
years. I could move with relaxed grace and throw any kind of punch, from
an orthodox straight one-two, jab-cross, to a left or right hook or a bunch
of them with my hands down low by my waist, to an overhand right or left
over a guy's guard. I slipped punches with my body when I was hooking
or caught them on my arms or in the air with my open gloves before they
reached me when I had my hands up. Or I could combine two boxing styles
to confuse a guy. I could switch and box left-handed, too, when the other
guy was a really good orthodox boxer and I couldn't get through his guard.
This often happened with fighters I worked out with over the years at Cal,
including a senior featherweight champ, who knew my style too well, and
the other coach at Cal.

In an attempt to make the college boys good fighters, I was used to taking
it easy, boxing mainly defensively, trying to let them punch without letting
them hurt me or punching them without hurting them. I came out to box my
older brother the same way, though I knew what a cut-throat killer he was.

We met in the middle of the ring and he stuck out a jab which I caught
on my right glove. He immediately threw two left hooks around my glove
to my face, catching me a glancing blow on the head with the first one. I
blocked the second one with my glove and danced back, saying, "Ah, trying
to hit me with that hook, huh?"

To be fair, I'd given him a mask to protect his face and my best gloves
so he could punch well, since I thought I could whip him, and because he
was my brother. Now, he was trying to take advantage of it and punch on
me, which didn't surprise me, although the power in his punch did. It was
stronger than I had thought it would be, since his starving body had lived
off its own muscle for so many years of dope addiction, and he was already
fifty-seven going on fifty-eight years old.

I decided to punch him back a little, just to teach him something. I moved
toward him and, when he threw out a jab, I caught it on my glove to time
it. Then I danced back and around the ring to confuse him. I then skipped
toward him again and dropped my head down low toward his waist with my
right hand held out to my side and stepped in close at the same time, giving
him a face target to make him jab. I kept my left arm and glove in front of
the left side of my face so he couldn't hit me with a counter right from that
side.

When he stuck out his jab this time, I was waiting for it. I dropped down
even lower to my left side, twisting my whole body to my left, pushing off
the ball of my right foot, which turned on a pivot and gave me the most
power I could possibly have, hooked with a long right hand, all my shoulder

and body weight in it, and drove my right fist into the ribs over his heart with a hard thump.

It knocked him back a step and his eyes blinked behind the mask. "Got yuh back, Al!" I said, grinning, letting him know we were even now.

He didn't grin back or act like a sport at all, which would have made it fun, not war. He just moved away with a tight look on his face. I could see how grim he looked even behind the mask and I knew I had gotten him good. I could stop him with that right hook. I'd stopped lots of big guys with it since I had learned it watching an old light-heavyweight pro from Richmond called Terry Lee. But I threw it with more power for my weight than Terry did. He was a defensive boxer who threw it quick under a guy's jab but didn't risk stepping in with it.

I boxed around Al then, noticing Claire's face sticking up over the top rope watching us closely. I didn't try to hit Al hard again—not yet! I was waiting to see how he'd box. Sure enough, he leaped in again, jabbed and threw the hardest hook he could throw. But I knew all about it already and blocked it with my right glove, keeping my right hand held up by my head.

I still didn't do anything back, just boxed around the ring enjoying myself, until he did it again, trying to nail me with the hook and then a hard right cross right after it. He was trying to hurt me. I blocked both shots.

"Okay, brother," I said to myself, "if you still want to punch on me, I'll punch on you!" I dropped in down low to my left toward his waist again, keeping my left glove over that side of my face and right glove down low by my right thigh so he'd have a target and have to jab. He did and caught me a light, glancing shot off my headgear as I drove that long right hook under his jab at the same exact time, smack, into the ribs over his heart again. I heard him grunt from the blow, then skip around the ring to get away. He moved well. My brother had graceful movements, too. Even in middle age, he still moved like a pro. We moved more alike now that he was older and couldn't bull his way around anymore.

"Gotcha again, Al!" I said, grinning again, still trying to make a game out of it now that we were even again. But he still didn't smile. He danced around till the pain went away, and as soon as he recovered, he tried to stiff jab me, throwing hard one-twos and that hard hook again, all of which I blocked with my arms and gloves.

He hadn't changed one bit. You weren't supposed to try and hurt your stablemates or your friends or green kids, let alone your brother. It was an unwritten code in any gym. Unless they tried to hurt you. Then you could get even, you could get 'um. I now understood why he stared at me when I gave him the best gloves and the headgear: He had come to beat me up, if he could. That gave me the right to get him, if I wanted to.

When the bell rang the second time, ending the two minute first round, I went over to my corner, got a swallow of water from Claire to rinse my mouth, spit it into the corner bucket, and glanced at Al in the other corner. He'd planned it, I could see. I was angry. Instead of being grateful for what I'd done for him, he was uptight over what I *wouldn't* do for him.

I walked around the ring with my head down, noticing Claire looking at me, but felt too unhappy to look back. Every contact with him was unpleasant, without exception. And here I was going for it again, playing his usual game of being used by him in some way, material or emotional. I wondered why I was letting him get away with it again and getting myself all worked up for nothing. What else did I expect of him? This is the way I first remembered him and this was the way it always was and this is the way it was always going to be and this was the way it was going to end. He would never really change. He had a warped personality and to expect something else from him was not only naive, but forever frustrating. So I decided to teach him a lesson. He had it coming for starting a fight.

As I waited for the bell, I said to myself, "Okay, Brother Al, I'm going to slow you down this next round. I'm going to punch on you a little bit, not let you slide anymore, so you won't be trying to punch on me anymore. Big Brother Al is going to get punched around this round, mask or no mask."

When the bell rang, I moved straight out toward him, dropped down to make him punch, slipped his jab, then stepped in and punched to his body with a right hook under his punch as he threw at my face.

I saw the movement, anticipated where the arm was going and slipped my own hook under it to the body, then pushed off hard with my feet and hurt him! Got him good! Thump to the ribs!

"That's for forty years of bullshit!" I said. He stared at me and charged and punched again. But I hooked again, too, though this time he used his other arm and glove to block his exposed side when he punched and blocked the hook. So I punched twice when he charged and punched again, once where he was blocking and once to the now exposed other side! Bam-bam! I got him with the second hook.

"That's for getting my nose broken for me at six!" I said. He stared at me again, but charged again. And, good fighter that he was, he threw two punches and covered both sides, one after the other with each free glove. So I then threw three hooks, one under each arm, throwing the third hook right where I'd thrown the first one. Bam-bam-bam! I hurt him so bad with it, he fell back against the ropes with his hands down.

"That's for punching on me at Auntie Dolly's house!" I said and stepped back to let his head clear, to let him catch his breath, but only for a second.

Then, with my gloves up by my face, I led off with a hard jab and started throwing a half-dozen straight left and right crosses to his head, slugging him with my hands held up in front of my face at all times, punching from there, giving him no way to get through to my face, catching him with every one of my crosses, just sticking them straight out in front of me, pop-pop-pop-pop-pop, knocking him back across the ring, making him run to get away.

Smaller and faster than he, I skipped after him, stayed right on him, catching him up against the ropes, throwing straight left and right crosses to the headmask, pounding on him there, knocking his head up over the ropes.

I could see his head bouncing back with each punch, but I wouldn't let up. I kept him there, blasting him with clean, neat shots, daring him to slug it out with me, knowing that the facemask allowed me to knock him around a bit, make his skull ring and brains spin with straight head blows without really marking him up. I could hurt him and teach him a lesson without killing him or knocking him out.

I kept him there, punching his masked face like a double-ended fast bag, saying, "That's for trying to beat me up in the gym after you got out of San Quentin and I was trying to help you, and again when I had the swollen hand in Big Basin and could only box one-handed!"

I kept punching him, talking all the time, without really hurting him until the one minute bell rang. Then I started throwing those straight left and right crosses again, saying, "And these are for trying to beat me up now, when I gave you the best gloves and a head mask to keep from hurting you. For not being grateful that I saved you from a cop! Or for writing to the judge for Ronnie! For putting me down for being poor in front of your girl! For coming on with Claire! For being a punk-rat and trying to set me up for a bust when I was putting myself out to save your son from reform school! So fight, punk! Fight! Fight! Fight! Fight!"

"I quit, Floyd! I quit!" he shouted from inside his mask, his head wobbling like a paddle ball at the end of my fist. "I'm too tired. I quit!"

I hit him one more time, just to let him know, then stepped back and watched him grab the top rope with one hand, turn, and, still holding onto the rope, stagger to his corner.

9

"Leaning in toward a guy's stomach like you do to hook under his jab is gonna get you knocked out some day," Al said.

I shook my head. I almost snorted. "I stop him with a TKO and he still has to have the last word," I said to George Buckingham, who was talking to me in the kitchen of my sister Annabelle's house in the Montclair Hills of Oakland at her yearly Christmas Eve party.

"Pretty good looking chick I got, huh?" Al said, then grinned, changing the subject after he got his licks in. He'd had all his teeth pulled in Walla Walla Prison in Washington and his false teeth made his mouth look wider than it used to. He hadn't said hello to me and I hadn't said hello to him either. But he'd come up to me in the kitchen when I was talking to George Buckingham, who was married to my cousin Hope's daughter Joyce, a nurse like her mother who'd wiped the blood off my face when Al had hit me at my aunt Dolly's birthday party.

I'd seen Al's date in the front room. She must have been in her late thirties, wearing a nicely tailored red dress, dark brown hair just touching her shoulders. Lipstick flared over the corners of her thin mouth, and her face looked hard, but she was pretty, probably a heroin addict he'd met at some Narcotics Anonymous meeting. Which meant that she was clean.

I nodded, then, trying to be polite, since he talked to me—even if it was to attack me and praise himself—I asked, "Where'd you meet her?"

"N.A.," he said, speaking out of the side of his twisted mouth.

"You've paid some dues," I said, not wanting to put her down, but making a comment on the fact that he still lived in a world of narcotics.

"I've got no regrets for anything I've done in my life," he said, ready to fight right away.

George and I looked at each other. George was short, but taller than me, a fair-haired, fair-skinned history professor.

Finally, trying not to hurt Al, but unable to keep quiet, I said, "Four of your kids committed suicide, Al! You hooked GeeGee and the direct cause of his death was heroin use! You have two hooked sons now. And Frankie and Ronnie have both gone back to jail!"

"I got no regrets," he said, then shut his mouth.

"Al!" I said. "You're talking about a lifetime of hurting people." My chest hurt trying to keep my voice down. "You used to steal money out of Mom's purse during the Depression when every penny counted! My first memory of you is in a cast from jumping off a tower to keep from being punished for stealing from Dad! You've been in reform school twice, county jails about ten times, two prisons—four counting self-commitments to Fort Worth and Leavenworth for drug addiction—half a dozen other drug addict institutions like Synanon, and the nuthouse at Napa. You must have been arrested at least fifty times, besides. All for crimes committed against people! You've got to have some regrets about something!"

He didn't answer, he just kept his lips pursed tight against his teeth. I shook my head and looked at George. Then I said, "What about me? Your brother? You've robbed me and cheated me all my life! You lost our apartment house by shooting all the rent money up your arm! You even tried to set me up for a bust when I'd taken your son into my own home to keep him out of reform school! You've cheated everybody you've known and manipulated every situation you could to your own benefit! To this very day! Right to this moment when you came up to get even with me and brag in order to shore up your fragile ego! I've been helping you since I went to Napa to see you and you haven't shown one ounce of gratitude for it!"

My face felt like it was going to burst with hot blood.

"You even helped break up Ginny and me because you were jealous of us and because I wouldn't give my wedding party in honor of Ronnie! When you wouldn't give him a party yourself!"

He finally looked down at the floor and opened his mouth like he wanted to talk, but couldn't.

I felt sorry for him. I lowered my voice and said, "Having regrets keeps me moral, Al. It keeps me from committing more transgressions than I would otherwise, because I feel guilty over *my* wrongs."

George looked at me with his light eyes and said, "I'm the same way. It helps me act better."

I thought I knew what George was talking about. He'd gone back to my cousin Joyce after having an affair with another woman when Joyce was pregnant.

"Having *no* regrets is a primary psychopathic trait, Al," I said. "Psychopaths have no regrets. I want to tell you that."

He met my gaze with a stony hard stare that still didn't soften. However, he did say, "Well, I do sometimes feel sorry for something I did."

I nodded my head and said, "If you feel sorry, that's having feelings and that means you have regrets."

But he shook his head and said, "I don't have any regrets, but I do have feelings."

"Then you're using the wrong word. Don't use the word regret, use another word," I said.

"I don't have any regrets," he said and swayed back and forth, switching his weight from side to side. "That's because I paid my dues to get to where I am and I don't have any regrets. And being a psychopath means to be violent and hurt people and I don't do that. You think you know who I am, but you don't know me now. I'm a better person now. You keep thinking I'm that person who was the dopefiend. But I'm not a dopefiend anymore."

"You may not be a dopefiend anymore, Al, but you still have those cheating dopefiend habits. Annabelle said you still had criminal traits because you cheated on your income tax and because you encouraged her son Fred to cheat on them, too. Now Fred owes them fifty thousand dollars. But you got out of it because you don't own anything and you're too old for them to be able to collect it!"

"I wouldn't call that psychopathic."

"Listen!" I said, pointing my finger at his chest. "To cause trouble for a brother over his wife is psychopathic, and ... "

"I don't have to take your word for it. I didn't do that. You just misunderstood."

"Why don't you admit that you did it, Al?" I said, my voice high, but still under control.

"You just misunderstood ... "

"Why can't you ever admit it when you've done wrong?" I said, my voice rising so high now I saw some faces turn to look at me. But I couldn't keep it down anymore. "Why do you persist on adding a lie to the act? Why don't you just admit you've done wrong? Isn't the eighth step in your NA program to make a list of all persons you've harmed and to be willing to make amends to them all? Isn't step nine to make direct amends to these people whenever possible, except when to do it would hurt them or others? Isn't the tenth step to keep taking inventory of yourself and when you're wrong, admit it?"

"I got no regrets," Al said and walked away.

Long after midnight, a few of us were in the front room just sitting around talking, when I noticed Al's date staring at me. She'd seen Claire and me dancing and evidently liked it.

Claire turned on every time we danced. It was romance time for us and as soon as we hit the darkened dance floor, we forgot everything else, got ourselves into a corner and hit it. I'd pull her to me and one-step till we got into the beat, with synchronized steps, my arm around her slender waist, our cheeks together, feeling the oneness of harmonic movement. We drifted off into a simultaneous sense of sound and movement, sight secondary, the perspective inside, interior, where the beat of the soul sounds.

I avoided looking at Al's date at first because I didn't want to give Al the pleasure of showing her off in front of me. But finally, she caught my eyes and smiled and said, "I like the way you dance."

"Thanks," I said, but didn't smile and didn't try to be nice back to her because of the tight feeling in me of hostility toward Al. She didn't say anymore, but I saw her look at me every once in a while.

Al must have seen her looking, too, because he said, "Why don't you take our picture, Claire?"

Claire looked at me, and though I knew that he was now going to make a big point of showing off that he could get a pretty woman, too, I nodded and Claire picked up her camera case, which was sitting behind the Christmas tree, and took out her little camera.

Al grinned and, pulling the woman up by the arm, stepped in front of the glimmering silver Christmas tree by the wall-wide windows of Annabelle's darkened sundeck. He knew I was sitting behind him in a big, stuffed leather chair, and as he posed for the picture, he let his hand slide down onto the woman's left buttock, then stuck his thumb out so that it pointed toward the crack of her ass.

I saw Al standing to one side of the picnic table at a family picnic in the Spring out at a place called Big Trees in the hills of Contra Costa County. He was talking to his son Ronny, who looked very thin with hollowed cheeks and dark-circled eyes.

"Hi, Uncle!" Ronnie said, but he avoided my eyes, which he usually did when he was hooked.

I smiled and said, "Hi, Ronnie!"

Al seemed to like that because he actually smiled at me.

Encouraged, I tried to return the friendliness. Because I regretted being cold to his date at Annabelle's, I asked, "Say, how's that pretty woman you were with Christmas Eve? Still seeing her?"

Al stared at me, but didn't speak for a moment. I could see Ronnie staring at me, too.

"Huh?" I asked again.

"She killed herself!" Al said.

I spun around and saw Claire standing behind me. She must have seen the shock on my face, her hazel eyes soft and sad. I stepped past her to get away fast, but she caught my hand and squeezed it, stopping me. I met her eyes again.

She smiled, looking so pretty, I suddenly saw how pale blue the clear sky was over her head and how the sun shone warmly down on me and her and on the green bushes and trees. Butterflies flickered over the grassy field. Deep orange poppies bloomed in the high, wild grass. It was all so beautiful, it was a crime to be sad.

I glanced back at Al. He spread his lips in a tight smile, just showing the edge of his false teeth. He looked so vulnerable, I stepped back and grabbed him, hugged him, then held him away from me and, squeezing his thick shoulders, said, "You don't shoot dope anymore! And you don't steal! And you don't go to jail! That's a lot! That's a lot! That's really a lot!"